The Smuggler's Girl

By Jennie Felton

The Smuggler's Girl

JENNIE FELTON

HEADLINE

First published in 2021
by HEADLINE PUBLISHING GROUP

1

Cataloguing in Publication Data is available from the British Library

ISBN 978 1 4722 7492 2

Typeset in Calisto by Avon DataSet Ltd, Arden Court, Alcester, Warwickshire

Printed and bound in Great Britain by Clays Ltd, Elcograf S.p.A.

Headline's policy is to use papers that are natural, renewable and recyclable
products and made from wood grown in well-managed forests and other
controlled sources. The logging and manufacturing processes are expected
to conform to the environmental regulations of the country of origin.

HEADLINE PUBLISHING GROUP
An Hachette UK Company
Carmelite House
50 Victoria Embankment
London EC4Y 0DZ

www.headline.co.uk
www.hachette.co.uk

It is almost eight years since I lost my darling husband, friend and soul mate after almost fifty years of happy marriage. He was a rock to me in every way, and always supported my writing career. Sadly he never lived to see me become Jennie Felton, so I am dedicating *The Smuggler's Girl* to him.

Terence Charles Tanner (Terry)
1936–2013

Acknowledgements

As we all know, 2020 was the most dreadful year; now, hopefully, there is light at the end of the tunnel.

I was so lucky to have my writing to keep me sane, though sometimes motivation was hard come by. And I was also so lucky to have my wonderful team behind me all the way.

So, as always, my grateful thanks to Rebecca Ritchie, my lovely agent, to Kate Byrne, my equally lovely editor, and all the team at Headline who have worked so hard to bring my books to the shelves: Rebecca Bader, Isobel Smith, Alara Delfosse, Martin Kerans, Sophie Ellis and Sophie Keefe.

I'm grateful too to Anne Mackle – *Books With Wine and Chocolate* – for her great reviews, and to everyone else who has reviewed me, from the professionals to my amazing readers. Thank you all so much for taking the time to put pen to paper – or rather keyboard to computer!

I hope my books have given my readers some light relief in the dark days we have been living through. And thank you all for your support. I couldn't continue without it!

A final note to say that my village of Porthmeor is a fictional one in terms of its location in Cornwall and I hope my readers won't mind my taking poetic licence with it!

Prologue

The dream was always the same. The roar of angry waves, the groan of tortured timbers, the deck heaving beneath her feet. The salt spray stinging her eyes, her cheeks, her throat when she dared raise her head from the folds of soaking-wet cloth in which her face was buried. The utter terror that consumed her. Invariably, she awoke screaming, and the salt taste on her lips was real, not sea spray but tears.

It came less often now than it had when she was a child, but when it did, it was no less vivid, the terror no less consuming. As her own scream jolted her awake, the aura of something terrible happening remained, paralysing her so that she was afraid of moving a muscle. But somehow she must. She couldn't allow herself to fall asleep again, couldn't slip back into that nightmare.

With shaking hands she pushed aside the covers, levered herself up to a sitting position and swung her legs over the edge of the bed, half expecting to feel wet boards beneath her feet, icy water swirling round her ankles. Instead her toes encountered the fabric knots of the rag rug. Emboldened, she took a step forward, and then another, crossing to the bedroom window, where she jerked open the curtains.

Dawn was breaking over the distant horizon, casting a hazy

rose-coloured light. She opened the window and leaned out, taking in deep breaths of the cool fresh air, and gradually the pounding of her heart lessened, her pulses quietened, as the horror of the dream faded with the lightening sky.

She turned to her dressing table, sinking down on to the three-legged wooden stool that stood before it, and buried her head in her arms.

Why? Why did she have this recurring nightmare? Why had she had it for as long as she could remember?

At last she raised her head, and her reflection in the wooden-framed free-standing looking glass stared back at her.

Auburn curls, coming loose from her nightcap to frame a heart-shaped face, still pale, and with the tracks of tears on her cheeks. Eyes blue as periwinkles, fanned with thick lashes that matched her hair. A small straight nose, a generous mouth. Her own familiar face, the face she saw every day when she brushed her hair or pinched colour into her cheeks.

And yet . . .

When she gazed into those eyes, it was as if they were not her eyes at all; she seemed to sink into them, deeper and deeper, until she could almost touch the soul behind them. An essence that was not her essence. A feeling of longing ached in her, a sense of loss, deep and all-consuming, overcame her. Tears rose again in her eyes, silent tears born of some unknown sadness, a sense that some part of her was missing, and the image blurred so she could no longer see it clearly.

This, too, was the same as it had always been. Inevitably, it followed the nightmare.

She wondered if perhaps she was a little insane, or at any rate on the edge of madness. But as the room slowly filled with the rosy light of a new day, she thrust aside the crazy thoughts that plagued her and rose to face it.

Chapter One

Zach Carver was deep in thought as he rode across the open moorland high above the waves that made lacy ripples on the sandy beaches and swirled around the outcrops of rock.

He had been summoned to Polruan House to meet with Godfrey Pendinnick, and that could mean only one thing. Another cargo of contraband was on its way to the south Cornish coast.

Zach didn't like Pendinnick, loathed the sideline he ran in the stormy winter months, luring unfortunate vessels on to the rocks that flanked Porthmeor Cove by silencing the warning bell and showing lights that led them to believe wrongly that this was a safe harbour. He suspected that Pendinnick had been behind the untimely death of Zach's own brother Josh and despised him for it. But Pendinnick ran one of the most successful smuggling operations in Cornwall, and if Zach was to be successful in his own endeavours, it was vital that he swallow his distaste and remain close to the man.

Already the alliance had meant him leaving the family farm north of Helston, and taking up lodgings at an inn near Marazion, one of a chain of safe houses along which silks, tobacco, French brandy and the like passed on their journey inland. He missed his own comfortable bed and his mother's

3

cooking, but they were small sacrifices if he was to obtain his objective.

Zach was twenty-four years old and blessed with the sort of looks that women seemed to find attractive. It was something he could scarcely be unaware of, yet it was still a puzzle to him. Yes, he stood a little over six feet tall, and was tanned and well muscled from the long years he'd worked on the farm in summer sun and the cold, salty winds of winter, but he didn't consider the face that looked back at him from his shaving mirror each morning to be handsome. His nose was, he thought, too large, and a little crooked from having been broken in a fight when he was sixteen years old, and though his jaw was square and well defined, he didn't care for the dimple in his chin. Perhaps that was the cause of him getting his nose broken – the drunken lout responsible had mistakenly taken him for a soft target. Zach still smiled to himself when he remembered the look of shock on the bully-boy's face as he'd returned the blow with interest and left him muddy, bloody and swearing in the gutter.

Neither did he follow fashion. He'd never taken to wearing a wig – they were uncomfortable, and harboured lice in his opinion – and he wore his thick dark brown hair tied back in a pigtail. As for day-to-day attire, he favoured wool and cord-uroy over more ornate materials, and riding boots over highly polished buckled shoes. As he cantered now across the mossy ground, choosing a path between the heather and gorse bushes, the open neck and billowing sleeves of his shirt rippled in the brisk breeze. He was revelling in the freedom and the solitude when two figures appeared on the horizon heading directly towards him.

Zach swore under his breath. If a major shipment of contraband was to be landed tonight, he didn't want to be seen heading for Polruan House. He pulled on the bridle, swinging an unwilling Gypsy at right angles to the path across the prickly ground with the intention of making a detour. As he approached the ruins of one of the old tin mines that proliferated here in Cornwall, he cast a glance over his shoulder. The two riders were still trotting along the path, but from this angle he was able to recognise them. The man sitting easily on the big black horse was Sam Penrose, coachman at Polruan House, and the young woman riding side-saddle and bumping uncomfortably on the dainty grey was Pendinnick's daughter Cecile. It hardly mattered if Sam saw him; the coachman knew Zach was a frequent visitor at Polruan House, and knew too that he could trust him to say nothing of what he'd seen. He'd confided in Zach over a jar of ale at the Wink – the tavern in Porthmeor village – that he and Cecile were in love, but they had to conduct their relationship in secret for fear of her father learning of it. Godfrey Pendinnick was fiercely protective of his daughter, and would certainly not approve of her consorting with the coach-man, who would most likely be dismissed on the spot.

Zach guessed how precious was the little time they were able to spend alone together, and the last thing he wanted was to intrude on their rendezvous.

Gorse bushes, bent and twisted by the winds off the sea, had grown up in the midst of the ruins of the old mine, and he steered Gypsy behind one of them, dismounted, and sat down with his back resting against a tumbledown wall so as to be out of sight. To his dismay, the two horses drew to a halt almost level with where he was skulking. He hoped it would not be too long before they moved on and he could go on his way.

Eventually his patience was rewarded when he peeked out and realised they were saying their goodbyes. Sam had dismounted and was standing beside Cecile, who was reaching down to him, and Zach turned away hurriedly as he saw their lips meet. The next time he risked a look, Sam had remounted and was setting off in the direction of Penzance, while Cecile sat motionless, watching him go, before turning back reluctantly towards Polruan.

He waited a few moments more, then rose and unhitched Gypsy. He had one foot in the stirrup when everything seemed to happen at once.

What had startled Cecile's mount he would never know – a rabbit scuttling across her path perhaps, or a bird flying up suddenly from the brush – but whatever it was, the horse reared, then took off at a breakneck pace in the direction of her stables and home, with Cecile clinging on for dear life.

Zach's heart jolted into his mouth. Sam had told him Cecile was no horsewoman and that she was terrified every time she took her grey mare out to meet him in secret – and not just because she was afraid of being caught out. 'The trouble is, Lady knows she's nervous,' he had said. 'She's a gentle beast, but Cecile unsettles her.'

How long could the girl hold on? Zach wondered. She had looked unsafe at a trot; now Lady was at full gallop. The slightest deviation in direction, and she would be thrown.

Without hesitation, he set out in pursuit, but before he could catch up, girl and horse had crested a slight rise and were out of sight. Beyond it, he knew, lay the steep and stony descent into Porthmeor Cove, a path it was wise to treat with caution, and certainly not at an unchecked gallop or even a canter. His concern grew sharper, and when he crested the rise himself, his worst fears were realised. The grey, Lady, was disappearing down the path in a cloud of dust, and he could see Cecile lying splayed out on the rocky cliff path.

As he began the descent, Zach slowed Gypsy to a safe pace so as to ensure his horse didn't stumble and perhaps break a leg.

It was a miracle that Lady seemed to have managed it safely, he thought.

Cecile lay in a tangle of skirts and petticoats. The tricorn hat she had been wearing had fallen off and her face was almost as white as her powdered wig, which was askew. Her eyes were open, wide and shocked, and her breathing shallow and panicked. Zach dismounted quickly and fell to his knees beside her, reaching for her hand.

'Miss Pendinnick?'

Her eyes skittered round to meet his, a little dazed and puzzled. Though he was a frequent visitor to Polruan House, their paths seldom crossed and she scarcely knew him.

For a moment it looked as if she didn't know what had happened either.

'I'm Zach Carver, an associate of your father's,' he said. 'You've taken a nasty fall. Are you hurt?'

'Lady . . .' Cecile tried to raise herself, an expression of panic in her periwinkle-blue eyes.

'Lie still for a minute,' Zach cautioned. 'Your horse is fine. The last I saw of her, she was heading for home at a gallop. She'll be back in the stables by now, no doubt.'

'Oh . . .' Cecile sank back on to the rough sward. 'Oh, thank goodness . . .'

'But what about you? Can you move your legs?' Zach had known those who had never walked again after taking a bad fall from horseback.

Cecile raised first one foot, then the other, experimentally. 'Yes. My knee hurts, and my ankle, but . . .'

'You'll hurt all over tomorrow, I expect,' Zach said. 'What about your arms and hands?'

The fine kid gloves she wore were scuffed and dirty – ruined as far as she was concerned, Zach guessed. But she was able to wiggle her fingers and lift her hand to try to straighten her wig.

Zach smiled. If Cecile was worried about her appearance, there couldn't be anything too seriously wrong with her.

'I think we'd better get you home,' he said. 'Your family are going to be worried about you when your horse returns without you.'

He helped her to her feet. Miraculously, she seemed to have escaped serious injury, but she was very shaken, trembling and, he noted as she swayed against his supporting arm, a little dizzy.

'You'd better ride,' he said. 'Don't worry, I won't let you fall again. But you'll have to sit astride. Can you manage that?'

'Oh!' she said, horrified. 'I don't think I can.' She smoothed her voluminous skirts down over her petticoats, and he saw the unmistakable shape of a hoop.

It seemed quite incongruous that while a lady riding side-saddle wore a tailored jacket, waistcoat, flounced cravat, tricorn hat and pigtailed wig just as gentlemen did, from the waist down she was attired in full skirts and hooped petticoat. Clearly there was no way Cecile could ride astride dressed like that.

'You'll have to take it off,' Zach said bluntly.

Colour rose in her pale cheeks. 'Oh . . . I couldn't!'

He shrugged. 'Well, do you want me to get you home or not?' She nodded. 'Take it off then. I'll turn my back.'

'You won't look?'

'That's what I just said.' Zach was beginning to feel a little irritated. The tartan silk skirt was voluminous enough in itself to protect Cecile's modesty and, in any case, desperate situations called for desperate measures.

He turned around, assessing the stony path that led down to the bay. He'd have to lead Gypsy until they reached safer ground. Whilst he himself might have been able to ride down if he took care, he didn't want to risk it with a dead weight like Cecile on board too.

When he turned back, the flounced hoop was lying on the sloping bank and Cecile stood waiting, eyes downcast, as if she was ashamed to be seen without it.

'Are you going to leave it there?' he asked.

She lifted her chin a shade. 'My maid can come and fetch it.'

'Right.' He made a stirrup with his hands. 'Come on. I'll hoist you up.'

She hesitated, then realised there was nothing for it but to do as he said. In a flurry of petticoats, she managed to sit almost astride Gypsy. Zach steadied her, and she slipped awkwardly into the saddle.

'Just hold on tight,' he warned. 'I'll do the rest.'

It was a slow descent down the cliff path, but at last they were on firmer ground, and before long they were on the tree-lined drive that led past a collection of outbuildings and down to Polruan House.

What a dismal place it was! Zach thought. No sunshine penetrated the thick foliage, and rooks cawed above where one might have expected the mewling of gulls. The door of the house was painted black, as were all the window frames, and a bell tower on the apex of the roof gave the building an oddly sinister feel.

As they approached, a woman appeared on the path that ran around the side of the house. No – not a woman; from her high powdered wig and purple silk gown to the tips of her embroidered slippers, she was every inch a lady.

'Aunt Cordelia!' Cecile cried.

The lady stopped, drawing herself up imperiously, her rouged face with its tiny black paper beauty spot blank with displeasure.

'Cecile! What can you be thinking of? You know you are forbidden to ride out without permission. And get down from that horse at once.'

'Aunt . . . is Lady home safe?'

The crimson lips tightened. 'No thanks to you.' She turned her steely gaze on Zach. 'And what are *you* thinking of, allowing my niece to sit astride a horse? Heaven only knows how such a thing could damage her.'

Zach had never liked Cordelia Pendinnick any more than he liked her brother, and now her lack of sympathy for her niece rankled with him so that he liked her even less.

'Miss Pendinnick was in no fit state to walk,' he said shortly. 'She took a bad fall. I came upon her and have seen her safe home, nothing more.'

'He was very kind,' Cecile said timorously.

'No doubt,' Miss Pendinnick sneered, and looked at Zach again. 'You'll want something for your trouble, I imagine. Parsons!' she called to a man in working clothes who had appeared around the side of the house. 'Go and find a half-sovereign if you will, so I may pay this man.'

'You insult me, madam,' Zach said coldly. 'I was on my way here in any case for a meeting with your brother.'

Before anything further could be said, he turned and led Gypsy towards the stables, where he allowed her to drink from the trough, then tied her to the hitching block. He was still fuming as he went into the house to meet Godfrey Pendinnick.

Godfrey Pendinnick sat at his leather-tooled desk overlooking the gardens that ran down to the cliff edge, a ledger and a stack of paperwork in front of him. He was a large man, run to fat from years of good living, and his bulbous, purple-veined nose bore witness to his fondness for good French cognac. Neither had any expense been spent on his attire. His waistcoat was brocaded, the stock tied twice around his neck and finished with a bow was of the finest silk, and his ample stomach struggled to escape from white buckskin breeches. From the pockets of the waistcoat hung a pair of fob watches, though one was in fact a dummy – a *fausse montre*, as it was known in France.

Godfrey could well afford to indulge himself in whatever took his fancy. Smuggling was a profitable business, even once the other members of the gang had been paid. The cargoes of brandy, fine wines, tobacco, tea, silk and Brussels lace all fetched good money, either from the local gentry or from the profitable markets inland, and wool would always find a buyer on the other side of the Channel if it was smuggled out on the vessels headed for France. Polruan House itself had been built with the proceeds of smuggling; not by Godfrey, but by the man who had taught him the tricks of the trade and bequeathed it to him in his will.

The illicit trade had made Godfrey a rich man, and the icing on the cake came from the goods that could be looted from ships lured on to the dangerous rocks in the cove during the winter months.

He looked up, startled, as the study door was suddenly thrown open and his sister Cordelia entered.

'Your daughter has been riding out alone,' she said without preamble. 'She's had a fall, but she seems relatively unhurt, though she is in a disgraceful state. I've sent her to clean herself up and make herself presentable, and told her that you will want to speak to her.'

'Dear me.' Godfrey shook his head despairingly. 'What am I to do with her?'

'Take her firmly in hand, I hope,' Cordelia said shortly. 'In the meantime, that man Carver is here to see you. He found her, it seems, and brought her home – riding astride his horse, if you please.'

Godfrey laid his pen down on the brass tray that held the inkwell. 'Yes, I'm expecting him,' he said, 'and if he brought her home safely, then we should be grateful to him, however he managed it. Perhaps you'd show him in, Cordelia. I'll speak to Cecile when we've finished our business.'

Cordelia sniffed. 'As you please.'

Zach was waiting in the hall outside the study. As Cordelia left, she motioned for him to enter.

'Ah, Carver, my friend. Do come in,' Godfrey greeted him. 'We have much to discuss.' As the door closed after him, he added in a low voice, 'And a busy and profitable night ahead of us, if I am not much mistaken.'

Chapter Two

'Well, miss, you're in a tidy state and no mistake.'

Bessie, Cecile's maid, crossed her arms across her ample chest and regarded her mistress sternly. She'd been in the employ of the Pendinnicks ever since they had moved into Polruan House and, as she had cared for Cecile as a child, it had been a natural progression to become her lady's maid when she was old enough to need one.

Tears sprang to Cecile's eyes. 'Oh, don't be cross with me, Bessie, please! It was just awful, and I was so frightened! Lady bolted and I couldn't stop her. I thought we were both going to die.'

'Heaven be praised you didn't. But you shouldn't have been up on the cliffs. You know you're no horsewoman. And don't think I don't know what you were doing up there, because I do. You can't pull the wool over my eyes, missy.'

Cecile dropped her chin, the guilt written plainly on her face.

'All this creeping about – mark my words, it'll come to no good,' the elderly maid went on. 'You used to be such a good girl, eager to please, and timid as a church mouse. I don't know what's got into you lately. Well,' she sniffed, 'I suppose I do. It's that Sam. He's turned your head. And you haven't got the good sense to realise it can't end well.'

'But I love him, Bessie!' Cecile cried, scrubbing at her wet cheeks with her fingers and leaving muddy streaks. 'If I wasn't able to see him sometimes, I couldn't bear it!'

'I know, I know.' Bessie sighed heavily. Cecile had no secrets from her; they were as close as mother and daughter, and her heart bled for the girl. She had no life here, no life at all, the only young person in the household, and between them her father and aunt had drummed all the spirit out of her. Bessie was only surprised she dared to carry on this affair under her father's nose, and was able to put aside her fear of riding in order to creep out and meet the man she was clearly in love with.

'Come on, let's get you out of those dirty clothes and make you presentable.'

Cecile's hands flew to her skirts, pressing them against her thighs, and hot colour flooded her cheeks. 'My hoop – I had to take it off to sit on Mr Carver's horse. But he swore he didn't look.'

Bessie clucked. 'I'm sure he didn't. He's a gentleman, that one. Handsome too. You'd do better to set your cap at him instead of the stable lad.'

'Sam isn't a stable lad. He's the coachman,' Cecile protested.

'But still a servant. Not someone your father would ever let you wed.' Bessie sighed, realising she was wasting her breath. 'Where is your hoop then?'

'Up on the cliff path. Would you fetch it for me, Bessie?'

'It's likely ruined by now.'

'But still . . . I can't leave it there for all to see . . .'

'Course I'll fetch it.' Bessie reached out and untied the flounced bow of Cecile's cravat. 'Now, are we going to get you cleaned up, or are you going to stay in those filthy things all day?'

* * *

By the time Bessie had washed Cecile's face, dressed her cuts and grazes and helped her into a fresh gown, Godfrey and Zach had concluded their business, so that when Cecile went to his study, her father was alone. Still badly shaken from her fall, she was nervous about facing him. Aunt Cordelia would have told him what had happened by now, and he would not be best pleased, to say the least of it. But she couldn't avoid him for ever, and the longer he had to think about it, the angrier he was likely to be.

'Papa . . .' She stood hesitantly in the doorway picking at the fine lace on the fancy sprigged apron she wore over her hooped and flounced skirts.

For what seemed to her never-ending moments, Godfrey continued with his work, his refusal to acknowledge her presence his way of showing his displeasure. Then he replaced his quill pen in the ink pot, pushed the ledger to the back of his desk, and looked up at her unsmiling over the top of his eyeglasses.

'Well, Cecile. What do you have to say for yourself?'

She cast her eyes down to the Persian rug beneath her slippered feet. 'I'm sorry, Papa.'

'What were you thinking?' His stern tone matched the expression on his paunchy face. 'You know you should not be out riding alone.'

'But Papa—'

'Sam knows very well you are not to take Lady out without someone to ensure you come to no harm. For two pins I'd give him his marching orders.'

'Sam wasn't there, Papa,' Cecile said swiftly. It was the truth – he had left the stables first, and she had followed later.

Godfrey's hooded eyes widened in disbelief. 'You saddled Lady yourself?'

Cecile was silent, biting her lip. In fact, Lady had been tacked up and ready and waiting for her – Sam had made sure of it before leaving himself. But she couldn't admit to that, of course, or her father would dismiss the coachman on the spot.

'Small wonder you took a tumble.' Godfrey gave an impatient shake of his head and powder flew from his wig, settling on the polished surface of the desk like fine dust. 'The girths, the bit and bridle – what do you know of such things? Except for watching as the horse is prepared for you, perhaps. I ask again – what were you thinking?'

'It's such a lovely day, I felt like being out in the sunshine,' Cecile offered.

'But to ride alone on the clifftop? You could have taken a turn in the grounds. The walled garden is always a suntrap at this time of day. If you wanted to take the air, that would have been by far the more suitable choice. Why, I didn't think you even cared much for riding.'

'I . . . well, I just felt like it, that's all,' Cecile said, with all the humility she could muster.

Godfrey shook his head again, and more powder flew, making Cecile's nose tickle.

'You might have been seriously injured, my girl. Killed, even. Promise your father you will never attempt something of the sort again, however inclined you feel to do so.'

Cecile crossed her fingers in the folds of the apron. 'I promise.'

'Very well. We'll say no more about it. Now, come here and give me your hand so I can be sure it is really you, unharmed, and not a ghost come to haunt me.'

She did as he asked, and he pulled her close, slipping an arm around her slender waist and resting his forehead against her shoulder.

'Oh, my dearest daughter, if I should lose you . . . I cannot abide the thought of it.'

The study door opened, and Cordelia stood there. Godfrey released Cecile, patting her hand and smiling.

'Run along now, and be sure to heed what I said.'

'Yes, Papa.'

Cecile crossed the room and slipped hastily past her aunt, who was regarding her with pinched lips and a cold stare.

As the door closed after her, Cordelia turned her gaze on Godfrey.

'You are too soft on that one. No wonder she thinks she can do as she pleases.'

'She's a good girl.' Godfrey's tone was defensive.

'She may play meek and mild, but she needs a firm hand.'

'Which I am sure you administer on my behalf.'

'Someone has to,' Cordelia said sharply. 'She's her mother's daughter, don't forget, and if you are not careful, she will break your heart, just as Marguerite did.'

Furious at the mention of his late wife, Godfrey raised his hand and brought it crashing down so sharply on the desk that the crystal inkwell juddered in its brass stand, his eyes flashing icy anger. 'That's enough, Cordelia. You go too far.'

Cordelia shrugged. She was too accustomed to her brother's sudden rages to be discomfited. 'You may refuse to allow Marguerite's name to be spoken, but you cannot deny she lives on in her daughter. It's why you insist on keeping Cecile close, yet forgive her follies, such as today's reckless escapade. But you would do well to remember it may not be just in her physical appearance that she resembles your sainted wife. She may also have inherited her wild and faithless ways. The best thing for all of us would be to marry her off so that we can be sure she will not bring trouble to our door.'

She turned away having delivered her parting shot and left the room before Godfrey could make any response.

* * *

Cordelia Pendinnick knew her brother only too well. As the two middle children of Squire Wilbur Pendinnick, they had always been close. With their elder brother Christopher heir to the entire estate, which encompassed six tenant farms and the village, and their younger sister Eliza babied and indulged, they had forged an alliance that had survived good times and bad.

Cordelia had never married, nor wanted to. When, as a young man, Godfrey left to go to sea, she remained at home, assisting her father and Christopher with the running of the estate, but living for the times when Godfrey had shore leave. And when he made captain, she often went to sea with him, standing at the prow, hair streaming out behind her in the salty wind, for all the world as if she were the painted figurehead that rode the storm beneath her. Those were the days when she was young and free, when she dressed in breeches, waistcoats and buckled shoes and wished she had been born a boy.

Those early trips were legitimate trading between England and France, but it wasn't long before Godfrey had realised the opportunity for making an income to supplement the wages he was paid by the ship's owner. Whenever there was room in the hold, he purchased tea, tobacco or rum to fill it, and sold his booty on in the inns and taverns of Penzance, his home port.

At first Cordelia had counselled against it. If Godfrey was caught, he would at the very least lose his livelihood – no honest trader wanted to be associated with a known smuggler. But when she saw the riches he was making, she agreed he was on to a good thing. She began to help him then, often taking on the negotiations with the French tradesmen and securing even better terms than Godfrey could manage. They were taken with her, those Frenchmen, this spirited English girl who was afraid of nothing and no one.

As he became more practised, Godfrey also became more ambitious. He wanted his own ship and his own gang, and before long he had found a way to get it.

Though smuggling was rife all around the Cornish coast, Mount's Bay, east of Penzance, was awash with the illegal trade. From Lizard Point to Land's End, the coast was peppered with hidden coves and inlets that provided perfect landing sites.

One of the most successful – and notorious – operations in the bay had been run in Porthmeor by the legendary Amos Fletcher. Tales abounded of his exploits, and of the grand house he had built on the cliffs above the village with the proceeds of his enterprise, which served both as his home and a hub for his illicit activities. Miraculously, he had never been brought to justice.

He was an old man now. His gang had long since been disbanded and he had become something of a recluse, alone in the great house but for an elderly housekeeper – who had once, some said, carried out duties that went beyond feeding him and laundering his bed sheets and linen. It was also rumoured that he was sitting on a small fortune. 'He does nothing these days but count his money,' Godfrey had heard it said, and it had whetted his appetite.

One November afternoon, he and Cordelia had paid the old man a visit. Sea mist had rolled in, so that only the bell tower and the chimney pots of Polruan House were visible, and the track that led up from the road below was slippery with a carpet of fallen leaves. They exchanged approving glances: Fletcher had chosen the perfect spot. Small wonder he had managed to keep his business hidden from the authorities for so long.

Cordelia reached for the bell pull beside the heavy oak front door and heard it ring somewhere inside the depths of the house. For a while there was silence but for the cawing of the rooks in the trees overhead, and she had begun to wonder if the house was unoccupied when she heard a faint shuffling sound, like slippers on flagstones, and the creak of bolts being drawn. The door juddered, but when it became obvious that the person on the other side was unable to get it open, Godfrey put his weight on it, and it gave grudgingly, scraping over the uneven floor.

An old woman stood in the hall beyond. Small, beady eyes seemed to have disappeared into folds of pallid flesh, multiple chins melted into the neckline of her gown.

'Yes?' Her tone was heavy with suspicion.

Godfrey removed his hat, holding it between his gloved hands like an offering. 'Would it be possible to speak to Mr Fletcher?'

'Mr Fletcher doesn't entertain visitors.' She made to try and close the door again, but once more her efforts were in vain and Cordelia managed to insinuate herself into the narrow gap.

'We won't detain him for long, I promise. But it is a matter of the greatest importance.'

Still the old woman stood her ground. Then, to Cordelia's surprise, the figure of a man, wizened and bent, leaning heavily on a cane, appeared in the hallway behind her.

'Who is it?' The voice was as scratchy as the cawing of the rooks. 'For the love of God, Hetty, I might as well be in a prison cell for all the company you allow me. That sounds like a pretty young voice from what I can hear of it. And fortune will surely be smiling on me if there's a pretty young face along with it.'

'How d'you know they don't mean you harm?' the woman, Hetty, demanded. 'How d'you know they won't rob you blind, or worse?'

'We just want to talk to you, Mr Fletcher,' Cordelia said in her sweetest tone. 'We are in the same line of business as you once were. Your success is legendary, and we'd so like to hear the stories you must have to tell.'

'Is that so?' The old man harrumphed loudly, then chuckled, his chest wheezing. 'Get out of the blasted way, Hetty, and let them in before I break my cane on your fat backside.'

Cordelia threw a triumphant glance at Godfrey over her shoulder. He thrust the door open wider, then closed it behind him as he followed his sister and Amos Fletcher into the house.

They didn't achieve their objective immediately, of course, any more than Rome was built in a day. But Amos Fletcher was only too delighted that their visits became a regular thing. He enjoyed recounting tales of his long-ago escapades and close-run brushes with the revenue men, chuckled at Godfrey's own stories – many highly embellished – and was flattered by Cordelia's rapt attention to every word he had to say. So when Godfrey eventually mentioned that he was looking to be able to buy at least one ship of his own, Amos was quick with his advice.

'What you need, my boy, is a backer. That's how I started. A local landowner put up the capital – I'll name no names, though his lordship's long gone to meet his maker. He took his cut but never did involve himself in the trade, except to have a word in the ear of the local magistrate if any of my gang looked like ending up before the bench for their trouble.'

Godfrey assumed a downcast expression. 'I don't know any landed gentry, I'm afraid.'

'Well, maybe I can help you there. I've got a nice little nest egg salted away, and no one to leave it to when I slip my mortal coil. Like I said, I was helped myself, so I reckon the least I can do is give something back. This house is ideally situated, too.

21

There's enough bays and inlets on this coast to put the revenue men off the scent, and plenty of hidey-holes.'

'Oh – I couldn't take your money!' Godfrey protested.

'Nonsense, my boy! You'll be doing me a favour, as long as you cut me in. I'll have more fun than I've had in years!'

It was true, Amos Fletcher seemed to take on a new lease of life as he explained to Godfrey what was required to mastermind a successful smuggling ring. It seemed only sensible that Cordelia should act as overseas agent, since she was already a familiar face amongst the foreign merchants, and Godfrey himself would be the banker and clerk. But he would also need a 'lander', who would be responsible for assembling pack animals – mules and horses – and human porters to move the contraband, and some brawny men to act as security guards.

A cutter was purchased, paid for by Amos, and the story was put about that she was to be used as a privateer – a ship that would give chase to smugglers and earn a reward for any contraband she was able to recover. Godfrey recruited a crew for the ship from amongst seamen he'd sailed with, and visited farmers and innkeepers drumming up support. Some of those who made up the land gang he was able to put together were the children and grandchildren of Fletcher's original enterprise. But Godfrey was careful to keep his distance from the landing site at Porthmeor in those early years. He and Cordelia took possession of an old rectory in Penzance, and he was able to live the life of a respectable shipowner. It was only much later, when Amos died at the ripe old age of eighty-four and left his entire estate to Godfrey, that he moved into Polruan House.

But by then his heart had been broken by Marguerite, the daughter of one of the French merchants he and Cordelia dealt with. Godfrey had fallen madly in love with her; so obsessed was he that he brokered an arranged marriage and brought her home to Penzance. Inevitably, everything had gone disastrously wrong, and now he was left with nothing but their daughter Cecile.

Cordelia had been desperately hurt when Marguerite had taken her place in her brother's life and his affections. He was no longer the man she had thought she knew so well, with whom she had shared everything, and she had come to loathe and despise the woman who had come between them.

She had been there for him, nevertheless, when his world had been torn apart, stepping seamlessly back into her old role, supporting him in every way. But to her chagrin, she had had to stand by helpless as Godfrey transferred his obsession with Marguerite to their daughter. He barely let Cecile out of his sight for fear of losing her too. Now, the jealousy Cordelia had felt towards her rival for Godfrey's affections was directed at her niece, and her bitterness manifested itself in her treatment of the girl.

Cecile was still trembling, and close to tears, when she returned to her own sitting room. The fall had shaken her badly and unleashed all the despair she usually tried so desperately to ignore.

Their situation was hopeless. Bessie was right when she said Godfrey would never allow her to wed Sam, and would most likely dismiss him on the spot if he came to suspect there was something between them. They'd talked about running away together but, as Sam had pointed out, with all Godfrey's connections they'd never even make it out of Cornwall unless they had a proper plan, and Godfrey would make sure they never saw one another again. He'd find a way, he'd promised, but deep down Cecile couldn't imagine what that might be. She feared she and Sam would never be together.

Oh, if only her mother were here! But she had died when Cecile was so young that she had only the most fleeting memory of a soft voice singing a lullaby, while sometimes the scent of the lavender bushes in the garden evoked a bittersweet recollection of warmth and love.

Thanks to Cordelia, there was not a single portrait of Marguerite on the walls of the house, and Cecile possessed just one memento – a locket she had found in a dresser drawer amongst keys and half-burned candles and other odds and ends. Somehow she had known she must keep her find secret. She had slipped it into her pocket, brought it to her room and hidden it in a blue silk reticule that she no longer used. Whenever she felt sad or in need of comfort, she would take it out and look at it.

She felt that need now. She fetched it from its hiding place, went to the brocaded chaise that stood beneath the window and sat, her back resting against its head, her feet drawn up beneath her skirts. Then she uncapped her hands and gazed at the locket, sterling silver on a length of black velvet ribbon, before carefully undoing the clasp and opening it to reveal the two tiny miniatures it contained.

Her mother must have loved her very much, Cecile reasoned, for both miniatures were of herself as a tiny child, one showing her right profile, the other her left, so that she appeared to be facing herself. Marguerite must have wanted to capture her daughter from every angle. Cecile's only regret was that she hadn't used one half for a picture of herself. That would have made it doubly precious.

No matter. She closed the locket, cupped it once more in her hands and pressed it to her heart.

'Help me, Mama, please help me,' she whispered. 'I love him so much.'

A feeling of peace enveloped her. She lay back, still clutching the locket, and closed her eyes. It never failed to work its magic. At times such as this, she could almost believe her mother was here with her. For that, she was truly grateful.

Chapter Three

'Hey, me lovely – you be at it again!'

The young man swaggering along the harbourside with the rolling gait of a seaman came to a stop as he reached the girl who sat gutting pilchards on the steps leading up to one of a row of fisherman's cottages.

She looked up, dropping the fish into one pail and dusting the blood and gore from her knife into another. 'Well, Billie Moxey, and aren't you the clever one!'

He grinned, and in the bright sunlight the furrows that had already begun etching themselves into his weather-tanned face deepened. 'I keeps me eyes open. Specially if they might light on the prettiest girl in Cornwall.'

'Oh, get along with you!'

Lise Bisset was well used to the Moxey boys – all five of them. She'd lived next door to them for as long as she could remember, and they'd grown up together. They were all rascals with a wicked twinkle in their eye, even Marco, the youngest at just twelve years old, but apart from Aaron – a year younger than Billie and a year older than her – who had an unpleasant side to his nature, they also possessed hearts of gold, just as their parents did. Lise thought of them almost as brothers, though she knew that beneath his tomfoolery and teasing, Billie, at least, would have liked it if her feelings for him had been more than that.

He leaned back casually against the low wall beside the stone steps, hands thrust into the pockets of his worn, salt-stained breeches, but his expression now was concerned.

'So if you be here cleaning the fish, Annie's no better then?'

Lise shook her head, and brushed back some of the thick chestnut hair that fell over her face. 'No. She can't seem to shake off this bad chest of hers. The Trevelyans have given me time off so I can be here with her.'

'That's kind of them.'

'They're good people. I was lucky to get a position with them and, as you know, I've worked my way up to parlourmaid. But if Annie's sick for long, well, they'll have to replace me, I should think.'

Even as she spoke, the wheezing and hawking of a coughing spasm could be heard from inside the house, and Lise dropped her knife into the bucket of fish guts and stood up, wiping her hands on the coarse sacking apron she wore over her skirts.

'I'd better go to her. Sometimes it's all she can do to catch her breath.'

'Yeah. You go on.'

Billie was unsure what else to say. His mother Gussie reckoned Annie was not long for this world, and from what Billie could hear of it, she wasn't far wrong. But he knew that Lise would be devastated if she lost her. It had been just the two of them since Annie's husband George had gone down with his fishing smack in a bad storm ten years or more since. Lise had no mother or father; but for Annie, she was alone in the world, and if Annie died, he didn't know what she'd do.

Unless . . .

Might it be he'd stand a chance with her if she had no one

else? He quickly pushed the thought aside, ashamed of thinking such a thing for even a moment. But for all that, he couldn't help the spark of hope that flared. He'd fancied Lise for as long as he could remember, but she seemed to think of him only as a friend. There was no one else as far as he could tell – for all the admiring glances she attracted from men and boys of all ages, he'd never seen her walk out with any of them. He couldn't understand it. But then that was Lise all over. A puzzle it was impossible to solve. A girl totally unlike any other he'd ever known.

Perhaps it was working for the Trevelyans, who lived in one of the big houses on the hill overlooking the town, that had made her different, he mused. Living cheek-by-jowl with the gentry, some of their fine ways had rubbed off on her. But Lise never affected airs and graces. Never thought she was better than anyone else. Never looked down on Annie, the fishwife, or on Billie's family.

She was just different. He couldn't say why, but she was. And it was that that drew him to her like a moth to a flame. He'd get his wings burned, he knew, but it made no difference. If ever Lise needed him, he'd be there. That was the way it had always been, and the way it would always be.

Billie sighed deeply, took one last look at the door through which Lise had disappeared, and headed for his own home.

'Annie?'

Lise hurried through the tiny kitchen to the living room beyond, where Annie lay on a bed Lise had made up for her on the sofa so she would not have to tackle the steep and narrow stairs. Annie's gnarled hands clutched her chest like claws as her body was racked with a fit of coughing, and her eyes, sunken in their dark-rimmed sockets, were closed.

Lise braced herself against the sofa, slipped her arms under Annie's and managed to haul her to a sitting position. As the coughing fit lessened and Annie sank back, exhausted, she fetched a cup of water and held it to the old woman's lips.

'Have a sip of this, and then you can have some of your medicine.'

Annie managed to drink a little, and Lise wiped away some water that had run down her chin. The medicine was on a small side table, and she uncorked the bottle and dribbled some of the potion into a spoon. But she couldn't help noticing that there was very little left.

'Have you been helping yourself to this?' she asked.

'No!' But Annie's expression was tinged with guilt, like a naughty child who'd been caught stealing biscuits.

'I think you have,' Lise reprimanded her gently. 'I think you've been drinking it straight out of the bottle. You know you shouldn't do that, Annie.'

'I like it,' Annie said mulishly.

'Well, there's not enough left to see you through the night. I'm going to have to go to the apothecary and get some more. But you must promise me you won't go on swigging it as if it was lemonade. Or gin,' she added, forcing a smile. 'I'll go next door and see if Mrs Moxey will come in and sit with you while I'm gone.'

'There's no need of that.'

'Maybe, but I'm fetching her all the same.'

'No!' Annie grasped Lise's hand. 'Don't go yet. There's something I have to—'

'You don't have to do anything but get better,' Lise interrupted her. 'What would I do without you, Annie? Now, not another word, or you'll start coughing again.'

She freed herself from Annie's grasp and went to the pottery

29

jar that stood on a corner of the mantelshelf. Counting out the money she'd need to pay the apothecary, she put it in a pocket in her reticule.

'Just behave yourself until I get back. And be sure Mrs Moxey will tell me if you don't,' she said, mock-sternly, and headed for the door.

'Well, this is a tidy how-d'ya-do and no mistake.'

Gussie Moxey settled herself with some difficulty in the chair beside Annie's bed. It hadn't been made with someone of her size and shape in mind. She and Annie could have hardly been more different in build: where Annie had always been skinny, even in the days before ill health had made her frail, Gussie seemed to overflow in all directions.

She'd made herself a jar of tea before sitting down, and offered one to Annie, but Annie hadn't wanted it. She didn't really want anything but her linctus, which slipped down nicely; it was all Lise could do to get a few spoonfuls of broth into her, and she'd eaten nothing solid for days now. 'Nothing tastes right,' she would say.

From the moment she'd arrived, Gussie could see Annie was agitated. She put it down to the coughing fit Lise had said she'd just had, and which Billie had reckoned he'd been able to hear right down on the harbour path. But when Gussie sat down, Annie reached over to grasp her plump knee, her mouth working as she summoned the energy to speak.

'Gussie . . . there's summat I've got to say to you . . .'

'You need to just stay quiet,' Gussie cautioned.

'No, listen, please. It's important.' Her tone was urgent, despairing almost. 'Lise won't let me speak and I'm not sure if I'm up to telling her. But I might not have long left, and she needs to know the truth.'

'She certainly do.' Gussie blew on her hot tea. 'She should'a bin told long ago.'

'Her mother didn't want that. She made me promise.'

'That was getting on for twenty years ago, Annie.'

'I know. But I always hoped . . .' Annie spluttered as a bit of phlegm caught in her throat.

'That she'd come back,' Gussie finished for her. 'And you didn't want Lise to know she'd just been abandoned.'

Annie recovered herself a little. 'I didn't, no. And truth to tell, I agreed t'was best to keep to ourselves how she and her sister came t'be here. But now . . .'

'How much does she know?' Gussie asked.

'Just that I took her and her mother in when her father was drownded. And she thinks her mother died of a broken heart.'

'Dear God, Annie!' Gussie shook her head in disbelief. The two women had been friends for as long as they'd been neighbours – thirty years and more – and she was familiar with Lise's story. But she'd never realised just how little Lise herself knew.

'So you're saying you want me to tell her everything if you aren't able to do it yourself?'

'Yes, Gussie . . . please, I'm begging you . . .'

'Course I will.' Gussie didn't relish the task, but it was the least she could do to set her old friend's mind at ease.

'Thanks.' Annie closed her eyes and sank back on the pillows, exhausted.

It was mid afternoon as Zach walked slowly along the St Ives waterfront. Godfrey Pendinnick had asked him to liaise with a man who was his contact on the north coast, and now he was killing an hour or so before the meeting was due to take place. He paused outside a chandler's shop, browsing the wares stacked outside – brooms and mops, reels of rope and cordage, and lanterns hanging on hooks above the frontage.

When he'd left home this morning, he hadn't anticipated trouble, and was unarmed, but now that he was on his way to meet a man he didn't know – maybe a ruthless and dangerous character who might have plans of his own – Zach thought he would like to have something he could use to defend himself should the need arise.

He ventured inside, breathing in the familiar smells of oil, turpentine, pitch and sail cloth all mingled together.

Chisels, planes and hammers lay in boxes along the counter, but it was the marlin spikes that caught Zach's eye. The wooden-handled knives with their metal blades tapering to a sharp point were exactly the sort of weapon he was looking for. It would fit nicely into his pocket and no one would be any the wiser.

When he had paid for his purchase and the chandler had wrapped it in a scrap of old sailcloth, Zach left the shop, tied Gypsy to a hitching post beside a drinking trough and headed into the narrow streets of the town. He didn't know the alehouse where the meeting was to take place – truth to tell, he scarcely knew St Ives at all – but Godfrey had provided him with clear directions, and he followed the landmarks deeper and deeper into the maze of streets and alleys, not much liking the feel of the district he found himself in, and glad of the marlin spike nestling in his pocket.

Just ahead of him, a young woman emerged from the doorway of an apothecary's shop and hurried away along the street. Zach might never have noticed her but for the thick tumble of auburn curls that cascaded over her shoulders, an unusual and welcome sight in these days of pompadour wigs and pigtails. Now that was something a man could run his hands through, he thought wistfully, and wondered who she was and where she came from. Perhaps she was a gypsy. Some-times the travelling folk came to Cornwall in the summer months to sell bunches of lucky white heather or tell fortunes at the fairs and Golowan festivals that were held during the summer months.

As he pondered, a rough-looking man emerged from the shadows of a doorway just in front of the young woman. She stepped to one side to pass him by, but he moved purposefully in the same direction. Instantly Zach was alert, his muscles tensing ready for action as he sensed trouble brewing. A moment later, his finely tuned instincts proved to be correct. In a flash the man had made a grab for the girl's reticule, snatching it from her arm so violently that she staggered and fell, then made off down the narrow street.

Zach didn't hesitate. Without a second's thought, he set off in pursuit. The man was moving awkwardly, as if one leg was a little shorter than the other, and Zach caught him easily with a flying tackle. The man went down heavily and Zach straddled him, wrenched the bag from his grasp, then hauled him to his feet and thrust him back against the wall of one of the higgledy-piggledy buildings that lined the street on either side, pinning him there with a hand around his scrawny throat.

'Rob a young lady, would you? And in broad daylight too? Take this as a lesson you won't forget.'

He brought his bunched fist up and hit the thief hard in the face, hearing the crunch as his nose broke, then turned away as the man crumpled and slid down the wall until he was sitting on the cobbles.

Zach retraced his steps. The young woman was bent double, retrieving a small package wrapped in brown paper that she must have dropped when she fell.

'Are you all right?' he asked.

'Yes, but my bag . . .'

'I took it off him. Here you are.'

As she straightened up, Zach experienced the strangest feeling of déjà vu. If it weren't for the flowing auburn hair and the cheap, unfashionable gown and shawl she was wearing, he could have been looking into the face of Cecile Pendinnick.

'Thank you so much!' As she took the reticule from him, that glorious hair fell across her face, hiding her features; then, without another word, she turned and hurried off in the direction she had been heading before she had been accosted, anxious, most likely, to get away from this rough district and the vagrants and vagabonds who frequented it.

Zach stared after her, puzzled and a little shocked by the girl's startling likeness to Cecile. He'd imagined it, surely. The jar of ale he'd had earlier must have gone to his head. And he had seen her face only fleetingly.

He gave himself a small shake. He didn't have time to wonder about it now if he wasn't going to be late for his meeting with Godfrey's associate.

As he set off along the street, the girl was disappearing into the distance and the thief was nowhere to be seen. He felt a quick stab of satisfaction that he'd been able to get her bag back from him and teach the thief a lesson into the bargain. And all without the marlin spike. Good. Zach much preferred employing his own strength to settle matters without having to resort to a weapon. But the men he was dealing with were a sight more dangerous than a lame thief and, for all he knew, he might yet need the spike before the night was over.

The Wink tavern in Porthmeor was filling up fast as the gang members who were to unload the incoming contraband and send it on its way inland congregated. Every nook and cranny, every settle, was filled with men enjoying a jar of ale before commencing their night's work.

Zach, who had been entrusted with the job of organising the operation, stood in the doorway, counting in his team. His assignation in St Ives had gone off without a hitch and he had ridden back before nightfall. When Sam arrived, however, he pulled him to one side.

'Did you know Cecile had a fall after you left her today?' Seeing the alarm on the coachman's face, he added: 'Don't fret, she isn't hurt bad, just shaken up, and some scrapes and bruises that'll be sore for a few days. I was heading for Polruan House. I found her on the cliff path and saw her safely home. Her horse had bolted.'

Sam swore. 'I thought Lady was a bit lathered up when I got back. I should have known something like this would happen. Cecile's frightened to death all the time she's in the saddle. Dear Lord, she could have broken her neck.'

'But she didn't. She's home now, and no harm done. But Cordelia is a witch and no mistake. She showed no concern for Cecile, just laid into her for riding out on her own.'

'She's a witch all right. Between her and Godfrey, Cecile's like a caged bird. I've got to get her away from there somehow, Zach, before they break her spirit completely – she's timid enough already, thanks to the way they treat her. But how in hell's name can I do it? If we got caught – and we would – he'd have me thrown into jail most like, and that would be the end of it. We'd never see one another again. It's bloody torture, and I don't see any end to it.'

'Well, go and get yourself a drink. We should be seeing some action soon. And get me one while you're about it.'

Just then, however, came the sound of a low-pitched whistle. To the uninitiated it might well have been the call of a night bird, but both Zach and Sam knew different. It was a signal from the lookout. The ship they were waiting for had been sighted.

'Looks like we're going to have to wait for that drink, unless you're real quick,' Zach said.

'I will be.' Sam was already disappearing into the Wink. 'Reckon I owe you that much, Zach, for what you did today.'

'No problem.' Zach's mind was already on what he had to do to ensure the operation ran smoothly. To fail would be to jeopardise everything he was working for.

As he issued orders to the men who had gathered, he forgot all about the girl he had seen in St Ives.

Noises from beneath her bedroom window woke Cecile. The sound of something heavy being dragged around the side of the house, and voices, low and indistinct, but unmistakably men with local accents. Though they invariably made her uncomfortable, those sounds, at the same time they drew her like a magnet. She slipped out of bed and padded to the window.

The moon was partly hidden by scudding clouds, but still gave enough light for her to make out the shapes of the men on the path and the large container they were dragging behind them. Others, carrying smaller, lighter packages – crates, a long roll wrapped in paper and straw – stepped on to the lawn that bordered the path to overtake them, and quickly disappeared from view. Still the men manoeuvring the heavy container struggled up the path, stopping only occasionally to wipe the sweat from their brows.

'Get a move on, can't you? We haven't got all night!' She recognised the voice as Zach's.

'Then give us a hand.' To her dismay, she realised one of the shadowy figures was Sam.

'Two old women could do better.' But Zach lent his strength

to their efforts, and soon the container, Zach, Sam and the other man had disappeared from her line of vision.

Shivering although it was a warm night, Cecile crept back to bed and pulled the covers over her head.

She'd known for a long time what went on under cover of darkness, and hated it. But to see Sam working with the smugglers was a low blow that had left her sickened and shaking.

Were nights like this what had driven her mother away? she wondered. Though she had been told her mother was dead, she'd somehow never quite believed it; why, she couldn't be sure. She'd seen the name etched on the simple headstone in the churchyard – Marguerite Pendinnick. She'd laid flowers there. But it didn't seem real to her. She couldn't believe her mother lay beneath that simple headstone – or perhaps she didn't want to believe it.

She squeezed her eyes tightly closed as if she could shut out what she had just seen, pressed her hands over her ears to block out the sounds of the activity below. Oh, if only she could get away from this place and never have to witness such scenes ever again! Her father loved her, and she supposed she loved him. But she didn't want to spend the rest of her life here, imprisoned in this house like a princess in a tower. She wanted to be free, to be with Sam, never again to have to watch him struggling with the contraband that financed her luxurious life.

Tears ran in slow rivers down Cecile's cheeks, and it was a long time before she fell asleep again.

Chapter Four

Although he had only had a few hours' sleep, Zach was awake early the morning following the landing of the smuggled cargo, his nerves still stretched tight and his head abuzz. He mentally ran over his part in the operation, checking that everything had been done right and he had done nothing to give Godfrey cause to dispense with his services. But all the while he kept thinking about the girl he had seen in St Ives. He simply couldn't understand why he should have imagined that she was so like Cecile as to be her double. The flowing auburn hair, the poor-quality gown and shawl could scarcely have been more unlike Cecile's powdered wig and expensive clothing, and yet . . . it might have been Cecile there in the alley, scrabbling on the cobbles for the package she had been carrying, and he was intrigued to the point where he couldn't get her out of his head.

When the opportunity arose, he'd revisit St Ives, he decided. Though the chances of running into her again were slim, he was almost certain it had been the apothecary's shop she'd emerged from when he'd first caught sight of her, and it was possible that she'd be known there. There couldn't be many girls with her glorious auburn hair in the town, surely?

His mind made up, he concentrated once more on the

previous night's work. Godfrey Pendinnick would be expecting him later so that they could discuss the operation, tie up any loose ends and send whatever contraband was still stored in the outbuildings at Polruan House on its way inland. Zach wanted to be sure he was prepared for any eventuality.

Unlike Zach, Godfrey Pendinnick had slept late. He wasn't as young as he used to be, he thought ruefully. Time was when he could have been up most of the night and still be fresh as a daisy next morning. Now, though his manservant had helped him out of his nightgown and into his day wear and wig, he still felt unready to face the world.

He could hear a dog barking on the lawns beneath his bedroom; he crossed to the window and opened the drapes. Yes, as he'd thought, Cecile was there playing with Moll, her spaniel. Godfrey didn't care for the dog – a silly, yapping thing, he thought it – but his florid features softened as he watched his daughter tossing a ball and chasing Moll around the garden. Dear God, she was so much like Marguerite! He could only hope that Cordelia was wrong, and his beloved daughter wouldn't break his heart as her mother had done.

Tears misted his eyes and he brushed them away impatiently. No sense pining. He'd loved her and lost her and that was an end of it. But his memories refused to be banished. He sank down into the brocaded chair beside the window, listening to Cecile's laughter as it floated up to him, and remembering.

From the very first moment he had set eyes on Marguerite, he was smitten. She had glowed like a bright jewel in the dark interior of her father's storehouse in the port of Brest, and he wanted her more than he had ever wanted anything in his life.

It was unusual for Godfrey to make the trip to France and

deal directly with the traders who supplied him with the goods he smuggled into England. It was Cordelia who was responsible for that part of the operation. But Cordelia had taken ill with a fever that had left her weak and in no fit state to make the crossing, let alone thrash out the finer points of the arrangement and secure a good bargain, and Godfrey had gone in her place.

Jacques Marchand was descended from a long line of merchants who had traded in Brest for centuries, hence his surname, which denoted the trade of his ancestors. He was a small, wiry man with beetling brows that almost met above dark, beady eyes and a small, straight nose; looking at him no one would have dreamed that he could have fathered a daughter as beautiful and magnetic as Marguerite. Godfrey had known him for years, but Marguerite had been scarcely more than a child when he had last seen her, and he had taken scant notice of the girl playing hide-and-seek with her brothers amongst the kegs of brandy and rolls of fine silks in her father's warehouse. The Marguerite he met now was a different matter entirely.

Though Marie Antoinette was the leader of fashion – her whims followed eagerly in France, and England too – and ladies were dressing their hair in ever more elaborate confections, adding height with pads of cotton wool and decorating the towering result with feathers, buckles and flowers, Marguerite had no time for such extravagance. Instead, her glorious auburn hair fell in shining waves and curls to her shoulders, and Godfrey, mesmerised, longed to reach out and touch it. Her complexion was creamy and clear; she had no need of the black silk or paper patches that so many women – and men too – wore to cover the blemishes that erupted as a result of the use of hair powder and too little cleansing. And neither were her skirts hooped; from a tiny waist they skimmed her hips alluringly.

Even as he talked business with her father, Godfrey could scarcely take his eyes off her. And before he left France for home, he had made up his mind. By hook or by crook he would make her his.

When he told Cordelia that he would be the one to deal with Monsieur Marchand from now on, she smiled archly.

'Ah, so you have met Marguerite, then,' she said.

A faint colour rose in Godfrey's cheeks. 'She was assisting her father in his warehouse.' His tone was defensive.

'And? You were struck by her beauty?'

'She's a fine-looking woman.'

'Who is betrothed to a soldier, I understand.' Her smile had become one of satisfaction. 'So I'm afraid, my dear brother, that your visits to France will be in vain.'

Godfrey's lip curled, his eyes as hard as clean-washed pebbles on the beach. 'Time will tell, Cordelia. Time will tell.'

With that, he turned and strode from the room.

Over the following weeks, Godfrey had visited Jacques Marchand far more often than his business required, on one pretext or another, and went out of his way to strike up a friendship with the merchant, whose English was good enough to make up for his own somewhat rusty expertise in the French language. Sometimes he stayed over for several days, occupying a spare room in the Marchand house. But for all his efforts, he was unable to make progress with his pursuit of Marguerite. She remained cool, aloof even, busying herself with some household task or bent over the sampler she was sewing so that that glorious auburn hair spilled over her face in tantalising curls. Often she retired early, leaving her father alone with Godfrey.

'She's gone to moon over Jean-Claude, I shouldn't wonder,' Jacques grumbled by way of explanation.

A flicker of unease pricked Godfrey's gut. The fiancé Cordelia had mentioned had never been in evidence when he was visiting, and he had begun to dare hope that the man was a spiteful invention of his sister's. It seemed he had been wrong.

'She has a beau?' he asked, trying to hide his dismay.

'Hmm,' Jacques grunted. 'More's the pity.'

'You don't approve of him?' Godfrey's hopes rose a shade.

'He's a nice enough fellow, but I'd be happier if she'd set her cap elsewhere,' the merchant said, reaching for his glass of brandy. 'He's a soldier to the marrow of his bones and away in India fighting to defend our holdings from you British. And getting the worst of it, by all accounts. We lost Chandannagar back in '57, and now it looks like we're going to lose Wandiwash. For all we know, Jean-Claude could have been killed or badly wounded already. If I can't persuade her different, my Marguerite is going to end up either a widow or caring for a cripple, and she deserves better than that.'

Godfrey, who knew nothing of the Anglo-French wars in India, took a sip from his own glass. 'But if she loves him . . .' he said nonchalantly, playing devil's advocate.

Jacques snorted, and brandy bubbled out over his lip and ran down his chin. 'Love! What does she know about love? She's nothing but a girl. It's a fancy, nothing more, and she'll grow out of it. That's what I'm hoping. Besides, love doesn't pay the bills, or put food on the table or clothes on your back, and that one will never earn more than I can afford to pay him. No, if she's any sense in that pretty head, she'll marry where money is. And until she chooses right, she'll never have my blessing.'

Both men were silent for a moment, Jacques wiping his chin with the back of his hand and taking another pull of his brandy, Godfrey digesting what his friend had just said. Then Jacques rose to refill his now empty glass and top up Godfrey's, muttering as he did so: 'And she'd better not take too long about it, or I'm done for.'

Godfrey looked up sharply, uncertain as to whether he had heard aright. 'What are you talking about, *mon ami?*'

For a long moment Jacques was silent again, sitting down heavily in his chair and sighing deeply. 'I have big problems,' he said at last, his voice so soft Godfrey had to lean forward to hear his words. 'I have many debts, and I don't know how I am going to pay them.'

'But I thought you had a thriving business here!' Godfrey said, surprised.

'It was doing well enough until I behaved foolishly.' The merchant couldn't meet his friend's eye, staring instead into his glass of brandy as if the answer to his problems could be found in its depths.

'Foolishly? How?' Godfrey asked.

At last Jacques looked up, and Godfrey saw the shame in his face.

'Have you never been tempted by the turn of the cards, my friend? And ended up chasing your losses?'

'No,' Godfrey said bluntly – and truthfully. He'd never had time for such things. He preferred to rely on his own wits to make his fortune.

'Then you are a wiser man than I,' Jacques said sorrowfully. 'At first I was lucky, but when my fortunes changed, I went on, wagering more and more in the hope of them favouring me again. That didn't happen, and now I am at the point where I stand to lose everything – my home, my business, my family's reputation. I don't have enough left to pay for the goods I have here in my warehouse, let alone more. I tell you, *mon ami*, I am at my wits' end as to what to do next.'

He sank his head in his hands, and did not see the smirk of satisfaction that twisted Godfrey's lips as he leaned forward in his chair, hands resting on his knees.

'How much do you need to get yourself out of this mess?' he asked.

'A great deal.' Jacques mentioned a sum that made Godfrey wince. But with his blood growing hot, money, even a sum such as this, was but the merest trifle.

'Supposing I was to make you a loan,' he said silkily. 'I would have to return to England to arrange it, but I dare say I could be back within the week. Can you hold off your debtors until then?'

Jacques raised his head, staring at him in disbelief. 'You'd do that? But . . .'

'I can well afford it,' Godfrey said easily. 'But I need to know it won't all go into the pockets of your . . . friends across the piquet table.'

'Oh, I'm done with that, never fear,' Jacques said emphatically. 'But I can scarcely believe you would trust me with so much . . . How can I ever thank you?'

'There is something . . .' Godfrey paused, pretending reluctance.

'Anything. Name it, my friend, and consider it done.'

'You said, I believe, that you would wish your daughter to marry a man of means?'

'I most certainly would.'

A faint smile twisted Godfrey's lips. 'So. Here he sits before you.'

'You?' The one word conveyed Jacques' surprise – disbelief, almost.

'She's a beautiful woman. I've long admired her. I would be honoured indeed to make her my wife.'

Jacques shook his head slowly. 'It's a kind and generous offer, but I don't know if she would be willing. You have my blessing to speak to her, but as I told you, her heart is set on Jean-Claude.'

Godfrey's eyes hardened, but his smile never faltered. 'And if I should make it a condition of the loan I have offered?'

Confusion and distress crumpled the merchant's face. Godfrey waited while the other man tried to find a way through his conflicting emotions.

'Well?' he said at last. 'Surely Marguerite would be only too glad to save her father from ruin?'

'I'll speak to her.' Jacques' voice was low and toneless.

'Good. And you had better make it soon. Your situation, it seems, worsens by the day, and my offer of assistance will not remain open for ever.'

Godfrey had been in little doubt as to the outcome of the conversation. Without the money he was able to provide, Jacques faced losing everything, and he could not imagine Marguerite allowing that if she could prevent it, no matter that her heart had been given elsewhere. And if she did, then Jacques had it in his power to enforce the match. It would not be an easy decision, Godfrey knew; the merchant idolised his daughter. But what future could he provide for her if he was bankrupted and disgraced? No, Godfrey felt confident that together father and daughter would conclude that the only way forward was to accept his proposal of marriage with good grace.

And so it had proved. The following day Jacques had come to him to say they could seal the bargain, and they had shaken hands upon it. Godfrey was to travel to England to do what was necessary to turn over the promised sum to Jacques, and when he left France to return home again, Marguerite would go with him. He could tell that Jacques regretted what he had been forced to do, and when the young woman was called to join them, she entered the room stiff and stony faced.

When Godfrey approached her and reached for her hand, she did not pull it away, allowing him to raise it to his lips and press a kiss against her cool, unresisting flesh. But all the time her eyes, icy blue and glittering with hatred, never left his.

Godfrey, however, was not deterred. The prize was his, and he liked nothing better than a challenge. He would enjoy every moment, just as he enjoyed breaking in a mettlesome horse.

Now, sitting in his brocaded chair listening to Cecile's laughter floating up from the lawns beneath his window, a smile flickered across his face as he remembered. Oh, he'd never broken Marguerite, but the pleasure he had gained from their encounters had been immense.

His blood ran hot as he recalled the first time he had taken her, in her cabin on the boat back to England.

He could see her still as she had been that night when he had thrown open the door without knocking – her corset half unlaced, that glorious auburn hair flowing over her bare shoulders. She had stiffened and grabbed her nightgown, which was lying on the bunk, holding it up before her, her face a picture of horror and outrage.

'How dare you!' she demanded.

A smile crossed his lips. 'I come to claim my husband's rights.'

Her eyes flashed cold blue fire. 'You are not my husband yet.'

'But soon I will be. What does a few days, or even weeks matter? We have a bargain, remember.'

'How could I forget?' Her tone was bitter.

A flash of anger ran through his veins, fuelling his hot desire. 'I see you need taming, my lady.'

He reached out and tore the nightgown from her grasp so that she was naked but for her corset, but this time she did not seek to cover herself, simply stood there, defiance in every line of her body and the set of her face. Then, as he came closer, she raised her hand and struck him full in the face.

Godfrey merely laughed, though his flesh burned where her fingers had connected with his cheek. He picked her up bodily and flung her on to the bunk, holding her down with one hand whilst removing his breeches. She fought him every step of the way, her nails raking his bare back, but she was no match for his strength, and her tigerish resistance only served to heighten his excitement and determination to make her his.

At last, when he was done, and rolled off her bruised and violated body, she pushed herself up on to her elbows, looking down at him not with tears or even shame, but with the same scorn as before.

'I hope you are satisfied, sir,' she said coldly.

And Godfrey had smiled as he gave her his reply. 'I will never be satisfied, my love. I could never get enough of you.'

Oh yes, they had been good years, though he knew she despised him. It had been enough to know that she was his, and he was her master. He was proud to have her on his arm and glad to have her in his bed on whatever terms. If she was unhappy, she never gave him the satisfaction of showing it. And to the outside world, she presented a serene face, whatever her hidden feelings might be.

What a woman she was, he thought now. If only Cecile had half her spirit! But at least she was still here, the living embodiment of her mother, and for that he could only be grateful.

He rose, opened the window, and called down to her. 'Cecile! You've been outside in the sun for long enough. Come inside, and we'll play a game of hide the ball with the dog in the parlour.'

Then he went downstairs to spend an hour or so with his beloved daughter before attending to the business of the day.

Chapter Five

Three days later, Zach rode into St Ives, the sun slanting low between the buildings that lined the narrow streets as he made his way towards the apothecary's shop.

The bell above the door jangled as he entered, and a wizened little man of middle age emerged from behind shelves filled with glass jars and bottles containing powders and brightly coloured potions.

'Yes, sir, how can I be of assistance?' he asked genially. 'Is what you require for yourself? Or for a friend or relative?'

His accent wasn't English, Zach thought, but no matter. It wasn't unusual to find a foreigner in a port such as St Ives.

'Neither,' he replied. 'I'm hoping you can help me with regard to a young lady who was a customer here a couple of days ago. I happened to catch a glimpse of her, and I feel sure she is an old friend of my sister's. Polly would so love to see her again if only I could find her.' He didn't like lying, but he was afraid the apothecary would be suspicious of him and refuse information if he told the truth.

'Ah!' The apothecary smiled and wagged a knowing finger in Zach's direction. 'You mean a young lady with beautiful red hair?'

Zach nodded.

'Then that was Lise Dupont. Is that the name of your sister's friend?'

'Indeed it is,' Zach said, pleased with himself. 'Could you tell me where I may find her?'

'Well, certainly. She's in here often enough for linctus and the like for the old woman she lives with.'

'And where might that be?'

'There's a rank of fisherman's cottages down by the harbour. Cockle Row, they call it. If you follow the road straight down to the water's edge and then turn to your left, you can't miss it.'

'Thank you. I am much obliged.'

As Zach turned to leave, the apothecary called after him: 'I hope you find old Annie better today. Please give her my regards.'

'I will,' Zach replied, and left the shop quickly before the apothecary could ask him any awkward questions.

'Would you like to sit outside for a bit? The sun's nice and warm, and the fresh air would do you good.'

Lise came in from the front garden, where she was peeling potatoes for the evening meal, and into the tiny sitting room where Annie was resting in an armchair. She was definitely a little better today; Lise had been able to get her up and dressed, and she couldn't help wondering if the apothecary had added something extra to the fresh bottle of linctus. She might even have begun to hope that Annie was improved sufficiently for her to return to work, had it not been for the unexpected caller this morning.

She had answered the knock at the door to find Mrs Trevelyan on the doorstep, looking utterly out of place here on the street of fisherman's cottages. She stood awkwardly, holding her skirts clear of the salty sand that covered the step, and Lise could only hope she hadn't been subjected to ribald comments as she'd walked along the harbour.

Lise had invited her employer in, flustered and feeling ashamed of her humble abode, and offered her a jar of tea, which Mrs Trevelyan had declined.

'You must be Annie,' she said, extending a gloved hand to the old woman. 'How are you feeling today?'

Annie bridled at the familiarity. 'I'm Mrs Parsons, yes. And I'm feeling more myself, thank you for asking.'

'I'm so glad.' Mrs Trevelyan showed no sign of discomfort. She was, in every sense, a lady. She turned to Lise. 'Would it be possible to have a few words in private?'

'Well . . . we'll have to go outside for that.' Already Lise had a pretty good idea of what was coming, and she thought it might be wise if it was said out of Annie's hearing. She didn't want the old woman flying off the handle and aiming some choice language in Mrs Trevelyan's direction. With some trepidation she led her employer back outside and closed the door after them.

'I expect you have come to find out when I'll be able to return to my duties,' she said. 'And I'm afraid the answer has to be that I honestly don't know. Annie certainly seems better today, but she's in no fit state to be left alone, and she might yet go downhill again.'

'Is there no one else who could care for her?' Mrs Trevelyan asked.

'No. There's a neighbour who pops in and sits with her for a bit if I have to go out, but I couldn't impose on her for more than that. And really someone needs to be within call all the time in case she has another coughing fit or wants something. This is the first day I've been able to get her out of her bed, and she's too weak to stand without help, let alone trying to get herself a drink or to the commode.'

Mrs Trevelyan nodded. 'Yes, I see. In that case, Lise, I'm afraid I have no option but to give you notice. I will be very sorry to see you go, and if ever a position arises in the future, then I would be only too happy to employ you again. But it's impossible to manage any longer short staffed as we are.'

It was just as Lise had feared, and her heart sank at the thought that she was going to lose a better position than she'd ever dared hope for. But what choice did she have? Annie had been like a second mother to her; now it was Lise's turn to care for her. If it meant she had to earn a living as a fishwife, so be it. Annie had survived on the meagre earnings since her husband had been lost along with his boat; Lise could do the same.

'I quite understand, Mrs Trevelyan,' she said. 'It's very good of you to have let me have the time off that you have, and it's not fair on the other girls. And thank you, too, for coming to speak to me yourself.'

'I wouldn't have dreamed of doing otherwise. You have been a valued member of the household for a long time, and it's I who should thank you.' Mrs Trevelyan patted Lise on the arm, then turned and went down the flight of stone steps to the harbour path.

Lise watched until she was out of sight, an elegant figure once again hitching up her skirts to avoid the dirt and puddles of seawater, then went back inside the house.

She told Annie only that Mrs Trevelyan had come to find out for herself when she might be able to return to work; she didn't want her to fret over being the reason she had lost her position. Now, suggesting that Annie might like to sit outside for a little while, she couldn't help thinking how ironic it was that she might be making a recovery just too late to save her from dismissal.

''Twould be good to smell the air,' the old woman said.

'Just wait there, then, and I'll take your chair out.'

She bundled the heavy old chair to the door and managed to manoeuvre it out by tipping it first one way then the other, then paused to catch her breath while working out the best place to put it so that it would be both on even ground and in a sunny spot.

'Moving house?'

It was Aaron Moxey, regarding her with some amusement from the path leading to the house next door.

'You know very well it's not that,' she retorted sharply. 'And if you were any kind of a gentleman, you'd come and lend me a hand instead of trying to be funny.'

'I've never made no pretence of bein' a gennelmun, unlike my brother, but I'll give you a hand if that's what you want.' Aaron crossed the path, and stood, hands on hips, eyeing up the chair. 'Where d'you want'un?'

Lise pointed to a spot with a good view over the harbour. 'There would be fine. But just be careful with it. Not too close to the steps. I don't want it to fall and get damaged.'

'Think I can't see that fer meself? Don't you trust me, Lise?'

Lise tossed her head. 'I've never trusted you, Aaron Moxey. Not since you locked me in the fisherman's hut.'

'You got a long memory! You couldn'a bin more than a nipper.'

'Maybe, but it's not something I'm ever likely to forget.' It was no more than the truth. The Moxey boys had been swimming in the sea, but Lise had been unable to do more than paddle, and, bored, she'd gone back up the beach to a row of fisherman's huts. The door of one of them was ajar, and she'd ventured inside, fascinated to see what lay behind the weathered walls and beneath the neatly thatched roof. It was dark inside, but she could make out the shape of creels lined up against the walls, and the strong smell of fish made her wrinkle her nose.

Suddenly a loud thud made her jump almost out of her skin, and what little light there had been was extinguished. She was in total darkness. The door had slammed shut, she realised. She stumbled towards it, searching for the latch, but the door refused to budge, no matter how hard she pulled on it. Something was preventing it from opening.

'Help!' she screamed, but the only response was the sound of a bolt screeching home, and an unpleasant laugh.

'That'll teach you!' It was Aaron. She'd know his voice anywhere.

'Aaron! Let me out!'

But he only laughed again, and she heard his footsteps crunching away.

Panic had set in then. She'd beaten on the door with her fists, terror and the overwhelming smell of fish making her nauseous, and the inky blackness closing in around her. She screamed and screamed until she was hoarse, but it seemed an eternity before the bolt was drawn and Billie stood there, looking bemused.

'What be you doing in there?'

'Aaron locked me in,' she sobbed. 'And then he went and left me.'

'Bastard! Wait till I get my hands on him . . . Are you all right?'

'I am now.' But she wasn't. Though her fierce pride was kicking in, she wanted nothing but to be home, with Annie. She headed back up the beach, only looking back when she reached the harbour wall; the last thing she saw was the two brothers rolling over and over on the sand. Billie was giving Aaron a beating, just as he'd promised.

It was just one of the mean tricks Aaron had played on her, though by far the worst. She'd had nightmares for weeks, and a fear of total darkness still haunted her. And though he was a young man now, not the cruel boy he'd once been, she still didn't like or trust him. She suspected he was mixed up in some of the nefarious dealings that went on in this part of the world. No, a leopard could never really change its spots.

Now, however, he positioned the chair exactly as she'd indicated and looked up at her with a wicked grin. On Billie the expression was disarming, but on Aaron it had an element of calculation.

'I take it this is fer Annie? D'you want me to help you get her out too?'

'Thanks, but no, you're all right. She's as light as a feather.'

And Annie wouldn't thank me for it, she added silently.

'The least we have to do with that Aaron the better,' the old woman always said. 'He's a wrong 'un, allus was, allus will be.'

Aaron shrugged. 'The offer's there if you want it. Don't say I never do anything for you.'

He sauntered away, heading for home, and Lise went to help Annie outside. She was so weak, Lise had to practically carry her. But at last she was settled in her chair, hawking at the phlegm that was still thick in her chest, and Lise returned to peeling the potatoes for supper.

Cordelia found Godfrey in his study, dozing in one of the easy chairs.

'Ha!' she said sharply. 'So this is what you do when you pretend to be working.'

Godfrey sat up, giving himself a little shake and straightening his wig, which had slipped to one side.

'The batter in that apple pudding Cook served was as heavy

as a waterlogged floor cloth,' he said. 'It settled most uncomfortably in my stomach.'

'Falling asleep in the chair won't help with that. A brisk walk would do you far more good.' She smirked. 'And in any case, I suspect the port you drank has far more to do with it than the pudding.'

Godfrey huffed impatiently. 'Just say what you've come to say and leave me in peace.'

'Very well.' Cordelia perched on the edge of a chair facing her brother. 'You remember how we were talking the other day about finding a husband for Cecile?'

'*You* made mention of it, yes. I don't recall having a conversation about it.'

'It really would be for the best,' Cordelia pressed on, regardless. 'And I have just the right man in mind. The vicar at Mousehole has recently lost his wife, and I hear he is struggling badly with her loss. I intend to visit him and make overtures on Cecile's behalf.'

'What?' Godfrey was almost speechless.

'He would make a most suitable husband for her, and I believe the life would suit her admirably too,' Cordelia stated. 'She can't remain here for ever, Godfrey. She's no longer a young woman, and will soon be just another old maid.'

'As you are,' Godfrey huffed.

'That is neither here nor there. What is right for me may be far from right for Cecile. As I said, I intend to speak to the vicar at the earliest opportunity, and I'll thank you not to try to prevent me.' With that, she turned and walked towards the door, leaving her brother fuming impotently.

Perhaps Cordelia was right. But the thought of his beloved daughter being wed and leaving the house was a dagger in his heart all the same.

* * *

Zach walked slowly along the harbour, looking at the row of cottages several feet above, reached by flights of stone steps at regular intervals. Two old men were sitting outside one, smoking clay pipes, and in the doorway of another a young woman was rocking a makeshift baby carriage. This is a fool's errand, he told himself. The chances of him clapping eyes on the girl who intrigued him so were next to nothing. Then, just as he was almost at the point of giving up, he saw her sitting with an older woman outside one of the houses a little further along the rank. There was no mistaking that auburn hair that gleamed in the sunlight and flowed like a molten river over her shoulders. She was bending over a tin bowl in her lap so he couldn't see her face, but no matter. It had to be her.

He slowed his pace, feigning interest in the fishing smacks pulled up on to the beach below the sea wall, ready for launching on the evening tide. Should he approach her? He doubted she'd recognise him; her glimpse of him would have been as fleeting as his of her before she'd fled. And unless he was close enough to get a good look at her face, he'd forever wonder if she was as like Cecile as he'd thought in that moment. Making up his mind, he walked slowly on along the harbourside.

As he reached the house where the two women sat, he glanced up and, at the same moment, so did the young woman.

'Good day to you.' He managed to keep his tone light and casual in spite of the jubilation he was feeling. He'd been right. The young woman looked exactly like Cecile.

'And to you.' But she was frowning slightly, a look of puzzled half recognition. Then, as he went to walk on, she called after him: 'Aren't you the man . . . ? Was it you, the other day?'

He stopped, feigning surprise, and turned.

'It was, wasn't it?' she said. 'You're the one who . . .' She hesitated, glancing at the old woman. 'Annie, I didn't tell you, but a ruffian tried to rob me when I was in town getting your linctus, and this young man came to my rescue.' She turned back to Zach. 'I was so anxious to get away, I'm afraid I didn't stop to thank you properly.'

'It was nothing.' Zach was still reeling from the girl's likeness to Cecile. 'I don't like to see vagabonds thieving from defenceless ladies.'

'What's all this?' the old woman wheezed. 'Why didn't you say, Lise?'

'I didn't want to worry you. There was no harm done, thanks to . . . I'm sorry, I don't know your name . . .'

'Zach Carver.'

'Zach. I don't know how to thank you.'

'I don't need thanking. Anyone would have done the same.'

'A lot wouldn't have. I really am so grateful. Can we offer you something to drink? A jar of tea, perhaps?

Zach hesitated. He would welcome the chance to get to know something about this girl. But he didn't think now was the time to push his luck.

'That's good of you, but I have to be somewhere. Perhaps if I'm down this way again?'

'Any time. Don't hesitate.'

'Thanks. And I'm glad I was able to help.'

With a smile and a nod, Zach turned and headed back the way he had come.

'Who was that you were talkin' to then?'

Aaron Moxey materialised on the path of the next-door cottage. He'd been eavesdropping, Lise realised.

'None of your business,' she said tartly.

'Seemed pretty friendly to me,' Aaron persisted. 'Our Billie won't be none too pleased, you inviting him in for tea.'

'It's none of his business either.' She glanced at the sky. The sun had disappeared behind a bank of cloud and the breeze coming off the sea had turned cold. Time to get Annie back inside before she caught a chill. 'If you want to make yourself useful, you can give me a hand getting Annie indoors,' she added.

To her surprise, he did as she asked. Hoping to find out a bit more about the stranger, she guessed. Well, he'd be out of luck.

The effort of returning inside was making Annie cough again, and Lise wondered whether it had been too much for her. When she recovered, however, her eyes were button-bright, though she had to press her hand to her chest in order to speak.

'Lucky for you that Zach sent the thief packing. He seems like a nice young man.'

'He certainly saved my bacon.' Lise plumped a pillow and set it behind Annie's thin shoulders.

'And we'll see him again, maybe.'

She gave a little shrug. 'I shouldn't think so. I thought it was only right to offer him some tea, but when I did, he was off before you could say Jack Robinson.'

Annie nodded sagely. 'Came looking for you, though, didn't he?'

'He was just out for a walk, by the look of it. And he was as surprised to see me as I was to see him.'

'Hmm.' Annie hawked into a kerchief. 'You can think what you like, but I reckon 'e came along here on purpose 'oping t'find you.'

'He wouldn't know where I lived,' Lise pointed out.

'There's ways and means. You're well known in St Ives, my

girl. And say what you like, I still think there was more to it than meets the eye. We'll find out soon enough if I'm right or not, and it's seldom I'm wrong when it comes to reading folk.' Annie leaned back against the pillow and closed her eyes, pointedly bringing the conversation to an end.

Lise went back outside to collect her pan of potatoes and bowl of pickings and found herself looking along the quayside, even though she knew the young man – Zach – was long gone. There was something about him that was stirring her in a way she hadn't been stirred since she was a young girl of sixteen or seventeen. His name had been Ahab and he'd been a fisherman, young, strong, tanned by the summer sun. The first time she'd seen him he'd been sitting on an upturned barrel mending his nets. He'd looked up and smiled at her, and that smile had started an excitement deep inside her that had lasted long after she was back at the cottage. She'd walked the same way the next day in the hope of seeing him again, and sure enough, there he was. This time he spoke to her, made conversation, and before she knew it, she was falling in love. He was her sun, her moon, her stars. She'd trusted him, given him her heart. And then, one day, he was gone without a word. Lise had been distraught, her world collapsing around her.

She'd got over him eventually, of course, but she'd never felt about anyone else the way she had felt about Ahab, and she'd made up her mind she never would. She never wanted to experience such heartbreak, such dark despair, ever again. And she'd shied away from any man who showed an interest in her, not trusting them, not trusting herself.

It shook her now that she was feeling that same twist of excitement, that same breathlessness she'd felt on first meeting Ahab. As if she was standing on the brink of something new and exciting. Well, it wasn't going to happen. Even if Annie was right and Zach did come back, she'd make sure she sent him packing.

Hardening her heart, she took the pan of potatoes into the kitchen and set it on the hob, refusing to give another thought to the young man who had unsettled her so.

Chapter Six

It was the following evening, and Zach had been to Polruan to discuss business with Godfrey. As he passed the stables, he saw Sam sitting on a bench outside, smoking a pipe and looking more downcast than he could ever remember seeing his friend.

'What's up with you?' he asked. 'You look as if you've lost a florin and found a sixpence.' When Sam didn't answer, merely shaking his head, he went on: 'What you need is a jar of ale. Let's go down to the Wink for a bit before I head home.'

Sam agreed, but the suggestion didn't seem to have cheered him up at all, and when Zach asked again what was troubling him, Sam pretended he hadn't heard.

The change in the weather that had threatened earlier had come to nothing; by the time they reached Porthmeor, it was soft dusk, the sky lit with just a faint rosy glow where it met the sea, and Zach suggested they take their drinks outside, where they could sit on a bench behind a rustic table.

He had decided it was useless to press his friend as to the reason for his glum mood. Sam would talk about it in his own good time and, in any case, Zach was impatient to share his own news, which he hoped might make Sam forget whatever was troubling him. When they were settled on the wooden bench, their drinks on the table before them, he began.

'Did you know Cecile's got a double?'

At his words, Sam spluttered into his ale. 'What?'

'She's got a double, I tell you. Her spitting image. Lives in St Ives. I couldn't believe it either when I saw her the other day. Some varmint was trying to steal her bag, and I went after the bastard and taught him a lesson he won't forget in a hurry. I didn't get to speak to her – she'd fled – and I thought my eyes must have been deceiving me. But I couldn't get it out of my head, so I went back to St Ives today and managed to track her down. She doesn't dress fine like Cecile, of course, doesn't wear a wig but, except for that, she's the dead spit of her.'

'Are you sure you aren't having me on?' Sam was regarding him suspiciously.

'Straight up.' Zach chuckled. 'You sure she's not leading a double life?'

Sam snorted derisively. 'She's hardly got one life, never mind two. I hope this other girl, whoever she is, has a better time of it than Cecile.'

'She might have her freedom, but she certainly doesn't have the advantages Cecile has,' Zach pointed out. 'Living in a fisherman's cottage, sometimes not knowing where her next meal is coming from and caring for a sick old woman can't be a lot of fun either.'

'Perhaps she'd like to swap places then,' Sam said sarcastically.

'What's got into you today, Sam?' Zach had finally had enough of his friend's ill temper. 'I've never known you to be quite this miserable.'

'Maybe I've got plenty to be miserable about,' Sam muttered.

'So tell me.' Zach took a drink of his ale, and Sam did the same. Then he raised his head, meeting Zach's eyes directly for the first time that evening.

'Pendinnick intends to marry her off. To the vicar of Mousehole, if you please. Cecile heard him and Cordelia talking about it. They want to get her out of harm's way, from the sound of it – and you know what that means.'

'Oh Sam.' Zach hardly knew what to say. No wonder Sam was in a dark place. This must have come as a dreadful shock to him. To lose the girl he loved, and to a man old enough to be her father, would leave him heartbroken. 'What did Cecile have to say about it?'

'She's in a terrible state, as you can imagine.'

'Do they know that she knows?' Zach asked.

'She doesn't think so. She was listening outside Godfrey's study door, and when she heard Cordelia bring the conversation to an end, saying she was going to speak to the vicar, she made a dash for it. I'm at my wits' end, Zach, trying to work out what to do. I think we're going to have to elope and hope we can go into hiding somewhere. I know the chances of us getting away with it are slim, but what choice do we have? We have no chance at all if they marry her off.'

Zach shook his head. 'I don't know what to suggest, Sam. If you decide to run away, you know I'll do whatever I can to help – create a diversion somehow, or tell them I saw you heading in the opposite direction to whichever way you've gone. It might buy you a little time.'

'And you'd lose your position with Pendinnick if he found out you'd sent him on a wild goose chase.'

Zach said nothing. He couldn't afford to fall out with Godfrey Pendinnick. Much as he wanted to assist Sam, he had to think of himself too.

The two friends finished their drinks in gloomy silence, then parted company and went their separate ways.

* * *

As he made his way back to Polruan the cloud of depression was still weighing Sam down. He'd been so delighted when Cecile had come out to the stables this morning with Moll at her heels and a carrot in her pocket for Lady, little knowing the awful news she was bringing with her. But he'd seen at once that something was very wrong. She'd ignored Lady's questing nose in her pocket, and looked to be on the point of tears. When she'd told him what she'd overheard, his heart had sunk like a stone, but he'd tried to comfort her, saying he'd think of something, that it would be all right in the end. But truth to tell, he couldn't see any way out that wouldn't end in disaster.

He hadn't wanted to share his news with Zach – he could hardly bear to think of it, let alone talk about it – but he was glad now that he had. At least it made him feel a little less alone. Perhaps between them they could come up with a plan.

As fragments of their conversation popped in and out of his head, like cards shifting in a shuffled pack, his mind went to what Zach had said when they'd first arrived at the Wink. A double. Cecile had a double living in St Ives. He couldn't imagine for a moment that there could be another woman alive who could match her, and certainly not one who lived in poverty in a fisherman's cottage. But incredible as it was, Zach had appeared to be perfectly serious.

Still pondering the mystery, he went through the gate that led from the cliff path on to the lawns of Polruan House, and quite suddenly a distant memory floated to him through the tangled web of his thoughts.

He was just a small boy, playing under the kitchen table, where his mother and her brother, Uncle Isaac, who had come over from Penzance to visit, were chatting over a pot of tea. He was pretending he was in a copper mine there in the dark under the table, and not paying much attention to the grown-ups until his mother mentioned their new neighbours up at Polruan House and asked Isaac if he knew them, since she believed they had come from Penzance.

Isaac had said yes, indeed he did know the man and his sister – and the little girl.

Sam had pricked up his ears then. He'd seen a child playing on the lawns and wondered if he could make friends with her and get himself invited into the grounds – the place had always fascinated him.

'Of course, there used to be two of them,' Isaac had continued.

Sam had sat up straight at that, and his head had bumped into the tabletop so violently that the teacups rattled. Ma had shooed him out, so he'd missed the rest of the conversation, but that evening he had overheard her talking to Pa. 'The poor man,' Pa said, and Ma said, 'Yes, 'tis very sad.' Later Sam had asked her about it, but she just said it wasn't talk for children, and after a bit he'd forgotten all about it.

Now, however, those snippets of conversation took on a new significance. *There used to be two of them.* Two little girls, he supposed. Could it be that Cecile had once had a sister, or even a twin? After he'd gone to work at Polruan and fallen in love with her, he had once asked her about her family, curious as to why it was only her, Godfrey and Cordelia. Her mother had died a long time ago, she had said, and he knew that was true because he had once seen her laying flowers in the churchyard, and when she'd left, he'd looked at the headstone. It had said *Marguerite Pendinnick, beloved wife of Godfrey*, and *mother of Cecile* and gave the date of her death, as 1764. But she'd made no mention of a sister.

It was possible, of course, that she might not know about her if she had been very young when whatever the tragedy was had taken place. But if Godfrey had lost a child as well as his wife, it could explain why he was so protective of Cecile, so possessive.

Curious and confused, Sam made up his mind to get to the bottom of it. He could ask Cecile again, a more direct question this time, but he didn't want to inadvertently cause her distress, especially as she might be totally ignorant of the existence of a sibling. His own mother was long dead, so he couldn't ask her. But Uncle Isaac was still alive, and still living in Penzance.

Sam decided that he would pay him a visit at the earliest opportunity.

To his shame, it was many years since Sam had visited his uncle, and he was shocked to see how frail and ill he looked. He had somehow imagined that Isaac would look exactly as he used to: upright, swarthy, well muscled from his years in the mines. The man he found sitting in a fireside chair was so thin his clothes seemed to hang on him, his cheeks sunken and his eyes rheumy.

He'd lost his sharp mind too, and seemed scarcely to know his nephew. It was only when Sam explained who he was that Isaac brightened. 'You're Alice's boy! My, how you've grown! And how is your ma? Keeping well, I hope.'

'Pa!' Lacey, his daughter, chipped in. 'You know very well she's been dead and gone for a long time. You went to the funeral, and Morwenna and me came with you.'

Sam exchanged a grateful glance with his cousin; he'd hardly known what to say. Lacey had changed almost beyond recognition too; the slender girl he remembered now had a thickened waist and the beginnings of a double chin.

'Pa do forget things,' she told him apologetically.

Sam's heart sank. 'It's my fault for not coming to see him before now,' he said. 'But my job keeps me busy, and if I'm ever in Penzance, I'm on Mr Pendinnick's time.'

'You be wi' *them*, be you?' she said, and Sam realised that not only was Godfrey still known well beyond Porthmeor, but from Lacey's rather dubious look, his occupation was common knowledge too.

'I'm coachman there,' he said swiftly, and made no mention of the nocturnal activities he was sometimes required to assist with.

'So what brings you here today?' his cousin asked, bustling to make a pot of tea.

'Truth to tell, 'tis about the Pendinnicks,' he said.

'The Pendinnicks!' The old man sat forward, wiping a dribble of spit from his chin with a bony finger and taking notice again. 'Live in Penzance, they do.'

'No, Pa, they went away from here. Must be getting on for twenty years since.'

'Oh ah, so they did.' Isaac plucked at his lip, exposing one yellowed tooth. 'No surprise there, really, seein' as what happened.'

Sam dropped to a crouch beside his uncle's chair, scarcely able to believe that the information he had come for was about to drop so easily into his lap. 'What did happen?' he asked.

'A bad business, that were. Drownded, all on 'em, bar one. 'Twas the wreckers were the cause of it, they reckoned. An' talk was that 'twas Pendinnick himself behind it. He couldn't 'ave known his wife and children were out there, caught in the storm. A bad business and no mistake.'

Sam was puzzled now. 'You mean his wife and children drowned?' he asked.

The old man nodded, but his eyes had clouded over and the few minutes of lucidity had passed. 'A bad business,' was all he kept saying, over and over, and Sam was afraid he would get no more out of him.

'I don't understand,' he said to Lacey as she handed him his jar of tea. 'Did Mr Pendinnick marry again after he lost his family?'

'I couldn't say.' Lacey took a seat and blew on her tea to cool it. 'I don't remember much about it. I was only a littl'un when it happened, an' it's all been forgotten for years now. Why do you ask?'

'Because Godfrey Pendinnick does have a daughter, Cecile. She's the reason I'm asking – we're sweethearts. But she can't be the child Uncle Isaac's talking about if that child was drowned.'

'Wait a bit.' Lacey set down her tea, looking thoughtful. 'I've got a funny feeling one of the girls was found half dead in the cove nearby where the ship went down. Pa!' She leaned across and shook her father's arm. 'Pa! Didn't they find one of the girls alive?'

''Tis no good askin' me. 'Tis all goin' again.' Isaac had retreated into the hinterland of his failing mind, but Sam was eager suddenly. *One of the girls*, Lacey had said. And that chimed with the words he remembered overhearing. *There used to be two of them*. He turned to his cousin.

'One of the girls,' he said. 'How many were there?'

'Just the two, as fur as I know.' Lacey reached for her tea again. 'Twins, if I remember rightly, but 'twas only the one who got found, and that would 'ave bin a miracle. They never did find the other one, nor Pendinnick's wife. Awful thing.' She shivered.

Sam, however, was jubilant. Cecile *had* had a twin! Somehow, miraculously, Cecile had been saved whilst her sister had supposedly drowned, along with their mother. But supposing she hadn't drowned at all! Supposing she too had survived, and was the girl Zach had seen in St Ives, who he claimed was Cecile's double?

As yet, though, he couldn't make sense of it. Why would she

be living in poverty in St Ives? And what about the mother? Had her body eventually been washed ashore? That would account for the grave in the churchyard. But if they had been living in Penzance at the time, why was she buried in Porthmeor? It was a complete puzzle, as well as being utterly unbelievable, like something out of a story.

After chatting some more with Lacey, he thanked her for the tea, promised to call again soon, and took his leave of her and his uncle. He couldn't wait to tell Zach what he had learned.

Once again the two friends were sitting on the bench outside the Wink, sharing a jug of ale, whilst Sam related the story he had pieced together from what Uncle Isaac and Lacey had said.

'So it seems Cecile had a twin,' he finished. 'D'you think she might be the girl you met in St Ives, washed up somewhere else where nobody knew who she was?'

'Possible, I suppose,' Zach said thoughtfully. 'An identical twin is the only explanation for her being so like Cecile.'

Sam took a quick swallow of his ale. 'She invited you back, didn't she?'

'She did say if I was ever in St Ives to call in for a cup of tea.' Zach sounded doubtful.

'Couldn't you take her up on it? I know it's a big favour, but it might give you the chance to find out a bit more about her.'

Zach smiled, thinking of the pretty girl with the flowing auburn hair. 'Not such a big favour actually. But what do you hope to gain from it?'

'I'm not sure. If she is Godfrey's lost child, and we could return her to him, perhaps he wouldn't keep Cecile so close. Or . . .' Sam hesitated. 'I know you were joking when you said she might like to change places with Cecile, but—'

'What are you talking about?' Zach demanded. 'Change places?'

'If she could pretend to be Cecile for just long enough for us to get clean away . . . I'd be forever in your debt, Zach – and hers, of course.'

'Have you taken leave of your senses? They may be identical, but she's not in Cecile's class! Her clothes, her hair . . . when have you ever seen Cecile without her wig?'

'If a wig and a change of clothes is all that's needed, then that's easily solved,' Sam said, and Zach could see that his friend was serious. 'Is she uncouth? Speaks badly?'

'No,' Zach admitted. 'There's something about her . . . It's almost as if she does have upper-class roots in her blood.'

'So there you be!' Sam said triumphantly. 'A few hours, that's all it would take, and we could be over Bodmin Moor and away.'

'I don't know, Sam . . .'

'What be you two doin' sitting out here in the dark?' A swarthy man was approaching, tankard of ale in hand, and swaying slightly, as if he'd already consumed too much.

'Keeping out of your way, Walter,' Zach said, but he knew the time for private conversation was over. Walter Freeman, one of Pendinnick's land crew, was noted for sticking like a limpet to whomever he'd targeted as next in line for his tall tales.

He drained the last of his ale and stood up. 'I'll think about it,' he told Sam, 'but for now I'd best be going.'

He walked away to where his horse was tethered, leaving Sam to the dubious pleasure of entertaining the garrulous Walter.

Zach was finding it impossible to sleep. Could Lise really be Godfrey's lost daughter? Cecile's twin? Unlikely as it seemed, it was really the only explanation for their startling likeness.

The plan Sam had suggested was madness, of course. How could a girl who lived in a fisherman's cottage masquerade as the daughter of gentlefolk, even for a few hours? And as for Godfrey loosening his hold over Cecile, if her twin came back from the dead, that was so much eyewash. He'd most likely try to run her life too and, although Zach had met her only briefly, he didn't think Lise would stand for that. From what he'd seen of her, she was too used to her freedom.

He thought too of what Sam had said about the girls and their mother drowning as a result of wreckers luring their ship on to the rocks. How ironic it would be if it had been Pendinnick's gang who had been the cause of him losing his wife and child! He felt no shred of pity, though, for a man who could indulge in such wickedness. He deserved to suffer the same grief as had so many others, widowed or orphaned out of sheer greed.

But if Pendinnick had known his family were out at sea, why had he allowed the operation to go ahead? Surely he would have realised there was always a chance that they would be guided to disaster by the false lights? And why were they aboard a boat without him in the first place?

Zach's curiosity was now thoroughly aroused. Gazing up from his bedroom window at the star-studded sky, listening to the distant roar of the surf on the shore, he came to a decision. He would take Lise up on her invitation to call again. It would be no hardship given what an attractive young woman she was. And he might find some answers to the multitude of unanswered questions.

Satisfied at last, he went back to bed and fell instantly into a deep and dreamless sleep.

Chapter Seven

Lise spread a clean sheet over Annie's bed, tucked it in and topped it with a blanket. The old woman was slowly improving, and Lise thought she should be able to make it up the stairs tonight. She'd sleep better in her own bed, and that would aid her recovery. She plumped up the pillows one last time, then picked up the heap of dirty linen and took it downstairs to the kitchen, where the copper was already on the boil. She poked the sheets and pillowcases into it with a long stick, added a blue bag and replaced the lid, before going into the tiny parlour, where Annie was sitting in her favourite chair.

'Your bed's all ready for you and the washing's on,' she said. 'It's a fine day, so it will dry nicely. Do you fancy a jar of tea, or something to eat?'

'I wouldn't mind a bit of bread and cheese,' Annie said. 'And perhaps a drop of ale?'

'You must be feeling better!' Lise said, smiling. Bread and cheese and a pint of ale was Annie's favourite mid-morning snack, but lately she hadn't wanted it – or anything else.

The kitchen was full of steam now, and the windows had misted over. Lise went to open one of them to let the fug out, and started in surprise. Heading up the path was the young man who had come to her rescue and then appeared so unexpectedly a few days later.

In spite of the fact that she had vowed she would never again allow her feelings to make her vulnerable to the sort of heartache Ahab had caused her, she had been unable to get Zach Carver out of her head. Every time she thought of him, a worm of excitement prickled inside her. And now here he was, almost as if her thoughts had conjured him up.

Her heart missed a beat, and as she hurried to the door, her hands flew to tidy her hair, which was tangled and damp from the steam from the copper.

'Well, this is a surprise!' she said, endeavouring not to let her sudden nervousness show.

'You did say to call if I was ever this way,' he reminded her.

'But I didn't really think you would . . .'

He smiled, a smile that crinkled the corners of his eyes. 'I can always go again.'

'No! Do come in, please!' Lise said hastily, afraid she had appeared unwelcoming, and then even more afraid that she sounded flustered now.

She opened the door wide, and Zach had to duck his head so as not to collide with the low lintel. In the tiny kitchen he seemed to be taller than she remembered, but every bit as devastatingly good looking, in spite of his nose being a little crooked, as if it had been broken at some time. Thick dark hair tied back in a ponytail, warm hazel eyes, strong chiselled jawline . . . Oh, that stupid flutter in her stomach!

She gathered herself together. 'Won't you sit down?'

'Thank you.' He took one of the two upright chairs set at the small oilcloth-covered table and glanced around the kitchen, empty but for the two of them.

'Your . . . grandmother? She's not . . . ?'

Given the state of Annie's health last time he was here, Lise realised Zach was half afraid she might have died, but couldn't bring himself to ask directly.

'She's in the sitting room, resting,' she said. 'She's been very ill but she seems to be on the mend now, thanks be to God. But she's not my grandmother. She's not really a relation at all, but she's like family to me. The only family I have.'

'Really?' Zach's eyes narrowed a fraction. 'It's good she's getting better then.'

'It's certainly a great relief.' She hesitated. 'Actually, I was just about to get her a jar of ale. Perhaps you'd like one too? Or I'll boil the kettle if you'd prefer tea.'

Zach smiled again, a smile that made the flutter inside her begin once more.

'Ale, if you can spare it.'

'Course we can. After what you did the other day, it would be a poor show if we couldn't. Maybe you'd like a bit of bread and cheese to go with it?'

'Oh – no, but thanks anyway.'

Lise poured three jars of ale. She didn't usually drink at this time of day, but she thought it might seem friendlier if she had one too. Not to mention steady her nerves!

'I'll just take Annie hers.'

She went into the little parlour and put the ale down on the stool beside Annie's chair. 'I'll bring your bread and cheese later,' she whispered. 'I've got a visitor.'

Annie gave her a knowing look. 'So I hear. That young man, if I'm not much mistaken.'

Lise put a finger to her lips. She didn't want the old woman to say something that would embarrass her.

Annie guessed her meaning. 'As if I would!' But she was still smiling with a mixture of amusement and satisfaction that at last Lise seemed to have taken a fancy to a young man. 'I can wait,' she said, reaching for her ale.

'So what brings you to St Ives today?' Lise asked as she took the chair across the table from Zach.

He held her glance for a moment as if deciding how to reply. Then: 'I had an invitation I couldn't refuse,' he said with a wicked twinkle.

A faint colour rose in Lise's cheeks. Was he saying he'd come especially to see her?

Zach took a pull of ale. 'So you are Lise – is that right?'

'Yes, Lise,' she managed. 'Lise Bisset.'

He cocked his head. 'That doesn't sound English.'

'It's not. My mother was French.' She took a small sip of her ale.

'But you said you had no family beyond . . . Annie, is that her name?'

'Annie. Yes. And no, I don't have any other family.' She didn't want to explain that her mother had disappeared when she was very young, and she had no idea what had happened to her.

It must have been evident in her tone because Zach said apologetically: 'I'm sorry. I ask too many questions.'

'Don't worry about it,' Lise said hastily, not wanting to make him feel uncomfortable. 'That's how it's been for a long time now – just me and Annie. I'm so used to it, I don't really think about it any more.' She sipped her ale. 'What about you? Do you have family?' She smiled. 'You see? I can be just as curious as you.'

'My family are farmers, up Helston way. And I had a brother.' Zach's face darkened.

'*Had* a brother?' Lise probed gently.

'Josh died a year or so ago.' He didn't elaborate, and Lise could see he was no more anxious to be explicit than she had been.

'I'm sorry,' she said. 'That must have been hard for you.'

'Yes, losing a sibling isn't something I'd wish on anyone.'

Lise was unaware that he was watching her closely as he said it. For some reason his words were plucking a chord somewhere deep inside her. She didn't ask if he had other brothers or sisters – she knew instinctively that he had not – and for a moment it was as if she was sharing his loss; not just empathising with him, but feeling the pain of a severed bond and the loneliness that followed.

Unsettled, she searched for a way to change the subject. 'How far have you come to visit?' she asked.

'I have lodgings in Marazion.' He seemed as relieved as she was not to be discussing family any more. 'The other day, though, I came from Penzance.'

Lise noticed he was watching her closely as he said it almost as if there was some special significance to Penzance and he wanted to see her reaction. But she must be imagining it. 'A long way,' she said lightly.

'Not so far when it's a journey I wanted to make.' He was back to flirting gently.

'You must have ridden then. Where is your horse?'

'Tethered to a hitching post in town.'

'What a shame! I'd have loved to see him – or her. I adore horses.'

'Her. Gypsy.' They were back on safer ground. 'Do you ride, then?'

Lise laughed. 'Certainly not! I've never been on a horse in my life. Fishing folk don't do much riding.'

'But you'd like to?'

What a strange question, she thought. 'I'd love to!' She gave a little laugh. 'But I wouldn't know how to even climb into the saddle.'

'Suppose I was to teach you?'

Something in the way he was looking at her told her he was not teasing, but making a serious suggestion. 'Really?' she asked incredulously.

'Really. If you want.'

'Oh, I want!' Her face had come alive. And much as the prospect of being on a horse thrilled her, it wasn't the only reason she was so delighted, even daring to wonder if his offer was an excuse to see her again.

'When would you be free?' Zach asked.

'As long as Annie doesn't get sick again, more or less any time,' she said ruefully. 'I've lost my position since I've had to take so much time off to care for her.'

'That's unfortunate. Or perhaps fortunate, depending on which way you look at it.' That wicked twinkle again. 'Shall we say tomorrow, then?' Seeing her startled look, he explained: 'It's just that I know I'll be free tomorrow. I can't always plan too far ahead.'

'Yes, all right. Where?'

'By the drinking trough in the centre of town? About this time?'

Lise nodded. She could scarcely believe this was happening. It seemed too good to be true.

He took his leave then, and she watched him go, dazed, but happier than she could ever remember feeling.

'Well, my girl, you seem to have found yourself an admirer.'

Annie had clearly been well enough to come through to the kitchen and was cutting herself a slice of bread and a chunk of cheese.

'He's going to teach me to ride!' Lise said.

'So I heard. Well, all I can say is watch your step.' Annie waved the bread knife to emphasise her words.

'I'm sure he won't let me fall and hurt myself,' Lise said.

'There's more ways t'get hurt than falling off a horse, as you well know,' Annie warned. 'He's a charmer, that one. And charmers can't always be trusted.'

Her words dissipated some of Lise's pleasure, and she replied sharply: 'Don't worry, I learned that the hard way. I'm not about to make the same mistake twice.'

Lise was not the only one to watch Zach's departure. Aaron Moxey had been sitting on the low sea wall, whittling at a piece of wood, when he'd seen Zach approaching and been struck again, as he had been that first time, that there was something familiar about him. He had ducked his head so as not to be recognised; if he and this man had met somewhere before, he wanted to know under what circumstances that might have been. It was only prudent, given the murky dealings Aaron was involved in, and secrecy came as second nature to him. When the stranger had disappeared into old Annie's cottage, Aaron had gone into his own home and stationed himself at the window so as to catch another glimpse of the man when he left.

His curiosity had gone unrewarded, though. The man had walked down the path without turning; all Aaron had seen was the back of him: tricorn hat, coat, britches and boots, all apparently of good quality, and a long dark pigtail.

It was the pigtail that had stirred recognition, he thought. Though a good many of his acquaintances wore them, few were as full as this man's – clean, too! The shine of his hair showed that he washed it more frequently than most. Aaron racked his brains. It would come to him, he was certain, and most likely at a moment when he was not thinking about it. Whistling to himself, he took his knife and the bit of wood he was fashioning into a teaspoon and went out to sit in the sun again.

* * *

Cordelia found Godfrey in his study, entering columns of figures in a leather-bound ledger.

'Proceeds from our last venture?' she enquired with a faint smile.

He snorted, and ink pooled from his quill on to the page. 'Now look what you've made me do.'

'Godfrey, you managed it all by yourself. Something's troubling you.'

'That dastardly Quinn has defaulted on his payments again.' Quinn was one of his customers up the line who wanted nothing but the best cognac and the finest silks. 'I am going to have to deploy a man – or a couple of men – who will ensure his debts are paid. This is the last time I deal with him. He's had his chances, and he'll live to regret trying to play me for a fool.'

'Excellent, my dear brother. You have not lost your touch, nor grown soft in your old age, I'm glad to see.'

'Less of the "old age",' Godfrey growled, though of late the years had begun to weigh heavily on him. 'And what are you doing dressed in the clothes you generally reserve for visiting?'

'I have had word from Cecile's intended,' she replied archly. 'I believe he is looking favourably on the suggestion, and he would like me to call and discuss the matter further.'

Godfrey's face darkened. 'The devil you will!'

Cordelia touched her black paper beauty spot with a gloved finger. 'I thought we were agreed. He would be a most suitable match for Cecile.'

'We talked about it, yes. But I don't remember giving it my blessing.'

Cordelia's lips tightened into a hard line. 'Whether you have or not is neither here nor there. My mind is quite made up. Though Cecile plays the meek and mild innocent, she is still her mother's daughter, and blood will out in time. You don't want her to bring disgrace to our door, do you? And that is what will occur, mark my words, if she is not kept in check. She needs a husband and children to curb any wildness she has inherited.'

'A husband and children did not curb Marguerite's wild ways,' Godfrey said bitterly.

'Godfrey, I do not have time to remain here and argue with you.' Cordelia reached for the doorknob, turning it. 'I am taking the carriage – I didn't think it would be fitting to arrive for a meeting such as this on horseback – so if you want to go out, you will just have to wait until I return, or take a horse yourself.'

With that, she marched out of the study, leaving Godfrey to shake his head helplessly. He might be the man of the house, he might be Cordelia's elder brother, but when it came down to it, it was she who ruled the roost, and had done ever since he had lost Marguerite. And before he had met her, he thought ruefully. Always, it seemed, it was Cordelia who made the decisions. Only over Marguerite had he thwarted her, and he didn't think she had ever forgiven him. It was the reason she was so anxious to marry Cecile off, he supposed. She reminded Cordelia too much of the woman he had loved more than he had loved his sister, and now he thought jealousy might well be behind her determination to have Cecile out of the house. She wanted to be the only one in his life, just as she always had been.

And when her mind was made up, there was no arguing with her.

Godfrey sighed, tried without success to remove the ink blot from his ledger and pushed it to one side.

He'd call on Dyfan Flinders, one of the roughest, most dangerous men in his gang, to deal with the debtor. Flinders would teach Quinn a lesson he wouldn't forget. That, at least,

Jennie Felton

was one aspect of his life where Godfrey still retained complete control, and he thanked the good Lord for it.

Sam was desperate to speak to Zach. He hadn't seen him all day, and when he went to the Wink that evening, there was no sign of him there either. There was only one thing for it. He decided to ride over to his friend's lodgings in Marazion.

He found Zach sitting on a bench outside the house enjoying a jar of ale.

'What are you doing here?' Zach asked when Sam rode up and dismounted.

'I have to talk to you.' Sam was clearly upset. 'Cordelia had me drive her to Mousehole today. She was going to see that old vicar they intend marrying Cecile off to. And she came out looking mighty pleased with herself. It's going to go ahead, Zach, if we can't do something to stop it. You have to help me, my friend! I can't lose her!'

'Come on, Sam, calm down.' Zach offered his jar of ale to his friend. 'Here – take this. I've had more than my fill, and you look as if you need it more than I do.'

Sam took the jar and drank thirstily. He had ridden hard, and the dust flying up from the track had made his throat dry as sawdust.

'Have you been able to see the girl in St Ives yet?' he asked, wiping his mouth with his sleeve.

'As it happens, I have,' Zach told him. 'I visited this morning.'
'And?'

'Well, there's little more to tell you as yet. Except it would seem that her mother was French.'

'French!' A glimmer of hope lit Sam's eyes. 'Cecile's a French name, isn't it? And Marguerite? You really think she could be the missing girl?'

'I think it's very likely.'

'Did you tell her about Cecile? Ask if she'll help us?'

'Hold your horses.' Zach raised a cautionary hand. 'It's far too soon for that.'

'But there's no time to waste . . .'

'It won't do any good to frighten her off,' Zach said reasonably. 'The wedding can't be imminent if they've only just begun talking about it, and even if it had been decided upon today, there would have to be at least a three-week wait for the banns to be read.'

'I s'pose . . .'

'Look, Sam, I'm seeing her again tomorrow,' Zach went on. 'I've promised to give her riding lessons; that will give me a good opportunity to get close to her. I can't promise anything, but I will try.'

Sam nodded, but he was clearly still agitated.

'Sit down, my friend, and I'll fetch us both another drink.' Zach vacated his seat and Sam took his place. 'It's no use you getting yourself into a lather about it. You need your wits about you. We both do if we're going to pull this off.'

He headed into the house for more ale. There was something he hadn't told Sam. Crazy as he still thought the idea of Lise swapping places with Cecile was, difficult as it was to see how such a stunt could be pulled off without ending in disaster, something had occurred to him.

If it did work, even for a day or so, it might be to his advantage too. Who knew? Lise might be the answer to his prayers and help him achieve the objective he had set his mind to. Progress at present was slow. But a spy within the household could be just what he needed.

Chapter Eight

Lise's first riding lesson had gone well. She had had no qualms about sitting astride Gypsy and, unlike Cecile, she had no hooped petticoats to hamper her. Without a hint of embarrassment, she hoisted up her skirts, exposing long bare legs, and slipped her booted feet into the stirrups Zach had adjusted to suit her, and yet at the same time she somehow maintained an almost ladylike demeanour.

'We'll just be walking to begin with,' Zach said. 'Don't be afraid – I won't let you fall.'

'I'm not afraid!' Lise had retorted, almost indignantly, and he could see she was not. This was not some young lady who had been cosseted and spoiled; Lise was a girl with spirit, who had known hardship and lived amongst ruffians and vagabonds as well as decent, honest fisherfolk.

When they reached the open moorland above the town, it wasn't long before Lise became impatient with the slow amble.

'Can't we go faster?' she asked.

Zach had to smile at her enthusiasm. 'We can try a trot if you like, but you'll find it bumpy and hard on your backside to begin with,' he warned her.

'I don't mind.'

'Very well. If you're sure.'

He quickened his stride, and Gypsy obligingly followed suit, trotting across the heather- and gorse-strewn turf. After a while, Zach slowed his pace and came to a halt.

'Well, how was that?' he asked.

Lise's hair was tangled and wind blown and there were roses in her cheeks. 'You were right about it being bumpy! Oh, my poor backside!' She shifted in the saddle as she said it, but she was laughing.

'Sit tight!' Zach was worried she might unseat herself. 'This is only your first lesson, remember.'

Again she shifted a little, easing the pressure on her tingling bottom. 'How could I forget? Ouch!'

'It'll be better when you've learned to rise to the trot.'

'And how do I do that?' Lise asked.

'Press down firmly in the stirrups and lift yourself up with the movement of the horse. Do you want to try it?'

'Of course.'

They set off again, Lise striving manfully to do as he said and failing miserably. Once or twice she thought she was getting the feel of it, then she was back to bumping again.

'Oh!' she cried in exasperation when Zach pulled on the reins and Gypsy returned to a walk. 'I can't do it!'

'You will, don't worry. Everyone bumps to begin with. We just need to persevere. But that's enough for one day, I think, or you'll have trouble walking tomorrow. Come on, down you get.' He held Gypsy steady, rubbing her neck while Lise slid to the ground. 'Do you want me to accompany you back to town?'

'Oh no, there's no need for that,' Lise said. 'I'm quite used to the walk. The house where I was employed was up here on the outskirts. And I've taken up too much of your time already.'

'My pleasure.'

And it had been, he thought as he watched her disappearing

into the distance. Her enjoyment had been infectious, and running alongside Gypsy with the sting of the salty breeze on his cheeks and the taste of it on his lips had given him a feeling of freedom that he had all but forgotten over the past year.

He was full of admiration, too, for her daring, and it occurred to him now that she had all the attributes she would need if she could be persuaded to carry out her part in Sam's crazy plan. It wasn't simply that she was identical to Cecile. Surprisingly, for a girl who had been raised by a fishwife, she had the posture and bearing of a lady, and also the spirit that Cecile lacked. And if he continued teaching her to ride, she wouldn't give herself away if she was required to sit a horse. He'd have to introduce her to the side-saddle, of course, and somehow she had to be coached in what would be expected of her if she was not to be rumbled straight away for an imposter.

As his doubts as to the enormity of what Sam had suggested returned, Zach's good humour dissipated. Sighing, he mounted Gypsy and kicked her to a gallop, heading back towards Porthmeor.

When Zach arrived at Polruan next morning, he found Godfrey waiting for him.

'I want you to ride to St Ives and seek out Dyfan Flinders, the man you met there on the day of our last delivery,' he said. 'I have a job for him.'

Godfrey always chose to refer to the illicit cargos as 'deliveries'.

'Very well.' Zach hadn't planned to go back to St Ives for a day or two; he'd thought he'd let Lise get over the stiffness and the sore bottom she was bound to be suffering from after yesterday's initial lesson, and in any case he didn't want to appear too eager. But if Godfrey wanted him to go to St Ives, then to St Ives he must go, and he didn't think it likely that he would run into Lise on an errand of this sort.

'What am I to tell him?' he asked.

'I want Horatio Quinn taken to task. He owes me money and needs teaching a lesson. If Flinders pays him a visit, I feel sure he will see the error of his ways.'

'And does Flinders know where to find him?' Zach was well aware that with Godfrey's operation so wide and far flung, those who worked for him in one area were not always familiar with those in another.

'He knows all right,' Godfrey growled. 'Quinn stole his wife away from him, so he'll have a score of his own to settle. But if he needs reminding, it's the Lion and Lamb in Camborne. Quinn's the innkeeper there.'

'And he's to spare no mercy?'

'You can tell him I don't care if Quinn ends up dead in a ditch as long as I get what I'm owed. And come straight back here, Zach. We've other matters to discuss.'

Once Zach had left, Godfrey sat back in his chair, sighing. That was one problem dealt with, and he needed to give the business his undivided attention. But it wasn't easy. He wasn't at all happy about this marriage that Cordelia was so eager to arrange between Cecile and the vicar of Mousehole. At least nothing had been decided yet. The man, Redmond, had seemingly not been averse to the suggestion, but had said he needed a little time to think it over. He would then contact the Pendinnicks and arrange to visit, and perhaps make Cecile's acquaintance.

The thought of losing her to another man was anathema to Godfrey, but he couldn't help wondering if Cordelia was right. If she was married to John Redmond, at least he would know where she was, and be able to exchange visits, whereas if she did take after her mother, she could be lost to him for ever, as Marguerite was. So far she had shown no such signs, but as Cordelia had said, Marguerite's blood did run in her veins.

I'm caught between the devil and the deep blue sea, Godfrey thought miserably, and made an enormous effort to apply himself to his work.

As he walked through the narrow streets of St Ives, Aaron Moxey was whistling a tune and singing the words in his head:

Bobby Shafto's gone to sea-ee,
Silver buckles at his knee-ee . . .

Then, as he turned a corner, he stopped, the song dying on his lips.

A little way ahead, two men were deep in conversation. One of them he knew well – Dyfan Flinders. Everyone in St Ives who was involved in shady business knew Dyfan. The other he recognised as Lise's mysterious visitor, and instantly his memory was jogged. He knew now where he'd seen the man before – a few days previous to that visit, in a tavern near the harbour.

He drew back into a doorway, a grin spreading across his face. Well, well! What would Miss Hoity-Toity think if she knew her admirer was mixed up with smugglers and wreckers? After watching the two men for a minute or two, he decided to chance his arm at an introduction.

As he emerged from the doorway, Dyfan happened to look in his direction and beckoned him over.

'Just the man. Come 'ere, Aaron.'

As Aaron joined them, Dyfan went on: 'This 'ere's Mr Carver, an associate of Mr Pendinnick over at Porthmeor. He's got a job wants doing, and I reckon two of us would be better'n one. What d'you say, Mr Carver? Will Mr Pendinnick pay for Aaron here to back me up?'

'As long as his instructions are carried out.' The stranger was looking Aaron up and down, and for a moment Aaron was concerned he might have recognised him. But he was pretty sure he'd kept well out of the way until Lise's visitor had gone and there was nothing in Mr Carver's manner to suggest otherwise.

Carver turned back to Dyfan. 'I can safely leave you to make your own arrangements, I presume?'

'You can that, Mr Carver. And thank Mr Pendinnick kindly for thinking of me. Rest assured, he won't be disappointed.'

Carver drew a dark red velvet pouch out of his pocket. 'Here's ten gold sovereigns to cover any expenses you may incur. You'll get the rest when this business is brought to a satisfactory conclusion. I bid you good day.'

With that, he turned and strode away.

Aaron was staring open mouthed at the velvet pouch. In all his life he'd never been so close to so much money all at once.

Dyfan chuckled. ''Tis no good you eyeing it like that. You'll get paid when the job's done, and not before.'

'How do I know that?' Aaron snarled. 'Maybe I'll think again 'bout helpin' you out.'

'Ah, you be sharper than I gived you credit fer, Aaron Moxey.' Dyfan chuckled again, opening the drawstring of the pouch and taking out two coins. 'That's just ter show goodwill. Don't spend it all at once.'

Realising he was not going to do any better, Aaron pocketed the coins, keeping his hand wrapped around them to be sure they were safe.

'We'll talk again then,' Dyfan said. 'The Hope and Anchor, six o'clock sharp. That suit you?'

Aaron nodded his agreement. He was whistling again as he walked home. It had certainly been a profitable morning – in more ways than one.

* * *

'Have ee said anything to Lise yet?' Gussie Moxey was giving Annie a straight look. She'd come round on purpose to ask Annie this very question.

'What about?' Annie asked, pretending not to understand.

'You know very well what. Not so long ago, when you were took bad, you tried to task me with tellin' 'er things she should'a bin told many years since, and I were worrying meself sick about it. It's your place, not mine, though I s'pose I'd have done it if I'd had to. So I be askin' ee, 'ave ee told 'er?'

'Not yet,' Annie said, looking guilty and uncomfortable. Gussie was right, she knew, but still she shrank from telling Lise the whole terrible story.

'Why not?' Gussie demanded.

'There be no rush, be there?' Annie said irritably. 'I'm better now.'

'And what if you take bad again? 'Twas touch-and-go this time, and another bout – well, anythin' could 'appen.'

'I'm not ready for the knackers' yard yet, Gussie.' Annie's tone was tart. 'I'll tell 'er in me own good time.'

'Well, you'd better make it soon.' Gussie folded her arms across her ample stomach and turned to see Aaron swinging his way along the rank of cottages. 'We'd best say no more now, but I'll be keepin' on at ee until 'tis done.'

'You two got nothing better to do than gossip?' Aaron called when he was within earshot. He was looking pleased with himself, Gussie thought.

'Get on wi' ee, ya cheeky little swine, or I'll 'ave yer guts for garters,' she threatened, but she was hiding a chuckle, her impatience with Annie forgotten. Rascals they might be, her boys, but she loved the bones of them.

* * *

'Come on, missy, you've got to eat summat or you'll waste away,' Bessie urged Cecile, whose bowl of soup lay untouched on the tray in front of her.

'I can't. If I do, I'll bring it right up again.' Cecile pushed herself away from the table.

She'd excused herself from lunching with her father and Aunt Cordelia as she usually did, pleading a headache, which was real enough, but the true reason was that she simply hadn't been able to bring herself to sit around the table with them. Now, alone in her room with only Bessie, her stomach was revolting at the thought of swallowing so much as a mouthful of the mutton broth. She was, she knew, literally sick with worry at the thought of what was being planned for her, and Bessie knew it too.

She'd confided in her that day when Cordelia had first broached the subject with her father and she'd been listening outside the door. She'd flown back to her room, shaking like a leaf in the wind, and unable to begin with to tell Bessie what was wrong. But with her maid's arms around her, her hand stroking her cheek, she'd stumbled out the gist of what she'd overheard.

'Oh Bessie, what am I to do?' she'd wept. 'They can't really mean to have me wed to some old man I don't know, can they? I love Sam! I want to be with him! I'd never see him again! Oh, I'll kill myself before I'd let it happen!'

'Hush, missy, don't say such things,' Bessie had said.

'I can't wed that old vicar! I can't!' Cecile had been inconsolable.

'You must tell Sam what's going on. Don't fret, me lovely. Between us we'll work summat out.'

Bessie repeated those words now, adding: 'It'll be all right, you'll see. Now please, my love, do try just a taste of this. You have to keep your strength up, or you'll be no good to man nor beast.'

Unwillingly Cecile accepted the spoon Bessie put at her lips. The first mouthful seemed to clot in her throat, but as she swallowed, she realised she was really very hungry. She hadn't eaten properly for days; now, slowly at first, and then ravenously, she finished the soup.

'See, that's better, i'nt it?' Bessie said approvingly. 'Now you'll be able to think straight, and we'll work something out, my precious.' She hesitated. 'They haven't mentioned it to you yet, have they?'

Cecile shook her head. 'I think they mean to have it all arranged before they do, so as not to give me a chance to object. They haven't any idea that I know what they're planning.'

'Well, you do, and that's all to the good.' Bessie cocked her head, listening. 'Isn't that Moll scraping at the door?'

'Oh yes, I think it is! Bessie, let her in, would you, please?'

The maid did as she asked, and the spaniel came running to Cecile, lifting her silky head to be stroked.

'Right.' Bessie picked up the tray bearing the empty soup bowl. 'I'm going to see to this now, and if I was you I'd take Moll outside for a bit. Go down to the stables and see Lady.' She inclined her head knowingly and gave Cecile what passed for a wink. She knew very well that Lady was not the main attraction at the stables.

Cecile smiled – the first time Bessie had seen her really smile for days.

'You know, Bessie, I think I will,' she said.

'What ails Cecile?' Godfrey asked. He'd been late coming in for luncheon and was displeased to find Cordelia alone in the dining room.

'A bad head – or so she says.' Cordelia was in a black mood. 'I'm afraid we're going to have trouble with her.'

'You think she's feigning it? But . . .' Godfrey hesitated, looking anxious. 'She hasn't been herself for days. I'm worried she's sickening for something.'

Cordelia tossed her head impatiently. 'Ha! Sick at the thought that her wings are going to be clipped, most like.'

'What?' Godfrey frowned. 'You don't mean . . . ? You haven't told her about our efforts to facilitate a match between her and the vicar of Mousehole, have you? We agreed to keep it from her until things were settled.'

Cordelia huffed again. 'She didn't need me to tell her. She overheard us talking, I believe, on the day we first discussed it. I think she was listening outside the study door. Oh, she beat a hasty retreat when she heard me leaving, but not hasty enough. I caught a glimpse of her skirts disappearing around the corner. One tends to forget that the hoop extends as far to the sides and rear as it does in the front.'

'Oh, dear, dear,' Godfrey murmured.

Cordelia shrugged. 'It will give her time to get used to the idea. I expect she knows, too, that I have been to make the proposal to Mr Redmond. Sam will have told her, no doubt.' She raised a crystal glass and sipped the wine she had already poured for herself. 'She's too friendly by half with that boy, spends far too much time down at the stables. You should put a stop to it, Godfrey.'

'For heaven's sake, Cordelia!' Godfrey's anxiety for his beloved daughter was making him as ill tempered as his sister. 'She loves that horse! I'm not about to stop her going to see Lady as well as everything else.'

Cordelia's eyes narrowed above the rim of her glass. 'You're not about to change your mind, I hope, Godfrey. I cannot stress enough that Cecile needs to be kept in check if we are not to encounter all the same problems Marguerite caused you.'

'No, Cordelia, I'm not about to change my mind,' Godfrey said wearily. 'I couldn't stand to see my daughter go the way of her mother.'

'Good.' Cordelia's tone was brisk. 'Then I'll ring for Maisie and have her bring our luncheon before it is quite spoiled.'

Chapter Nine

By the time Lise had had four more lessons, she had mastered the trot and the canter – 'Much easier!' she'd said – and she'd soon be ready to attempt a full gallop. She was enjoying herself enormously and, for all her determination never again to allow herself to give her heart to a man, she had to admit that it wasn't just the riding that was making her happy. She looked forward to seeing Zach with the same excited anticipation as she did to feeling the wind in her hair and Gypsy's easy, rhythmic stride eating up the heather-strewn moorland; felt a little thrill run through her at his touch when he steadied her as she dismounted. And she thought about him far too often.

She tried to heed Annie's warning that all too often charmers weren't to be trusted, and reminded herself of the heartache Ahab had brought her. But she was fighting a losing battle, and she knew it.

Zach wasn't Ahab – nothing like him. He was reliable, or certainly seemed to be, where Ahab had been unpredictable. From the very start she'd never been sure whether Ahab would let her down over some planned meeting, whereas Zach was always there waiting for her in the appointed place. Where Ahab had been impatient for her kisses – and more – Zach had not pressured her in any way. And would Ahab have stepped in to chase an assailant who had tried to steal her bag? She doubted it. He would have been too anxious not to risk his pretty-boy looks by tangling with a ruffian.

She felt safe with Zach. Safe, and cared for. She knew next to nothing about him beyond that he worked for a gentleman in Porthmeor and had lodgings in Marazion, that his family were farmers, and he had once had a brother. There had been little opportunity for conversation, and when she had tried to probe further, he had been annoyingly vague. But that just meant that he was a private person, as she herself was. It didn't mean he had anything to hide, and the slight air of mystery only added to the attraction she felt towards him. And all the while, she was dizzy with the feeling that she was standing on a cliff edge, about to plunge into something wonderful.

Lise was falling in love, and there was nothing she could do to stop herself.

Zach had enjoyed the lessons too. Besides being a very attractive young lady, Lise was good company, and her enthusiasm for learning to ride was still every bit as infectious as it had been that first day. But he knew he couldn't afford to become emotionally involved. If they were ever to try to put Sam's crazy plan into action, he knew she could be walking into a dangerous situation, especially if he was to ask for her help in achieving his objective too. Godfrey was a ruthless man who guarded his empire jealously. If Zach grew too fond of her, he would never be able to allow her to take such a risk. If nothing ever came of it, then things could well be different. But for the moment, he must harden his heart, and consider her, and all that they were sharing, as merely a means to an end. Nothing could be allowed to stand between him and the vow he'd made a year ago.

* * *

Unbeknown to Zach, Sam and Cecile's problem was becoming increasingly urgent. That very day, Mr Redmond had sent word that he had come to a decision with regard to the marriage proposal and would like to call at Polruan House to meet the prospective bride and talk over arrangements with Godfrey and Cordelia. Cecile had run straight out to the stables, distraught, and when Sam and Zach met that evening at the Wink, Sam was in a terrible way.

'Have you mentioned the situation to Lise yet?' he asked, his voice ragged with anxiety.

Zach felt his heart sink. He'd known this moment would come but, now that it had, his reluctance was far stronger than he'd expected.

'Not yet, no. And I still know next to nothing about her. I've probed a bit but, truth to tell, she seems to know very little herself beyond the fact that her father drowned at sea and old Annie took her and her mother in. I asked where her mother is now, but she didn't seem to want to say. She just kicked Gypsy into a canter and left me standing. I've been treading carefully since then.'

'Well, the time for that is over,' Sam said. 'We have to move, and quickly, or I'll lose my lovely Cecile for ever.'

'Does she know the plan yet?' Zach asked.

Sam shook his head. 'All I've said is that I'll think of something.'

'So they're both in the dark.'

'I've been wondering about that.' Sam took a long pull of his beer.

Zach experienced a glimmer of hope that his friend had come to his senses and realised just how crazy his suggestion was. But it soon became apparent that that was not what he meant.

'I'm thinking that the best way would be to bring them face

to face. If they really are sisters, surely there would be a bond between them? Wouldn't your Lise be more likely to agree to the plan if she saw how much it mattered to Cecile?'

'She's not my Lise,' Zach retorted.

Sam, however, was not listening. 'The Golowan festivals will be held next week. Suppose Cecile could get Godfrey to allow her to go to one of them? And you could take Lise.'

Golowan was the Cornish word for light and rejoicing; the fire festivals were an old-established tradition, and Sam knew Cecile would love to attend one of the celebrations that took place each year at midsummer. She'd told him the previous year how she'd stood on the lawn of Polruan House and gazed enthralled at the night sky, all aglow from the dozens of bonfires burning on the cairns and hills high above the cove, and how she longed to witness the old rituals that were enacted, even though in these more enlightened times few people still believed in witches and their curses and spells. The tar barrels that were set alight, the townsfolk processing through the streets carrying flaming torches, then joining hands and dancing in circles around the bonfires to protect themselves from evil. She'd even heard that sometimes one or two of the wilder youths would leap through the dying flames in a display of bravado, and Sam had been able to confirm to her that this was true.

'How likely is it, do you think, that Godfrey would allow Cecile to go out with you after dark?' Zach asked, his tone sceptical.

'Not at all likely. But if Bessie were to come along as chaperone . . . Bessie knows all about us.' Sam had clearly given this some thought.

'And what am I supposed to tell Lise?'

'That's up to you. But nothing that might scare her off. And I reckon we ought to go to the one at Penzance. It's the biggest and best for miles around. Come on, my friend. We've got to get things moving or it's going to be too late.'

'Very well,' Zach said reluctantly. 'I'll see what I can do.' He was still doubtful about the plan, but he didn't want to put too much of a damper on his friend's hopes.

'What would you say to something a little different to a riding lesson?' Zach asked Lise.

'Something different?' She gave him a quizzical look.

'Next week is Penzance Golowan. It's a great occasion all around that part of the coast, and the Penzance celebrations are among the best. I generally go to one or another since I've been in these parts, and I'm thinking that this year I could take you.'

'Penzance! It's a long way. How would we get there?'

'I reckon Gypsy's strong enough to carry both of us.'

'Are you sure? It won't lame her?'

'You can't weigh more than a feather mattress. Course it won't lame her. I shan't take her into Penzance, though. She wouldn't care for the firecrackers. I know a farmer close enough to the town – I'll leave her there and I can walk back and fetch her when the celebrations have died down.'

A little prickle of excitement tickled deep inside Lise. For all her good intentions, she'd been secretly hoping he might suggest meeting sometime when they weren't concentrating on the riding lessons, and had even begun to dare to hope that he might feel something for her. Why else would he come all this way to spend time teaching her to ride? she reasoned. Why else would he trust her with his horse? And now . . .

He had asked her to go with him to Penzance for the Golowan! Surely, surely it must mean that he cared for her, a little, at least! As Lise's feet flew her back down into the valley where St Ives nestled between the moorland and the sea, her heart was singing, and it never occurred to her that Zach might have had an ulterior motive for the invitation.

Cecile, too, was bubbling with excitement. When she'd visited the stables that morning, Sam had mentioned the idea of attending the Golowan festival in Penzance. He hadn't gone into detail; simply said there was someone he wanted her to meet there, someone who might be able to assist them in eloping, and however much she had begged him to tell her more, he had only shaken his head and remained silent. Could it be, she wondered, that he had it in mind that they should make their escape during the celebrations?

'Just make sure you persuade your father to let you go,' he instructed her. 'He must know how you've longed to be a part of it all.'

'That's true,' Cecile agreed. 'I'll do my very best, never fear.'

She'd hurried back to the house and found her father in his study. As she came bursting in, Godfrey lowered the newspaper he had been reading and looked at her over the top of his eyeglasses, which were rapidly sliding down his nose.

'Good gracious, Cecile! Whatever is it? Where's the fire?'

Cecile giggled. 'It's nothing like that. But I've just heard that the Golowan festival is being held next week in Penzance, and oh – can I go, Papa, *please*?'

Godfrey frowned. 'I'm not entirely sure that's a good idea, my dear.'

'But, Papa – why?'

Godfrey gave up the unequal struggle with his glasses and removed them entirely. 'Quite apart from the danger the fires pose, all kinds of undesirables frequent such events and things can become very unpleasant. They are no place for a young lady.'

'But if Sam drove me there, he'd make sure I came to no harm,' she argued. 'And before you say it wouldn't be proper for me to be alone with him after dark, Bessie could come too, to act as my chaperone.' She hesitated, then played what she hoped was her trump card. 'Please, Papa! I don't suppose I'll ever have the chance again if I'm to wed Mr Redmond. The clergy don't agree with what they think are heathen practices, do they?'

Godfrey sighed. He didn't like the idea one bit, but it would be good to see Cecile happy. He'd been worried about her the last few days. And if it meant she might be more ready to accept her betrothal to the vicar, then perhaps it could prove a good thing.

'I'm not at all happy about this, Cecile,' he said warily, 'but if you talk to Bessie, and she agrees to accompany you, then I will speak to Sam and give him explicit instructions as to what he is to do to ensure your safety. You will not go close to the fires, and you will keep your distance from the torches and any firecrackers. In short, I will not have you exposed to danger. Do I make myself clear?'

'Oh, Papa – yes! Thank you! Thank you!' Cecile ran to him and threw her arms around his neck, tears of joy and relief filling her eyes.

Bessie would agree, she felt sure. She could talk her maid into anything. Even helping her and Sam to run away together . . .

Everything that had seemed like a hopeless dream was now within reach. Trembling with excitement, Cecile ran out to the stables to tell Sam that her father had agreed to her suggestion.

The night of the Penzance Golowan was fine and clear, a sliver of new moon hanging in a star-studded black velvet sky, and the breeze off the sea was warm and perfumed with the scents of the moors as it blew from coast to coast.

Zach hoisted Lise up into the saddle, then mounted behind her, so that when he took the reins in his hands, his arms circled her waist and her spine rested against his broad chest.

'Hold on tight now!' he warned her as he kicked Gypsy to a canter, but by now Lise had grown so accustomed to gripping the horse's flanks with her knees that it came as second nature, and she tangled one hand in Gypsy's thick mane whilst holding on with the other to the bonnet she had worn for the occasion.

By the time they had reached the farm where Zach was leaving Gypsy, and walked to the point where the town lay spread out beneath them, the fire barrels were already alight, their bright flames marking the path of the main street and beyond, and bonfires on the cairns and hills around Mount's Bay lit up the night sky. Zach slipped an arm round Lise's waist to guide her through the crowd of men, women and boys making their way up from the quay and keep her at a safe distance from those who were swinging flaming torches made from tarred and pitched canvas attached to sturdy poles and chains. Though the practice was undoubtedly dangerous, it was an accepted fact that everyone would ignore the town crier's warnings, just as they did the banning of firecrackers.

Zach was keeping a sharp lookout for Sam and Cecile, even though they'd agreed not to meet up until the procession had reached its destination. He didn't want Lise and Cecile to come face to face until Lise had had time to enjoy the celebrations.

Something was happening. The crowds were gravitating to either side of the main street, leaving a channel down the centre. It was not unlike the story of the parting of the Red Sea as Moses was leading the Israelites out of slavery in Egypt. The town crier, fresh from his fruitless warnings, strutted along the narrow aisle ringing his bell, and not far behind him came a creature the like of which Lise had never before seen.

102

'What is it?' she gasped, round eyed, and Zach laughed.

'It's Old Penglaze, the 'Obby 'Oss,' he said. 'You better watch out. He's known for grabbing a pretty young miss who takes his fancy.'

Even as he said it, Lise heard some girls screaming and saw them scuttling away. She gazed in disbelief as the bizarre creature came nearer. Its head was a horse's skull, made, no doubt, of wood, and somehow, as it capered and bounded, its mouth opened and shut with a loud snapping noise. Beneath the head a cloth made of horsehide fell almost to the ground, completely hiding the man who must be inside the contraption. As it drew level with them, the horrible creature stopped, and the giant head turned towards Lise.

With a gasp of horror, she took a step backwards, and instantly Zach's arms came around her, pulling her close. For a sickening moment the great head nudged hers, and she gasped again, turning her face away from the fetid odour of the hide and closing her eyes to shut out the grotesque sight of that clacking mouth.

Thankfully, when she opened them again, the horrible creature had moved on, but Zach was still holding her so close that, as she turned her head, her cheek brushed his chin.

'All right?' he asked, his breath warm against her ear.

'Yes – now that it's gone! Oh, I didn't care for that at all!' Her heart was still beating fast, but from the amazing closeness of Zach now, not from fear of the 'Obby 'Oss.

'It's not like you to be afraid, Lise.'

'No. Not a lot frightens me.' She was wondering if she'd reacted that way for quite a different reason – that she had hoped Zach would protect her from the monster. And as he released his hold on her, she was filled with a sense of loss and regret. But he did take her hand, and that felt good too.

103

'There's a fair tomorrow down on the quayside, with boat rides and all kinds of entertainment,' he said. 'You might like that better. There's always a chance the 'Obby 'Oss might put in an appearance, but he wouldn't be nearly as frightening in broad daylight.'

Lise ignored the reference to the weird creature. 'I'd like to take a boat ride.'

'Good.' Zach squeezed her hand. 'Shall we follow the procession then?'

In the swathes of light thrown by the blazing tar barrels and the flaming torches, his face was all planes and shadows, and an unfamiliar sensation twisted deep within Lise. Not trusting herself to speak, she nodded, and they followed the crowds along the narrow street.

By the time they reached the town square, folk were already beginning to link hands to form circles around the bigger tar barrels.

'Come on.' Zach pulled Lise towards one, and a couple of dancers separated to allow them to join in.

The heat emanating from the bonfire was making Lise's face burn, but it was as nothing compared to the glowing warmth inside her. She felt as if she was floating on a cloud of unreality, soaring above the intoxicating scenes below, anchored only by Zach's firm grasp of her hand.

The dance slowed, the circle began to break up, and Lise and Zach moved across the square, past the stone market cross, towards a space where the crowd was thinner. A man and two women stood on the edge of the gathering, watching the celebrations. Just as Lise and Zach neared them, two revellers whose torches were still flaming fiercely passed between them, illuminating the trio. A plump elderly woman, a slightly built man, and . . .

Lise stopped short, eyes widening in shock, unable to believe what she was seeing. But for the younger woman's high powdered wig, she might have been looking at herself in her bedroom mirror.

'Lise?' Zach's hand tightened on hers, drawing her towards the trio, and, totally dumbstruck, she had no choice but to follow.

Close to, the likeness was unmistakable. The young man was whispering something into the girl's ear, but for a long moment she remained motionless, Lise's shock reflected in the identical features as the two women gazed at one another. Lise took a step forward, her hand outstretched and, once again, for a seeming eternity, the two of them seemed to be carved in stone. Then the other girl's hand flew to her mouth and she turned and fled, pushing her way through the sparse crowd.

'Cecile!' The young man cast a desperate glance at Zach and Lise, then set off in pursuit, with the old woman, clearly bewildered, blundering after them.

'What . . . ?' Lise turned agonised eyes on Zach.

'I'm sorry.' He sounded genuinely distressed. 'I should have warned you.'

'But who . . . ? I don't understand . . .'

Zach led her through the few revellers who still lingered to a deserted alley, then turned her to face him. 'Lise, I believe that girl is a sister you never knew you had. Looking so alike, as you do, what other explanation could there be? And you knew it, didn't you? The moment you looked into one another's faces.'

For a moment, Lise couldn't speak. Her *sister*? No! It couldn't be! And yet suddenly she was remembering the odd feeling that overcame her sometimes when she brushed her hair in front of her looking glass, the feeling that the eyes she was looking into were not her own, an essence that was not her essence. And the ache of longing that almost always followed, a sense of deep and all-consuming loss. Had she once had a sister – a twin, even – from whom she had somehow been separated, and who she still remembered in the deepest parts of her brain and in her heart, despite her conscious mind forgetting?

'Both of you have French names, too,' Zach was continuing urgently.

Lise returned to the present with a jolt. 'You know her?' she asked, shocked all over again.

'Her name is Cecile,' Zach said. 'And she is in desperate need of your help.'

'You arranged for us to meet.' Ice-cold disbelief coursed through Lise's veins, making her shiver in spite of the heat of the bonfires. 'That was your purpose in bringing me here!'

The guilt on his face gave her her answer with no need of words, and suddenly the disbelief was replaced by anger. 'How dare you?' she blazed. 'You've just been using me! My riding lessons – everything! How could you do that?' She raised her eyes, which flashed with a fury that for the moment was hiding her hurt. 'Is she your lover? The girl who looks just like me?'

'No! Lise . . . listen to me, please.' He gripped her arm; with a sharp movement, she wrenched it away.

'Leave me alone! I never want to see you again!' She pushed past him, heading up the alley into which Cecile had disappeared.

'Lise – wait! How will you get home?' Zach called after her, but she was gone, swallowed up by a group of raucous merry-makers.

Chapter Ten

Sam had left the carriage at a coaching inn on the road from Porthmeor to Penzance. Now, he urged the horses to a canter as he drove back to the spot where he had left Cecile and Bessie. Cecile had clung to him, weeping, begging him not to leave her, but Bessie had taken the shaking girl in her arms, holding her close to her ample bosom and soothing her gently.

'Just make haste,' she'd instructed Sam, her tone so sharp he had known she was blaming him for Cecile's distress.

As well she might! he thought. But she couldn't blame him more than he was blaming himself. He should have explained to her the reason he was taking her to Penzance. Not knowing where to begin was no excuse. Coming face to face with a sister whose existence she had known nothing about had been too shocking. He could only hope and pray that he hadn't ruined everything.

Cecile and Bessie had walked a little further up the road from where he had left them, to a spot where the flat moorland on either side would make it easier for him to turn the carriage. He did so, then jumped down and went to Cecile, who instantly clung to him.

'It's all right, my love.' He wiped the tears from her cheeks with his fingers. 'Come on, I'll take you home.'

'Not before you tell me what the divil is goin' on!' Bessie said in the same sharp tone she had used before. 'And not in this state, either. The master and Miss Cordelia will 'ave me guts fer garters if they sees her like this.'

'We'll pull in somewhere quiet on the way. We need to put some distance between us and the town or the fireworks could spook the horses.' He lifted Cecile up into the carriage and was about to help Bessie to follow, but she shrugged him away impatiently and heaved herself up into the seat beside Cecile.

'Mind you do,' she snapped over her shoulder.

Not another word was spoken until they drew into the courtyard of a coaching inn and Sam led them through an archway into a grassed space that might have been busy on any other evening but was deserted tonight.

'We can talk here,' he said, dreading the conversation that was to come.

'Go on then.' Bessie sat down on a bench, pulling Cecile down beside her, and Sam dragged across a rustic chair and sat facing them.

Ignoring Bessie, he reached over and took Cecile's hand. 'How much do you remember of when you were very small? Being on a boat caught in a storm at sea, perhaps?'

Cecile shook her head, puzzled, but Bessie turned her head sharply, suddenly alert.

'What's that?'

Again Sam ignored her, concentrating only on Cecile. 'You must have been very frightened. And cold. And wet.'

Cecile shivered, but still she shook her head. It was Bessie who spoke.

'You used to have nightmares, my pet. Don't you remember those nightmares when you were afraid to go back to sleep, and you'd creep into my bed and cuddle up wi' me?'

Cecile shivered again, more violently. 'I don't have them any more, though. And I don't want to think about them! Don't make me, Bessie, please!'

Bessie turned to Sam, aggressive once more. 'What's all this about, anyway? You'll only upset the lass again with such talk. And what's it got to do with that girl in Penzance giving her a fright?'

'It's important, Bessie. Didn't you notice something about her? The very thing that shocked Cecile so?'

Bessie snorted. 'In the dark? With all that smoke and fire? Me poor old eyes were waterin' and stingin' like billy-o, and they're not what they once was, anyways.'

'You saw her clearly, though, didn't you, Cecile?' Sam said gently. 'Do you remember I told you there was someone I wanted you to meet in Penzance? Someone who could help us run away together?'

'Yes, but . . .'

'The thing is, Cecile, I believe that girl is your sister. I think you had a twin who was with you and your mother on the boat that night when it was lost in the storm. Someone must have got you to shore – when daylight came, you were found on the beach. Just you. Your sister was missing and everyone assumed she must have drowned, your mother too. But I don't think she did. Somehow she too was saved. And tonight, for the first time in all these years, the two of you met, and you recognised one another. Of course you did!' He squeezed her hand. 'I should have warned you. I should have known what a shock it would be. And for that I'm truly sorry. But can't you see how she can help you to escape? If she could take your place for just long enough for us to get clean away . . .'

For a long moment Cecile was silent, simply bewildered. Then: 'Really?' she whispered.

'If I'm right, as I'm certain I am, then yes, I do believe she will help us. Isn't that what any sister would do?'

Cecile was crying again, overcome with emotion, and Bessie stepped in. Flabbergasted as she was, her first thought was, as always, for the young woman she loved as her own daughter.

'That's quite enough for tonight, Sam. I don't know what to think about what you've said, but the rest will keep till tomorrow. Now, dry your eyes, my angel, and try to compose yourself. And perhaps Sam will go into the inn and fetch us a drop of brandy. Truth to tell, I could do with one meself.'

Sam rose. 'I'll do that, Bessie.'

As he strode off across the courtyard, he glanced back. Bessie's arm was still around Cecile and their heads were close together as they talked, no doubt, about the startling revelations he had just made.

Shaking with shock and anger, Lise scrambled up the cliff path. The heartache and hurt would soon follow, she knew. Already she could feel it in the tears that ached in her throat, but for the moment it was outrage that consumed her, along with disbelief. She'd trusted Zach, even allowed herself to have feelings for him that she'd sworn she would never again entertain for any man. And all the time he had been playing her like a fiddle. Everything she'd believed about him had been nothing but a sham, leading up to the meeting he had engineered tonight. But why? Why had he done such a thing? He'd denied the girl was his lover, but why else would he go to such lengths to bring them together? And who was she, this young lady who, Lise was beginning to believe, must be related to her, since the face that had looked back into hers was identical to the one she saw each morning in her bedroom mirror. From her attire it was clear she was well off, to say the least. But what had Zach meant when he said she was in desperate need of Lise's help?

But for all the questions and confusion that were swirling around in her brain, the anger at Zach still burned strong, and when she reached the farm where he had stabled Gypsy it erupted into determination. 'How will you get home?' he'd called after her. Well, he'd find out how when he returned to the farm himself and found his horse missing. Let him be the one forced to walk back to wherever it was he came from. He'd taught her to ride to suit his own purposes; now he could reap the consequences.

He hadn't unsaddled Gypsy; Lise rubbed the horse's nose, patted her neck and led her to a mounting block in the farmyard. Once astride the mare, she rode out on to the moor, kicked Gypsy to a canter, and headed for St Ives.

When Zach reached the farm and found Gypsy missing, he guessed at once what had happened and, for all his dismay at the thought of having to walk the five miles or so back to Marazion, he couldn't help but admire Lise's resourcefulness, and feel relief that she had a means of getting home. And the fact that he had been so concerned about her told him that he did indeed have feelings for her that went beyond where he'd intended they should.

What a disaster this had turned out to be! Zach cursed himself for having gone along with Sam's crazy plan. He'd doubted from the outset that it could work, and now, with Lise totally alienated, it lay in tatters. But that scarcely mattered. It was Lise's parting words – 'I never want to see you again' – that had cut him to the quick. She'd meant it, he had no doubt, and who could blame her? She'd been right when she'd said he'd used her, and now he was bitterly regretting it.

He wondered, too, what had happened when Sam had caught

up with Cecile. Had he been able to calm her down, or had she still been in a state when they got back to Polruan? If he was dismissed for allowing Cecile to become so upset, Zach would never forgive himself for not insisting his friend give up his crazy plan; Sam might lose both his livelihood and the girl he loved in one fell swoop.

On the point of setting out for Marazion, he had another thought. Polruan was closer by two or so miles; he could find a place to sleep in one of the outbuildings and hopefully set his mind at rest as to the situation there. And provided Sam hadn't been thrown out, perhaps he'd lend Zach a horse to ride to St Ives tomorrow and collect Gypsy. She'd be safe enough until then; he couldn't believe for a moment that Lise would let any harm come to her, however furious she might be with her owner.

His mind made up, he turned and strode out along the road that led to Polruan House.

Zach found his friend sitting on an upturned barrel outside the stables, his head in his hands.

He looked up when he felt Zach's hand on his shoulder, his eyes, in the bright moonlight, sparking with desperate hope.

'Zach! Were you able to talk Lise into helping us?'

Zach gazed at him in utter disbelief. 'Surely you can't mean to continue with this, Sam? You saw what happened tonight.'

'Cecile was taken by surprise. You know how easily upset she is. But she's better now. I talked to her, explained, and—'

'You told her what you planned?'

'Yes. And that if Lise is her long-lost sister, as we believe, she'll help us to run away without being caught before we even reach the Devon border.'

Zach shook his head. 'Sam, I'm sorry, but it's not going to work. Lise is furious to think she's been used – which she has been – and she's hightailed it off back to St Ives. On my horse. There's no way she'll be a part of this now.'

Sam rose and caught him by the shoulders, his eyes blazing. 'No! I can't give up on this! It's our only hope! If you're any sort of a friend, you'll help us. Talk to Lise, make her see how vital it is she plays her part.'

Zach shrugged helplessly. 'It won't do any good, Sam. Lise has a mind of her own, and when it's made up . . . Besides, you must know that even if she did agree, she'd be spotted as an imposter long before you could make good your escape.'

'Not if Cecile could coach her in the ways of the house and how she needs to behave. In Cecile's wigs and dresses, she'd fool anyone! For the love of God, Zach, you have to do this for us!'

Zach sighed, defeated. He had little hope of success, but he realised his friend would never forgive him if he turned his back on him now. 'All right, I'll do my best, Sam. I doubt Lise will even speak to me, but I'll try. Provided you lend me a horse tomorrow to get to St Ives.'

'Anything!'

'What do you say we go down to the Wink and get a drink? I could do with it, and so could you. And then I suggest we hunker down for the night and try to get some sleep so as to face whatever tomorrow may bring.'

'I'll be forever in your debt,' Sam said, clapping him on the back.

But his gratitude did nothing to lift Zach's dark mood.

Lise had almost reached St Ives when she realised she hadn't thought about how she would stable Gypsy for the night. She didn't want to leave her tethered for hours to the hitching post Zach used when he rode into town; the poor thing might be tired, and want to lie down. She eased the horse to a walk, thinking furiously. There must be livery stables somewhere in town, but she had no idea where, and she wasn't sure where the nearest coaching inn was either. Was she going to have to spend a night on the moors, or swallow her pride and return Gypsy to the farm from which she had taken her? Really she couldn't think of any other option, until a thought suddenly struck her.

Her former employers, the Trevelyans, had horses – of course they did! Did she dare go to them for help? She'd always got on well with them, and they had been very good to her, giving her time off to care for Annie until her prolonged absence had forced them to give her notice. But to turn up unexpectedly at this time of night . . . was it too much to ask?

Well, nothing ventured, nothing gained! she told herself, and turned Gypsy in the direction of the Trevelyans' home.

When she reached it, she was relieved to see lamps still burning at the windows, but she was still full of trepidation as she dismounted, approached the door and knocked. The door was opened by a girl in maid's uniform, who was staring in amazement at the sight of a young woman standing on the doorstep holding the reins of a horse.

'Lawks! What in the world . . . ?' she exclaimed, before recovering herself.

Taking her courage in both hands, Lise asked for Mrs Trevelyan.

'She's abed.' The maid was still gazing in disbelief at the horse.

'Mr Trevelyan, then?' Now that she was here, Lise wasn't going to give up so easily.

'Who shall I say?' the girl asked.

'Lise Bisset.'

She scuttled off and Lise waited nervously. After a few minutes, the master of the house appeared in the doorway.

'Lise! What on earth brings you here at this hour? And what . . . ?' He gesticulated in the direction of Gypsy.

'I was wondering if I could ask you a really big favour . . .' Lise went on to explain the bare bones of what had happened, without mentioning that she had taken the horse without the owner's permission. 'Just until tomorrow,' she finished. 'I'll come back for her then.'

To her enormous relief, Mr Trevelyan did not hesitate in agreeing.

'You're in luck. We've a spare stall in the stable. Wait while I put my boots on and I'll come with you. Ned has gone to the Golowan and I don't suppose he'll be back yet awhile.'

'Thank you so much! And I'm sorry to put you to such trouble,' Lise said, but Mr Trevelyan had already disappeared into the house.

'Can it really be true?' Cecile asked wonderingly. 'Is it possible that all my life I've had a sister I knew nothing about?'

'When you've lived as long as I have, my angel, you'll know anything's possible. Now, let's get you into this nightgown before you catch a chill.' Bessie held up the voluminous garment and beckoned Cecile with a jerk of her head.

'It's a warm night! I could sleep in my chemise and come to no harm.' But Cecile lifted her arms obediently anyway, and Bessie slipped the nightgown over her head and tugged at the hem to pull it down.

The minute it was in place, Cecile crossed to her dressing chest, retrieved her precious locket and snicked it open.

'Look. I always thought this was a likeness of me, pictured on both sides. But . . . might it be me and . . . her? That girl? My . . . sister?'

'Where did you get that?' Bessie asked sharply.

115

Cecile's face clouded. 'I found it in a drawer in the dresser. I think it must have belonged to my mother. Oh, please don't tell Papa! He'll never talk to me about her and I think he might be cross if he knew I had it.'

'I won't say a word.' But Bessie still looked troubled. The locket had reminded her of something Sam had said that didn't quite add up.

'So do you think it might be a likeness of my sister on the one side, and me on the other? If so, we're not just alike, we are the same age! Which would mean we must be twins!'

Bessie shook her head impatiently. 'I really couldn't say. But it's time you were in bed and asleep. You've had a busy day, and a hard one, and you need to get your rest if you're not to fade clean away. Come on now, 'op in and I'll tuck you up.'

Obediently, Cecile did as she was bid, but her thoughts were still racing, and her hopes were high. Was it possible that if the strange girl was her twin, she would help her and Sam to elope? Excitement swelled in her chest, almost taking her breath, and it was a long time before her eyelids began to droop. Eventually, however, she fell asleep, still clutching the precious locket that was a link to her mama, and now, perhaps, to her twin sister too.

With Gypsy safely stabled, Lise set off at a run down into the town, anxious now only to get home. She was hoping fervently that Annie would already be in bed; she didn't feel like talking to anyone until she had had a chance to put her chaotic thoughts in some sort of order. But as she approached the cottage, she saw that a lamp was burning in the little sitting room, and Annie appeared in the doorway.

'Well? Did you have a fine time? Let's have a jar of tea and you can tell me all about it.' She must have been waiting up especially, and there would be no escaping her interest however much Lise would have liked to.

'It's been . . .' Lise paused, unable to think of a suitable word to describe the events of the night. 'You were right to warn me to be careful of Zach. He's been using me. But there's more. Far more. Tonight he took me to meet a girl who looks exactly like me. A girl he reckons needs my help. A girl he says is my sister.' She stopped, then turned to Annie. 'Could that be true? Is there something you've never told me?'

Annie swung round abruptly, and the expression on her face told Lise she had hit the nail on the head.

'Annie?' she prompted.

For a moment or two the old woman was silent, seeming almost to shrink into herself, and when she spoke, her voice rasped with emotion. 'I should'a told you long ago, but your ma didn't want me to. I didn't agree with her, but I've done what she asked. Now – well, it looks like things have changed and the time has come. Let me make the tea first and then we'll talk.'

Lise pulled one of the chairs out from under the kitchen table and sat down, waiting. At last Annie set the tea on the table and seated herself opposite.

'It's a long tale, my love, and a sad one. but I reckon you already know that, don't you?'

Lise nodded, and at last Annie began to relate Marguerite's story.

Chapter Eleven

Four years of marriage to Godfrey Pendinnick had done nothing to change Marguerite's feelings for him; in fact, if possible, she hated him more than ever. He, on the other hand, was still obsessed with her, and doted on their identical twin daughters, Lise and Cecile, who, to Marguerite's enormous relief, bore no resemblance whatever to their father, but were so much like her that he might have had nothing to do with their conception at all.

Not that she had ever been able to forget that dreadful night when she was accompanying him back to England and he had taken her by force. How could she, when they shared a bed, and he still demanded his conjugal rights? She'd grown used to that now, and lay cold and unyielding beneath him, the only way she could show her distaste for him. Sometimes this roused him to anger, but she didn't fear him, and his frustration at her lack of response gave her satisfaction.

In the beginning, she had tried to imagine he was her beloved Jean-Claude, but that proved impossible. The dusty smell of the powder in his hair was repellent to her, his breath stank of cigars and brandy, and his flabby body could hardly have been more different to Jean-Claude's lean and muscled frame. Pretending only made the reality more odious, and reawakened both memories and her longing for the man she loved so that it was all she could do to hold back the tears – and that she was determined to do. Wretched as she was, she would not let him see her cry.

She took care, too, never to allow her unhappiness to show when she was with her children. They were her pride and joy, and she resolved that their lives should be happy and secure. Fortunately, Godfrey was as besotted with them as she was and saw they wanted for nothing. It was left to her to scold them if they were naughty, to limit their sweetmeats, and to take a firm hand if their demands were unreasonable. Disciplining them came hard to her, but she didn't want them to grow up spoiled, which was what she thought would happen if it were left to Godfrey.

Cordelia was another thorn in her side. Godfrey's sister clearly resented her, and made no effort to hide her dislike and disdain. She ignored Marguerite as far as was possible, and when she spoke to her it was in icy tones. She was spiteful, too, in her remarks and in other ways; when Marguerite mislaid something – her embroidery scissors, a hair ornament that disappeared from where she had left it, a child's shoe – she felt certain Cordelia was responsible, and could well imagine her smirk of satisfaction as she hid it where it would never be found.

Eventually she had told Godfrey of her suspicions, and although he had defended his sister and pooh-poohed the suggestion, she had heard him berating Cordelia behind the closed door of the room he used as a study. Cordelia had come flouncing out tossing an angry 'How dare you?' in Marguerite's direction, but from that day on nothing more had gone missing. Godfrey had taken her part as she had known he would, but it only served to make Cordelia more jealous of her.

Aside from all this, Marguerite's life was an easy one. With a cook to prepare meals and a maid to light the fires each morning and attend to the chores, her time was her own, and she liked to take the children out each day when the weather permitted. She loved the time they were able to spend together away from the oppressive atmosphere in the house, and the girls enjoyed their outings to the harbour or the town. Had she been with Jean-Claude rather than the hateful Godfrey, she would have thought herself the luckiest woman alive, and even as things stood, she knew she must count her blessings, chief among them her two beautiful, beloved daughters.

Marguerite, Lise and Cecile were in the garden at the front of the old rectory. They hadn't ventured far today, as the skies were overcast with threatening rain clouds and the March wind blowing off the sea was cold and gusty, but Marguerite had thought the girls needed to get some fresh air and use up some of their boundless energy. She was standing in a sheltered spot behind the summer house, watching as they ran around the lawns gathering primroses that grew in clumps in the borders.

'Mama! Mama! Who's that man?'

'Where?' Marguerite emerged from her nook, puzzled and a little alarmed. Might it be one of the smuggling gang? If it was, she didn't want him anywhere near her children – they were ruthless men, and dangerous. Though she had always known from his dealings with her father that Godfrey engaged in shipping contraband, since she had come to Cornwall she had learned of the wrecking activity that was carried on in this part of the world, and the wickedness of it had turned her stomach and made her despise him the more. She felt sure that if there was money to be made, Godfrey would stop at nothing to grow his fortune.

'By the gate.' Lise had stayed where she was, gazing curiously in the direction of the stranger, while Cecile scuttled to her mother, clutching at her skirts.

'It's all right.' Marguerite smoothed the child's thick auburn curls reassuringly. 'Go indoors. You too, Lise!' she called.

Reluctantly Lise retreated, and the twins headed for the house, hand in hand, though Lise was still stealing sly glances over her shoulder.

The man remained where he was, as if waiting, and Marguerite approached, walking purposefully across the lawn. Then she came to an abrupt halt, her eyes widening in disbelief, her heart pounding in her breast.

'Jean-Claude!' She spoke his name softly, wonderingly, thinking this must be nothing more than an illusion.

'Marguerite!'

It was him! It was! She flew across the grass and into his open arms.

As he kissed her hungrily she melted into him, disbelieving yet at the same time ecstatic. The familiar scent of him in her nostrils, the feel of his hard muscles beneath her hands set her pulses racing and her senses swimming.

When at last he raised his lips from hers, she realised she was trembling like a leaf in the breeze and her eyes were misted with tears of joy.

'Oh, Jean-Claude, I thought you were dead! I can't believe you're here! How did you find me?'

'When I returned to France, your father told me everything. How could he have done such a thing, Marguerite? He as good as sold you! What sort of a father could do something like that?'

'He was desperate. He stood to lose everything. I can't find it in my heart to blame him.' It was true. For all the misery he had caused her, Marguerite still loved her father dearly.

'You are more forgiving than I,' Jean-Claude said grimly.

'Though I believe he has lived to regret it. He begged me to bring you home. And that I mean to do.'

'Oh . . . !' She was breathless with the wonder of it, but also suddenly dreadfully afraid as cold reality washed over her in a sobering tide. Casting a quick fearful glance towards the house, she tugged on his arm. 'They mustn't see you. Come with me!'

Jean-Claude stood his ground. 'But I want to see him, the bastard!'

Marguerite pulled at his arm again, more urgently. 'You don't know what he's like. The men who work for him. He'd set them on you without a second thought.'

'I've been fighting a war, Marguerite. I'll take on any man.'

'A gang of them? Armed? They have blood on their hands and . . .' she raised a hand and touched the livid scar that ran across his cheek, 'you've been wounded. Please, Jean-Claude, for me!'

Reluctantly he allowed her to draw him into the shadow of the summer house. 'How has it been for you?' he asked anxiously.

She laughed, a small, bitter sound. 'How do you think? He's a monster, and his sister is no better. But at least he has given me two beautiful daughters.'

'Was that them?'

'Lise and Cecile. They are twins, and they are almost four years old.' She swallowed the emotional tears that threatened to overwhelm her. 'Oh, Jean-Claude, I've missed you so much! But why has it been so long? I thought the war in India was over a year and more ago.'

'It was. Unfortunately, I caught a tropical disease, as well as being wounded. I was kept isolated for a long time. But I'm here now, and I'm taking you home.'

'If only you could!' A solitary tear escaped and ran down Marguerite's cheek. 'But it's impossible.'

'Nothing is impossible if you are determined enough.' Jean-Claude wiped away the tear with the tip of his finger. 'The boat that brought me over from France is moored in the harbour and waiting for me to return. She's called *Ma Belle Jeanne*. Come with me, Marguerite!'

'And the children?'

'Of course!' It wasn't something he'd reckoned on, but it made no difference. 'You must not attract suspicion, though, by packing a valise. We can buy everything you need when we reach France.'

Surely, surely this couldn't really be happening! The enormity of it was beyond her wildest dreams! 'Oh yes! Please!' But the moment the words were out, her skin crawled with apprehension, as if some sixth sense was issuing a warning. Instinctively she peeped out again from the shelter of the summer house, and froze, horrified.

Cordelia was approaching the lawn. At any moment she would be able to see them there.

'I have to go!' Marguerite whispered urgently. 'My sister-in-law . . .'

Jean-Claude nodded, understanding. He gave her hand a quick squeeze. 'The *Ma Belle Jeanne*,' he whispered.

'I'll find you.'

She stepped out from the hiding place and hurried towards Cordelia, desperate to somehow head her off. 'Oh, so you have decided to enjoy the spring sunshine too!' she called in a gay tone that belied her fast-beating heart and trembling stomach. 'You must come and see the blossom on the blackthorn!'

Cordelia, however, was in no mood to admire the burgeoning of the trees that flanked the old rectory. 'The girls said there was a man in the garden,' she said, her tone heavy with suspicion. 'Who was it? And where is he now?'

'Oh – it was just a stranger who'd become lost,' Marguerite lied. 'He's gone on his way now.'

'Really?' Cordelia was still looking around, her lips pinched, her eyes narrow with suspicion, and Marguerite felt sick with fear. But Jean-Claude must have crept further around the building so as to be well out of sight, or maybe even ventured inside.

'It does happen sometimes, doesn't it? And there are the people who think the rector still lives here. Why, just last week I had to redirect a young couple who had come to speak to him about the reading of their banns! I think that's what they wanted . . .' She knew she was babbling inanely and somehow got a grip on herself. 'So you didn't come out to enjoy the sunshine at all,' she said. 'You wanted to see for yourself if we had a trespasser.'

'One cannot be too careful in these times,' Cordelia said stiffly. 'Who knows what rogues and vagabonds are lurking?'

At any other time Marguerite might have thought that rich, given the business she and her brother were mixed up in. For the moment, however, she was too caught up in diverting Cordelia's attention so that Jean-Claude could make his escape unseen.

'Well, he's gone now, so you've no need to worry any further,' she said, and linked her arm through her sister-in-law's. 'Shall we go and see what the children are up to?'

Cordelia shrugged away. 'I have work to do,' she said haughtily. And to Marguerite's immense relief, she strode off towards the house. But Marguerite didn't dare to go back to Jean-Claude. She couldn't risk raising Cordelia's suspicions any higher than they had already been raised. She knew where to find him now, and she would go to the ends of the earth to be with him.

Though she was still trembling from the narrowness of their escape, a wild, delirious joy leapt in her heart. Jean-Claude hadn't abandoned her to her fate. He loved her. He'd come for her and would take her and the children home to France. At last, it seemed dawn was breaking into the long, dark night she had lived through these last years.

In a daze, Marguerite hurried upstairs to the children's room. Jean-Claude had warned her not to pack a valise, but she couldn't go without a change of clothes for them. She found a soft bag and slipped some underwear and a clean nightgown for each of them into it, along with a couple of their favourite toys, then took it across the landing to the bedroom she shared with Godfrey to fetch a few bits and pieces for herself. At the sight of the four-poster bed with its heavy drapes, a feeling of immense relief filled her. Only one more night lying beside her despised husband; only one more night of submitting to his insatiable demands. Tomorrow she would take the children for a walk into town as she so often did, go to the harbour and find the boat she and Jean-Claude would escape on. She could scarcely believe this was really happening. She half expected to wake and find it was nothing but a lovely dream.

She fetched her hairbrush and a couple of combs from the dressing table, and a lace-trimmed chemise from her underwear drawer, and was just putting it all into the bag when the creak of a floorboard made her spin round, her heart leaping into her mouth. No one was there, but she'd carelessly left the bedroom door open. Anyone on the landing would have had a clear view of her packing her things. She hurried to the door, looking out. There was no one in sight, but the air was heavy with the overpowering scent of the rose water that Cordelia used on her wig to disguise the smell of sweat and dirt.

Trembling, Marguerite grabbed the bag from the bed and stuffed it into the bottom of her clothes chest, covering it with the garments that were stored there. As she stepped back out on to the landing, a board creaked loudly beneath her feet, undoubtedly the same one that had alerted her that she was being watched. She was in no doubt now. She'd failed to allay Cordelia's suspicions about the strange man the children had seen in the garden, and the woman had been doing some surreptitious investigating. She couldn't know, of course, what Marguerite and Jean-Claude had planned, but she would be watching her sister-in-law like a hawk, which could spell utter disaster. For now, though, there was nothing Marguerite could do except try to behave normally and hope that would satisfy Cordelia.

Full of trepidation, she went downstairs. Of Cordelia there was no sign. She found the children, anxious to keep them close, and suggested they play a game of chequers. Young as they were, they were learning fast, and Godfrey approved of this way of improving their minds. And it would help to still her whirling thoughts and all her hopes and fears for a little while at least.

For much of the rest of the day, Marguerite could feel Cordelia watching her surreptitiously from beneath those hooded lids, though she said nothing. And that night Godfrey was so late to bed that for once he did not press her for his conjugal rights. He was busy planning his next consignment of contraband, she guessed, for she had heard the low murmur of men's voices coming from the parlour when she passed it on her way to bed.

Unsurprisingly, sleep was impossible for her, but she feigned it anyway. Eventually she dozed fitfully before being wide awake again long before dawn. And though she could scarcely bring herself to eat a mouthful of the coddled eggs and cold meats that comprised breakfast, she made sure that Lise and Cecile had their fill. Who knew when they would get another square meal?

Once again she could feel Cordelia watching her closely, her lips curled into an unpleasant sneer; once again the woman said nothing. When the long-case clock in the hall struck ten, Marguerite dressed the children in their warmest clothes. She retrieved the soft bag from her bedroom chest and slung it around her, hiding it beneath her heaviest cloak. She had no need to explain to either Godfrey or Cordelia that she was taking the children for their daily constitutional; regular as it was, they would not question it and, in any case, the two of them were closeted in the parlour, presumably discussing the venture Godfrey had been planning the previous day.

'Where are we going today, Mama?' Lise asked as they set out.

'To the harbour. To see the boats. We might even go on one.' Marguerite's heart was thumping in her chest and she held tightly to her little daughters' hands, one on either side of her, leading them towards what she hoped would be a wonderful new life for all of them.

The reunion with Jean-Claude when she reached the harbour was joyful, but to her dismay, he told her their departure would have to be delayed, as the boat had been in need of some repairs to one of the masts, and it would be late afternoon before they were completed.

Marguerite spent the day in a state of anxiety, terrified that when she did not return home for luncheon, a search party would be sent out to look for her and the twins. But it was something else entirely that was worrying Jean-Claude. The skies, which had been clear and blue, were darkening, and the wind was freshening. It looked to him as if a storm was brewing.

'We might have to wait until it's passed,' he told Marguerite.

'We daren't do that!' Marguerite cried, horrified. 'We must get away today, or it will be too late! Godfrey has many friends in the town, and we're bound to have been seen by someone.'

Doubtful though he was about the wisdom of setting sail with conditions worsening, Jean-Claude at last agreed. The old saying 'Caught between the devil and the deep blue sea' had never been more apt, he remarked to Marguerite.

And so it was that with night falling earlier than usual because of the heavy cloud cover, *Ma Belle Jeanne* embarked on what was to be her last fateful voyage.

High seas washed over the decks, and the masts and timbers creaked as gigantic waves buffeted the boat.

'It's no use. We'll have to turn back,' Jean-Claude shouted over the roar of the wind.

Marguerite nodded. It would be impossible to reach France tonight, and as the vessel heeled and tossed, she was now more frightened for her life and those of her children than of anything Godfrey could do to them. She hugged Lise and Cecile close; Cecile had been violently seasick, and both of them were crying.

'Head for shore!' Jean-Claude instructed the captain, who had been as unwilling as he himself to venture out with the storm brewing. Instantly the man issued orders to his crew, who lost no time in complying. Only one looked bewildered: a Cornishman taken on to replace a seaman who had disappeared whilst they were awaiting the completion of the repairs. He spoke no French, so Marguerite translated for him, and he hastened to do as he was bid.

With the wind behind them now, they raced towards the shore, but it was lost to sight in the darkness and sea spray.

'These are dangerous waters.' The captain was straining his eyes, searching for a glimpse of a safe harbour, and Marguerite knew that he meant the rocks that lay beneath the surface in many places along the coast. In the four and a half years she had lived here, there had been many shipwrecks; even some fishing boats had been lost, though their crews knew the bays and inlets like the backs of their own hands.

Suddenly she saw what looked like lights flickering in the darkness ahead of them.

'Thank God!' She felt Jean-Claude's arm, which had been around her shoulders, relax a little. 'That's harbour lights if I'm not mistaken.'

It was impossible to know which port they were heading towards, however. All sense of direction had been lost as the boat tossed and turned in the angry winds. But they were approaching the lights fast, the crew eager to reach dry land.

Then, just as Marguerite thought they would soon be safe, the boat reared suddenly like a frisky mare, and at the same moment she heard a terrifying rending sound. The vessel shuddered violently so that she lost her footing and slipped on the flooded deck, taking Lise down with her.

'Sweet Jesus, we're holed!' the captain yelled. Already the water was rising on the deck as it poured in through the gash torn in the boat. 'Abandon ship! Get out while you can!'

The outline of a cove was visible now in the light of a dozen lanterns; there were men on the beach.

Jean-Claude pulled Marguerite and Lise to their feet, then lifted a weeping Cecile in his arms. 'I'll get her to shore and come back for you. Those people will help us.'

Tears of terror misted Marguerite's eyes; she choked them

back. Cecile's head was buried in Jean-Claude's chest, and Marguerite pressed her lips to her little daughter's neck. 'Be a brave girl, Cecile. We'll all be together again soon.'

Over Cecile's head her eyes met Jean-Claude's. 'I love you!' he mouthed, and moved to the rail.

'I love you too!' she called after him, though whether he heard her over the pounding of the waves she didn't know.

Clutching Lise tightly, she watched Jean-Claude swim towards shore. With the strong tide it was slow progress as he strove to keep Cecile's head above water, and several times he disappeared from view. He'd been sucked around the headland, away from the beach where the lights showed, but Marguerite felt sure there would be another cove on the other side, and she prayed he would reach it safely. A few moments later she sent up a prayer of thanks as the moon emerged from behind the thick scudding clouds, allowing her to see him swimming back around the headland.

There was another figure in the water, a crewman who had abandoned ship and was making for the bay and, with a sudden icy rush of horror, Marguerite realised that the men on the beach, rather than going to his aid, were hurling a volley of stones, aiming for his bobbing head! Dear God – wreckers! And when Jean-Claude rounded the headland on his way back for her and Lise, he would be a target too!

She screamed, one hand pressed to her heart, the other burying Lise's face in the folds of her skirts, but the sound was lost in the roar of the wind and the waves. The moon disappeared behind another cloud, and when it re-emerged, there was no sign of anyone in the water. 'Jean-Claude!' she sobbed. 'Where are you?'

'He won't be back, m'dear. The bastards got him.' It was the Cornish seaman, taking her by the arm. 'Come on, we're sinking fast. I'll do my best to get you and the littl'un to safety.'

Marguerite hesitated, still staring at the stretch of water between the stricken ship and the shore in the hope of catching sight of Jean-Claude even now, but there was no sign of life. The boat was heeling over as water poured in through the gashes in her hull, and the Cornishman pulled on her arm. 'Come on, fer Christ's sake!'

Somehow they made it across the slippery deck and the Cornishman lowered himself into the water. 'Get on your back and hold the littl'un's head up high,' he shouted to Marguerite. 'Leave the rest to me.'

As she did as he said, Marguerite felt a tug on her hair so violent she thought it would be torn out by the roots. Waves washed over her face as her rescuer began to swim strongly away from the sinking vessel, making her cough and fight for breath, but she concentrated on holding Lise as high as she could. She felt as if she was about to lose consciousness, but she fought it with all her strength. If she let go of Lise, it would be the end for the child.

How long they were in the water Marguerite would never know. She wasn't even aware of the direction they were moving in. In fact, the tide had turned and the current was sweeping them in the opposite direction to the one it had taken Jean-Claude and Cecile, to yet another secluded bay. But after what seemed an endless stretch of time, she felt sludgy sand beneath her feet. The Cornishman had taken Lise from her arms, and Marguerite rolled on to her stomach, coughing and retching. When she had recovered a little, she saw that the heroic crewman was working on Lise to expel the seawater she had swallowed. Marguerite crawled towards them, shivering as much from desperate dread as from the chill of her sea-soaked garments.

'Is she . . . ?'

For long moments the Cornishman made no reply, then, as Lise stirred, gasping and vomiting, he glanced up. 'She'll live. But we'd best get you home, and warm and dry, or there's no telling—'

'We can't go home!' Even in this desperate situation, she could not contemplate going back to Godfrey and Cordelia.

The Cornishman did not question her. 'Then we'll find shelter at the nearest inn, and think again tomorrow. I reckon it might be best if I took you back to St Ives with me.'

Chapter Twelve

'So now you know,' Annie said. 'Your mam were tryin' to escape from Penzance wi' you and your sister, an' go back to France with the man she loved. But it all ended in disaster. You've already guessed, I reckon, that it were my George what saved 'er life, and yours. That be 'ow you came to live with us. Yer poor mam 'ad nowhere else to go, bar going back to *him*, and I wouldn't have seen her out on the streets.'

'Oh Annie . . .' Lise's head was spinning; she hardly knew what to say. 'It's all so . . . unbelievable! But the storm . . . I've had this dream, ever since I was a little girl, clear as you like. I'm on the deck of a ship, soaked to the skin and frightened to death. It stops there, though. Your George got Mama and me to shore, you say, but in the dream I'm never in the sea.'

'I don't reckon you knew much about that,' Annie said. 'From what George said, you was half drownded. You don't remember anything about it when you're awake, do you?'

'I didn't, no, but now it's beginning to come back. And I've always had this strange feeling, too. That . . . oh, I don't know how to describe it . . . that part of me was missing.'

Annie nodded knowingly. 'That'll be right. They do say it's a terrible thing for twins to be separated, 'specially ones that are the spit image of one another.'

'So what happened to my sister? Mama thought she had drowned, I suppose, like Jean-Claude.'

A wary look came into Annie's eyes. If Lise hadn't been so taken up with trying to piece together all the disparate parts of the story, she might have noticed, and wondered if the old woman really had told her everything.

'But she didn't drown,' she went on. 'She must have been found in the cove where Jean-Claude had left her. Whoever took her in must be wealthy. She was wearing fancy clothes, and a powdered wig, like the gentry do. But who . . . ?' Her eyes widened as the thought struck her. 'Her father. She was recognised and taken back to her father!'

'Mebbe,' Annie said, non-committal.

'That must be it! And who did you say he was?'

This was one question the old woman couldn't avoid. 'Godfrey Pendinnick.'

A fresh wave of shock ran through Lise's veins. She hadn't really taken in the name while listening to Annie's story; now it struck her like a hammer blow.

Godfrey Pendinnick. She had a feeling Zach had once mentioned that name as being the man he worked for.

'He's her father? And mine?'

'Accordin' to what your mama told me, and I have no reason to doubt her. But he's a scoundrel, me darlin'. Made his fortune smuggling – and worse. He isn't above wrecking. You know what that is, don't you? Luring ships on to the rocks, making sure there ain't any survivors to tell the tale, then looting the cargo. And like I told you, that's what 'appened the night you got wrecked. The captain was making for lights on the shore thinking it were a safe haven, and, well, you know what the upshot of that was. My George always reckoned it were Pendinnick's doing.'

'You mean he deliberately wrecked the boat? With his wife and children aboard?' Lise was horrified.

'I'm not saying that, and neither did George. But 'twas Pendinnick behind it, for sure. He was king of that coast, and still is. And now, my lovely, 'tis long past time I was abed, and you're done in too. Here.' Annie went to the dresser and got out a quarter-bottle of brandy. 'Take this with you and have a nip. It'll help you sleep.'

Lise had spent a good deal of the night standing by the open window in her bedroom, breathing in fresh salty air and allowing the breeze to cool her hot cheeks. She was in too much turmoil to sleep, the story Annie had told her running around and around in her head alongside the events of the evening and the situation she now found herself in.

The dream wasn't just a dream; it was a forgotten memory. The strange feeling that consumed her sometimes when she looked at her reflection was another. Somewhere deep inside she had known she had lost a twin sister. But if that sister was Cecile it must mean they shared a father too. Godfrey Pendinnick, an evil man who might well have been the cause of the disaster. A man who ran smuggling enterprises and encouraged wrecking. The man Zach worked for. And that made him every bit as bad as his employer. He had tricked her into meeting her sister whilst pretending interest in her. How despicable was that? To think she had begun to allow herself to fall in love with him!

But what had been his purpose? Her sister needed help, he'd said. Lise couldn't imagine what that might mean. What could she offer a young woman who had everything? It sounded very suspicious. Was it just another lie to inveigle her into some conspiracy to which she would never agree under normal circumstances?

Her head was aching, her eyes burning with tiredness, and at last, as dawn was beginning to lighten the sky, she lay down on her bed, pulled the covers up to her chin and instantly fell asleep.

'Lise! Wake up!'

As Annie shook her shoulder, Lise came to with a start. 'What . . . ?'

'There's someone here to see you.' Annie's lips were pressed together disapprovingly. 'I told him you was still abed, but 'e won't listen to me. Says he won't be goin' anywhere till 'e's seen you.'

Although Annie had not mentioned Zach's name, Lise was in no doubt as to who it was who had come calling. She rubbed her heavy eyes, winced at the throbbing pain in her temple, and pulled herself to a sitting position. She had no wish to see Zach, but since she had stolen his horse last night, she should at least tell him where he could find her.

'Tell him I'll be down in a minute.'

She dressed hastily, pulled a brush through her tangled hair and descended the narrow stairs. Annie had not asked Zach in, but had left the door open so that as she crossed the kitchen, Lise could see him silhouetted against the bright morning sunshine. Her heart twisted painfully and she knew that in spite of everything, she still had feelings for him.

Steeling herself, she approached him. 'I suppose you've come for Gypsy. You'll find her in the stables at the place I used to work. I pointed it out to you once, didn't I?'

'She's unharmed, I hope?' Zach's cold tone matched hers.

'Of course. You taught me well, even if it was all part of a plan to trick me into meeting . . . my sister.'

'That's how it began,' Zach admitted.

'And ended,' she said shortly. 'I told you last night I never wanted to see you again, and I meant it. Now that you know where to find Gypsy, I'd be obliged if you'd go,'

'We need to talk.' It was as if Zach hadn't heard her, or was ignoring what she'd said. 'Things are not always as they seem. Besides, I'd have thought you'd want to learn a little, at least, about Cecile and the plight she finds herself in.'

Lise hesitated. However devious Zach had been, she was in no doubt now that Cecile was her sister. He seized his opportunity.

'Won't you walk with me, and I can tell you everything you wish to know.'

Still she hesitated, before curiosity and a sense of obligation to her twin got the better of her. She nodded curtly. 'Very well. Wait while I fetch a wrap.' Fine as the weather was, there was still a chill in the breeze coming off the sea.

'You're not going with him, are you?' asked Annie, who had clearly been eavesdropping, as Lise went back into the kitchen.

'Just this once. I need to know why it is that my sister needs my help.'

'Sister or not, you don't want anything to do with them Pendinnicks.'

A wary note in Annie's tone gave Lise pause for thought. Had she told her the whole story? Or was she keeping something back? Something she didn't want Lise to know?

'If Pendinnick was responsible for the wreck that was the cause of all this, then I certainly won't be engaging with him,' she said. 'But Cecile is still my sister. I lost her once. I can't lose her again.'

'On your own head be it,' Annie muttered.

Lise ignored her and fetched her wrap, joining Zach at the door. 'Why do we have to walk anyway?' she asked.

'Because I want to be sure no one overhears what I have to say to you.'

'You mean Annie? She's only concerned for me, that's all.'

Zach glanced at the adjoining cottages. 'Walls have ears,' he said cryptically. 'Come on. I'll explain once we're well out of earshot.'

They walked in silence until they reached a deserted spot where unattended boats bobbed in the gentle swell. Out at sea, a cloud of herring gulls followed a fishing smack, their mewing cries carrying to shore on the stiff breeze.

'So?' Lise challenged Zach. 'What have you got to say to me that can't be overheard?'

'Let's sit down.' Zach indicated the low harbour wall, and Lise, tired from her sleepless night, was glad to concur. Zach sat beside her, but at a distance, and she was glad of that too. If he had come too close, she would have quickly stood up again. 'So where do you want to begin?'

'I thought we were going to talk about my sister, and why she is in need of my help.'

'Very well. You have to understand, Lise, that she has had a very different upbringing to yours—'

'I imagine so,' Lise interposed, her tone sarcastic.

'I don't just mean that materially she has wanted for nothing,' Zach continued, unfazed. 'And given the option, I know which life I would choose. You have your freedom; she's like a bird in a cage. You have Annie; you've told me she's like a mother to you, and it's clear she loves you dearly. Cecile has her father, who no doubt does love her, but shows it in ways that aren't conducive to happiness. He's possessive, demanding, controlling. And Cordelia, his sister, who lives with them, treats Cecile very badly. The poor girl has no friends, except for Bessie, her maid, and Sam, the coachman. She and Sam have fallen in love, but

138

there is no way her father would sanction a relationship with him. And now I think either Godfrey or Cordelia might have begun to suspect that something is going on between them, for arrangements are being made for her to wed a man of the cloth, a widower much older than her, whom she scarcely knows and certainly does not love.' He paused, letting Lise absorb all he had told her.

'Well, I'm sorry for her,' she said at last. 'It does sound as if I was the lucky one. But I don't see what help I could possibly be.'

'I'll do my best to explain.' Zach shifted on the wall, looking away from her now. 'Sam is my friend. He's as desperate as she is for them to be together, and when I told him I had seen a girl in St Ives who was Cecile's double, he remembered hearing – a long time ago – that she had once had a twin sister who was believed dead, drowned along with her mother. This wasn't common knowledge locally, since it was only afterwards that the family moved to Porthmeor, but Sam had an uncle in Penzance, where they had lived previously, and he was able to confirm the story. Sam begged me to try to find you. He'd come up with the idea of persuading you to take Cecile's place for just long enough to enable her to escape unnoticed, giving them the chance to run away together.'

'That's insane!' Lise gasped, incredulous.

'That's what I thought at first,' Zach said, 'but the more I think about it, the more I believe it could work. You're identical. It gave me quite a start when I first saw you, that day when the rogue tried to rob you.'

'So you took your chance. You chased him and got my reticule back just so that you could speak to me.' Her anger had returned, and with it the deep hurt that Zach was not at all the man she had thought him, and that he had planned from the very beginning to use her.

'That's not so,' Zach said swiftly. 'I was behind you. I didn't see your face until I returned your reticule to you.'

'Hah!' Lise snorted. 'And why would I believe you – a smuggler and worse?'

Zach's expression hardened. 'It's the truth, but you must believe what you will.'

'The whole idea is madness!' Lise said. 'Surely our father and this . . . what was her name? Cordelia? . . . would know at once, however alike we might be. Cecile has pretty manners, no doubt, while I am just common hoi polloi. When she rides, she rides side-saddle, I imagine. I have no idea of the layout of the house, or the daily routines. I could never carry off such a deception, and I can't believe you are serious in thinking I could.'

'You and Cecile would have to meet a few times, of course, to allow her to school you in what you would need to know. I can teach you to ride side-saddle, and if you take to it as you took to riding astride, it will pose no problem whatsoever. As for how to behave, I'm sure you are not as ignorant as you would have me believe. You've worked in a grand house. Set tables, no doubt, served dishes. I'd wager you'd never let yourself down in polite company. You already speak and behave as a lady. Think about it, at least. Think about your sister, forced into a marriage of convenience, torn apart from the man she loves. Are you not able to find it in your heart to do this for her?'

Lise was silent for a long moment. Then: 'How would I meet her?' she asked.

'The stables at Polruan would be the safest place,' Zach said. 'She often goes there to visit her horse. Lady is a gentle beast and Cecile loves her, though she doesn't often ride; unlike you, she is somewhat timid, the result of the way she's been raised, I imagine. That's something else you would need to be careful of:

to keep your somewhat wild ways well hidden. We'll choose the moments for those meetings carefully, just as we will a good time for you to take her place. So, will you do it?'

'You have it all worked out, I see,' Lise said with a touch of bitterness. 'But then, you're very practised in deception, are you not? I would never have entertained meeting with you if I had suspected for a second that you were involved in smuggling and wrecking. Don't deny it – I learned last night that the man you work for is behind all that goes on around this coast. So my answer is no. I won't do it. I very much doubt it would work, and it would be reckless and dangerous to tangle with such a man, even if he is my father.'

'He's your father all right. You can trust me on that.'

'Trust you? I think not! Why, you are every bit as bad as he is. Don't pretend that working for him is anything other than aiding him in his wicked ways.'

Zach's mouth tightened. 'All is not always as it seems,' he said quietly.

Something in his tone rang true, but Lise's trust in him was so bruised she was determined not to allow him to deceive her again. 'Nothing in this whole charade has been as it seemed,' she said abruptly.

'Lise.' He reached out as if to touch her arm, then withdrew swiftly as she jerked away. 'Not everything has been a charade, as you put it. I admit that in the beginning the reason I sought you out was at Sam's behest, crazy as I thought his plan. But as I got to know you, I found myself growing fond of you, and admiring you more and more. You are not only beautiful to look at, you are beautiful within too. And courageous, spirited, and dutiful to your friend Annie. There was no deception with regard to my feelings for you.'

An imp twisted in Lise's gut, but she did her best to ignore it.

141

'Don't think you can worm your way back into my favour with fine words.'

'That is not my intention, though I am hoping I can yet persuade you to change your mind.' Zach's voice was steady, earnest. 'There is another reason for me pressing you to do this, and it has nothing to do with Sam and Cecile's heartfelt desire to be together. But in order to explain what it is, I need to tell you the true reason I am in Pendinnick's employ. You don't trust me, I know, and I don't blame you for that. But if I am to tell you the whole truth, *I* must trust *you*. With my very life.' He paused, looking directly into her face. 'Can I trust you, Lise?'

His tone, the expression on his rugged face were both so serious that in spite of herself, Lise was not only intrigued, but impressed. Had she been misjudging him? Was there truly some reason why he was working for her father that was not what she had thought and could put his life in danger if he revealed it?

'Lise?' he prompted.

Still she hesitated, disturbed by the turn this conversation had taken. Then, returning his gaze, she nodded. 'You can trust me.'

Zach took a good look around, ensuring there was still no one else in the vicinity, which reassured Lise that what he was about to say was for her ears alone.

'I told you once that I had a brother,' he began in a low voice. 'Josh was a year older than me, and a riding officer, working for the Revenue and Customs. His job was to patrol the moors and the coastline and apprehend those who were up to no good, which made him an enemy of the smuggling gangs and wreckers. One day he failed to return home. His horse was found wandering, but of Josh there was no sign. We suspected at once that he had been set upon by a party of lawless men, perhaps secreting goods for illegal shipping abroad, or transporting a cargo of contraband inland, but we had not a shred of proof, and neither did his employers. His body was never found; doubtless it was either tossed over a cliff or dumped in one of the old mine shafts, but no one could be held responsible for it. I made up my mind then that I would see that justice was served, and my brother's death avenged.'

Horrified as she was by what he was telling her, Lise was in no doubt that Zach was speaking the truth. It was not uncommon for riding officers to be attacked, even murdered; they did a dangerous job and they and everyone else knew it.

'I was still living at home, helping my father with the farm, when Josh disappeared,' Zach continued. 'I came down to Mount's Bay, not disclosing my identity, and learned that the kingpin of the smuggling operation hereabouts is Godfrey Pendinnick. No one would speak a word against him, however, probe as I might. Many have done well out of the illicit trade and would lose half their livelihoods if a stop were to be put to his activities, and many more are rightly afraid of him. Besides, even if I were able to bring him before the justices on one charge or another, it's likely he would be let off lightly. He has plenty of friends in high places. But I had also learned that the gangs of wreckers who lure ships on to the rocks are controlled by Pendinnick too. Most often these gangs do away with any survivors, and then strip the wreck of whatever cargo she was carrying. This, I am glad to say, is treated far more seriously by the courts, the case even heard in another district if needs be, and the perpetrators face severe consequences.

'Nothing can bring Josh back, of course, but to see Pendinnick jailed for a very long time would at least give me some satisfaction. So I set out to infiltrate his set-up. Whilst I pretend to be working for him, in reality I am seeking evidence that will bring him to justice, and deliver his just deserts.'

'But how?' Lise asked. 'What good can you achieve by aligning yourself with such wickedness?'

'My object in the beginning was to gather information about illicit landings and alert the authorities in the hope that the culprits would be caught red handed. But as I said, Godfrey has friends in high places – justices, even some officials in the Customs and Revenue who are not above corruption. But when I had established myself in Porthmeor, I learned something very interesting. Along with the loot, the wreckers are under instruction to take trophies from the ships they run aground, and these are delivered to Polruan House.'

'Trophies?' Lise asked, puzzled.

'A figurehead, a ship's bell, even a piece of board bearing the name of the stricken vessel, for the purpose of satisfying Pendinnick's warped sense of achievement. I realised that if I could locate this macabre collection, it would provide proof of his involvement in the much more serious offence of wrecking.'

'But you haven't found it yet?'

'So far, no, but my access to possible hiding places is limited. I have had no opportunity to search the upper rooms, the attic or the cellars. I have thought of asking for Cecile's help, but as I mentioned, she is not the bravest of young ladies.' He paused, his eyes returning to Lise's. 'You, on the other hand . . .'

In that moment, Lise understood. Why Zach had decided to go along with Sam's outrageous plan. Why he had cultivated her. And why he was now revealing secrets that could place him in mortal danger. He didn't just want her to pretend to be her sister so that Cecile could run away with her lover; he was hoping she could keep it up for long enough to search for the trophies he needed as evidence to convict the leader of the wrecking gang.

Had he given any other reason for asking her to take Cecile's place, she would have refused. Not even sympathy for her sister could have persuaded her; if the plan failed, it could prove disastrous for them both. But now . . .

Lise was thinking about what Annie had told her. That she believed it was Godfrey Pendinnick's gang of wreckers who had been responsible for the sinking of the ship on which her mother had been seeking to escape from her loveless marriage to this monster. If there was any way she could gain retribution, however risky it might be, Lise was going to take it.

She returned Zach's gaze, the set of her chin determined, her eyes flashing brilliant blue fire.

'I'll do it,' she said.

Chapter Thirteen

The minute Lise got back, having parted company with Zach, Annie demanded to know why she hadn't just told him where he could find his horse and sent him away 'with a flea in his ear'. Reluctantly Lise explained. She knew Annie wouldn't approve, but even so she was unprepared for the vehemence of old woman's reaction. Her eyes went wide with horror, and one bony hand flew to her throat, while the other clenched and unclenched in the folds of her skirts.

'No! You mustn't go there!' Her tone was shrill. 'It's not safe!'

'It's a risk, I know,' Lise conceded. 'But I'm sure I won't come to any harm. And how can I refuse to at least try to help my sister? And get to know her, and how she's lived, at the same time?'

'Risk?' Annie repeated harshly. 'You'd be walking into mortal danger! That man . . . you don't know what he's capable of!'

'You mean the wrecking?'

'And the rest.'

'What?' Lise was puzzled.

'Never you mind. There's things that man 'as done that's even worse. Things I don't want to talk about, not now, not ever.'

146

'Annie, you're frightening me.'

'And you should be frightened, my girl. Now, let's say no more about it. And for goodness' sake, tell me you'll put this daft notion out of your head, and forget all about going to that place.'

'I'm sorry, Annie, but no. My mind's made up.'

The kitchen door creaked as it opened a crack and a voice she recognised calling 'Coo-ee!' stopped Lise in her tracks. Gussie Moxey.

Their neighbour often came round to share a jar of tea with Annie, but Lise was annoyed, and dismayed too, that she should have chosen such an inopportune moment today. No doubt she had seen Zach arrive and the two of them walk off together, and she was eager to learn who he was and whether there was a romance in the offing, but the last thing Lise wanted was for Annie to blurt out the truth. Gussie might be her best and most trusted friend, but the more people who knew what she and Zach planned, the greater the risk.

'Don't say a word to Gussie!' she whispered urgently, but Annie was too agitated to listen, and when Gussie sensed the tension in the kitchen and asked: 'Whatever be the matter?' the old woman didn't hesitate.

'You'll never guess what this one be thinking of doing! Goin' to Polruan! To change places with her sister! You tell 'er, Gussie. Tell 'er that she'd be nothin' but a lamb to the slaughter!'

'Oh dearie me.' Gussie was chewing her lip, a little dribble of spittle running down the first of her multiple chins. 'That bain't a good idea, me babs.'

Lise looked from one to the other of them. Gussie, it seemed, knew she had a twin or she would have exhibited surprise at Annie's words. Did she know too why Annie was so horrified at the very idea that she should visit what was after all her rightful home? What harm her own father was likely to cause her? 'Will somebody please tell me what you're talking about?' she demanded.

'Can't you just take my word fer it and leave it, my girl? Don't you know what's good fer you?'

'No, Annie,' Lise said. 'This has gone far enough. It's only right I should know what you're keeping from me.'

'Oh my lovely . . .' All the colour had drained from Annie's face, and she swayed suddenly, reaching out for the back of one of the kitchen chairs to support herself.

'Be you aw right?' Gussie made a grab for her friend, catching her as Annie's legs crumpled beneath her.

'She's faint.' All her questions forgotten momentarily, Lise grasped Annie's other arm. 'Sit her down!'

Between them they manoeuvred Annie on to the chair, and Lise pushed her head down between her knees, a trick she'd learned while working for Mrs Trevelyan, who was given to fainting fits. Gussie hurried to fetch a cup of water.

After a few minutes, Annie recovered herself a little, and they supported her into the little parlour and sat her down in a comfortable chair.

'Oh dearie dear, I come over all funny,' she said shakily.

'Because you was gettin' in a stew.' Gussie threw Lise a straight look as if to warn her not to continue with the subject.

As if she would! Anxious as Lise was to know why Annie couldn't bring herself to explain her vehement objection, she couldn't pursue it while the old woman was in this state. 'Just sit quietly until you feel better,' she urged her. 'I'll make you a nice jar of tea.'

'If you'm sure you be aw right now, I'd best be getting home,' Gussie said, and followed Lise into the kitchen, where she wagged a finger at her.

'Let me know 'ow she is. An' don't you be upsettin' 'er agin,' she warned before bustling out of the door, dashing any hopes Lise might have had of asking her what she knew. For the moment, her questions would have to remain unanswered.

Aaron Moxey was sitting on his doorstep, drinking the last of his tea and trying to hear what was going on in the cottage next door. From his bedroom window he'd seen Lise and the man he now knew as Zach Carver walking together from the far end of the quay, but by the time he got downstairs, Lise had gone indoors and Carver was disappearing in the direction of the town. He'd cut himself a slice of bread and slathered it with dripping, then made a jar of tea. He'd offered one to Gussie, but she'd declined. She was going round to Annie's, she said, taking off her apron. That suited Aaron very well. Sometimes when the weather was fine, as it was today, Annie would leave the door open, and since both she and Gussie were a little hard of hearing, they talked to one another in loud voices. If he took his breakfast out and ate it sitting on the doorstep, he might well overhear something of interest pertaining to Carver's visit.

Ever since he'd been introduced to Carver by Dyfan Flinders, he'd been curious to know what connection there was between Lise and a man in the employ of Godfrey Pendinnick. He couldn't believe she could be involved in any way with Pendinnick's trade; she had no time for that kind of thing, as she'd made clear more than once when she or Annie had suspected he was up to no good. And she wouldn't be likely to be stepping out with Carver if she knew who he worked for and what he did. She'd been taken in by his good looks and his fine clothes, Aaron supposed, and it was small wonder that he could afford them on what Pendinnick would pay him. Aaron had seen what Carver had given Dyfan even before they'd finished the job, and though he didn't know what the balance had been, he guessed it must have been generous, since Dyfan had parted with another three gold sovereigns to cover his part in getting what was owed to Pendinnick out of Horatio Quinn. It had been the easiest money he'd ever earned in his life, holding the innkeeper while Dyfan beat him almost senseless, and he felt no guilt over it, just eagerness to get the chance again. And maybe, if he played his cards right, it would come his way. If he could get to know Carver, perhaps he could get himself taken on in his own right, not just as Dyfan's sidekick. If he was lucky, he could end up earning enough money to buy fine clothes, too. Stand his pals a jug of ale now and then. Buy his mother a few trinkets.

''Aven't you got any work to go to?' she asked now, taking off her apron and giving him a straight look.

Aaron shrugged. 'I'm going down to give our Billie a hand with his catch when he gets back. I'll have me breakfast outside so I can keep an eye out for him.' It was a lie, of course, but he was glad of the excuse for sitting on the doorstep.

As he sat down and took a bite of his bread and lard, he heard Annie's voice, shaky and shrill. He stopped chewing and cocked his head to listen. Annoyingly, he couldn't make out what she was saying, but she certainly sounded upset about something. It wasn't like Annie to raise her voice in anger.

'Move yourself then and let me get out.'

It was Gussie, behind him. He very nearly warned her that there was something of a to-do going on next door, but decided against it. He didn't want her to change her mind; if the row was about Carver, she'd likely find out about it, and he could pump her even if he wasn't able to overhear what was being said himself.

He got up to let her pass. Things had gone a bit quieter, and as she bustled to her neighbour's door, Gussie seemed blissfully unaware of anything wrong. He watched as she pushed it open without bothering to knock, and heard her call out her usual greeting. 'Coo-ee!' Then, to his disappointment, she closed the door behind her. Still, the kitchen window was open, and he shuffled along as far as he could, straining his ears. Lise was saying something, and then Annie was shouting again. 'Can't you just take my word fer it and leave it, my girl? Don't you know what's good fer you?'

'No, Annie . . .' The rest of whatever it was Lise said was lost to him, and he shuffled back again, not wanting to be caught lurking beneath the window should his mother leave the house unexpectedly.

He waited another ten minutes or so, but everything seemed to have gone quiet, and he went back to the kitchen for a second jar of tea. As he was making it, Gussie came in, huffing and puffing and looking anxious.

'What's goin' on next door?' he asked.

'Annie took bad.' She gesticulated towards the tea. 'Do one for me, will you? I never did get a jar round there.'

'So what's the matter with 'er?' he asked disingenuously as he poured her tea.

'Came over faint, that's all. An' I thought you was keeping an eye out for your brother. He could be back by now, and you wouldn't be any the wiser.'

Aaron realised he was going to get no more out of her. But he'd find out what it was sooner or later. You couldn't live so close and not get to know one another's business. It was something to do with Carver, he was sure of it. And once he knew exactly what, he might be able to use it to his advantage.

* * *

151

After collecting Gypsy from the Trevelyans' home, Zach rode straight to Polruan House with Sam's horse on a leading rein. He found Sam, and Cecile too, in the stables.

'Well?' Sam asked anxiously.

'It was a close-run thing, but she'll do it,' Zach said.

'Oh yes, yes!' Cecile clapped her hands, bubbling with excitement, and Sam nodded, relieved. Given the disastrous way the meeting last night had turned out, he had been very afraid their plan would fail before it had even begun, and quite apart from his own hopes being cruelly dashed, he'd dreaded to think how upset Cecile would be. When he'd left her in Bessie's care, her shock at coming face to face with her mirror image had been forgotten in her excitement that she had a sister she'd never known about, and that there really might be a way in which she and Sam could be together.

'We need to decide how we are going to make this work,' he said now.

'I think it would be best if I brought Lise here.' Zach wiped his hands on the seat of his breeches. 'As long as she is able to sneak in unseen, it should be safe enough, and since Cecile spends a good deal of time here with Lady, no one would suspect, would they? The two of them can get to know one another, and Cecile can talk Lise through the habits of the household.'

'Oh yes!' Cecile clapped her hands together again. 'I can't wait to meet her – my very own sister! As for how we can pass her off as me, I'll give her some of my gowns and a spare wig!'

Sam frowned. 'How will you manage that?'

'I can wear one gown over another – Bessie will help me – and hide the wig in a saddlebag. Oh, it's all so exciting! It will work, I know it will!'

'Let's not get ahead of ourselves,' Zach cautioned. 'You'll

have to give Lise a lot of tuition. We can't risk her making some fundamental error and being caught out before you are well away.'

He didn't add that he was hoping she would be able to carry on the deception long enough to look for the trophies from the wrecks. He hadn't even confided that to Sam; playing his cards close to his chest was the safest way for both Lise and himself. And he couldn't trust Cecile not to let something slip in her frenzied excitement. Already Bessie knew what was planned, it seemed, and although he didn't think she would say or do anything to give Cecile away, he couldn't be sure how far her loyalty would extend when it came to Lise. She had, after all, been in Pendinnick's employ for many years

No, best to keep his own counsel for the time being. And he must remember to warn Lise not to mention anything of what he had told her. She, now, was as anxious as he was to find the evidence he needed to obtain long-overdue justice for both his brother and her family.

Annie had never really made a full recovery from the chesty illness that had almost killed her. Although to all intents and purposes she had shaken it off, she still tired easily and had lost some of her wiry strength. For almost an hour after the fainting fit, she was pale and shaky, and remained in the easy chair, simply staring into space.

'I think I'll go and lie down for a bit,' she said eventually.

Lise followed her up the stairs to make sure she didn't stumble, settled her on her bed, and pulled the curtain partway across the window, through which the noonday sun was streaming.

'Is there anything else you want?' she asked.

'No. I just want to rest my eyes.'

Annie made no mention of the earlier upset and, anxious though she was to discover what it had all been about, Lise knew this was not the time to raise the subject.

'Well, just call if you need me.'

'Don't worry about me. Just go on and do whatever you've got to do. I'll be all right.' Annie sounded drowsy already; Lise guessed she would soon be asleep.

Downstairs she made a start on preparing dinner, then decided to pop round to tell Gussie how Annie was. And who knew? She might be able to find out from Gussie what it was that had upset Annie so, and what it was she was keeping from her. Gussie knew, she felt certain.

Their neighbour was in her kitchen, peeling onions for a stew. When Lise knocked on her door, she opened it, wiping her eyes on her sleeve. 'Bliddy onions allus makes me cry,' she explained. 'You comin' in or what?'

'Just for a minute,' Lise said. 'I don't want to leave Annie on her own for too long, though she seems much better. She's having a rest on her bed, and I think a nap will do her good.'

'I 'spec so,' Gussie agreed. 'That were a nasty turn, though. I've never seen 'er so upset. And you should 'ave known better'n to keep on at her.'

It was Lise's opportunity to broach the subject, and she took it. 'Then perhaps you can enlighten me. She's hiding something from me, something to do with Mr Pendinnick, and I think you know what it is.'

'What gives you that idea?' Gussie blustered, but a slow flush was creeping up her neck and into her flabby cheeks, and something in her expression told Lise that she was on the right track.

'If it concerns me, I've a right to know,' she persisted. 'And it does, doesn't it? Look, I already know he's my father. She told me that last night. She even told me that her George suspected it was Pendinnick's gang that was behind our ship being wrecked. And she told me the story of how he rescued me and Mama and brought us here to St Ives. She was a bit reluctant, but she told me all about it, and it didn't upset her the way she got upset this morning. So I know there's more to it, and I mean to find out what it is. If you're a friend to her, which I know full well you are, you'll tell me, so that I won't have to ask her again.'

Gussie chewed her lip for a moment, considering. Then she nodded. 'I do know, aye. And when she was at death's door with that cough and fever, she made me promise that if anything happened to 'er, I'd tell ee what ee wanted to know. Straight up, I've allus thought she should'a told you a long time ago. But 'twas her decision. I even spoke to 'er about it when she got better, said it was 'er place, not mine, to tell you, an' I'm glad she's told you as much as she 'as. This, though . . . well, I can see she might want to spare you if she can. And why she was in such a state at the idea of you goin' to Polruan. So mebbe it'd be for the best if I did say. But don't you go faintin' on me an' all.'

'I'm not the fainting kind,' Lise said bluntly. 'Go on, please.'

'We'll get a nip of brandy ready just in case. I could do wi' one meself an all.' Gussie fetched a small bottle and two mugs. 'Don't ee ever wonder what became of your mama?' she asked as she poured two generous measures.

Lise frowned. 'She died. When I was a child. She never recovered from being shipwrecked, is what Annie's always told me.'

'An' her grave? 'Ave you ever seed 'er grave?'

'Annie said George buried her up on the moors. They didn't have the money for a proper funeral.'

'Well I can tell you, none o' that's true.' Gussie took a long pull of her brandy as if to give her the courage to go on. 'Your

155

mama didn't die here in St Ives. An' she made a decent recovery from the shipwreck, though she were pretty bad for a bit. No, what she couldn't get over was losing your sister, and when George heard from one of his shipmates that the littl'un hadn't drowned like we all thought, but 'ad been found washed up in a cove and taken back to 'er father, well, nothing could 'ave stopped 'er. She left you 'ere wi' Annie, and went off to Polruan. And . . .' she gulped down the rest of her brandy, 'the fact is she never came back.'

'You mean . . . she's still there?' Lise asked, startled.

'Oh dearie me, no. She ain't never bin seen since. He must 'ave done away wi' 'er, old Pendinnick. And Annie's affrighted that if you go there, the same thing'll 'appen t'you.'

Annie must have woken up feeling better. When Lise returned from talking to Gussie Moxey, she found the old woman in the kitchen, continuing with the preparations for dinner that she'd begun. There was more colour in her cheeks, but she was tight lipped as she banged a pot of vegetables on the hob and turned to Lise.

'She's told you, I suppose. She didn't think I was up to it.'

Lise flew to Gussie's defence. 'She was afraid you'd have another funny turn if I started asking you questions again.'

Annie didn't comment on that. Instead she said: 'So now you know why I don't want you going to that place. You'll come to harm, just like your mother did. I hope you'll see sense, and forget all about it.'

'I'm sorry,' Lise said. She was very afraid of upsetting Annie again, but she couldn't lie to her.

'Sorry you ever thought about doing something so bliddy silly?'

'No.' Lise drew a deep breath. 'Sorry that I can't do what

you want. That evil man has to be stopped one way or another. I was set on it before, but now . . . I'm more determined than ever. I have to do what I can to get justice, not just for what he did all those years ago, but for Mama. You must see that, surely?'

For a long moment Annie was silent, then she sighed. 'I should've known better than to try and stop you, Lise. I should've known 'twould be useless. I wish you were a lot less reckless, but I s'pose if you were, 'twouldn't be you. But for the love o' God take care, and come back safe to me.'

Lise went to the woman who had been a second mother to her, put her arms around her thin frame and hugged her. 'It'll be all right, Annie, you'll see. At least I'm prepared. I know what he's capable of. But if anything should go wrong, I want you to know how grateful I am for all you've done for me. And how much I love you.'

Tears were running down Annie's wrinkled cheeks. 'Just come back safe,' she repeated.

Chapter Fourteen

'I can't believe you are really my sister!' Cecile reached for Lise's hands, squeezing them tightly between her own. 'I am so sorry I ran away that first time I saw you, but it was such a shock!'

Zach had taken Lise to Polruan House, and the twins were meeting in the stables. 'It was for me too,' Lise admitted. 'And yet somehow I always knew there were two of us. As if part of me was missing. Did you feel that too?'

'I don't know . . . maybe. I should have guessed. I found a locket of Mama's in a dresser drawer and there were miniatures inside of what looked the same little girl. I thought they were both of me, pictured from different sides, but now I know I was wrong. One was me, and one was you.'

Lise frowned. 'You have a locket of Mama's?'

'It must be hers. Aunt Cordelia doesn't wear that kind of ornament. And the colour of the little girls' hair and eyes . . . it's us, Lise, when we were very small. I'll bring it and show it to you next time we meet. I keep it in a safe place in my room. I do wear it sometimes when I visit Mama's grave, but I keep it well hidden under my bodice. I don't think Papa or Aunt Cordelia know I have it.'

'Mama's grave?' Lise was alert suddenly, her senses tingling.

So it was true, then. Her mother had come here to Polruan in order to find Cecile, and had never left alive.

'It's in Porthmeor churchyard. I'd take you there, but we mustn't be seen together.'

'Perhaps Zach will take me when I'm pretending to be you.' Lise thought she would dearly love to see her mother's last resting place.

'I can never thank you enough for what you are doing for me,' Cecile said. 'And the sad thing is that we shall be parted again. I do so want to be with Sam, of course, but I wish you could be there too.'

'When this is all over, I'll come and find you,' Lise promised. 'We will get to know one another properly as sisters. But perhaps now we should begin going over some of the things I need to know. How much time do we have? Has anything more been said about your marriage to this . . . ?'

'Mr Redmond. Nothing has been finalised as yet. Papa seems a little reluctant, though Aunt Cordelia is pressing him hard to make the necessary arrangements.' She smiled ruefully. 'She wants to be rid of me, I think. She wants it to be just her and Papa, as it was before he married Mama.'

'Well, we must hope we have enough time to prepare properly,' Lise said. 'But I can only pray that if Papa truly believes me to be you, he won't force me into a carriage and deliver me to Mr Redmond himself!'

Cecile giggled. 'I don't believe he would do such a thing. But Aunt Cordelia might!'

'Hmm.' Lise was thinking she was not much looking forward to meeting Aunt Cordelia.

The stable door opened and sunlight poured in to illuminate even the darkest corners. Zach and Sam were back.

'So how are you two getting on?' Zach enquired.

'We've only just begun!' Lise retorted. 'We have to get to know one another first.'

'Yes, we do,' Cecile echoed.

Zach smiled. 'That will be no problem, I imagine. Already you speak as one. But talk about what Lise must do to carry this off first.'

'Very well,' Cecile said meekly. 'Where shall I begin?'

'Run through a day's routine, perhaps?' Zach suggested.

'Oh, that will be easy. Bessie will tell Lise all she needs to know. You'll love Bessie, and she is completely on my side.'

'She knows?' Lise asked, wary suddenly.

'Don't look like that.' Cecile pouted. 'She won't say a word to anyone. I could trust her with my very life.'

'That,' Lise said drily, 'is exactly what you are asking me to do.'

'She's gone, then,' Gussie Moxey said flatly as a distraught Annie tapped at her door and came into the kitchen, where she was elbow deep in a sinkful of soapy water. From her window she'd seen Lise leave with the young man who had become such a frequent caller of late. 'Not fer good, though, I'm guessin'. Not yet.'

'No, she'll be back later. At least I hope she will. I'm beside meself with worry, Gussie, and that's a fact. The good Lord alone knows what danger she's in, and I blame meself.'

'Whatever for? It's not your fault,' Gussie objected.

'It is though. If I hadn't been bad – an' so fond o' me bliddy linctus – she wouldn't have had to go into town for more, and that Zach would never 'ave set eyes on 'er. I'd been guzzling it all day, and Lise was afraid there wouldn't be enough left if I had a bad turn after the apothecary'd shut up shop for the night. 'Twas only chance that 'e seed her and realised . . . well, who she must be. No, if she 'adn't been in town that afternoon, she'd never have fallen into his clutches. Besotted with him, she was. She's seen through 'im now, o' course, when it's too late and he's got her mixed up with that wicked lot. An' her mind's set on going through with it since she found out 'twas them that did for her poor mother. I'll never forgive meself, Gussie, if harm comes to her, like it did to my lovely Marguerite.'

'Let's 'ope it don't come to that. Sit down, do, Annie. I'll make ee a jar o' tea.' Gussie wiped her hands on a dish rag. 'Or mebbe you'd like someut a bit stronger. I ain't got any o' that linctus you'm so partial to, but I have got a nice bottle o' brandy our Aaron brought home t'other day.' She went to the dresser, got it out and plonked it on the kitchen table.

Annie's eyes nearly popped out of her head. She'd never set eyes on a whole bottle before; the most she'd ever been able to afford was a quarter. Even the label was impressive.

'Cogg-nack,' she said, working out the unfamiliar word, and feeling proud that her George had taught her her letters.

'I don't think that's what our Aaron called it,' Gussie said doubtfully. 'Sounded more like "yak". I thought it was a mighty good name for it, seeing as 'ow I couldn't stop yakking after I'd had a glass.' She laughed, her multiple chins quivering like half-set custard. 'An' don't think it's like that stuff you keep for when you're took bilious. This won't burn your insides out, but it'll do you good. Go on, try it.'

Annie took a cautious sip, and then another. Gussie was right. It slipped down her throat as easily as her cough linctus. 'Where did 'e get this?' she asked, licking her lips appreciatively.

Gussie snorted. 'Not from one of the taverns in town, you can bet on that. But where our Aaron's concerned, you don't ask too many questions. I'm guessin' 'tis bootleg. He were out half the night wi' that no-good Dyfan Flinders, an' when he

161

came back, this is what he gave me.' She paused, taking another nip of the brandy. 'I do worry what 'e's up to, though, an' that's the truth.' She lowered her voice. 'Don't repeat this, whatever you do, but when I washed the shirt he'd 'ad on, there was blood on it.'

'Oh, dear, dear.' Annie couldn't say she was surprised. Aaron had always been a wrong'un, from the time he was a nipper. But she couldn't get worked up about what he had done to earn a bottle of liquor as fine as this one when she was so worried about Lise.

'Ah well, he's grown now, and he won't listen to me, if ever he did. I just hope and pray he don't get 'imself into bad trouble.' Gussie picked up the bottle and her glass and headed for the little living room. 'Let's sit and enjoy this in comfort. No sense frettin' over what can't be changed, either of us.'

As soon as Annie and his mother had left the kitchen, Marco, the youngest of the Moxey boys, crept down the stairs and out of the door. He was supposed to have been out on the quay helping Billie unload his catch, but he'd seen Aaron going to meet him and thought the two of them could manage quite easily without him. He wanted to make a ship in a bottle as his friend Jack Ivors had done, and the first step was to draw out the template, adjusting it to the size of the bottle. He'd scrounged one from the local tavern and decided a tall ship would be the best fit, but he was no artist and he kept getting the dimensions wrong. He'd been skulking up in the bedroom he shared with his brothers, trying yet again to draw an even shape for the hull, when he heard Annie's voice downstairs. She and his ma seemed to spend a lot of time in one another's houses and usually he made himself scarce, bored with their idle chit-chat. Today, however, was different.

Annie sounded distressed about something. 'I'm beside meself with worry, Gussie. The good Lord alone knows what danger she's in, and I blame meself.' Who were they talking about? Not Lise, surely? Lise wasn't the sort to get herself into trouble. Curious, Marco crept along the landing to the top of the stairs so as to be sure he didn't miss anything, and there he stayed until the conversation turned to Aaron and the brandy he'd brought home for Ma. Aaron's doings were of no interest to him, and he went back to his room until he heard the two women go into the living room and shut the door behind them. Then he abandoned his template and tools and slipped quietly down the stairs and out of the house, eager to find his brothers, tell them what he'd overheard and ask them what they made of it.

He found them unloading the last of Billie's catch.

'What kept you then?' Aaron asked, chewing on a wad of baccy.

'Don't mither him,' Billie said equably. 'He helps me out more often than you do.'

'An' I wanted to get on with my ship in a bottle,' Marco said, catching his breath after running the length of the quay at full tilt. 'But never mind that now. I just 'eard Ma and Annie-next-door talkin'.'

The two older Moxeys rolled their eyes at one another. They were used to the old women's gossip.

'No – listen! An' don't look so pleased wi' yourself, Aaron. Ma knows you were up to no good gettin' that bottle o' brandy you gave her.'

Aaron chortled. 'Tell me summat I don't know! There's no flies on Ma.'

'That's not all, though. They was on about Lise an' that fellow that's been visiting 'er.'

That got his brothers' attention. Both stopped what they were doing and looked at him, and Marco, still breathless, from excitement now as well as from his dash along the quayside, related everything he had overheard.

'See?' Aaron said to Billie when Marco had finished. 'Didn't I tell you that Carver was up to no good?' His tone was triumphant.

'So you were right,' Billie said impatiently. He'd dismissed it flatly when Aaron had first told him, smirking, that Lise was associating with a man who worked for one of the most influential smugglers in Cornwall. Lise wasn't that sort of girl, he'd said, flying to her defence. 'Whatever, it sounds from what Marco says as if she's got herself into all kinds of trouble an' Annie's in a devil of a state about it. Tell me again what she said, Marco.'

Marco was beginning to become a little muddled. The conversation that had been so clear in his head was slipping away from him like a dream on waking.

'She's in his clutches,' he said. That bit was clear enough; it was the sort of phrase that stuck in your mind. 'Annie'd never forgive herself if harm came to her. An' something about the same thing that happened to 'er mother. But she 'asn't got a mother, 'as she? It's only 'er an' Annie.'

'Not s'far as I knows,' Aaron said, but Billie was looking thoughtful. Marco's words were ringing distant bells, bringing back memories that had long since been forgotten. Another woman in the cottage next door, a woman who had fascinated him because she spoke with a funny accent, different to his mother and father, or anyone he knew. And her hair . . . Suddenly a picture rose in his mind of flowing auburn locks. Or was he imagining that because he was seeing Lise in his mind's eye?

'There was a woman, a lot younger than Annie,' he said slowly. ''Tis so long ago – I was only a nipper. I ain't thought about her for years. She just faded out of my life, I suppose, an' I forgot she were ever there.'

'I don't remember 'er,' Aaron objected.

'I don't s'pose you would. You'd 'ave bin too young. It seems like a bit of a dream to me, an' I'm older than you. An' Lise 'as never mentioned 'er. Nor a father, neither. Mebbe he was one o' them. A smuggler. An' she were mixed up wi' them too.'

''Tis all very interestin'. Good fer you, our littl'un.' Aaron winked at Marco, then turned to Billie. 'I'll find out, never fear. Next time I see Dyfan, I'll get it out o' him.'

Billie bent double, flinging the last of the catch into the barrel on the quay. 'I'm not waitin' for that if Lise is in danger. I'm goin' to ask Ma right now.'

'No! You can't!' Marco squealed. 'She'll know I were listenin'!'

Billie didn't answer. Already he was striding off along the quay.

By the time Billie got home Annie had already left, but Gussie was still in the sitting room, nursing another tot of cognac. He wasn't in the mood to waste words.

'What's goin' on wi' Lise?'

Gussie looked up at him blearily. 'Where d'you get that from?' Her voice was slightly slurred and Billie wondered how much she'd had to drink.

'Is it true what our Marco says? That she's got herself into some sort of pickle? Danger, even?'

'So that little toad was listening, was 'e? I'll give him listen! He'll get a clip round the ear fer 'is trouble!'

165

'Never mind that. Is it right?'

Gussie drank the last of her brandy, reached for the bottle and poured herself another.

'What are you doing, Ma, drinkin' that in the middle of the day?' Billie reached out and took the mug from her hand before she could stop him.

'Ya cheeky little beggar!' She glared at him. 'An' you're not too big for a clip round the ear neither!'

Billie moved away out of her reach. 'If there's something up with Lise, I want to know about it.'

'It's none o' yer business. You don't want to get mixed up with lawless sorts, even if our Aaron is. Not you, Billie. An' if you've got any sense, you'll forget about Lise. She's a fetching little thing, I know, but she'll only break your heart. Get you into all sorts of trouble. She's not fer you, an' the sooner you get that into your head the better.'

Billie could see he was getting nowhere by being aggressive. Instead he resorted to pleading. 'Ma. Tell me, I beg you.'

But still Gussie remained tight lipped. 'I'm sayin' nothing. I've said too much already. If I'd kept me mouth shut when Lise come to me wi' 'er questions, we mightn't be where we are now. So go on, go back and see t'yer catch, and earn some money t'put food on the table. And don't come pestering me, because my lips are sealed.'

With that, she got up, swaying slightly, and pushed past him. Frustrated, Billy realised that whatever was behind all this, he was going to learn nothing from his mother.

'Where is Cecile? I need to see her urgently.'

Having called her niece's name in all corners of the house, to no avail, Cordelia had gone in search of Bessie, and found her in her room mending a seam in one of Cecile's petticoats.

'Oh, she's . . .' Bessie broke off. She knew very well where Cecile was – at the stables, meeting her sister. But she didn't want to say anything in case Cordelia took it into her head to go there to find her. That would be a disaster in the making. Bessie hurriedly jabbed her needle through the fine silk and dumped the petticoat on top of her workbox. 'I'll go. Don't trouble yourself. But what am I to tell her?'

'That wherever she's hiding she is to come back immediately. Mr Redmond is expected, and I want her neat and tidy and looking her best, not dishevelled from playing with her dog or whatever it is she is doing.'

Mr Redmond. Cecile's intended. Bessie's heart sank. So they were going ahead with it. She could only hope the plan Sam and Zach had concocted would work.

'She'll be . . . excited, I dare say,' she ventured.

Cordelia sneered. 'Whatever her reaction, the matter is decided,' she said haughtily. 'So please, don't encourage her to think differently.'

'As if I would!' Bessie said with pretended affront, and hurried downstairs and out to the stables.

As she had expected, Cecile was horrified. Her hand flew to her mouth, her eyes wide and distressed above it.

'I can't see him! I can't!'

'You've got no choice, missy,' Bessie said. 'It's all arranged, yer aunt said. And you don't want to go upsetting the apple cart, do you?'

'She's right.' Sam took her other hand, squeezing it. 'Just try to act normal. And remember, we have a way out of this now, thanks to your sister.'

'Oh, I know!' Cecile turned to Lise. 'How will I ever be able to thank you!' She turned back to Sam, her face crumpling. 'But

I don't want to see that man! Suppose he tries to kiss me? Or worse?'

'I'm sure he won't do that,' Bessie said comfortingly. 'He's a man of the cloth. He knows how a gentleman should behave.'

Lise wasn't at all sure that was true, but she wasn't going to say so. 'Be brave and he'll respect you,' she encouraged Cecile. 'One afternoon can't be so bad. Especially if you remember you have the rest of your life with Sam.'

Cecile smiled a watery smile. 'Yes. That's what I must think of.'

As the two girls hugged goodbye, a tide of emotion swept through Lise's veins. This was what she had been missing all these years, this closeness that brought understanding without the need for words, the feeling of being whole, not missing a part of herself. Yes, they would soon be separated again, but it wouldn't be for ever, and knowing now what they both did, it would be quite different.

Bessie tapped Cecile on the shoulder. 'Come on, miss. You'd better get back to the house before your aunt comes looking for you.'

Reluctantly Lise released her sister. 'Bessie's right,' she said. 'We can't risk being caught together.'

Cecile nodded, but she was looking over her shoulder at Lise as Bessie led her out of the stable.

Chapter Fifteen

Cecile sat stiffly on the very edge of a brocaded chair, hands folded in her lap, eyes downcast, hoping to give the impression of modesty, whereas the truth was that she couldn't bear to look at John Redmond, who was sitting opposite her.

He was, she thought, the strangest-looking man she had ever seen. Tall and bony, with an oddly narrow head topped by an ill-fitting wig. His nose was hooked, like a bird's beak, his lips thin, and his waxy skin appeared too tightly stretched over the bones of his face. His teeth were crooked, yellowed and slightly protruding, while his eyes, magnified behind thick glasses, looked unnaturally large. He reminded her of the wolf disguised as Granny in the tale of Little Red Riding Hood, Cecile thought. She'd never liked the story when it had been read to her from her Perrault book of fairy tales; it had made her shudder then and it made her shudder now. Small wonder his wife had taken sick and died; the same fate would befall Cecile herself if she were forced to marry this man.

'I expect your aunt has told you, now that the decision has been made, that we are anxious to proceed to matrimony without delay. My children and my parishioners have been left bereft since the passing of my good wife; a woman's hand is sorely missed. And if I may make so bold, I too have suffered greatly. You, my dear, are young, and so very fair. You will bring light and comfort into all our lives.'

'Yes, sir,' Cecile whispered.

'Not "sir", my dear. If you are to be my wife, you must call me John. And I shall call you Cecile, though to the outside world you will be Mistress Redmond.' He chuckled softly. 'And "dearest Mama" to my children and any we may be fortunate enough to bring into this world. What do you say to that?'

Cecile gave a tiny shake of her head. Words were quite beyond her. The thought of lying with this revolting man, having him get children on her, was making nausea rise in her throat.

Mr Redmond smiled thinly, raising a bony hand as if about to confer a blessing. 'Perhaps I have spoken too soon of my hopes for the future. You are young and innocent, and I believe I have shocked you. If that is the case, my sincerest apologies. But you need have no fear of what lies ahead. I shall lead you, teach you, and the good Lord will be with us every step of the way to closer and ever closer union in his love.'

'Wonderful.' Somehow Cecile managed to form the single word.

'Good. Then we understand one another.' He rose, pulled her to her feet also, and raised her hand. A shudder ran through her as his lips touched the back of it, cold and moist, but she managed to control herself so that he did not – she hoped! – notice.

'Now, your father and I have details to discuss, things that would bore and confuse you. Women were not made to bother their pretty heads with such matters. But I look forward to meeting you again, and furthering our acquaintance. And even more to our wedding day.'

Once again he lowered his lips to her hand and Cecile was

forced to swallow the lump of disgust that rose in her throat. Only when she was alone did she bury her face in her hands, half sobbing, half retching. And only when she reached the sanctuary of her room did she allow the tears to come, hot and blinding.

She couldn't marry him! Wouldn't! She prayed Sam's plan would work out, but if not, she would run away anyway; where, she didn't know. But if she died from exposure out on the moors, she didn't care. Anything, anything would be better than to be forced to marry that revolting man. Look at his face across the table three times a day. Be forced to endure his kisses. Lie with him at night . . .

She opened the locket that had belonged to her mother and gazed through tear-blurred eyes at the likenesses of the two little girls. Two halves of one whole. She wasn't alone now. Whatever befell her, she had her sister, after all these long years.

Once again Zach and Sam had met at the Wink, and once again Sam was growing ever more desperate.

'Now that bliddy vicar's been to see Cecile, we need to act fast, before it's too late.'

'You're anxious, I know, but we daren't even attempt it until Lise is ready. That way lies failure, maybe even disaster,' Zach warned. 'It's gone well so far, but that's just the beginning. If Lise is anything less than totally convincing, we will be putting her in danger, of her life, perhaps.'

Sam sighed impatiently. 'You're not going to spike the plan, I hope. You care for her, don't you? I've seen the way you look at her.'

Annoyed that his friend should be thinking only of himself and Cecile, Zach took a long pull of his ale before replying. 'We've agreed to do this, and do it we will. As for any feelings I

171

may have for Lise, that's neither here nor there. But I won't have her put at risk unnecessarily.'

'So you do care for her.' Sam couldn't let it go. 'Does she care for you?'

Zach laughed shortly and bitterly. 'She's barely speaking to me, if you really want to know. She hasn't forgiven me for engineering that first meeting between her and Cecile. She thinks I tricked and deceived her. She's doing this for her sister's sake, so the least you can do is have a care for her safety.'

It was the closest the two friends had ever come to a serious falling-out, and Sam realised that if he didn't change his attitude, Zach might call the whole thing off.

'You're right. It's just that the thought of that old devil with Cecile makes me sick to my stomach. She's a brave girl, Lise. I wouldn't want to think of her coming to harm.'

'We'll agree on that,' Zach said. 'So let's think about the detail here. I can bring Lise up to Polruan most days, if you think Cecile can get away so they can meet.'

'She's in the habit of visiting the stables every morning, so it shouldn't arouse suspicion. But one of us should keep a lookout so Lise can hide in an empty stall should anyone come. This morning was a close-run thing. If it had been Cordelia rather than Bessie, well . . .' Sam broke off, huffing breath over his top lip.

'Agreed. But best it should be you. You can find something to do outside, whereas I have no more right to be there than Lise.' Zach set his ale down on the bench beside him before continuing. 'And there's something else worrying me. When you and Cecile have gone and Lise has taken her place, it will very likely be difficult for me to communicate with her. I can go to the house when I have an excuse – if Godfrey summons me, or if I can concoct a reason to see him – but that won't be every day. She will be left to fend for herself. And I won't even know if she is safe.'

'It won't be for long, though, will it?' Sam said. 'Just long enough for Cecile and me to get well away.'

'The longer the better, surely?' Still Zach was unwilling to divulge his other reason for wanting Lise to remain in the house. 'What we need,' he went on, 'is a go-between. Would Bessie act for us, do you think?'

'Bessie's loyalty is to Cecile,' Sam said doubtfully. 'And how would she manage it?'

'She could find some excuse to go into the village, surely? Or for a walk?'

'I suppose.'

'And there is yet another angle to be considered.' Zach reached for his ale and took a long pull. 'With Lise taking her place here, hopefully Cecile will not be missed. But there has to be some explanation for your absence or questions will be raised.'

'I'll give it some thought.'

'Good. But you see now that this isn't something that can be rushed into.'

'Yes. I can see that,' Sam said, a little shamefaced. 'And thanks, Zach – for everything.'

Cordelia and Godfrey were lingering over dessert, little chocolate soufflés served with thick cream, but although this was one of Cecile's favourites, she had hardly touched hers, just as she had picked at her guinea fowl and vegetables, and had excused herself to go to her room.

'What can be amiss with the girl?' Cordelia exclaimed bad temperedly. 'Mr Redmond was very taken with her. She should be pleased and flattered. Instead she is in a sulk.'

'Perhaps she was less taken with him,' Godfrey ventured.

'He will make her a most suitable husband,' Cordelia returned coldly. 'He will provide well for her, and he is old enough to be able to take her in hand. Our worries that she may take after her mother will be at an end.'

'Hmm. Old enough, certainly.' Godfrey's tone was far from complimentary. 'Don't you think it might be possible for us to find a suitable match for her who is closer to her in age?'

'And who, may I ask? Do you know of a single eligible young gentleman in these parts who might be, as you put it, suitable? No, Godfrey, Mr Redmond is by far and away the best solution to our problem, and the sooner she is safely wed to him the better.'

'I wasn't aware the problem was so pressing,' Godfrey protested mildly, and it was Cordelia's turn to scoff.

'That is because you are so blinkered where Cecile is concerned,' she pronounced. 'No, it is much for the best that we proceed with the match with all due speed. What arrangements did you and Mr Redmond reach?'

Godfrey sighed and laid down his spoon. 'The banns will be called for the first time on Sunday week. The wedding date is yet to be set, but it can be any time once the three weeks' notice are up. So it seems, Cordelia, you are about to get your way in this. Just as you always have,' he added quietly.

Cordelia made no response. She had no need. The satisfied smirk on her rouged lips spoke for her.

In the contrasting setting of the cottage kitchen, Lise and Annie were finishing their supper of fresh mackerel and boiled potatoes, and they too were talking about the events of the day.

On fine balmy evenings such as this, they often sat outside once the dishes had been cleared away, but Annie had warned

Lise she didn't think it would be a good idea today.

'You want to keep out of Billie's way, and Aaron's too,' she had said. 'Gussie said the pair of them have been asking questions, specially Billie – you know how much he thinks of you. It seems me and Gussie wasn't careful enough this morning, and young Marco overheard some o' what we was sayin'.'

'And what were you saying?' Lise asked, alarmed.

'How worried I am about you and what you're planning. I know, I know.' Annie shook her head, guilty but apologetic. 'But I was goin' out o' me mind. I had to chew it over with somebody, and Gussie's me best friend.'

'You know, Annie, nobody else must know of this,' Lise said distractedly. 'Did you actually say what is going to happen?'

'I don't think so. I don't really recall *what* I said, I were in such a state about it. But if I did, and Marco heard, then he'd have told his brothers and they wouldn't have pestered Gussie with the questions they did.'

'She didn't answer them?'

'She wouldn't do that. You can trust Gussie. Didn't she keep the secrets about you to herself all these years? No, she won't say a word to anyone. But I reckon it's best if you keep out o' the way of the boys for a bit or they might well start plaguing you as well. An' you'd better not let them see you with that Zach again, either.'

'I'm meeting him tomorrow up on the edge of the moors. There's no chance Billie or Aaron will see us.'

Annie nodded. 'Yes, well, I still think 'twould be best if we stopped in 'ere tonight.'

She was right, Lise supposed, but more than anything she wished she could go for a walk, alone with her thoughts, while the fresh sea breeze cleared her head. Since leaving Polruan, she had had not a single moment to herself to analyse her confused emotions. After she had helped Annie clear away the dirty dishes, she went to the window that looked out on to the quay-side path, watching for Billie. Surely soon he would be taking the smack out for his night's fishing, and when the coast was clear she could venture outside herself. Aaron might or might not go with his brother, but she could handle him if she ran into him. He was used to her cutting remarks, and would think nothing of it when she brushed him off. Billie, though, was a different matter. She didn't want to hurt his feelings any more than she already had by being unable to return his feelings for her.

At last he emerged from the house next door, swinging his carry-all and striding out towards the end of the harbour, where his boat was moored. And for a wonder, Aaron was with him. When they were out of sight, Lise collected her wrap, explained that it was now safe for her to venture out, and left the cottage, walking along the quay in the opposite direction to the one Billie and Aaron had gone in.

At the far end, she scrambled down on to the beach. Her feet sank into the soft sand and the wind tangled her hair about her face. As she walked, she pondered on the strange turn her simple life had taken, and her emotions churned like the waves buffeting the cliffs. She felt elation that she and her long-lost sister had been reunited, the joy that had lifted her when their hands had touched and their hearts met. Sadness that if things worked out as they had planned, they would again be separated, for a while at least, and gratitude that she could do something to bring Cecile happiness. The prospect of taking her place did not frighten Lise as perhaps it should; a strange excitement prickled inside her at the challenge she was to undertake, along with a steely determination to do as Zach had asked, so that the wicked man Annie believed had been the instigator of the disastrous shipwreck, and also behind the disappearance of her mother, could at long last be brought to face the justice he so richly deserved.

With the thought of Zach, her turbulent emotions took yet another turn. She'd barely spoken to him today and, when she had, her tone had been cold. She'd come to trust him, been on the point of giving her heart to him just as she had given it to her first and only love, and he had lied to her and deceived her. She couldn't, wouldn't, put herself through that kind of torment again.

And yet her treacherous heart was still ready to betray her. It softened when he was near, so it was all she could do to maintain her icy distance. Her skin prickled as if a gentle breeze rippled over it if their hands touched. Desire had twisted deep inside her as they had galloped over the moors from St Ives to Porthmeor, his arms encircling her waist, so it was all she could do not to give way to it. It was another good reason for her to take Cecile's place.

At Polruan House she would be living her sister's life, not her own. And with her concentration focused on carrying off her deception and her time taken up with searching for the proof of her father's perfidy, perhaps she would be able to begin to forget Zach Carver. With her whole heart she hoped it would be so.

The lathered horse slithered down the steep path to Polruan House, the rider keeping his seat with difficulty. At the great front door beneath the bell tower, he dismounted and knocked, sending a flurry of rooks cawing into the sky above the over-hanging trees.

It was Bessie who opened the door, puzzled and a little alarmed. It was unusual for anyone to call at the front of the house at this late hour; any activity when shipments of contraband were being unloaded took place at the rear. She didn't recognise the man who stood on the doorstep, but despite his dishevelled attire, he looked respectable enough and she opened the door a little wider.

'Yes? What do ee want?'

'I've ridden in some haste from Trevarric. I have news for Mr Pendinnick of his father.'

'Oh!' Bessie's suspicion gave way to dismay. Trevarric was the family home of the Pendinnicks, and from the urgency with which the man – clearly one of the squire's servants – spoke, she could hardly believe that he was the bearer of good news. 'You'd better come in.'

The man stood his ground, still holding on to the reins of his horse.

'I'm under orders to go straight back. Will you give him a message? Squire's on his deathbed, doctor reckons, and if Mr and Miss Pendinnick want to see him afore he breathes his last, they'd best come without delay.'

'Oh!' Bessie gasped, her hand going to her throat. 'What . . . ?'

'I'm not party to that. All I knows is 'e's bin abed fer a week'r more. Will ee tell Mr Pendinnick, an' I can be on me way.'

'I will so.'

As the servant put his foot in the stirrup, Bessie hurried into the house.

'Drat it!' Godfrey exclaimed bad temperedly. 'I'd best go right away. But I can't be gone long. Another shipment is due any day. The old man's been sickening for years now with the dropsy. How like him to take a turn for the worse at the least convenient moment. Will you come with me, Cordelia?'

His sister's thin lips twisted into a sneer. 'I would think I would be the last person Papa would wish to see on his deathbed. No, you go alone, Godfrey. And good luck to you!'

Godfrey huffed. 'I've a mind not to go at all. There's nothing I stand to gain. The estate all passes to Christopher.'

Cordelia smiled enigmatically. 'But should our brother predecease you, it could still be yours, since he has sired only daughters.'

'More of your scheming before the old man is cold in his grave?' Godfrey moved impatiently. 'I suppose I will have to saddle my horse myself. Sam is no doubt drinking himself senseless at the Wink.'

Without another word, he strode out of the room. The tight smile still on her lips, Cordelia watched him go.

Chapter Sixteen

Dawn was breaking as Godfrey rode back down the track to
Polruan House and led his tired horse into the stables, where he
was surprised to find Sam asleep on a blanket laid over a pile of
hay. He gave him a sharp kick in the ribs, and the coachman
started awake, grunting.

'What are you doing here?' Godfrey demanded irritably.

Sam rubbed his bleary eyes. 'When I saw your horse was out,
I reckoned I ought to wait for you.'

'Well, as you are here, you can unsaddle and stable him.'

'Yes, sir.' Sam took the reins, but even before he had begun
to untack the horse, Godfrey had left the stable.

Sam wondered idly where he had been half the night, but
even though he had worked for Godfrey for some years now,
much of the man's doings was a mystery to him, and in any case
it was none of his business. Godfrey could have been arranging
some shady deal or taking his pleasure with a woman, he neither
knew nor cared.

He finished his task, made sure the horse had water and hay,
and lay down again, yawning, to resume his interrupted sleep.

Cordelia, too, had been awaiting her brother's return and had
fallen asleep in one of the brocaded chairs in the drawing room.

She was awakened by the clatter of his boots on the bare boards of the entrance hall. Her neck was stiff and her head aching and her feet felt bristly and yet at the same time numb.

'Is that you, Godfrey?' she called, rubbing her neck and wriggling her feet to try to restore them to life.

He appeared in the doorway, dishevelled, his wig awry and mud splatters spotting his breeches. 'Has no one in this household gone to bed tonight?' His tone was irritable and weary.

Cordelia raised an eyebrow. 'How am I expected to sleep with our father on his deathbed and you attending him?'

'I wouldn't have thought you would be minded to pay heed to any of that,' Godfrey said coldly. 'In fact I expect you to feel no sorrow when I tell you that his suffering is at an end.'

'Ah. So the doctor was right for once.' Cordelia had no patience with doctors in general and Dr Meek, the Pendinnick family physician, in particular. Charlatans, all of them, in her opinion.

'A fool could have known he was unlikely to see the new day,' Godfrey responded tetchily. 'He barely knew I was there.'

'So you could have saved yourself a long and tiring journey.'

'Unlike you, Cordelia, I have a sense of duty. He is my father, and yours, whatever your differences. And now I am going to my bed and you, I think, should go to yours.'

'Tell me first. Did he have any last words of import?' Cordelia's eyes were narrowed, catlike.

Already halfway to the door, Godfrey turned to look at her. 'There is no change to the will or the inheritance. How can there be? Christopher is the rightful heir to the estate. You know that.'

'I am not a fool, Godfrey,' Cordelia said silkily, but Godfrey had already gone, loosening his stock as he went. Sometimes even he was shocked by his sister's coldness. She had a heart of ice, he thought, and had never forgiven her father for his open opposition to the life she had chosen, any more than he had forgiven her for walking away from the family home and, as he saw it, bringing disgrace to their door. As an unmarried woman she should have stepped in when her mother died, and taken over her place in the household. Instead she had cavorted about dressed like a boy until at last she had settled down with Godfrey, with whom she was unhealthily obsessed, in the squire's opinion.

She had wanted to know of his last words. What would she have said if he had told her? But he hadn't been able to bring himself to repeat them to her, and he doubted he ever would.

Godfrey had been warned before he entered the bedchamber that his father had developed a high fever and was hallucinating, and his younger sister Eliza, sitting at the bedside, had confirmed it.

'You mustn't be alarmed, but he is drifting in and out of delirium,' she said. She was holding one of her father's hands on top of the bed covers, and her eyes were red and puffy from weeping. At least there was someone who would mourn him, Godfrey thought.

The sight of his father left Godfrey in no doubt that he was nearing the end. The dropsy that had plagued him for years appeared to have spread upwards; the bed covers scarcely concealed the vast bulk beneath them, and his face and neck were swollen with fluid. Even his eyelids were puffed, so they were half closed as if he was falling asleep, yet his free hand moved restlessly, plucking at the sheets, while the other worked spasmodically beneath Eliza's comforting fingers.

'Godfrey's here, Papa,' she said softly, and it seemed he made an effort to open those heavy eyes as he mumbled, 'Godfrey . . .'

'Yes, Papa, that's nice, isn't it?'

'My boy . . .'

'Papa.' Godfrey scarcely knew what to say. It would be ludicrous to enquire how his father was feeling, inappropriate to speak of mundane matters and morbid to make any reference to imminent death. No priest would be called to administer last rites – the squire had turned his back on the faith in which he had been raised long ago. 'It's good to see you, Papa,' he said at last. 'I've neglected you. I should have come long ago.'

'And good to see you,' the old man muttered.

As Godfrey struggled to find some other platitude, his father suddenly tensed, his whole body going rigid, and he raised a hand, pointing.

'A horse? There's a horse by my bed!'

'No, Papa—' Godfrey began, but Eliza silenced him with a shake of her head.

'It's Blackie come to see you,' she said soothingly. Blackie had been Squire Pendinnick's favourite steed. 'Is it Blackie, Papa?'

But the squire's attention had shifted. His half-closed eyes had swivelled towards the window, where the heavy drapes had been drawn to shut out the dark night, and an expression of agitation creased his swollen face.

'What is it, Papa?' Eliza asked gently, but her father was now focused entirely on whatever, or whoever, he was seeing in his confused mind.

'You!' he grated. 'What are you doing here? Get out! Get her out!'

'Papa, please. You're safe. No one is going to harm you . . .' In vain Eliza tried to calm him. But once again his voice rang out, hoarse but strong.

'Delia. Get away from me, d'you hear? Leave me! Go!' And he collapsed back on to the pillows, frothing at the mouth.

183

Papa's last words, Godfrey thought, as he kicked off his boots and discarded his muddied clothing in a heap on the floor of his bedroom. Delia was the diminutive form of her name that the family had used for Cordelia when she was a child. His father had hallucinated that she was in his room. And far from being pleased to see her, he had become dreadfully distressed.

Godfrey had had no opportunity to wonder just why his father had reacted thus. After a family discussion, he had left for Polruan. There was little more to be done tonight except await the arrival of the woman who would wash the body and lay it out; arrangements for the funeral would have to wait until tomorrow.

Now, exhausted, he climbed into his bed and was asleep the moment his head touched the pillow.

When Lise and Zach arrived at the stables next morning, they found Sam and Cecile deep in conversation, Cecile looking downcast, Sam animated.

'This is it!' he exclaimed as they went into the dim interior, where the air was full of the sweet, pungent smell of hay and excrement. 'Our chance is nigh!' He grinned at their puzzled expressions. 'Old Squire Pendinnick died last night. I wondered where the divil Godfrey had gone until the middle of the night – I bedded down here in the stables, but he didn't explain himself when he returned. I didn't have an answer till Cecile came and told me. The old man's snuffed it at last.'

Lise felt a strange sinking sensation in the pit of her stomach. The man who had died must be her grandfather, and she had never known he existed, much less met him. Now she never would. And he was Cecile's grandfather too. 'How are you faring?' she asked her sister anxiously.

Cecile nodded. 'I didn't know him very well, but it still makes me sad that he's no longer with us.'

Lise squeezed her hand. 'Of course you're sad. That's only natural.'

Sam shook his head. 'I've been trying to tell her she ought to be on top of the world! It'll give us our best chance at getting away without being missed. Her father and Cordelia are bound to go to the funeral and it'll leave the coast clear.'

'They may want me to go with them,' Cecile said anxiously.

'You can get out of that easily enough. Just make out you're poorly.'

'But they'll need you to drive the carriage. They'd know something was up if you took ill too.'

Sam's face fell. He hadn't thought of that.

'Perhaps if you were to give notice, you could leave now and come back for her on the day of the funeral, whenever that may be,' Zach suggested.

'But if there's a different coachman, we won't be able to use this as a meeting place,' Lise pointed out.

'I'll offer to step in,' Zach said. 'Godfrey is used to me doing whatever odd tasks need to be done. There's a cargo of contraband expected any day now, but that excepted, I don't know that I have any other duties to perform.'

'It could work,' Sam said thoughtfully, and Lise's heart sank. Though she still couldn't bring herself to trust Zach as she had before he had deceived her into meeting Cecile, she hated the thought of having to begin her impersonation of her sister without him being nearby. Was her determination to ignore her feelings for him beginning to weaken? Or was it just that she knew he was anxious for her to succeed as much for his own ends as for Cecile and Sam?

'On second thoughts, it might be best to wait until we've

taken delivery of the contraband and sent it on its way,' Zach said thoughtfully. 'Should I be needed in connection with that, and if you give notice too soon, someone else might be brought in to take your place.' He turned to Cecile. 'You have no idea when the funeral will be?'

'I don't think anything will have been arranged yet. It was only last night that Grandpapa died.'

'So four or five days at least?' Zach surmised. 'Hopefully the distribution will all be sorted before then. And I agree, Sam, when Godfrey and Cordelia are both away does seem like too good an opportunity to miss. Apart from anything else, it will give Lise a chance to acquaint herself with the layout of the house. Having it described to her seemed like the best we could do, but if she can actually familiarise herself with it, she's much less likely to make a mistake that could give her away.'

'Oh, are you really going to do this for me?' Cecile gazed from Lise to Zach and back again, tears of gratitude shining in her eyes.

In spite of the qualms that had so recently assailed her, Lise squeezed her sister's hand. 'Of course we are.'

'Now I'd better present myself at the house and see what I have to do in preparation for the landing.' Zach turned for the door, turned back briefly. 'And you, ladies, had better get down to talking over everything Lise needs to know. Time may be very short indeed.'

'She's meeting that man who works for Pendinnick.'

Aaron Moxey was waiting when Billie got home after unloading his catch, a triumphant grin spread across his good-looking face.

'What?' Billie was tired, and not in the best of tempers. He'd been late returning to harbour, and many of the merchants he relied on to relieve him of much of his catch had already done their business with other fishermen and departed. He'd been forced to sell to small local businesses at reduced rates or risk having to toss most of his night's work back into the ocean.

'Lise. She left early just like she has these past days. I saw her go. An' I followed 'er.' Aaron's grin grew even wider.

'What is the matter with you? What if she'd seen you?' Billie said irritably, but his curiosity was aroused just the same.

'Well, she didn't. In too much of a hurry to meet her lover, if you ask me. She headed up to the moors an' 'e was there waiting. Zach Carver, same fella as came to see Dyfan about that job we did for Pendinnick. She got up on his horse wi' 'im an' they rode off. Heading for Porthmeor, if you ask me.'

'I'm not asking you,' Billie snapped. 'But I am tellin' you. Lise would never get 'erself mixed up with any funny business. Unlike you.'

Aaron shrugged. 'Suit yerself. Just don't say I didn't warn you. An' don't be so smug about how I make a livin'. I reckon I'll be a rich man when you're still struggling to earn a crust, if I'm not much mistaken.'

He mooched off, leaving Billie both fuming and concerned. Whatever his brother's failings, he believed him when he said he'd followed Lise and seen her meeting the mysterious stranger. He could only hope, for her sake, that she wasn't getting herself into something she couldn't handle.

As he entered Polruan House by the side door, Zach heard raised voices coming from Godfrey's study. Godfrey and Cordelia. He was about to retreat until the violent disagreement was over, when Cordelia's voice, loud and shrill, carried clearly through the partly open study door.

'I will *not*, Godfrey. I refuse absolutely to pretend sorrow at that man's death. To attend his funeral and shed false tears would be nothing short of hypocritical.'

Zach stopped short, then took a couple of cautious steps closer, anxious to hear what was to come, but wary of being caught eavesdropping.

'*That man*, as you call him, is your father! What harm would it do you to pay your respects? It's the least his tenants will expect – that his children are there to see him laid to rest. Think of the talk it will cause if you are absent.'

Cordelia laughed scathingly. 'When have I ever cared what folk said about me? You, on the other hand, like to be recognised as a gentleman of means and morals, though you and I know the plain, unvarnished truth. Your morals are sadly lacking, and as for your means – well, if it were not for my help in the very beginning and since, you would still be nothing but the master of someone else's ship. Speaking of which, is it not likely you will be occupied with the dispersal of our latest cargo at about the same time as the funeral will almost certainly take place? Will it be wise even for *you* to attend?'

'I've had word the shipment will arrive tomorrow night if the weather stays fair. All will be dealt with in good time before I have to leave for the funeral. Even the sainted Christopher will not be able to hasten matters beyond the customary four or five days.'

'Well, go if you must, and make excuses for me as you will.'

'I hope you may yet accompany me, Cordelia, but I dare say your mind is made up and nothing I can say will change it.'

Guessing Cordelia would be emerging from the study imminently, Zach retreated to the end of the passage, hoping to make it appear that he had only just arrived. Sure enough, a moment later Cordelia stalked out of the study in a swish of stiff petticoats, but to his relief she did not so much as glance in his direction. He waited a minute or so, then approached the door and tapped on it respectfully.

'Come!'

Apart from his colour being even higher than usual, there was little about Godfrey to show for the bitter argument between him and his sister.

'Ah, Carver, my man, you have arrived at a most opportune time,' he greeted Zach. 'I have a task for you. The cargo we have been waiting for is expected tomorrow night. You will need to spread the word that our little band will be required then, and I would also like you to ride to St Ives and once again enlist the help of Dyfan Flinders. He is a most useful man, strong, and not afraid to do whatever is necessary should we encounter any trouble. Perhaps he can also bring one or two of his cronies to swell our number. This is an important consignment, of great value, and I want it dealt with as swiftly and safely as possible.'

'I'll see to it, sir.' Zach was thinking more about conveying what he had overheard to Sam, Lise and Cecile than he was about doing as Godfrey asked.

'Good man.' A sharp nod indicated that the interview was at an end.

As he closed the door behind him, Zach glimpsed Godfrey taking a bottle from his desk drawer – good cognac, he guessed – and taking a quick slurp without even bothering to find a glass.

As he rode to St Ives, his arms encircling Lise, who sat astride Gypsy in front of him, Zach's jaw was set tight, his discomfort with the plan growing to deep-seated concern. It was only now that he had come to realise just how much he cared for this girl, and for her safety.

When he had returned to the stables and told his co-conspirators that Cordelia was adamant she would not attend the funeral, they had been dismayed, but after some discussion they had unanimously agreed that they should take advantage of the opportunity that Godfrey's absence would afford them. Surely it was he who would be most likely to remark anything strange about his daughter's behaviour? Cordelia had so little time for her niece, it would be typical of her to ignore 'Cecile' as much as possible.

It was then that Zach had felt the first stirrings of distaste at what he had talked Lise into doing. He knew all too well the danger she would be in, and now, as he rode in silence, seeing the wind tangle her hair, feeling the warmth of her body pressed against his, inhaling the sweet scent of her, he knew he wanted no part of this. Perhaps, if he was going to the funeral alone, Godfrey would ride, rather than take the carriage, and Sam and Cecile could slip away unnoticed. If they could make it across the moors before he returned, there would be no need to involve Lise. And as for his own motive for wanting a spy in the camp, nothing warranted risking her life.

When they reached the slopes overlooking St Ives, he drew Gypsy to a halt. They had decided it would be safest not to be seen together in the town, and now Lise slithered gracefully from his grasp and stood for a moment stroking Gypsy's neck.

'So, I have just a few more days to learn all I need to,' she said.

'Are you certain you're still agreeable to doing this?' Zach asked.

Her gaze met his, direct and unwavering. 'Of course.'

He sighed, dismounting himself and taking her arm with his free hand whilst holding the reins with the other. 'I don't think you should, Lise. It's too dangerous. You don't know what that family are capable of.'

'Don't I?' she returned sharply, lifting her chin. 'I think having lost my mother and my sister because of them I am as aware as you as to what they are capable of.'

'There is no need for you to put yourself in harm's way,' Zach insisted. 'I will search the house myself while Godfrey is away.'

'But Cordelia will still be there,' Lise argued. 'If she should catch you . . .'

Zach smiled grimly. 'I think I am a match for Cordelia. And I am not willing to risk your life in this way.'

'I am the one who should decide what risks I take with my life.' Lise's mouth was set in a firm line. 'I'm doing it, Zach, whatever you say. If I can be convincing enough to make them believe I am Cecile, I shall have time, as well as opportunity, on my side. I can search far more thoroughly than you could in one short day. Besides, Cecile is my sister. I don't want to let her down. And I am determined to do whatever I can to discover my mother's fate, and see my father brought to justice.' With that, she shook her arm free of Zach's grasp. 'Be here to take me to Polruan tomorrow, or I will never forgive you,' she said fiercely before turning and walking away, heading for St Ives, leaving Zach fuming helplessly.

Chapter Seventeen

When Lise climbed the hill to the moor next morning, Zach was waiting.

'You came then,' she greeted him.

'Not that I wanted to. You left me no choice,' he said shortly. 'You haven't changed your mind, I presume?'

'No,' Lise said quietly.

'You know, don't you, that you will be totally alone most of the time? I won't be able to protect you.'

'Yes, I do know, but I have to do this.' Her eyes met Zach's, pleading with him to understand.

Touched by his concern for her, which warmed her heart, she had lain awake much of the night thinking about him and wondering if she had been wrong to blame him so bitterly for tricking her into meeting Cecile. Had her anger been an instinctive defence against losing her heart to him? Had she been so afraid of it being broken as it had been once before that she had used it as an excuse, a shield to protect herself from her own vulnerability?

But it hadn't prevented the quivers of excitement that ran through her veins whenever she saw him, nor the prickles of warmth when she leaned back against his strong body as she rode in front of him astride Gypsy, nor the sensitivity of her skin to his touch as he lifted her up on to the horse, or handed her down.

It was happening again now. The magnetism between them was undeniable. If only they had met under better circumstances, how different things might have been! But as it was, she had to remain strong. She mustn't let her heart rule her head. Never mind her fear of being hurt again; she couldn't allow herself to be distracted in any way from what she had to do, the part she had agreed to play.

'I'm out o' me mind with worry, Gussie, an' that's the truth.'

Annie had gone next door, as she so often did, to share her anxiety for Lise's safety over a jar of tea with her friend.

'I'm sure you be, Annie. I'm worried about our Aaron too. That Dyfan Flinders was here yesterday, wanting him to go over to Porthmeor tonight to help out wi' unloading a cargo Pendinnick's expecting, and we all know what sort'a shipment that is! I don't like 'im bein' mixed up wi' that lawless crew any more'n you like Lise goin' there. But there's nothing either of us can do about it, so we'd best not waste time nor effort worrying about it.'

'Oh my life! There'll be a whole lot more scoundrels thereabouts if that's goin' on!' Annie wrung her hands together in her apron. 'Whatever is goin' to become of 'er, Gussie?'

Gussie shook her head. 'She's worldly wise, Annie, and sharp as a knife. I reckon she can take care of 'erself. And anyway, like I say, there's nothin' you can do about it, so just drink up yer tea and calm down or you'll do yourself a mischief.'

'I s'pose you'm right,' Annie said, and wished she could believe it.

'I won't be able to stay with you today,' Zach told Lise when they arrived at Polruan and met Sam and Cecile in the stables.

'I have work to do, gathering the troops for the delivery tonight.'

Cecile shivered. 'I hate it! All of it! But at least tonight will be the last time I'll have to witness it,' she added, her face brightening.

'The funeral is tomorrow,' Sam said by way of explanation.

'Tomorrow! That's quick!' Zach looked less than pleased at the news. He turned to Lise. 'Will you be ready?'

'I'll have to be.' Lise, too, was shocked at the speed with which arrangements had been made, and daunted by the thought that she had only one more day before she had to enter the fray.

'Surely Godfrey will still be tied up with the distribution?' Zach said, hoping, no doubt, that Pendinnick would be unwilling to leave a job half done, and the whole plan would be abandoned, for the time being at least.

'No, he's still going, but at least I now know he's riding Satan, not taking the carriage,' Sam informed him. 'As you know, most of the stuff will be sent on its way under cover of darkness, and Cordelia will attend to the bookwork, which will keep her occupied most of the day. You'll be busy, though, Zach, I shouldn't wonder. It may be you won't be around to collect Lise in the morning and, if that is the case, I can do the honours once Godfrey has left.'

'Very well.' Zach agreed, but his expression was grim. 'You might need to take her home today too when you've finished here. I've no idea what time I will be able to get away. And now I'd better go up to the house and get my orders.'

Lise's heart dropped like a stone. The thought that she might have to take her sister's place without seeing Zach again made her sick inside.

'You will try, though, won't you?' she begged before she could stop herself.

'It may well be I have to see a man in St Ives,' Zach said. 'If so, I'll try and arrange it to kill two birds with one stone.' His eyes locked with hers, and she took comfort from his direct gaze.

Then he was gone, and she was left alone with Sam and Cecile.

'You haven't furnished me with any of your gowns yet, or a wig,' she said to her sister. 'I can hardly pretend to be you dressed as I am.'

'We've thought of that.' Clearly Sam and Cecile had done some planning in her absence. 'We can simply swap our attire here.'

Lise looked doubtfully at the intricate fastenings of the bodice of the blue silk gown Cecile was wearing, and the full hooped skirt. 'I don't know that I'll be able to manage it. You'll have to help me.'

'Oh, Bessie will do that.' Cecile laughed. 'I don't think I could dress myself without her assistance either. And she will make sure the wig is sitting right, too. That can be tricky.'

Imagining that heavy concoction on her head instead of feeling the breeze in her flowing locks made Lise grimace. 'I don't know how you put up with it.'

Cecile shrugged. 'You'll soon get used to it, and it will feel strange when you're not wearing it. But there is something I want to give you today.' She reached inside the neckline of her gown. 'This is Mama's locket that I told you about. I found it in a dresser drawer and I keep it in my room, but I don't often wear it because I don't want Aunt Cordelia to know I have it – I think it would anger her. But I now know that the likenesses it contains are of the two of us, and I want you to have it. I'd like to think it might help to keep you safe. As if Mama is watching over you.'

She pressed the locket into Lise's hand, and wonderingly Lise snicked it open with her fingernail. She'd never before seen a likeness of herself as a young child, and she gazed at it in awe.

'We were so alike, even then!' she said. 'I wonder which is you and which is me?'

'I don't know.' Cecile smiled. 'We were very sweet, weren't we? But please, take care of it. I wouldn't like it to be lost, or confiscated by Cordelia.'

'Of course I will,' Lise promised. 'And when we meet again, as I hope and trust we will, I'll return it to you.'

'Oh, we'll decide when the time comes. You have as much right to it as I – more! I will never be able to thank you enough for what you are doing for Sam and me. This would be just a small token of my appreciation.'

'Thank you so much.' Unexpectedly, tears filled Lise's eyes; she blinked them away. 'But one more thing. Can you tell me where I will find Mama's grave? I'd like to visit it.'

'It's in the village churchyard. In the shadow of the church tower. The headstone is very simple, but I've kept it clean of dirt and moss, so the inscription is still clear: "Marguerite Pendinnick, beloved wife of Godfrey, and mother of Cecile".'

The tears threatened again, and this time Lise was unable to stop one from sliding down her cheek.

Cecile reached out and took her hand. 'It's very upsetting, I know. But the important thing is we have found one another now. Mama would be very happy for us.'

Lise nodded, and in that moment the two sisters experienced the precious closeness that had once been between them.

Sam interrupted their reverie. 'Hey, you two, let's get down to business. Time is short.'

Lise smiled ruefully. 'That's true. I need you to tell me all I still have to know to prevent me from making some stupid error and being discovered as an imposter.'

* * *

To Lise's disappointment, Zach had been dispatched to ride to some of the drop-off points in the chain of distribution of the expected cargo, which according to Godfrey included many rolls of fine silk as well as cognac, tobacco and tea. Thus he was not available to take her back to St Ives when her tuition session ended. Instead she had to ride with Sam and, much as she liked him, she desperately missed that time she spent with Zach.

'Be sure to be here in good time tomorrow,' Sam instructed as he set her down. 'If Zach's still tied up, I'll come for you as soon as the master leaves, and there will be no time to waste.'

As she walked the rest of the way home, she wondered how long it would be before she would see St Ives again after tomorrow. If ever. It was a daunting thought, but Lise was as determined as she had ever been. She would find the proof of her father's wicked activities that Zach required. And she would do all she could to discover the cause of her mother's death.

Godfrey Pendinnick was in a furious rage. All the arrangements had been made to receive the expected cargo. The lookouts had been at their posts for hours, watching for the first sight of the clipper that would bring the contraband to Porthmeor Cove; the men who would unload it and the pack animals who would transport it on its way were ready and waiting, and the recipients along the distribution chain had been alerted and would have their own plans in place. But the ship had not come.

'Goddammit to hell! Where are they?' he fumed.

'Perhaps there has been some misunderstanding in the line of communication,' Zach suggested.

'Codswallop! There has been no misunderstanding. It was all arranged, clear as daylight. That shipment is bought and paid for, and since the sea is calm as a mill pond, I want to know why it has failed to arrive as planned.'

'You'd like me to go to France and investigate?' Leaving Porthmeor while Lise was at Polruan House was the last thing Zach wanted to do, but he felt duty bound to offer.

'No,' Godfrey snapped. 'If it doesn't arrive tonight, I'll go myself when I return from the burial. We'll give it another hour, and if there is no report of a sighting from the lookout, you may as well disband the troops. But tell them to be back tomorrow night just to be sure there was no confusion over dates.'

'I'll see to it, sir,' Zach promised.

'Good.' Godfrey swore viciously. 'But it will be another fruitless operation, I fear. That scoundrel of a middleman has fleeced me, if I'm not much mistaken. I should have known better than to trade with someone other than my usual contacts. But he will rue the day he crossed Godfrey Pendinnick, make no mistake of that. I shall take Dyfan Flinders with me; he'll make short work of recovering my losses and making that French scoundrel pay for his trickery.'

'He deserves everything he gets,' Zach said, though privately he was sickened by Pendinnick's planned revenge. But at the same time, his hopes rose. If the cargo failed to arrive and his employer went to France, it would give Lise a few more days free of the scrutiny of her father.

'I'm off to my bed then.' Godfrey stamped his booted feet, shaking off wet caked sand. 'I have an early start tomorrow, and had I known I had been taken for a fool, I could have been there several hours since.'

Without wishing Zach goodnight, he stomped off, pausing only occasionally to cock his ear in the vain hope he might yet hear a whistle or hoot that would tell him the clipper had been sighted, and looking back over his shoulder for any lights.

Zach went in search of Sam, and found him in a group of men waiting in the shelter of the overhanging cliffs. He briefed them that they would be stood down in an hour's time if the consignment had not arrived, but would be required again the following night. The men grumbled amongst themselves at the wasted time and the possibility that there might be no payment for tonight, and Zach did his best to calm them, fearing that the mood might turn ugly.

'Mr Pendinnick will travel to France in person if it fails to arrive,' he told them. 'He'll see you right, have no fear.'

'He better 'ad!' One of the most outspoken of the men shook his fist warningly, and another, a peacemaker, interceded.

'He ain't never let us down yet, Judd. No use gettin' in a flux about it till we knows what's gone wrong.'

'I s'pose,' Judd said heavily.

Hoping the flashpoint was safely passed, Zach pulled Sam to one side.

'It helps our plan, though,' he said in a whisper. 'Pendinnick means to go to France immediately on his return from the burial, so it will allow more time for Lise to find her way round the house and accustom herself to the ways of the family. And since it seems unlikely we will have any cargo to unload tonight, I shall be able to collect her myself in the morning.'

'Right.' Sam sounded relieved, and Zach guessed he wanted to be here to take care of Cecile and calm any fears she might have.

'Now – where's young Tommy Firks? I want him to run over to the lookouts and tell them that when they see a flare from here on the beach, they can pack up and go home.'

Cecile sat on the edge of her bed, a wrap over her nightgown, her feet bare, expecting to hear activity outside her window at any moment. The night was clear, the stars bright, and it would be no use trying to sleep until it was over – if she was able to sleep at all, which she doubted. Her stomach was tied in knots, her emotions a strange mixture of excitement, apprehension and – though she could not be sure why – sadness. Perhaps it was because she would be leaving her little dog Moll behind. She hoped fervently that someone would be kind to her, and play the games she loved – and treat dear Lady well too. Perhaps it was because it would be a long while, if ever, before she and Lise could be together again, a long while before they could begin to re-create the closeness they had once shared, enjoy the unbreakable bond between them. Or perhaps it was because she would be leaving the place where Mama lay. She wished she had found the time to visit the grave in the last few hectic days. But at least Lise had said she would go there.

Thinking of Mama made her long for the comfort the locket had brought her when she had felt sad and lonely. She would miss it, she knew, but giving it to Lise had seemed the right thing to do. She had meant it when she had told Lise she would never be able to repay her for what she was doing. She deserved the locket; she had earned it a million times over.

Cecile looked at the soft bag lying in the corner beside her dresser, which she had packed with underwear, skirts and bodices, and a simple wrap. It was all she could take with her, all she needed. She lay back on the bed, thinking of Sam, imagining his arms around her and her head lying on his chest, and her eyelids began to droop. Although she had anticipated she would spend a wakeful night, she soon drifted into sleep, to dream of the future Lise was making possible.

Lise, too, was awake. She should try to sleep, she knew. Tomorrow she had a long and testing day ahead of her and, for all her bravado, she felt sick with apprehension. Could she really do this? It would have been easy enough to pass herself off as her twin with friends and acquaintances, but the two people she had to convince were the very two people who knew Cecile best in the whole world. And if the deception was discovered, what would happen to her? She was in little doubt she would meet the same fate as her mother.

She drew out the locket Cecile had given to her, opening it and gazing at the two identical likenesses, and as she did so, a warmth filled her, and a sense of peace drove away her fear. It was as if Cecile were here with her, close as the two little girls were when the locket was fastened shut, and Mama too.

She bathed in the warmth and the peace, and when eventually she fell asleep, it was with her fingers curled around the locket, pressing it to her heart.

Chapter Eighteen

The stables at Polruan were a hub of frenzied activity, the very air heavy with a sense of purpose, nervous tension and anticipation.

Because the expected shipment had failed to arrive last night, Zach had been able to collect Lise from their usual meeting place on the moors above St Ives, and her heart had leapt when she saw him waiting for her. But the chemistry between them had been somewhat lost in apprehension, a sense of unreality, and a gut-wrenching feeling of inevitability that this was actually going to happen.

Sam, Cecile and Bessie had been waiting for them; Godfrey had left early, waking Sam to tack up Satan, and then riding off at a furious pace, his mood every bit as sour as it had been the previous night. Cordelia, it seemed, had remained abed, and Cecile had eaten breakfast alone before bidding a tearful farewell to Moll, burying her face in the dog's coat and stroking her silky ears.

Now it was time for the transformation of one sister to the other. With a mind for Lise's comfort, Cecile had chosen to wear her newest gown, emerald-green satin. It still had ruffles at the neck and sleeves, but instead of the unwieldy hooped skirts, it had a small bustle, while the front of the gown fell easily from a high waist. Cecile had persuaded Aunt Cordelia to allow her to deviate from the styles the older woman still favoured and follow the latest trend in fashion, and now she was glad for Lise's sake that she had. She only wished her aunt had given her blessing to abandoning the heavy powdered wig too. 'Whatever next!' Cordelia had exclaimed, horrified, when Cecile had suggested it.

With Zach and Sam banished from the stable, Bessie began helping the sisters to swap their clothes, though for the sake of modesty both retained their own shifts. Lise would be able to use one of Cecile's when she next undressed, and she would hide hers beneath the heaps of underwear in her twin's drawer. When it was time to put on the powdered wig, she shuddered, wincing as Bessie tucked all her own hair out of sight. Cecile, meanwhile, was delighting in the wonderful feeling of her locks flowing free.

'You can come back in now!' Bessie called.

'Good Lord!' Zach exclaimed as he and Sam re-entered the stables.

Sam shook his head in amazement. 'Truly, if I didn't know better, I'd swear you were Cecile!' he said to Lise.

'Really?' she asked, desperate for confirmation.

'Absolutely! It is truly amazing!' he reaffirmed, but Zach added a note of caution.

'Just remember Cecile is far less outspoken than you. You have to play meek and compliant if you are not to arouse suspicion.'

Lise smiled uncertainly. 'Just now, I *feel* meek! Don't worry, I shall be too afraid of putting a foot wrong to behave like my usual self.'

'And hopefully that will become a habit.'

'It's strange,' she went on, 'but I really do feel different.' She ran her fingers over the wig and the little mobcap Bessie had settled on top of it, and stroked the flowing satin of her skirts. 'I don't feel like me at all.'

Bessie stood back for a moment, admiring her handiwork with satisfaction, before uttering a deep sigh. 'I'd best be gettin' back afore I'm missed. Come 'ere, me darlin'.' She pulled Cecile into her ample bosom, hugging her close before eventually letting her go. 'Just you take good care of her, Sam. And you, my lovely, well, I hope you gets the happiness you deserves.' Then, tears shining in her eyes, she turned and left the stables.

'Are you two both ready, then?' Sam was impatient to be away.

'You can stay here a little longer if you'd care to,' Zach told Lise. 'Cordelia is used to Cecile spending time with Lady each morning. But remember, when you do go up to the house, tell her you think Sam must have accompanied Godfrey. That will explain why he and his horse are gone, and no one will know different until Godfrey's return. That should give Sam and Cecile time to put some distance between themselves and the house.' He turned to Sam. 'Where do you plan to head?'

'As far as we can get before both Cecile and my horse grow too tired,' Sam replied. 'Then we'll look for an inn where we can rest before going on.'

'I'd be cautious concerning the wisdom of such a plan,' Zach warned. 'A good many inns and hostelries between here and the Devon border are stopping-off places for smuggled cargo. You'll know some and I could warn you against others, but far from all.'

Sam shrugged helplessly. 'If we are reduced to sleeping under the stars, then so be it.'

'I have a better plan. The farm I still call home is north of Helston, just outside the village of St Godolphin, and about sixteen miles from here as the crow flies. If you explain to my ma and pa that you are a friend of mine and I have suggested you take shelter with them before pressing on, I know they will be willing to accommodate you. They are good people, you can trust them, and the farm is isolated enough not to pose any danger of you being discovered there. If you make for Camborne and Redruth, you should find St Godolphin signposted along the way.'

Sam's face cleared. 'That would be capital. If you think they will believe me.'

'If you wait while I go up to the house, I'll find paper and write a short note,' Zach said. He glanced at Lise. 'Perhaps you'd like to come with me? I can show you the way Cecile would go in and, if Cordelia is still abed, the downstairs rooms. If she is up and about, I can be the one to lie about Sam's absence.'

Much as she would have liked to postpone the start of her deception for as long as possible, Lise knew the offer was too good to refuse. Having Zach beside her when she crossed the threshold would give her comfort and courage.

'Very well,' she said.

'But make haste,' Sam urged Zach. 'I'll saddle up Zeus, and then we must be on our way.'

Zach nodded, Lise hugged Cecile one last time, and they set off towards the house.

At the side door, Zach paused, his hand on the latch. 'Your bedroom is right above us on this side of the house. Remember that if you get disorientated.' He reached out and lifted her chin with his fingers, looking directly into her eyes. 'Just take care, Lise. Don't risk doing anything to put yourself in danger. Nothing, but nothing is worth that.'

Under his touch, Lise felt her chin quiver, and a frisson of awareness ran like a bolt of lightning through her veins and prickled on her skin. He'd talked her into doing this to further his efforts to gain justice for his brother, but now, when the chance of achieving just that was closer than it had ever been, he was telling her he didn't want to put her in harm's way. In that moment she knew that she had been right to question her anger towards him. He did care for her. Perhaps his feelings had taken him unawares, just as her own had crept up on her. It didn't matter now. But she must let him know she no longer blamed him for the situation, that she regretted the way she had behaved towards him these last days, that she hoped they could be friends again – and maybe more.

'I'm sorry, Zach,' she said softly. 'I shouldn't have been so horrid to you, but . . . I think I was trying to keep my distance because I was afraid of the feelings I was experiencing for you. Once, long ago, I was badly hurt, and I didn't want to ever be in a position where I could be hurt like that again.'

'Oh, Lise . . .' He moved his fingers up to her cheek, tracing the lines of her cheekbone, her nose and then her lips, as if committing them to memory. He lowered his head so that his face was shadowed by his tricorn hat. 'I just wish with all my heart that you wouldn't do this. I can't bear the thought of harm befalling you. And I could never live with myself if . . .' He broke off.

'You are not forcing me to do anything,' Lise said. 'I have my own reasons, as well you know. I'll be careful, I promise, but if anything should happen to me, you are not to blame yourself. I forbid it!'

He looked up then, and in his eyes, and the softening of his face, she saw what she could almost believe was love. He lifted her chin again, but his time leaned towards her, so close that she could no longer see him clearly, only feel his breath on her cheek and his hand caressing the back of her neck, drawing her closer still. And then his lips were on hers, a gentle pressure at first that hardened into a kiss that was almost savage in its intensity.

Lise's heart pounded in her chest and little thrills ran through the deepest parts of her. Her arms went round him, feeling the rough broadcloth of his coat and the hard muscles beneath it. For long moments they remained there, two figures merged into one, until at last he pulled back.

'Just come back to me safely, do you hear?' he said, his tone rough; then, with a decisive movement, he opened the door.

Bessie was in the hallway, carrying a chafing dish. She swung round when she heard footsteps behind her, and put a chubby finger to her lips, nodding in the direction of what Lise was to learn was the breakfast room. 'She's up,' she mouthed.

Zach nodded wordlessly, then spoke in normal tones. 'So how did you find Lady today, Miss Pendinnick?'

Swallowing hard, Lise took her cue. 'Oh, beautiful, as always. She does so enjoy her carrot! She fair nibbled my fingers off in her eagerness to get it! But I think Sam must have left with Papa. His horse is gone, as well as Satan, and so is he.'

Zach rewarded her with a brief smile of appreciation. 'I must find your Aunt Cordelia and discuss business. Why don't you go and play with Moll? You don't want to be party to such boring talk.'

A commanding voice billowed out of the breakfast room. 'Here, Carver!'

'Miss Pendinnick!' With a last encouraging wink at Lise, Zach moved away.

Left alone, Lise experienced a moment's panic, then took a firm grip on herself. 'Moll?' she called. 'Moll? Where are you?'

A few moments later, the little dog scuttled into the hall, tail wagging. She came to a halt in front of Lise, cocking her head and regarding her with a bemused look.

'Moll! There you are!' Lise bent to stroke the silky head, anxious to establish a bond and afraid that her deception might be revealed by the dog, which sniffed curiously at her skirts, then, to Lise's enormous relief, began to respond to her petting.

'Shall we go to my room, Moll? I'm sure we left your ball there,' Lise said, loudly enough for her voice to carry into the breakfast room, and hoping that the ball was indeed there, as Cecile had told her.

Instantly Moll headed for the staircase, leading the way, and Lise was able to follow without fear of taking a wrong turn.

As she opened the door before which Moll stood expectantly, Lise almost gasped aloud. Why, it would be possible to fit the whole of Annie's cottage into this one room! And the furniture and furnishings! Unlike the mishmash of bits and pieces in her own bedroom, everything here matched! The carved headboard of the bed, the night tables, the chest of drawers and dressing chest, all were of a reddish-brown wood edged with decorative borders in what looked like gold leaf. A similar border surrounded a mirror that hung above the chest. The bed covering was of heavy cream satin, with tan cushions and frilled flounces, while the rich window drapes continued the theme, clearly made to match perfectly. At the foot of the bed was an ottoman, upholstered in the same fabric, but this time richly embroidered; and carpets the like of which Lise had never seen covered much of the polished wooden floor.

Lise could scarcely believe she would look at herself in that incredible mirror, sleep tonight in that bed, wake to such opulence. Cecile must love Sam very much to leave it all behind.

'Aw right, ducks?' Bessie materialised behind her, urging her into the room and shutting the door behind her. 'Nice, ain't it? Cherry wood, that is, with gold and silver leaf, and all the way from Italy. An' will you look at that carpet!' She indicated the one that lay between the bed and the dressing chest. 'An Axminster, that is. Just see how many flowers you can find – there's roses, daffodils and tulips, even morning glory. Many a happy hour Cecile spent as a child tracing them out with her little finger. And when she was older, she'd draw them and cut them out – she were goin' ter make 'er own carpet, she reckoned.'

'Oh, I did something similar!' Lise exclaimed. 'I used to draw people – ladies, mostly, in fine clothes – and I planned to make a frieze to decorate my room! I never did finish it and I don't know what became of it.'

Bessie smiled benignly. 'No more did Cecile.' She crossed to the door, opening it a crack and peeping out before shutting it again. 'You'd better be careful,' she cautioned. 'I know I've been guilty of it meself, but it ain't a good idea to talk about Cecile, nor about yerself, fer that matter. You're supposed t'be 'er, remember, and walls have ears.'

'You're right,' Lise said, chastened. 'It's going to take a bit of getting used to, but I must think before I speak.'

Moll had been scrabbling under the bed, half hidden by the flounced covers that reached to the floor; now she emerged, her ball in her mouth, trotted over to Lise and dropped it at her feet.

'Why don't you go out on the lawn with her?' Bessie suggested. 'That's what Cecile would do, a fine day like this.'

'Will you come with me?'

Bessie shook her head. 'Can't do that, miss. I got work to do. You can get out on to the lawn from the French windows in the parlour – down to the end of the passage, turn left, and you can't miss it. Go on, you'll be fine, just so long as you don't forget yourself.'

209

* * *

It had been the strangest day Lise could ever remember. She had spent a long while playing with Moll and exploring the gardens, putting off the moment when she would have to go into the house and meet Cordelia. When Zach had left, walking across the lawns, he hadn't approached her, merely tipping his hat as he passed some ten feet away. He and Cecile weren't supposed to be more than acquaintances, she guessed, and Cordelia might have seen from one of the windows if he had shown any more familiarity.

When she could dally no longer, and with Moll at last tiring of chasing her ball, she retraced her steps into the house. Cordelia was nowhere to be seen, and, heart racing, Lise made her way along the passage. Through the parlour door she spotted her aunt sitting at a small escritoire, pen in hand, with what she guessed was either a ledger or a book of records in front of her. Cecile had warned her that Cordelia didn't like to be disturbed when she was working, and, relieved, Lise simply called, 'Good morning, Aunt,' as she passed the door.

'Good morning, Cecile.' Cordelia's tone was clipped and unwelcoming, confirming what Cecile had said.

This was as good a chance as she would get to explore the house and familiarise herself with the layout of the rooms, Lise decided. Cecile had given her a carefully drawn plan, which she had committed to memory, but there was no substitute for seeing where everything was for herself. The door to what she recalled from the plan was her father's study was closed, and she didn't venture inside; she would have no plausible excuse for being there if she was caught. She did explore the dining room, however, and was amazed all over again.

The walls, she discovered, were covered in crimson silk, the hangings cream brocade tied back with heavy red braided cords

with tassels, and a circular pattern of gold leaf had been sten-
cilled around the light fitting – a candelabra that was suspended
over a highly polished mahogany table. Eight matching chairs
were positioned around it, their seats upholstered in crimson
and their legs finishing with a ball-and-claw base, and dark-
stained floorboards surrounded the brightly patterned rugs.
Artwork in elaborate frames hung on the walls, along with a
large tapestry.

Although it must be approaching time for luncheon, the table
was not set, and Lise guessed that since it would be only Cordelia
and herself, they would eat in what Cecile had called the
breakfast room. As she went in search of it, she met Bessie in the
passage, carrying a steaming mug of soup and a platter of cold
cuts on a tray.

'Ah! There you be!' She thrust the tray at Lise.

'For me?' Lise said, startled.

'No, fer Miss Cordelia. She intends working on while she
eats – she do often do that – and I thought as 'ow you might
take it to her.'

'Oh . . .' The quiver began again in Lise's stomach, but she
couldn't avoid her aunt for ever, and at least if Cordelia was
working, she wouldn't be expected to talk much to her.

'Good lass.' Bessie nodded approvingly. 'I'll bring yours
along to the breakfast room – unless you want to have it upstairs,
that is?'

'The breakfast room, please,' Lise said. She might as well
begin to get used to eating there.

Balancing the tray carefully on one arm, she tapped at the
parlour door.

'You've no need to knock, Bessie. Just come!' The commanding voice was daunting. Shaking inwardly, but outwardly
calm, Lise entered the room.

'It's me, Aunt.'

Cordelia looked up from the ledger she was poring over, her rouged lips twisted into a sneer. 'So I see. Leave the tray on the table. I'll fetch it when I'm ready.'

'But the soup will go cold . . .' Lise ventured.

'And if I take it now, no doubt I'll burn my tongue.' Cordelia's tone was impatient. 'Just do as I say, can't you?' And without so much as a thank-you, she bent once more over the ledger.

Though shocked by her aunt's rude attitude, Lise couldn't help feeling relief. It appeared she wasn't going to have to see much of Cordelia at all and, as far as she was concerned, the less the better!

She ate her own luncheon in the breakfast room, Moll sitting expectantly at her knee, and though she guessed such a thing would be disapproved of she slipped the dog a few bits of baked ham. She would need Moll on her side if she was to carry out the deception successfully.

The afternoon passed much as the morning had, but when the time for dinner approached, Lise realised she would have to face her aunt for the first time across the table.

'Should I change my gown?' she asked Bessie, but the maid told her that wouldn't be necessary, and Lise was already seated at the big table, where just two places had been set, when Cordelia swept into the room.

'Hungry, eh?' she barked.

'A little.' Lise attempted a smile. 'And you must be too. You've had a busy day.'

'All my days are busy, as well you know.' Cordelia was silent as a fish course was served, then pointed at the dish and spoke sharply. 'Is that not a bone? What is Cook thinking of? Take this away and tell her to remove it if she wants to retain her position here.'

The girl departed hastily, and Cordelia snorted. 'Servants! Lazy good-for-nothings, the lot of them. I hope you will be more fortunate when you are wed to Mr Redmond.'

'I hope so too,' Lise said. In all the preparations, she had quite forgotten that Cecile was betrothed to the vicar.

Somewhere in the house a clock chimed the hour, and Cordelia sniffed impatiently. 'I suppose your papa is drowning his sorrows with the rest of the family. The burial must have been over long ago. No doubt he'll arrive home in his cups and stinking of brandy. And he wondered why I had no desire to accompany him.'

Lise said nothing, waiting for the offending fish to be returned to Cordelia before beginning to pick at her own.

For the most part the meal passed in silence, and Lise thought she could well understand why Cecile had been so anxious to escape. There was precious little joy in this household. Some-how she managed to work her way through the fish and meat courses, but by the time an apple pie and cream were brought to the table, she didn't think she could swallow another mouthful. Her nerves were wound tight, and her head was beginning to ache.

'Do you think I might be excused, Aunt?' she asked tentatively.

Cordelia poured cream on to a generous slice of pie. 'You need to eat more, my girl. These last few weeks you seem to be wasting away.'

'I'm perfectly well, Aunt,' Lise said. 'I just—'

Cordelia waved her fork. 'Oh, go if you must. Your company is hardly stimulating.'

After a moment's hesitation when she wondered anxiously if she had done something to arouse her aunt's suspicion, Lise bunched her napkin, laid it on the table and rose.

'Thank you, Aunt,' she said meekly. Then she turned and fled the dining room and the unpleasant atmosphere Cordelia generated, and, with Moll at her heels, escaped to her room.

Lise must have been dozing. She'd thought she'd never sleep, but when she was awakened by the sound of horse's hooves on the path outside her window, she came to with such a jolt that she realised she must have done. She pushed aside the covers, got out of bed in one swift movement and rushed across to the window, her bare feet sinking into the soft rug. She'd left the heavy drapes open; now she pulled aside the fine gauze behind them and looked out. As she did so, a commanding voice, the male equivalent of Cordelia's, shouted impatiently for Sam, and cursed loudly when he failed to appear.

'Dammit, where is the good-for-nothing?'

It was Godfrey, home at last from his father's burial – and the worse for drink, by the sound of it. Cordelia had been right when she supposed he had stayed late drinking with other family members. Lise opened the window and leaned out as far as she dared, anxious to catch her first glimpse of him. She could see nothing of his face, which was turned away from her, but her impression of his physique was that he was portly and his hat sat slightly askew on his bewigged head. As she watched, he rose in the stirrups, presumably to dismount, but then toppled forward. The horse reared, startled, and he lost his balance, one foot still in the stirrup, the other flailing wildly. Horrified, Lise clapped her hand over her mouth as he fell heavily, landing on his side, then rolling on to his back and lying motionless.

Without stopping to think, she grabbed a wrap she had draped over the bedside chair and ran out on to the landing. She wasn't sure which bedroom was Cordelia's, so she banged on both doors, shouting a warning, before hurrying downstairs, out of the side door and towards the supine figure.

'Papa!' The familiarity came to her lips so easily it was as if Cecile was speaking for her.

She'd come here to gain revenge on the monster responsible for the loss of her family, but now, fearing him badly injured, perhaps even dead, the only thought in her head was that this man was her father and she must go to his assistance.

Chapter Nineteen

As they rode north, Lise was constantly on Cecile's mind. It was only natural, she supposed. The bond between them was unbreakable, even though they had been parted for so many years. Once they had lain curled up together in Mama's womb and, after they came into the world, in their crib. For a while, as they had grown, they had played together, slept together, laughed and cried together, each feeling the other's joy and pain as if they were one. Now, after the lonely years, it was just the same, and this new separation was a niggling ache deep inside her.

She was also afraid they might encounter someone who would recognise them, but Sam had given Porthmeor a wide berth, and once they were out on the moors they were able to see far enough ahead to make a detour if another horse and rider or wagon appeared on the horizon. By the time they reached the hamlet of Sithney, just north-west of Helston, Sam thought it was safe enough for them to stop and rest so as to water Zeus and buy pasties for themselves. There would be other well-organised smuggling gangs on this side of Mount's Bay, operating out of Church Cove, Mullion and the Lizard, he said, and it was unlikely that contraband from Porthmeor would be brought this way. But still the nagging concern for Lise's welfare haunted Cecile.

She was growing very tired too, her thighs aching from the hours of sitting astride Zeus. Sweat was trickling down between her breasts, and her head had begun to ache dully. Would they never arrive at their destination? she wondered as they headed north-east again, Sam getting his bearings by the position of the sun. And then, at last, just as it was beginning to sink behind them, they saw the sign for St Godolphin and a small cluster of houses that must be the hamlet itself, and then the farm, nestling in a fold of gently undulating land.

'That's it!' Sam exclaimed. 'We're nearly there! Would you like a little rest before we go down? Just as long as we make it before dark.'

'Oh, yes, please!'

He lifted her down, and she leaned against Zeus's strong flank as she ran her fingers through wind-tousled hair, then wetted her handkerchief and brushed at the dust she imagined must be staining her cheeks. She didn't know if she could bear to get back on the horse. Could they walk the remaining distance? And what sort of welcome would await them?

The thought occurred to her suddenly, out of the blue. It was not one she had entertained as they had planned their escape, nor in all the turmoil of the long day she had just lived through. Now, however, it flashed into her mind, making her fearful again.

'You do think we're doing the right thing in going there, do you?' she ventured.

'Certainly.' Sam frowned. 'Why would you think otherwise?'

Cecile frowned. 'He's your friend, I know. And he certainly *seems* to have been helping us. But . . . he does work for Papa, after all. That makes him a fortune seeker, doesn't it?'

Sam was silent for a long moment. 'There's something I've kept from you, Cecile. I think Zach is working for your father

217

for a reason. Did you know his brother was a riding officer, working for the Revenue and Customs? He disappeared a year or so ago, and was never seen again. Zach told me about it one night when we were drinking at the Wink, not long after he came here; he believed his brother had met his end at the hands of the smugglers and wreckers hereabouts. I had to agree; he wouldn't be the first, and he won't be the last. Zach has never mentioned it since – I think he only did so then because of the quantity of ale he'd consumed – but I think the reason he obtained employment with your pa was so as to find evidence that would bring him to justice. Zach is no fortune seeker. In my opinion he is a bereaved brother looking to avenge the death of a loved one.'

Cecile had turned pale as he spoke. 'You can't believe my father is a murderer, surely?' she said, shocked and horrified.

Sam took her hand. 'I don't know what to believe, Cecile. There is no doubt too many lawmen have met their deaths because they sought to put a stop to what goes on under cover of darkness. To be truthful, it wouldn't surprise me. I don't say your father himself has thrown anyone down a mine shaft, or over a cliff. He wouldn't do his own dirty work, but it would be done with his blessing.'

'No!' Cecile jerked her hand away, wrapping her arms around herself. 'How can you think such a thing? I can't believe it! I won't!'

That Godfrey had made his fortune from criminal activity she didn't doubt. She knew all too well what went on, and she hated it. But this . . . Never! He was still her father and, despite everything, she loved him. She couldn't bear to think of him being betrayed by someone he trusted.

'Why didn't you tell me Zach was an enemy in the camp?' she demanded.

'And have you run to your father and put Zach's life in danger? I couldn't be party to that. He is my friend, and yours. Isn't it thanks to him that Lise has taken your place to allow us to escape? Didn't he suggest we find our way to his home rather than risk staying in one of the hostelries that work with the smugglers? Zach is a man of principle. I trust him, and you must too.'

Tears sprang to Cecile's eyes. She no longer knew who, or what, to believe. Her father conducted his business with a ruthless efficiency, it was true, but she couldn't accept he would condone the murder of any man. She loved Sam with all her heart, but there were secrets he had kept from her. And Zach . . . Whatever Sam said, Zach was a cuckoo in the nest. Exhausted as she was, it was all too much for her.

Sam put an arm around her, but she shrank away, feeling she no longer knew him. 'Please don't,' she whispered, distressed.

'Come on, my love, don't be foolish,' he said gently. 'You're tired and hungry, you are making mountains out of molehills. Let's go down to the farm – you'll see things in a different light when you've had something to eat and drink, and slept in a comfortable bed.'

She swallowed hard. Really, what choice did she have? 'Very well,' she said softly, and this time she did not pull away from Sam as he hoisted her back on to the horse. But she did sit stiffly in the saddle, not leaning into him. She wasn't ready yet to forgive or forget that he had known about Zach's treachery and hidden it from her.

On their way down to the farm, they passed sheep grazing on the rough grass, and some late lambs skipped and frolicked nearby. They came at last to a low stone building with a barn, a pigsty and a stable flanking it. Sam dismounted and helped Cecile down, then rapped on the farmhouse door. It was opened by a rosy-cheeked woman whom they guessed immediately must be Zach's mother.

'Yes?' She gazed at them curiously. 'Lost, be you?'

'We're friends of Zach's,' Sam said. 'I have a note from him confirming that.' He produced it, and when she had read it, Zach's mother clucked her tongue sympathetically.

'Oh my, you poor dears! Come in, do, and have someut to sustain yourselves. Tad!' she called into the house. 'We've visitors, and their poor nag needs unsaddling and watering too.'

In the homely kitchen, she bustled about, offering them ale to drink and setting a pan over the fire to make them supper.

'Eggs from our own hens, and bacon from one of our porkers,' she told them as the delicious aroma set their taste buds watering. 'That'll set you up, and when you've had your fill, you'll be ready for bed, I shouldn't wonder, if you've come all that way. There's only the one bedroom besides mine and Tad's, but you're welcome to that. Or one of you could sleep down here on the couch if that'd suit you better.'

Cecile sat silent, her eyes downcast, and Sam answered for both of them.

'We'll be happy to share a room, Mrs Carver. We're to be wed as soon as we can find a priest.'

'Well, if you be sure,' she said, and Cecile didn't like to raise any objection.

Neither of them spoke as they climbed the bare wooden staircase to the room that Zach had once presumably shared with his brother. When they saw that it had only the one bed, Sam sensed Cecile's reluctance.

'I'll sleep on the floor,' he offered.

'No, you won't. You need to be fit to ride on tomorrow,' Cecile replied, but there was no warmth in her tone.

'Well, I'll wait outside while you get yourself ready,' Sam

said, knowing she would not want him to see her undress.

Once the door had closed after him, Cecile took off Lise's outerwear – far easier than her own complicated gowns! – then slipped into bed still wearing her shift and pulled the covers up to her chin. A few minutes later, Sam re-entered the room, undressed himself, and climbed in beside her. She lay awkward and rigid, as close to the edge of the bed as she dared.

'Goodnight, Sam.'

'Night.' It wasn't at all the way he'd imagined his first night with Cecile in a shared bed would be, but he was afraid to make any move towards her. He didn't want to risk her rebuttal – she had made her displeasure with him all too clear – and besides, he was dog tired too. Within a few minutes of his head touching the pillow, he had drifted off, but sleep eluded Cecile.

Around and around in her mind went the things Sam had said about Zach's reasons for seeking employment with her father. She still couldn't believe it. Yes, Godfrey engaged in criminal activity, but he had never been anything other than a loving father to her. It was his devotion, she knew, that would have made him object to a match with Sam, and seek to ensure her well-being by way of a marriage that, however unwelcome to her, would provide her with security and a good living. But what if he really was as ruthless as Sam had suggested? What if he would stop at nothing to achieve his aims? Could it be that she had exposed her sister to unknown peril through her own selfish desire? And how could she blame Sam, the man she loved so dearly, for his loyalty to his friend? Really, it was no more than she would expect of him.

Longing for him suddenly, for the old closeness, she inched away from the edge of the bed and curled her body around his. He stirred in his sleep, an arm snaking over her shoulder as he turned towards her. She lay motionless.

'Cecile?' he murmured sleepily.

'I love you, Sam,' she whispered into his shoulder, and tasted the salt of his skin on her lips.

'Mmm.' It was a contented sigh.

As she burrowed into him, loving the feel of the warmth emanating from his body, Cecile's eyes began to close. She'd tell him tomorrow that she was sorry for being angry with him. Lise would come to no harm. And she and Sam would be free to spend the rest of their lives together.

Peaceful at last, she slept.

Lise dropped to her knees beside Godfrey's supine figure. One leg was twisted awkwardly beneath him, and by the light of the moon she saw blood pooling on the cobbles from a gash on his forehead. His wig had slipped to one side so that it covered the other side of his face, and he smelled strongly of rum. He appeared to be senseless,

'Papa!' she said again, taking his wrist and feeling for a pulse. For a long moment she was unable to find it, and her own heart seemed to stop beating. Was he dead? Then she felt it, thready but ticking irregularly beneath her fingers. Close beside her, Satan stamped impatiently, and Lise was afraid he might land a kick on one of them, or even trample Godfrey where he lay.

She scrambled to her feet, taking Satan's bridle and leading him into the stable, the door of which was open. As she emerged, Cordelia came running along the passageway, her haste totally unlike her usual dignified pace.

'Godfrey!' She dropped to her knees beside him just as Lise had done. 'Sweet Jesus, Godfrey! What have you done?'

'He fell. I saw it from my window. He was trying to dismount, but he somehow caught his foot in the stirrup and—'

'Drunk, I suppose.' Momentarily she was the old Cordelia,

sharp, scathing. 'And where is that wretched boy when he's needed? Sam! Sam – where are you? Find him, Cecile, and tell him to ride for Dr Meek.' Then her voice softened again as she raised her brother's head to cradle it in her lap, careless of the blood soaking her nightgown. 'Lie still, Godfrey. The doctor will soon be here and he'll see to it that you are fine.'

Lise stood for a moment, uncertain of what to do or say. 'Sam's not here,' she ventured.

'But he went to the burial with Godfrey!' Cordelia looked around, puzzled, as if she could make him materialise out of the darkness. 'Where is he?'

'I don't know.'

'Dr Meek! We must call for Dr Meek!' Cordelia's voice was rising again, panicked now.

'Shall I go for him?' Even as she said it, Lise realised she had no idea where to find the doctor. It wasn't information that she, or anyone else, had anticipated needing. But to her relief, Cordelia snapped back sharply.

'Don't be ridiculous! Lady won't be saddled, and you know you are scarcely safe riding in broad daylight, let alone at night! Dear God, what is to be done? He's out cold! Godfrey! Godfrey – speak to me!'

As if on cue, Pendinnick groaned, shifted slightly and mumbled incoherently.

'I'll fetch water,' Lise suggested. 'And perhaps some brandy?'

'He's had more than enough liquor for one night,' Cordelia snorted. 'But just a little might help him to rally. You know where it is.'

It would be in his study, Lise guessed. 'Hold on, Papa,' she urged him, and hurried into the house, where she almost collided with a portly figure clad in a nightgown and wrap and carrying a lighted candle.

'What in the world be goin' on?' she demanded.

'Bessie!' The maid must have been woken by all the commotion, and Lise had never been more glad to see her. 'Oh, Bessie, it's Papa! He's had a bad fall from his horse, and I'm to fetch brandy to try and rouse him, and something to stem the bleeding from his head.'

Bessie gathered herself together with surprising alacrity. 'Leave the brandy to me. You'll find what you need in the kitchen. Now – where be he? Out by the stables, I s'pose.'

Without waiting for a reply, she bustled off in the direction of Godfrey's study, while Lise headed for the kitchen, where she poured water into a bowl. In a cupboard she found an old sheet that had been cut up to make dusters, and she grabbed several of them, hurrying back outside. A few moments later, Bessie emerged from the house with a glass of brandy, which she handed to Cordelia. Godfrey seemed to be coming to, and he gulped at the liquor and managed to swallow a little, though some dribbled down his chin. As Cordelia wiped it away, he muttered something, then tried to move, groaning in pain as he did so.

Cordelia raised anxious eyes to Bessie. 'We can't find Sam. Do you know where he might be?'

'Lawks, miss, I'm not his keeper!' Bessie's tone was indignant, hiding the fact that she knew very well where Sam was.

'Damn the boy!' Godfrey grunted. He still sounded groggy, but at least now he appearing to be regaining his senses. 'Where is he?'

'We don't know, Godfrey. We thought he was with you,' Cordelia said.

'What? No! Why would he be?'

'Well, wherever he is, you can't remain out here.' Cordelia, too, was beginning to revert to her usual air of authority. 'We have to get you inside.'

'Dammit, woman, I've broken my blasted leg!'

'We don't know that, Godfrey. It may just be that you have twisted it badly. Let us get you up. We'll support you. Try not to put any weight on it, but we need you to help yourself.' Cordelia wound her arm through his and round his back to encircle his waist. 'Cecile – take his other side.'

Lise did as she was bid. Though she was slightly built, she was far stronger than she looked, and slowly, painfully, they managed to reach the house, Bessie following. It was clear that Godfrey would be unable to climb the stairs, so they supported him into his study, where he collapsed with a groan on to a chaise that flanked the wall.

The effort had started his head bleeding again; Bessie pressed a rolled cloth tightly against the wound while Cordelia fed him a few more sips of brandy, and at last he lay quietly, eyes closed.

'We can do no more tonight,' Cordelia said. 'I'll remain here with him; you two may as well go to bed.'

'Very good, miss.' Bessie was quick to agree, but Lise hesitated. She couldn't believe how responsible she suddenly felt for her father, who now seemed less of a monster and more an old man with human faults and frailties.

'Go to bed, Cecile,' Cordelia said firmly. 'You've done well, and we may need your help on the morrow.'

With one last look at her father, Lise left the room.

By the time Lise came downstairs the following morning, the gardener's boy had arrived for work and been sent to fetch the doctor. Godfrey, raised on pillows, had drunk his tea and, with Cordelia's help, managed a little milky porridge, and Cordelia herself was in the breakfast room, picking at a plate of fresh fruit topped with thick cream.

'How is Papa?' Lise asked anxiously.

'Go and see for yourself.' Cordelia speared a segment of apple with the point of her knife. 'He passed a restless night, but he is well enough to ask for you – and to fret over the missing cargo. He's still saying he intends to go to France the moment he can stand, though in my opinion that is unlikely to be for some time. But we'll know more when Dr Meek has attended.'

'I'll go and wish him good morning.'

As Lise entered the study, Godfrey managed a pained smile, and held out his arms to her.

'Cecile, my dearest one! Come and give your poor wounded father a loving kiss.'

Something within Lise recoiled; the compassion she had felt last night had vanished with the light of day. Her father he might be, but he was still a stranger to her, a stranger she believed to be an evil man. But she was in no doubt as to how Cecile would respond, and she had no choice but to do the same.

She crossed to Godfrey, took his outstretched hands and kissed him on the cheek, wincing inwardly when he pulled her into an embrace, and enormously relieved when he stiffened suddenly, groaning, and released her. Then he reached for her hands again, this time holding her at arm's length.

'It is so good to see you, my dearest daughter. I feared last night that I was done for and would never see you again.'

'I was with you, Papa. Have you forgotten?'

'My love, I thought it was but a dream. The dream I so often have of your dear mama. Oh, Cecile, you grow more like her with every passing day.'

'Really, Papa?'

'You could be she reincarnated.'

A shiver ran down Lise's spine, but before she could reply the door opened and Cordelia entered along with a short, tubby man who carried a medical bag.

'Well, well, Godfrey! What ails you, my friend?' he asked heartily. 'Let's have a look at you and see what the damage is.'

Cordelia nodded abruptly in Lise's direction, dismissing her, and with some relief she left her aunt, her father and the doctor to their consultation.

Lise was feeding Moll titbits from the breakfast table when she heard voices in the passage, followed by the sound of the front door being opened and then closed. The doctor had gone, then. After seeing him out, Cordelia returned to the study, but she must have left the door open, because now Lise was able to make out the conversation.

'You heard what Dr Meek said. You must not even attempt to put any weight on your leg for a matter of weeks, if not months, or you could be crippled for life. There is not the faintest possibility of you voyaging to France for some time to come.' Cordelia's tone was strident as always.

'Then you must go for me.' Godfrey spoke just as loudly. 'You have always been more than capable in managing the Frogs, and you'll do it again. Take Dyfan Flinders with you – he can take care of any trouble. Or, on reflection, Zach Carver. It's high time he became acquainted with the business on the other side of La Manche. And I have no doubt he is handy enough with his fists if the need arises. Yes, have Carver accompany you. And if that miserable crook of a contact proves difficult, Flinders can go later and teach him a lesson he won't easily forget.'

Lise froze, still clutching the chunk of ham, and Moll leapt and snatched at it, her sharp little teeth catching Lise's fingers. But she scarcely noticed the pain, so shocked was she by what she had overheard.

It wasn't that she was concerned about Cordelia going to

France; she thought her father, poorly as he was, was less likely to become suspicious of her than his sister. No, it was that Zach would be going too. He had warned Lise he might not be around to help her if she ran into trouble, but she hadn't anticipated the breadth of the English Channel between them! And supposing she located the evidence he sought? What was she to do about it?

Never in her life had she felt more alone than she did in that moment.

Chapter Twenty

Annie was sitting on the wall outside her cottage gutting fish when Billie, who had passed her a few minutes earlier on his way home, came rushing out again and approached her.

'Ma says Lise didn't come home last night,' he burst out. 'Where is she?'

Annie looked up, and he saw the anxiety in her faded eyes.

'I don't know,' she said, but instinct told him she wasn't speaking the truth. Annie was as transparent as the day was long.

'Don't lie to me, Annie,' he said abruptly. 'Where is she?'

Annie dropped the fish and her knife into the bucket beside her and wiped her hands on her apron. 'I can't tell you, Billie,' she said pleadingly. 'I can't tell anyone. Her life may depend on it.'

Billie's jaw dropped. 'What are you talking about?'

Annie simply shook her head, and he went on: 'It's that Zach Carver, isn't it? Our Aaron said he's mixed up with the smugglers. What has he got her into?'

'Not smuggling,' Annie protested.

'Then what? He's trouble, I know it.'

Annie's eyes filled with tears, a sight so unusual it shocked Billie all over again.

'I'd tell you if I could, Billie, and that's a fact. But I'm sworn to secrecy.'

'I'd do nothing to harm her, you know that!' Billie said, his voice rising as anxiety shattered his patience. 'For God's sake, Annie!'

Annie leaned across and touched his arm. 'Oh, I do know. I knows how you care fer her, and right now she could do with a man she can trust to look out for her. But there be nothing you can do. They'm dangerous men she's tangling with, and likely armed. You wouldn't stand a cat's chance in hell if you crossed them. You'd end up down the bottom of a mine shaft, I shouldn't wonder.'

'I'm not afraid of them,' Billie said through gritted teeth.

'Then you should be. And not just for yerself. If you go blundering in and give the game away, it won't be just you down that mine shaft, it'll be Lise as well. She's safe enough just as long as she don't get caught out.'

'You be talking in riddles!' Billie said, exasperated.

'An' that's the way it's got to be till she's done what she has to, and is away from that place. I can't say more.' She gave him a warning glance. 'And not a word to your Aaron, either. He might be your brother, but the company 'e keeps . . .'

'You saying Aaron's mixed up in this?' Billie demanded.

'No, I'm not sayin' that. But he can't be blabbin'. I mean it, Billie. If anything should happen to that girl . . . Now, get on wi' you. It's best not Aaron nor nobody else sees you talkin' to me fer too long. Go on!' She shooed him away as if he was a gull after her fish.

Billie went, puzzled and desperately concerned. He wouldn't say anything to Aaron, or even his mother for that matter. But Gussie had already noticed Lise's absence, and Aaron would be sure to as well. And there was not a thing he could do about that.

* * *

Lise had passed the morning visiting Lady to take the horse her expected carrot, and playing with Moll, though her mind was on neither. She had also spent an hour sitting dutifully at her father's side. He seemed only vaguely aware of her presence, and she guessed the doctor had given him some medication to ease his pain, which was also making him drowsy. This was all to the good; he was unlikely to notice anything that didn't ring true in her impersonation of Cecile, and if the doctor continued to dose him up, it would make it easier for her to begin her search once Cordelia had left for France.

She had seen little of her aunt, almost as little as the previous day, for Cordelia was busy with preparations for her trip. Lise supposed Zach would be doing the same – Dicken, the gardener's boy, had been sent with a message for him – and thinking of it made her stomach clench uncomfortably, while the feeling of isolation washed over her again. Why, oh why, had Zach been chosen to accompany Cordelia rather than the man who was, from what she had overheard, a thug of some kind? Surely it would have been easier to take this man in the first place, rather than send him later if things turned awkward? It made no sense. But with Zach on the other side of the Channel, Lise would be left totally alone and friendless.

Was this what her mother had felt before she had made her desperate break for freedom – the break for freedom that had resulted in disaster? Yet she had returned, risking everything, in order to find Cecile. And that too had ended badly. Had she been imprisoned here until her death? How alone she would have felt then, how friendless.

Suddenly Lise knew what she wanted, more than anything, to do. She would visit her mother's grave and take flowers to show she was not forgotten, and was loved dearly. Perhaps

Mama would know somehow that she was there and send her some token of comfort; give her the courage she felt she was lacking. Besides, it might be her last chance to visit her mother's resting place. Making up her mind, she went in search of Cordelia, whom she found in Godfrey's study, leafing through paperwork, extracting some sheets and placing them in a binder.

'I'm going to the churchyard to place flowers on Mama's grave,' she said, feeling sure Cecile would not need to ask permission.

Cordelia's lips tightened into a hard line, and Lise remembered Cecile mentioning that their aunt did not approve of her continuing devotion to her dead mother. 'I don't think there was much love lost between them,' she had said, and Lise could tell from her aunt's reaction that it was not far from the truth.

'Don't be too long about it,' she said sharply. 'Luncheon will be in less than an hour, and Cook is preparing a fish pie and a soufflé; she will not be best pleased if it is left to spoil.'

Remembering the incident with the fish bone, Lise couldn't help thinking Cordelia hadn't much cared for the cook's feelings then. But she was coming to realise her aunt was a law unto herself.

'I'll be back,' she promised.

Lise cut some yellow roses from a bush in the garden. Following the directions she had memorised, she was able to find the churchyard without difficulty. It was a pleasant walk, and she found herself enjoying the views of the rugged coastline, so unlike the gentle harbour of St Ives. The churchyard was peaceful, sunlight filtering through the branches of the trees that bordered it, and with well-kept open spaces between neat rows of graves. Some were recent enough for their occupants to still have family to mourn them, judging by the fresh flowers, some in stone vases, some in glass jars, that adorned them. Others were clearly much older, their headstones listing and weeds growing up between the sparse gravel that covered the bare earth. One, a huge box-like edifice, was crumbling, and so green with lichen and moss it was impossible to decipher the inscription.

She took the winding path towards the little church, and there, in the shadow of the tower, she found Marguerite's grave, just as Cecile had said she would. For a moment she simply stood there; then she sank to her knees on the soft grass that surrounded the grave. Cecile had kept it well tended, and some fading blooms in a vase beneath the headstone showed she had visited very recently. Lise removed them, wishing she had thought to bring fresh water, and hoping there was enough left in the vase to sustain her roses.

When she was done, she sat back on her heels.

'For you, Mama,' she said softly. 'Do you recognise me? I am Lise, not Cecile. But I remember you so well, and I have never stopped loving you and missing you. Now there is something I have to do, and I will do it, however afraid I may be. Please, Mama, will you help me?'

She held her breath, waiting. A breeze rustled the leaves of the trees, a blackbird called, a couple of gulls mewed overhead. Otherwise the quiet was undisturbed, the silence complete. What had she expected? A white feather fluttering down? A butterfly alighting on her face or hand? Mama's voice speaking inside her head? Or just to feel a lightening of the load around her heart? A sense of peace?

But there was nothing. She saw nothing, heard nothing, felt nothing. It was as if Mama was never here, never had been.

Tears pricked Lise's eyes. Stupid, stupid, stupid. Mama was

dead, and that was an end to it. She leaned forward once more to straighten one of the roses that had fallen askew. A thorn pricked her finger, drawing a bright drop of blood, and as she raised it to her lips to suck it away she thought: is this the sign that I sought? If so, it can mean only one thing. Bloodshed.

She shivered, her skin crawling with gooseflesh, then a voice spoke behind her.

'Lise?'

Her heart leapt, and she spun round, disbelieving.

'Zach!'

He was here, just when she needed him most.

'What are you doing here?' she asked.

He reached out his hand, pulling her to her feet and into his arms. The scent of him was in her nostrils, a scent that was totally masculine, not overlaid with the odour of a powdered wig; and the taste of him, soap and salt, was on her lips. At last she raised her head, looking into his face and loving everything about it: the strong jaw and cheekbones, the generous mouth, the little lines etched by the sun and the wind into the skin around his mouth and eyes.

'How did you find me?' she asked.

'I went to Polruan to finalise arrangements for tomorrow – you do know I have to go to France tomorrow? – and Cordelia told me you were visiting your mother's grave.'

'Oh.' Lise was faintly surprised. Had he asked where she was – where *Cecile* was? She'd thought they were supposed to be acquaintances, not friends. Or had Cordelia volunteered the information – and if so, why? A worm of unease stirred in her stomach, but before she could ask, Zach's mouth was on hers, kissing her until she was breathless and could think of nothing but his nearness.

'I couldn't leave without seeing you,' he said when he finally released her. 'Finalising arrangements with Cordelia was simply an excuse.'

'Oh, Zach . . .'

His eyes met hers, holding them. 'I have serious concerns for your safety, Lise. As I told you, I don't want you putting yourself at risk this way. This would be the perfect opportunity for you to leave Polruan and go home. Sam and Cecile should be safely away by now, and with Cordelia out of the country and Godfrey incapacitated your absence would be unlikely to be reported for another few days at least, which would give them even more time to put a good distance between themselves and your father's empire. Please, as soon as we sail for France, take Lady and return to St Ives.'

She tore her eyes from his. 'I can't do that, Zach. Not when we are so close. We must do all we can to stop this evil that has brought tragedy to both our families, and many others beside. This may be an opportunity for escape, but it is also an opportunity better than we dared hope for me to search the house for the evidence you seek. I can't let it slip through my fingers.'

He was silent for a long moment, then he nodded, resigned to the fact that she was not going to change her mind. He took her hands in his. 'If there's nothing I can say to dissuade you, then so be it,' he said. 'Just make me one promise – that if you do discover what we seek, tell no one, do nothing until my return. Then, when you are safely far away from here, I will make my move.'

'That's an easy promise to make,' she said with a smile. 'Who would I tell? I trust no one but you. And any trophy from a ship would most likely be too weighty for me to lift, let alone secrete out of the house.'

'That's true enough,' he conceded. 'But for the love of God

235

take care, Lise. Do nothing to arouse suspicion. I love you. I can't lose you now.'

Her heart felt as if it were a candle melting as it was consumed by the flame. 'And I love you. You must stay safe too. You are in more danger than I, I think, in a strange land surrounded by evil people.'

He grinned at her crookedly. 'I'll do my best. And now I must leave you. We can't risk being seen together.'

'I should be going back too,' Lise said regretfully. 'Aunt warned me not to be late for lunch.'

Zach took her in his arms once more, his kiss gentle and loving, a promise of things to come. The churchyard was quiet and still, but for a bird swooping up suddenly from the branches of a tree as if startled. Lise watched Zach walk away, then turned once more to her mother's gravestone.

'I hope I am luckier in love than you were, Mama,' she said softly. 'And God willing I shall live my life as best I can for you.'

Then she too left the churchyard, and made her way back to Polruan House.

Cecile was feeling unwell.

She and Sam had left the farmhouse soon after they had eaten a hearty breakfast of home-cured ham, eggs, and crusty bread hot from the oven, with the good wishes of Zach's parents ringing in their ears and the pannier bag stuffed with a stone bottle full of water and enough food to last them for the day at least, and possibly longer.

'How can we ever thank you?' Sam had said, and in reply Zach's mother had hugged Cecile.

'By taking care of this little one,' she had said. 'And by finding the happiness you so richly deserve.'

It was a hot summer's day, and as they journeyed north-east the sun beat down on them mercilessly. Here, inland, there was no cooling sea breeze to offset it, and by the time it was at its noonday height, Cecile was beginning to feel both sick and a little dizzy.

'Dare we stop for a little while?' she asked.

'When we find some shade,' Sam replied. 'Zeus needs to rest, too. You're light as a feather, I grant you, but it's still an extra load for him to bear, and in this heat . . .' His voice tailed away.

All around them the moors stretched bare and daunting, the only trees twisted and stunted, and not a building of any kind as far as the eye could see. Sam had kept well away from the road, but now he thought he would do well to return to it in the hope of coming across a hamlet, an isolated farmhouse with outbuildings where they could shelter from the pitiless glare of the sun, or even a coaching inn. Though there was always the risk that it might be one of the stopping-off points for Pendinnick's booty on its way north, it was far enough from Porthmeor for there to be any likelihood of Cecile being recognised, especially dressed as she was in Lise's clothing, and with her hair loose. In any case, as long as their change of identity had not been rumbled, no one would yet be looking for her.

Sure enough, eventually he spotted a hostelry at the roadside some way ahead. On reaching it he pulled in, dismounted, and helped Cecile down. As her feet touched the ground, she swayed, and Sam had to support her to keep her from falling. Her cheeks, nose and chin were scorched by the sun, but he could see that beneath it she was deathly pale. Worried, he helped her inside, called for a jar of water for her and ale for himself, and left her sitting on a wooden settle while he went back to attend to Zeus.

By the time he returned, she seemed to have recovered herself a little, and he sat beside her, drinking his ale and watching her anxiously.

'I'm sorry,' she said.

'You've nothing to apologise for! It's my fault for riding so far, and in that heat. I should have found somewhere for you to rest before now.'

'There was nowhere. You had no choice,' she reassured him.

'We'll tarry here until it's cooler.' He finished his ale and indicated her mug. 'Would you like more water, or perhaps a cider? And what about something to eat?'

'Water, please. But I don't think I could manage food, and in any case, we have plenty in the pannier.'

'True.' He headed for the bar.

The innkeeper was a swarthy man with bulging muscles, his face almost hidden by bushy black whiskers and an untidy beard.

'Would you object if we brought in our own food?' Sam asked as the man replenished their mugs.

He shrugged his big shoulders. 'Do as you like.'

'Thanks.' But Sam didn't like the way the man was shooting suspicious looks at him from beneath the thick eyebrows that almost met across the bridge of his nose.

'Where be you headed?' he asked as he took payment.

Sam thought quickly. 'Launceston. To visit our cousins.'

'An' where do ee come from?'

'Helston.'

Feeling distinctly uncomfortable, Sam returned to Cecile. The innkeeper's eyes rested on her speculatively.

'I'll fetch the food, seeing as how I've asked if I could, but I think it would be best to be on our way as soon as you're feeling better. That one asks too many questions for my liking.'

Cecile's eyes filled with alarm. 'You think he knows who I am?'

'No, but if your father's men come looking for us, he'll give us away in a flash if there's a reward for information.'

Cecile shuddered at the thought of riding on under the merciless sun, but she was even more frightened by the thought of being found. 'We must go.'

'Are you sure?'

'Yes!' She managed a weak smile. 'I'm stronger than I look.'

'I hope so.'

But Sam was beginning to doubt the wisdom of this whole exercise. Cecile was clearly not well; more hours in the saddle could only make her worse, and he had no idea where or when they would find a safe haven where she could recover. But returning now to Polruan across the desolate, sun-baked moor was out of the question. He could only pray that they would come across safe refuge before too long.

Chapter Twenty-One

By the time Lise rose next morning, Cordelia had already left for France, and though Lise had seen little of her in the previous two days, the house felt curiously empty without her powerful presence. But it was as nothing compared to the void that had been created by knowing that Zach, too, would be far away by now, and her fears for his safety. He might be concerned for her, but she thought he was in far greater danger. With her father confined to bed, she couldn't believe he posed any great threat, while Zach might face real peril when he and Cordelia confronted the man who had cheated Godfrey. He was undoubtedly a rogue, and would certainly have cronies and henchmen at his beck and call. Lise suppressed a shudder as she pictured Zach lying beaten and bloodied in some French alley, set upon by violent men. In a fair fight he would be able to take care of himself, she knew, but it would be a different story if he was heavily outnumbered.

She gave herself a little shake. Worrying about Zach would do no good and would distract her from her own role in this pantomime.

She looked in on her father, who was still sleeping, ate breakfast alone, wondering how Cecile and Sam were faring, visited Lady with the carrot she would be expecting, and looked in again on her father. He was awake now, but strangely confused.

'Marguerite,' he said, holding out his hands to her.

Lise dropped a kiss on his cheek, but managed to avoid being drawn into a hug. 'It's Cecile, Papa,' she said patiently. 'Marguerite has been dead for many years.'

'Oh yes. Cecile. Of course, my love.' But he both looked and sounded vacant, and she couldn't help wondering exactly what the potion the doctor had prescribed was, or if Cordelia had for some reason deliberately administered more than the proper dose.

'Would you like some breakfast?' she asked.

'Breakfast? At this time of day?'

'It's morning, Papa.'

'Really? I thought . . . And where is Cordelia? She always breakfasts with me.'

'Cordelia has gone to France to recover your losses,' Lise reminded him. 'Had you forgotten?'

'No, no, of course not!' he responded irritably. 'I hope she teaches that rogue a lesson he won't forget.' Then, after this brief moment of lucidity, he seemed to relapse again. 'Find your aunt. Have her come to me. I'm hungry and thirsty, and so will she be.'

Shaking her head, Lise went in search of Bessie. 'Papa's awake, and says he's hungry. But he is behaving very strangely, and talking nonsense.'

'Hmm.' Bessie snorted. 'Lucky fer you, I dare say.'

Lise knew what she meant – that it was less likely he would notice any slips she made if he was woozy. She was also feeling strangely responsible for him again. 'I'll take him his tea and sit with him while he drinks it to ensure he doesn't spill it on himself,' she said.

Bessie nodded approvingly. 'Ye're a good girl.'

She poured tea from a pot Cook had left sitting on the table, and Lise returned to her father's study, where she raised him on his pillow before placing the mug in his hand.

'Careful now, Papa,' she cautioned, steadying it as he held it shakily and looking round the study for anything that might be a trophy from one of the ships his gang were responsible for wrecking. She didn't really expect there would be. He wasn't likely to display such a thing here, where he saw colleagues and employees – and if he did, Zach would have seen it when he visited to take his instructions. There were numerous drawers in his desk, of course, which he probably kept locked, but she could hardly investigate now, and even if she did, and found something, it would only be some small item, the provenance of which was not likely to be easily identifiable. No, as Zach had suggested, it was something much larger she must search for – a figurehead, perhaps, from the prow, or a ship's bell inscribed with its name – and she must begin today. Time was short, and she would never have a better chance.

There was a tap on the door, and Bessie came in with a tray – coddled eggs and muffins.

''Ere you be, sir. Now, make a good breakfast. You got to keep yer strength up.'

Godfrey frowned, raking her face with puzzled eyes. 'Who are you?' he demanded.

'Why, sir, I'm Bessie. You'da know that.'

'Bessie?' he repeated, bemused. 'It can't be. Bessie is just a girl. You are old!'

Bessie glanced at Lise, raising her eyebrows. 'Older!' she corrected him tartly. 'As we all be, if I may make s'bold. I'll bring y'a looking glass so you can see yourself if you don't believe me.'

'You're confused, Papa,' Lise said gently. 'You thought I was Mama, didn't you?'

Godfrey snorted. 'If you say so.'

'Now, are you going to try some breakfast? You said you were hungry.'

With another look at Lise and a shake of her head, Bessie left the study. Lise placed the tray on her father's lap and began helping him to the egg and muffin.

Cordelia stood at the prow of the vessel taking her to France, watching the waves breaking over the bows, tasting the salt wind and feeling the sting of spray on her cheeks. She remembered the glory days when Godfrey had been a sea captain and she had accompanied him on his voyages, standing just where she stood now. How happy she had been then! How she had loved the freedom of the boy's clothes she had worn, the breeches and boots, and her hair tied in a pigtail – no heavy wig then! And how she had relished the feeling of being mistress of all she surveyed, not least Godfrey's heart.

What would Zach Carver think if she could turn back the clock and have him see her as she had been then? Would he be shocked? Or excited, as Godfrey had been?

She turned to look at Carver, standing by the rail watching out, as she was, for the first glimpse of the French coast, and lust stirred deep inside her. He was a fine figure of a man and no mistake. He was not Godfrey, of course, but oh, it had been so long . . . Her gaze moved lasciviously over him, taking in the strong lines of his face, his windswept hair, a thick, rich brown, his broad shoulders, his narrow hips in their tight breeches, the muscles that rippled in his arms as he shaded his eyes the better to catch his first glimpse of land.

She sighed. What an old fool she was to think he might look

twice at a woman of her age! No amount of rouge, no silk or paper beauty spot, could hide the blemishes and wrinkles that marred what had once been a fine complexion. No corset could quite conceal the thickening of her waist, nor uplift her sagging breasts.

But no matter. A small satisfied smile lifted the corners of Cordelia's painted lips. One day, very soon, everything would be as it used to be. One day, very soon, she would be the sole mistress of Polruan House again.

And of Godfrey's heart.

'Try to eat something, my love. For me,' Sam pleaded, offering Cecile what remained of the food Zach's parents had packed for them, but even as he said it, he knew it was no use.

After fleeing the coaching inn, they had eventually found shelter in an abandoned shepherd's hut, and Sam had hoped that a night's rest, however far from comfortable it might be, would see her recover some of her strength. But as they lay close together on his coat, which was serving as a mattress, the heat radiating from her body was as hot as the noonday sun, and her skin felt clammy to the touch. She'd been restless, her breathing rapid and shallow, and she had woken once crying out with a cramp in the muscles of her leg.

He'd been shocked to see by the light of day how pale she was, though her nose and the skin over her cheekbones was scorched and blistering, and she was dizzy when she tried to stand.

The sun yesterday had been too much for her, he thought, castigating himself for having ridden so far for so long when it had been beating down relentlessly, though he didn't know what he could have done differently.

'I couldn't eat anything,' she said now. 'I feel very sick and my head is pounding. But I am really thirsty.'

Sam shook the water bottle. It was almost empty. He passed it to Cecile, who upended it and drank as if her life depended on it.

'I'm sorry!' she wailed as she lowered it again. 'I think it's all gone. What about you?'

'Don't worry about me.' Sam was thirsty too, but Cecile's need was greater than his. 'We must find water soon, though. We can't survive without it.'

'Oh Sam, what are we to do?' Cecile asked, sounding close to tears.

'I'll go and look for a stream and refill the bottle. And Zeus can drink too. You rest here, where it's cool.'

Plainly it would be folly for Cecile to even attempt to go further in her present state.

'Very well,' she agreed, and sank back down on to Sam's coat.

'While I'm about it, I'll see if there's somewhere we can find food and shelter. So don't worry if I'm gone for some time.'

'I won't. I think I need to sleep again.' She already sounded drowsy.

'Do that.' Sam brushed her hair off her clammy forehead and kissed her gently. 'I love you, Cecile. I am so sorry to have brought you to this.'

'Don't say that,' she murmured. 'I wouldn't be anywhere else. And I love you too.'

Sam left the shack and saddled Zeus. Cecile heard the creak of leather as he mounted the horse, and fading hoofbeats on the hard turf that seemed to keep time with the pounding of her head, before she drifted into a deep and dreamless sleep.

* * *

Lise had remained with her father while he finished his breakfast, and then read to him for a little while until he became drowsy.

'Would you like to be left alone for a while, Papa?' she asked when she saw his eyes drooping. 'I won't be far away, and neither will Bessie.' She placed the little silver bell Cordelia had left for him within easy reach. 'Just ring this if you need anything.'

'Yes, my dearest.'

Did he still think she was Marguerite? Lise wondered. Perhaps it wasn't just his leg he'd injured when he fell from his horse. Certainly he'd cut his face. Could he have suffered a serious blow to his head? And what would that mean? Without doubt, his memory was affected and his thought processes disturbed, but he'd seemed lucid enough last night when he'd told Cordelia she would have to go to France in his place.

Lise frowned. She'd heard of people who had died from head injuries, sometimes days later. Annie had once spoken of a sailor who'd been knocked over by a swinging boom. 'When the brain's addled, it can bleed,' she'd said. 'An' that poor man, well, 'twere runnin' out'a his eyes, I'm told.' Lise had been horrified just imagining it, and the memory made her shudder now. But there was no blood running out of Godfrey's eyes, or down his nose, for that matter, though she'd never known anyone to die of a nosebleed. Satisfied, she left him sleeping and determined to begin her search now, while the going was good.

But where to begin? Was it possible Bessie had seen something during her long years of service with the Pendinnicks without realising its significance? She would have to ask in a roundabout way, of course. Make her questions sound like innocent curiosity. Armed with a cup of tea, she went in search of the maid and found her in her room darning stockings.

'Papa's asleep at last,' she said, taking a seat facing Bessie.

'I've left the little bell by his side, so perhaps you could listen out for it. I will too, of course, but if I am outside playing with Moll, I might not hear it.'

'My hearing's not what it used to be,' Bessie said ruefully, and Lise smiled inwardly, thinking that she had certainly heard the commotion the other night. But alerting Bessie was not the main reason she was here.

'Perhaps it would be best if I remained in the house then,' she said.

'Reckon it would. An' I've got a lot of mending to do.' Bessie bit off the cotton with her teeth, put down the stocking and reached for another.

'Papa used to be a sea captain, Cecile said.' Lise was trying to gently steer the conversation in the direction she wanted. 'I think that is very romantic. Did you work for him then?'

Bessie glanced up. 'Not then, no. I was with the squire – his father – back in those days, then when he and Miss Cordelia moved here with Cecile, they needed a nursemaid for her and took me on.'

'Did he regret giving up the sea, do you think? Did he keep mementoes of those days?' Though she kept her tone light and conversational, Lise was watching Bessie closely, and was disappointed when the old woman shook her head.

'I really couldn't say. I've never seen anything like that. But then I don't suppose I would. I've no call to go into his rooms. Keeping them clean and tidy is the maid's job, not mine.'

'Of course. How silly of me!' Lise said quickly, afraid she might have caused offence.

But Bessie's thoughts had taken off in a different direction. 'I wonder if Miss Cordelia and Mr Carver have reached France yet?'

Lise's heart twisted at the mention of Zach's name, and

anxiety for his safety along with an ache of longing twisted deep inside her once more. Oh, if only he were here! If only she didn't feel so alone!

She thought suddenly of the locket Cecile had given her. Afraid that Cordelia would notice if she had been wearing it, she had hidden it in a drawer in the bedroom that held Cecile's undergarments. Now, however, she thought it would be safe to fasten it around her neck. Perhaps it would somehow aid her in her search. She hadn't felt her mother's presence when she visited the grave, but maybe she would find some connection through the locket.

'I must leave you in peace,' she said to Bessie.

'You don't have to,' Bessie said, but Lise rose anyway.

'I'm sure you can work faster without my chatter,' she said.

In her room – Cecile's room – she retrieved the locket. Then, gathering her determination, she headed for what she considered the most obvious place to start her search: Godfrey's bedroom.

Having grown used to the grandeur of Cecile's room, it was no surprise to her that Godfrey's was every bit as luxurious. The bed was similar in design, but the drapes and curtains were a rich ruby red, and the dressing table was larger, and topped with a triptych mirror. It had three drawers on either side of a central cubbyhole, each of which Lise slid open, but as she had suspected, they contained nothing of interest. She had a faint hope that something might be concealed within the big wardrobe, but it appeared only to contain Godfrey's coats, breeches and boots. She knelt down to lift the ruby flounces that reached the floor on three sides of the bed, and peered beneath, but there was nothing to be seen there but an ornately decorated china chamber pot. Only one possible hiding place remained – a wooden panel that had been let into a recess in the wall and hid what must be a cupboard or maybe even a priest hole. But it refused to open, and the only key she could find didn't appear to fit. Either there was another key hidden somewhere, or the cupboard hadn't been in use for a very long time; in any case, it didn't look big enough to house the kind of trophy Zach hoped to find.

Lise went next to what she now knew to be Cordelia's bedroom, with similar lack of success. A narrow staircase in the centre of the landing led up to what she imagined must be the servants' quarters – almost certainly Godfrey wouldn't conceal anything of note there. Instead, she went back downstairs, where she investigated various chests and armoires that seemed to occupy every likely corner of the rambling passages, but again found nothing.

This was turning into a fool's errand, she thought, disappointed. There was nowhere else she could look, and if Zach had already searched the outbuildings where the contraband was sometimes stored, then it seemed likely there was nothing to find.

Suddenly it occurred to her that she hadn't seen Moll for some time; until now, the little dog seemed to have been at her heels practically the whole time. 'Moll?' she called, but there was no response, no clatter of paws, no snuffling nose. Lise looked around anxiously and noticed that the side door was open. Someone must have gone out or come in and neglected to close it properly. She didn't like the thought of Moll being outside unsupervised. The gardens lay too close to the cliff edge for comfort, and if the dog should lose her footing and fall . . . It didn't bear thinking about.

Her quest forgotten for the moment, Lise hurried out, again calling for the little dog. She hurried down the path towards the lawns, panic rising in her throat like gall. And there, to her enormous relief, she spotted Moll lying on the grass, chewing on

249

an enormous marrow bone that she was holding between her paws.

'There you are!' she cried. 'I thought I'd lost you!'

Moll looked up, guilty at having been caught with her prize, and Lise took her by the collar. 'Come on. You're coming inside. And no, you can't bring that with you.'

Bent double, she dragged a reluctant Moll to the side door. As she leaned forward to push it open, something caught her eye.

A door, low in the wall, beside the step. She hadn't noticed it before; now she felt a twist of excitement in her gut. A cellar! It probably reached all the way beneath the house, and maybe there was even a passageway that led down to the cove. It would be a perfect hiding place for a large artefact.

Lise was just about to shut Moll inside the house so that she could investigate when she heard the distinctive tinkle of the bell she had left for her father to ring if he needed anything. She swore, something she almost never did; a word she had heard the Moxey boys use when they were annoyed about something. She would have to go to Godfrey. For now, this further search would have to wait.

Chapter Twenty-Two

'I think I have found a place we can seek refuge.'

It was early evening, and Sam had just returned from another expedition to check the area around the shack where Cecile had been resting all day. His first absence had been short; he had found a stream without too much difficulty, allowed Zeus to drink and scooped up enough to quench his own thirst with his cupped hands, then managed to fill the water bottle. It wasn't easy; the recent hot sunshine had reduced the stream to little more than a trickle. He had then gone straight back to take the water to Cecile, who was, he knew, in desperate need. When she had almost emptied the bottle, he had gone back for more, and eventually, as the day wore on, she began to recover a little, though she was still weak.

He had waited until late afternoon to venture out again. Storm clouds had begun to gather; he hoped they would bring welcome rain and usher in a cooler day tomorrow.

And then he had seen the rough stone building in a fold of the moors. He ventured closer. Was it another inn? But it was well off the beaten track, and when he neared it, he came upon a little shrine containing an image of the Virgin Mary and a weathered wooden sign. The building was a nunnery.

Sam was staggered to find a religious community living out

here, so far from civilisation. Were they a closed order? A bell hung at the entrance and, tempted though he was to ring it and seek food, he decided not to disturb the nuns tonight when they might well be at Vespers. Better to return tomorrow with Cecile if she was well enough to make the journey.

'They won't turn us away, surely,' he said now. 'They will be good people, who will help us.'

Cecile clasped her hands together, and closed her eyes as if in prayer. 'Thank God.'

'And who knows?' Sam went on. 'There may be a priest there.'

'A priest?' Cecile hadn't known Sam was religious.

He covered her clasped hands with his own and looked into her eyes, a small smile playing around his mouth. 'To marry us,' he said softly. 'That is what we want, is it not?'

'Oh, Sam!' Tears filled Cecile's eyes, tears now of happiness. 'That would be the most wonderful thing!'

'And no one would be able to tear us apart again. Ever.'

What had turned into a nightmare was now a dream again. A dream that had once seemed impossible but that was now almost within reach.

Lise was feeling frustrated. All afternoon and evening Godfrey had been exceptionally demanding, refusing to let her leave his side. She had had no opportunity to explore the cellar, and by the time Bessie bustled in and announced firmly that he must rest, dusk had fallen and Lise knew it would be far too dark to do so tonight.

'Have you had your medication, sir?' Bessie picked up the bottle and spoon from where they lay on a side table, and it occurred to Lise that as far as she knew, he hadn't had any all day.

'I don't want the stuff,' he said grumpily. 'It makes me dozy.'

'But it'll ensure you have a pain-free night,' Lise said, and took the bottle from Bessie. 'I'll see he takes it, don't worry.'

'Very well, miss. I'll leave you to it. And then you'd best be away to your bed too.'

As she approached her father, Lise wondered if she dared give him a double dose as she suspected Cordelia had done. If he hadn't had what he had been prescribed during the day, it couldn't hurt, surely? But she couldn't bring herself to do it. Who knew what the result of an overdose might be? Though she was determined to get justice for all those whose lives he had destroyed, she didn't want him dead. Far better that he was forced to face the consequences of his evil actions.

'Open your mouth for me now, Papa,' she instructed.

Godfrey's fleshy lips remained resolutely closed, but there was a wicked glint in his eye as he looked up at her. 'Make me, my sweetest.'

Squirming inwardly, Lise parted them a little, but before she could slip the spoon inside, they closed over her fingers, sucking on them. All the while his eyes never left her face.

Lise jerked away, sickened, and the spoonful of medication spilled on to the rug that lay over him. Somehow she managed to regain some semblance of control.

'Papa, you are very naughty! Now see what you have made me do.'

He only smiled at her, that lascivious smile that turned her stomach. 'Try again, my dearest. You enjoyed it, didn't you?'

'I did not. And if you try it again, I shall call Bessie to come and help me. Or Agnes.' Agnes was the kitchen maid, a big-boned, gawky girl with uneven yellow teeth, a bad squint and a faceful of angry spots. Godfrey wouldn't try that trick with her, Lise knew.

'Very well, my dearest.'

This time as she put the spoon to his lips he opened them obediently and she was able to trickle the syrupy liquid into his mouth. But all the while his eyes were on her face, favouring her with a knowing look.

Lise made up her mind. She would take her chance and give him just a bit extra. She couldn't bear to endure any more of his suggestive behaviour. Was this what Cecile had to put up with? she wondered. Or had the blow to his head awakened some perverted desire, as well as confusing him?

'Have just a little more, Papa,' she urged, pouring half a spoonful. Again he took it, then reached for her hands, pulling her towards him. Lise just managed to turn her head in time to avoid his lips meeting hers; the kiss landed on her cheek, and she pulled away, forcing a smile.

'Good night, Papa. Sleep well,' she said, and escaped to her room.

Sam woke early the next morning, hungry and stiff from another night on the hard ground. He propped himself up on one elbow to look at Cecile, who was still sleeping beside him, and gently brushed her hair away from her forehead. Her skin felt cool now and he knew she'd had a much better night. Not even the relentless patter of rain on the roof of the shack had disturbed her. Relief coursed through him. There had been a time yesterday when he'd thought he was going to lose her.

He got up carefully so as not to wake her, and went to the door of the shack. The rain had stopped now, but the moist air was full of the fresh scent of it. He breathed in deeply, letting it fill his lungs and clear his head. He was in hopes that Cecile would be well enough to resume their journey today; if not, he would ride back to the nunnery and beg food and water.

'Sam? Sam – where are you?' Cecile's voice, panicked, called from inside the shack.

'Here, my lovely. You didn't think I'd run off and left you, did you?'

'I don't know . . . For a minute . . .'

'How are you feeling?' he asked.

'Better, I think. My head isn't aching so. But I do feel . . .' She covered her mouth with her hand to suppress the nausea that was stirring in her stomach.

'I expect you are just hungry. I know I am. Do you think you'll be able to ride with me to the nunnery once you have had the chance to wake up properly?'

She nodded. 'I will have to. We can't stay here for ever, can we?'

'No, we cannot. There is no sun to speak of as yet. I believe we could make it before the clouds clear and the heat of the day builds. Shall we set out, then?'

Cecile nodded her agreement. She wasn't looking forward to getting back on to Zeus, but it had to be done if, as she had said, they weren't to stay for ever in this shack in the middle of nowhere.

Lise was dreading facing her father again, but she knew that if she was to keep up the pretence of being Cecile, she must. She'd slept badly, tormented by dreams of his fleshy lips trapping her finger that remained with her as a suffocating aura when she woke, and fears that she might have done him some harm by giving him more than just the one spoonful of his medication.

'Is Papa awake?' she asked Bessie when her maid came to help her dress.

'Still sleeping when I looked in on 'im,' Bessie replied, easing one of Cecile's gowns over her shoulders.

Lise heaved a silent sigh of relief. Surely Bessie would have noticed if he had passed away? But she held her breath all the same when she went downstairs and looked in on him herself a few minutes later.

To her immense relief, she saw that Bessie was right. Godfrey was asleep and snoring, his mouth open, his chins quivering in time. Leaving him, she repeated the pattern of the previous day, feeding scraps of ham and cheese to Moll as she breakfasted alone, visiting Lady, and then looking in on her father again. He was awake now, but seemingly in an irritable mood, asking her snappily why she hadn't been by his side when he woke, complaining that his throat was dry – hardly surprising, Lise thought, since he had been sleeping with his mouth open – and uttering curses as he tried to move his leg.

'I'll fetch you some tea, and something to eat, Papa,' she said soothingly, whilst thinking she much preferred his bad temper to his unseemly behaviour towards her.

'Don't be too long about it. A man could die of hunger and thirst,' he snapped.

'You are very impatient, Papa.' Steeling herself, Lise dropped a quick kiss on his cheek and withdrew before he could try to engage her in a hug, or worse.

'And you are unusually sharp with me, Cecile,' he said. 'That tone is very unlike you.'

Annoyed with herself for forgetting Zach's warning that Cecile was meek and mild where she herself was outspoken, Lise set her face in what she hoped was an expression of contrition. 'I'm sorry, Papa. I do not know what came over me to speak to you so.'

He smirked, seemingly satisfied, and Lise went to the kitchen, where Cook was toasting muffins in front of the open fire. She must be more careful, she reminded herself. But not for much longer, perhaps. If she could discover the whereabouts of the trophies Zach sought, then she could make her escape from this house, where the sun never seemed to shine, and rooks cawed in the trees with not a single gull in sight.

When she had helped Godfrey with his breakfast, she fetched the bottle of medication and a spoon.

'You missed your doses yesterday. No wonder your leg is causing you pain. Now, are you going to behave yourself if I give it to you?'

Godfrey shifted position, and groaned. 'I suppose I must.'

'Here you are then.' Lise somehow overcame her revulsion and put the spoon to his lips once more. To her relief, he swallowed the medicine without any of yesterday's game-playing. 'That's much better,' she said. 'Would you like me to read to you?'

'If you wish.'

She took up the book and settled in a chair beside the chaise, willing him to fall asleep soon.

By the time they reached the nunnery, Cecile was feeling ill once again. Sam helped her dismount and sat her down on a tussock of grass with her back to a stone wall whilst he rang the heavy bell at the entrance.

By the light of day he could see that the building had every appearance of a manor house: long and low, with a central section that jutted out from the rest of the house and a turreted attic room at the top. To one side he saw a collection of outbuildings, one of which boasted a large cross over its door – the chapel, perhaps?

He rang the bell again, and a door to the left of the central section opened. A young woman stood there, modestly clad all in pale grey but for the pristine white of her coif and wimple.

'Yes?' she said, curiously but not unkindly.

Overawed suddenly, Sam was struck dumb, uncertain as to how he could explain their situation to a Bride of Christ, as he had heard nuns described. Then inspiration struck.

'My sister is in need of help,' he managed at last, gesturing towards Cecile and hoping she would not give the game away.

'Oh!' The nun hadn't seen Cecile; now her violet eyes widened in horror. 'Oh, the poor young lady! What is wrong?'

'She rode too far and for too long in the hot sun,' Sam said.

The nun frowned, looking up at the overcast grey sky.

'Two days ago,' Sam explained, reading her mind. 'When she became ill, we took shelter in a shack out on the moors.'

'Two days! With no sustenance?'

'We had a little food, and I was able to get some water from a stream. But we have had nothing since.'

'Then we must help you.' The nun opened the door more widely. 'Is she able to stand? Bring her inside and I will fetch Sister Bridget. She will know what to do.'

As the nun disappeared in search of assistance, Sam helped Cecile to her feet and into the dark hallway of the house.

At first Lise hadn't noticed the roughly hewn keyhole in the door to the cellar, but after struggling to open it without success for some minutes, she saw it, and her heart sank.

She had hurried out as soon as the medication had taken effect, waiting only to make sure no one was in the vicinity to see what she was about to do. Now she groaned in frustration. Unless she could find the right key, she would be unable to explore the cellar. But where might it be? She'd seen some hanging on hooks in the kitchen, but they had all looked new and shiny, whereas she guessed the one that fitted this lock would be old and rusty.

Perhaps it was in one of the drawers in her father's desk. Whatever was down there, be it contraband or what she was seeking, he wouldn't want any of the servants having access to it. She went back to the study, where Godfrey was sleeping, thanks to the potion, and opened each drawer in turn, finding paperwork, writing implements, even a brass candle-snuffer, but no key.

His bedroom, then. Her heart was thudding as she opened the door and began her search, but it was just as fruitless. Without much hope of success, she went to Cordelia's room, searching the dressing table and chest of drawers and once again finding nothing. On the point of giving up, she noticed a cream silk reticule lavishly embroidered with gold thread hanging from the handle of one of the wardrobe doors. Hardly the sort of bag Cordelia would take with her if she was going down to the dusty, dirty cellar, but all the same, for some reason Lise felt drawn to it. She slipped her hand inside and was startled when her fingers encountered rough metal. Her heart leapt, and she drew the object out, terrified of disappointment. But lying in the palm of her hand was indeed a key. Whether or not it fitted the cellar door she had yet to find out, but it was certainly a likely candidate.

Suddenly she felt the need to be wearing her mother's locket when she investigated the cellar – she hadn't put it on yet today. As she went along the passage to her room, she saw that the door was ajar. She pushed it open and gasped in surprise. Sitting on the bed, head in hands, was Bessie.

'Bessie?' she said, and the old maid looked up sharply. Her eyes were red and puffy, and she quickly wiped them with the back of her hand.

'Oh, I'm sorry, miss. I shouldn't be here, I know, but . . . I do miss Miss Cecile so, and I feel close to her in her room . . .'

Lise went to the bed and sat down beside Bessie, taking one of her plump, care-worn hands. 'It *is* her room, Bessie, and you have far more right to be here than I.'

Bessie sniffed and wiped her nose on the sleeve of her gown. 'You're a good girl, but for all that, you ain't Miss Cecile. Cared for 'er since she was a little girl, I has, and I can't help but think of 'er as me own.'

'I know.'

'Where d'you reckon she is now? She will be safe and happy, won't she?'

'I'm sure she's far away by now and happier than she's ever been,' Lise consoled the maid. 'Stay here just as long as you like if it helps. I'll leave you in peace.'

She rose and left the room. It didn't seem right to parade the locket in front of Bessie just now. Besides, the key was burning a hole in her pocket, begging to be tried in the cellar door.

She hurried down the stairs and out of the side door. Her hands were trembling so much that it was all she could do to fit the key into the keyhole, and a moment longer before she could bring herself to see if it would turn.

The lock was stiff, but Lise felt sure something in the mechanism had moved slightly. She tried again, wrapping her pinafore round the protruding end of the key to give her a better grip. And . . . yes! It was turning. Metal scraped on metal until, with a final click, it gave. Lise's heart was pounding now as she straightened and pushed at the door. Still it resisted, but she put all her weight behind it, and gradually it scraped over the block of stone it was resting on and opened far enough for her to squeeze through.

She found herself at the top of a flight of stone steps. It was dark, the only light filtering in through a couple of gratings in the wall, and she had to wait a few moments for her eyes to accustom themselves to the gloom before she dared venture carefully down the steps.

The cellar smelled of damp and disuse, the floor rocky and uneven, with what felt like sand beneath her feet in the hollows. It was narrow, with a distinct downward tilt, and Lise suspected she had been right when she had wondered if there was a secret path here leading down to the beach. At one point it widened out and she was able to make out random shapes stored against the rocky walls. Suddenly the breath caught in her throat and she took an involuntary step backwards. A giant head on an arched neck was almost close enough to touch; it seemed to be reaching out as if to bite her.

As her initial fright subsided, it was replaced by curiosity and a jolt of excitement. She reached out and touched the object, tracing its outline with her fingers. It was made of wood, a woman's face surrounded by ringlets and, even in the dim light, she could see they were painted gold.

Her heart came into her mouth with a gigantic leap. A ship's figurehead. Exactly what Zach had said he was seeking. Most likely there would be other trophies here too, but she scarcely needed to look any further. She would lock the cellar again, return the key to where she had found it, and escape, her task completed. When Zach returned from France, she would tell him of her discovery and he would decide on the best course of action to achieve the retribution they both sought.

She felt her way back to the cellar steps and had just started up them when the door above her was thrown fully open and daylight flooded in, almost blinding her. She gasped, and almost lost her footing, but somehow saved herself. Someone was there, at the top of the steps, a dark shape against the grey light of day. She heard a rustle of silk, smelled a perfume she recognised, and panic flooded her veins.

'Ha! Just as I thought! I knew you were up to something.' Cordelia's strident tones echoed around the rock walls of the cellar, and Lise backed away, cornered, as her aunt came down the steps towards her.

Chapter Twenty-Three

'You thought I was still in France, I'll wager. How very unfortunate for you that I returned before you expected me.' There was a smirk in Cordelia's voice.

Lise stood frozen in shock while her thoughts ran in dizzying circles. What explanation could she give for being here? Why had Cordelia come to the cellar? And if she was back in England, did that mean Zach was too?

Before she could find her voice, Cordelia descended the last few steps, holding the lantern high so that it illuminated the ship's figurehead in all its faded glory.

'Ah! So you have found *Ma Belle Jeanne*, I see. No doubt that is what you sought.'

Lise swallowed at the knot of nerves in her throat. 'I don't know what you mean.'

'No? Oh, I rather think you do. But let me refresh your memory. She was taken from the ship that was carrying you, your sister, your mother and her lover after it was wrecked by my men.' She smirked again. 'I have kept it all these years as proof of my success.'

Lise's eyes widened. It was almost beyond belief that this figurehead belonged to the ship that she had seen so often in her disturbing dreams. That when she had stood on the prow with her head buried in her mother's skirts while the wild sea drenched the decks with spray, this very effigy had been right beneath her feet. And then, as Cordelia's words sank in, she felt another jolt of shock.

'*You?*'

'Yes, my dear. Me. Surely you did not think your father would countenance the wrecking of a ship bearing his beloved Marguerite?'

'But she was leaving him . . .'

'Even so. He would have sought her out, dispatched her lover in the most painful way possible, and brought her home. I couldn't allow that. Marguerite stole Godfrey from me. She stole my life. Before he met her, he and I were everything to one another. The floozy destroyed all that. I wanted her gone from our lives for ever.'

The hatred in Cordelia's voice was so venomous Lise could be left in no doubt but that she was speaking the truth.

'But how did you . . . ?' She didn't finish the sentence. A dozen questions were battling inside her head.

'How did I know? I know a lot of things, my dear. I watch, and I listen. I saw her in the gardens with a man I knew must be her lover. I was outside the bedroom door when she was packing your things. I followed her when she took you and your sister down to the harbour. And I was there when you all set sail. It was folly, of course. The storm clouds were already gathering, but I assume they were afraid that if they did not leave, Marguerite would be found and taken back to Godfrey. And so I sent word to my followers and had them make ready the flares and silence the warning bell. I knew the ship would be forced to seek harbour before the night was out.'

Cordelia paused, letting Lise absorb her revelations. 'And now,' she said, 'all that is left is for me to decide what is to be done with you. I think perhaps a spell here in the dark is called for while I think on it.' She dug into the pocket of her gown and drew out the rusty key, waving it tantalisingly at Lise in the light of the lamp.

Lise's eyes widened in horror, and fear, white-hot, rushed through her veins. She had left the key in the lock, never expecting for one moment that she was in danger of being locked in. Surely her aunt couldn't mean to leave her here? But a woman who could do what Cordelia had just confessed to – boasted of – was capable of anything.

'You can't!' she said hoarsely. 'Papa—'

Cordelia laughed shortly. 'He will not miss you. He will sleep soundly all the while, I have made sure of that.'

She turned for the steps. There was no way Lise could reach them first. And if she followed Cordelia up them, her aunt could send her tumbling with a sharp push – she was a big-boned woman, and strong. Somehow she must distract her. Gain time. For the moment, the only thing she could think of was to keep her talking. If Zach had returned too, maybe he was in the house; maybe he would come in search of her and see the open door. It was a desperately slim hope, but it was the only one she had.

'Why would you want to do this, Aunt?' she asked, striving for an even tone. 'What does it matter that I have found where your treasures are hidden? I have no one to tell your secret to – I scarcely leave this house, you know that.'

Cordelia turned back, and in the light of the lamp, Lise could see that she was smiling again, a tight-lipped, triumphant smile.

'Oh, my dear, what a good little actress you are. Really, you have missed your calling. You should have used your talents to join a troupe of travelling entertainers. Do you really think I was taken in by your charade?'

Lise's blood ran cold. 'What do you mean?' she whispered.

'That you are not Cecile, of course. You are the long-lost twin Marguerite left at home in St Ives when she came here to try to take Cecile away with her. Your name is Lise, I believe. Oh, I was taken in at first, I admit. But it didn't take me long to become suspicious, and when I began looking for them, the telltale signs became obvious. The tilt of your head and the flash of your eyes. The way you ran to your father when he fell from his horse – Cecile would never have done that. She is far too timid. She would have called for help and hung back while I tended Godfrey. But I suppose most telling of all were the looks exchanged between you and Carver. Cecile has never looked at him that way, nor he at her. Do you know where Cecile is, by the way? She has run off with that coachman who has gone missing, I suppose. Well, good luck to her. I hope she never returns. With the two of you out of way, I shall have Godfrey to myself once more. Soon everything will be as it once was.'

Again she began to move towards the steps; again Lise searched desperately for something to say that would delay the moment.

'I never knew the name of the ship that was wrecked until you told me just now. Or that you had kept the figurehead. Why would I have been seeking it?'

The ploy worked. Cordelia, it seemed, could not resist the temptation to boast about how clever she had been.

'Because Carver asked you to, of course. I never trusted him, though Godfrey was utterly taken in. I suspected he had some ulterior motive for worming his way in here at Polruan, and made enquiries of my own. I learned that he had a brother, a riding officer, who threatened our business interests and had to be dealt with appropriately. It would have been useless to warn Godfrey without proof – he was so taken with the scoundrel he would simply have rejected out of hand my advice to have Carver disposed of as his brother was. I bided my time, watching his every move, saw him behaving suspiciously, poking around in places he had no business to be, and guessed what he was about. And still I waited, waited for him to provide me with incontrovertible evidence, as I knew he would eventually.

'When I realised you were not Cecile, I suspected that you and he were working together, and it was not long before my suspicions were confirmed. I needed to catch you out in whatever it was you were here to do, and Godfrey's accident gave me the perfect opportunity. I sailed for France, taking Carver with me, but I had the ship bring me back as soon as was practicable, leaving him behind.' Her painted mouth twisted into a sneer. 'Rest assured I have arranged for him to be dealt with as he deserves.'

Lise gasped. 'No! Oh, please, no!'

'I am afraid so. He cannot be allowed to return and cause more trouble. Not even for the sake of young love.' She smiled again, that cruel smirk of satisfaction. 'Oh yes, I saw the two of you together in the churchyard. Carver came here on the pretext of finalising arrangements for our voyage and asked your whereabouts, oh so casually, but I saw through his excuse. And I was right. I followed him, and of course he came straight to you. A most touching scene. You laying flowers on what you believed to be your mother's last resting place, he comforting you. Oh, very touching. But for the fact, of course, that she is not there.'

Lise shook her head, utterly bewildered now as well as afraid. 'What do you mean – she's not there?'

'She had the misfortune to fall down a disused mine shaft. Godfrey was away on business at the time, and I had the grave dug and the funeral held before he came home. Except that all the coffin contained was rocks and pebbles. I told him she had taken ill and died, and he believed me.'

'You killed her! You killed my mother!' Lise gasped.

Cordelia shrugged. 'She stole Godfrey from me. She had to die.' She paused, then her lips twisted into a cruel smile as she continued: 'Ah yes. I think that is what I will do with you. It would be fitting indeed for you to meet the same fate as she did. Gone for ever down a mine shaft. And when Godfrey recovers, I shall tell him the same story. That you – Cecile – died whilst he was incapacitated, and have been buried alongside your mother. He will be sad, of course, but I shall be here to comfort him.

'And now, my dear, I think it is time I left you. I have arrangements to make, and I am sure you would like to be alone to contemplate all you have learned today.'

Without further ado, she turned and climbed the steps. The door scraped over the top one, the key turned in the lock and the cellar was plunged into near darkness. Lise's shaking legs would no longer support her. Overcome with utter despair, she sank to the ground, her back against the rock wall, and buried her head in her hands.

Sister Bridget was a small, bird-like woman of indeterminate age whose face peeked out from beneath her coif. A silver crucifix hung around her neck, and a rosary dangled from her belt. Her eyes narrowed slightly as she looked at Cecile.

'My dear, Sister Margaret tells me you are unwell . . . and oh, I can see that for myself. Come with me.' She indicated that they should follow her, and Sam supported Cecile along a passage where religious pictures hung to a long, narrow room set with a long refectory table and wooden benches.

'Be seated and I will fetch you something to eat and drink.'

She turned to the nun who had answered the ringing of the bell, and who was hovering anxiously. 'Remain with them, Sister Margaret, if you please.'

Sam wondered if perhaps the nuns didn't quite trust a man inside the convent; he could, after all, be a rogue using the excuse of a sick friend to gain entry. But Sister Margaret didn't seem afraid of him, simply nervous that Cecile might faint, or worse.

'I must apologise for the intrusion,' he said clumsily.

'Think nothing of it. Your sister could not continue on her way in her present condition.' Sister Margaret fiddled with her rosary. 'It is not often that we are presented with an opportunity to help our fellow humans in their hour of need far out on the moors as we live. And we have few visitors except for the priest who comes to administer the Holy Mass and hear our confessions.'

'He isn't resident here then?' Sam asked.

'Oh no!' The young nun looked quite shocked at such a suggestion, and Sam was glad he had introduced Cecile as his sister.

Sister Bridget was soon back with a jug of water and a platter of bread, cheese and pickles.

'I'm afraid we live very simply here,' she said, setting it down on the table. 'But I hope this is acceptable.'

'More than acceptable!' Sam poured water into a mug and passed it to Cecile, who drank thirstily.

Sister Bridget turned to the younger nun. 'You may go about your duties now, Margaret.' Sister Margaret left the refectory, rather reluctantly, Sam thought, and Sister Bridget took a seat at the table opposite them.

'So where do you hail from, and what is your destination?' she asked. Her eyes, sharp and watchful, seemed to rest on

269

Cecile, though she was clearly in no fit state for conversation.

'We have travelled from Helston on our way to visit cousins in Launceston.' Sam repeated the lie he had told the innkeeper previously. This time it slid more easily off his tongue, and he hoped it had satisfied the nun.

'I see. Well, I do not think it would be advisable for you to continue on your journey until your . . . ?'

'Sister,' Sam supplied.

'Until your sister has recovered from whatever ails her. When you have eaten and drunk your fill, I will find a cell where she may rest as long as she needs to, but I am afraid I cannot offer *you* accommodation. It would be against our regulations.'

Sam had expected as much. 'I understand. And I assure you, I am well able to fend for myself.' Seeing the anguish in Cecile's eyes, he touched her arm. 'I won't be far away, and I'll call and ask after you every day. Then as soon as you are well, we can go on.'

Cecile forced a smile. She knew she had no choice but to remain here until she had regained her strength.

An hour later, she was settled in a tiny cell, bare but for a table and chair, and a cot with a crucifix mounted on the wall beside it, and Sam had been allowed in to bid her goodbye.

'You'll be well taken care of,' he said, and kissed her forehead, not daring to touch her lips with Sister Bridget standing in the doorway. He was already concerned at the looks she had continued to give Cecile as they ate their meal. He couldn't believe that news of their elopement had reached this isolated place, but the nun's apparent interest was making him uncomfortable.

Pushing his reservations to the back of his mind, he thanked Sister Bridget, raised a hand in farewell to Cecile and left the nunnery.

* * *

The Moxey family were eating their evening meal when they were disturbed by a loud rapping at the door.

'See 'oo that be, our Billie,' Gussie said through a mouthful of fried fish, and Billie obliged.

A moment later, he was back, his face like thunder. 'It's fer you, Aaron. That Dyfan Flinders.'

'Oh, my life. I 'oped we'd seed the last of 'im,' Gussie groaned.

'He's trouble, that one.' Billie took up his knife and fork. 'Seems like he's got a job for our Aaron.'

'What's that then?'

'How should I know? You'll have to ask him.'

'That I shall,' Gussie said with determination, and when Aaron returned to the table, she wasted no time.

'What does 'e want ee fer, then? I 'ope you told 'im no, whatever it be. The sort 'e mixes with, you'll end up in a ditch before long, wi' the livin' daylights beaten out o' you.'

Aaron grinned. 'Not this time, Ma. It's an easy job, this one. Just some woman as needs teachin' a lesson.'

'A woman? Whatever next! When did you turn into a woman-beater?' Gussie demanded.

'Who said anythin' about beating?' Aaron stuffed the last of his fish into his mouth. 'I gotta go. Dyfan's waiting for me an' I can't afford to turn 'im down. The Pendinnicks pay well.' With that he grabbed his coat from the back of his chair and went out.

Billie's blood had turned to ice at the mention of the Pendinnicks. He'd been out of his mind with worry about Lise ever since she'd disappeared so mysteriously, thinking of Annie's words when he'd questioned her. She'd warned him off, told him Lise's life could be in danger, talked in riddles. He had suspected from the outset that the danger came from the

271

Pendinnicks and their ruthless cronies; he knew that Zach Carver, who had taken such an interest in Lise, worked for and with them. Now all his suspicions and anxiety crystallised. A woman who had to be taught a lesson. Supposing that woman was Lise? Aaron had intimated that no harm was intended to be caused to her, but Billie didn't believe that for one moment. It might be what Dyfan Flinders had told Aaron, but Billie didn't trust him one little bit. If Flinders had worried that Aaron might baulk if he knew what he was to be party to, he'd say anything, and the promise of a good payout would do the rest.

Billie put down his knife and fork. 'I'm sorry, Ma, but I'm going too.'

'Oh, our Billie!' Gussie wailed.

Marco, too, was on his feet, his young face alight with excitement. 'And me!'

'Not a chance,' Billie said before a horrified Gussie could find her tongue. 'This is men's work.' He shrugged into his coat. 'Don't worry, Ma. I'm just goin' to follow to begin with. See what they're up to. But if I have to interfere, I will.'

'But yer fishin' . . .' Gussie attempted once more to dissuade him.

But Billie wasn't listening.

Chapter Twenty-Four

For a while, Lise had remained where she sat, her thoughts racing.

Cordelia. It was Cordelia, not her father, who was the brains behind the various enterprises, the evil driving force behind the wreckers. It was she, not Godfrey, who had taken trophies, she who gloated over them in secret, and of that Lise was glad. Oh, her father was complicit, yes, but she could at least comfort herself that his worst traits might be weakness and greed, rather than ruthless cruelty. And it explained, of course, why she had found the key in Cordelia's room and not her father's. She should have realised then that Cordelia was their most dangerous enemy, but it wouldn't have saved her from being discovered here in the cellar. She had believed her aunt was still in France; had underestimated her acute perception and her deviousness. And so had Zach. They had done their best to avoid suspicion, but it had not been good enough. And now she was a prisoner, and Zach . . . She hardly dared think about what had happened to Zach. But avoiding imagining what he might have endured didn't do anything to ease the unbearable pain in her heart at the knowledge that she had, in all likelihood, lost him for ever.

Whatever Cordelia had planned for her, she was no longer afraid. If Zach was dead, then she didn't want to go on living.

Eventually, when her eyes had grown accustomed to the gloom, she had picked herself up and made a careful investigation of her surroundings. Besides the figurehead of the ship from her dreams, she found a ship's bell and yet another figurehead – this one an angel, judging by the wings that sprouted from behind the shoulders – and also a chest containing smaller items. Some, she guessed, were personal belongings of some of the men whose lives had been claimed. Really, Cordelia's wickedness knew no bounds.

Hours passed. How many Lise did not know; she had lost all count of time. But judging by the change in the light that filtered in through the grating high up in the wall, it must now be late afternoon. She was hungry, having eaten nothing since breakfast, and she began to wonder if Cordelia meant to simply leave her here to starve. The thought of that was much worse than being thrown down a disused mine shaft as it seemed her mother had been. Given their depth, she would almost certainly die when she hit the bottom – if she had not been murdered first.

She thought back to when she had visited her mother's grave and remembered how she had had no sense of being close to her there. That, at least, had now been explained. Wherever Marguerite lay, it was not in Porthmeor churchyard. Oh, Mama, did she lock you up here too before disposing of you? Lise wondered.

A sound interrupted her reverie – the creak of the key turning in the lock, the scrape of the door on the rock step. Lise scrambled to her feet as three figures descended the steps. First came Cordelia, once again lighting the way with her lamp. Behind her were two men; one of them, short, squat and rough in appearance, she had never seen before. But her breath caught in her throat as she recognised the other. It was none other than Aaron Moxey.

* * *

'So. This is the young lady I want you to take care of. My niece. As you see, she is slightly built, so should give you no trouble.' Cordelia's tone was cold and hard and, by the light of the lamp, Lise could make out the cruel twist of her lips.

Could they see her? And if they could, was the light good enough for Aaron to recognise her? Surely – surely – he would do no harm to the girl who had lived next door since they were children? But in the wig and Cecile's fine clothes, she no longer looked like the Lise he knew, and besides, when had he ever had any scruples? The unkind tricks he used to play on her flashed through her mind, especially the occasion when he had shut her in the shed on the beach. Her situation now almost mirrored that, and the same terror she had felt then flooded her veins now.

Cordelia was speaking again, addressing the short, squat man. 'Do you recall the mine shaft where her mother was disposed of, Flinders?'

'I bain't sure that I do, miss.' The man's voice was rough. ''Twas a long while ago, an' I were nobbut a lad. I just followed where Stannard led, and did as I was bid.'

'Well, if you cannot remember exactly, any other one will suffice. Although I must say, the poetic justice of them being together in death rather appeals to me.' She drew a length of thick cord from her apron pocket. 'Bind her wrists.'

The man – Flinders – grinned. 'With pleasure, Miss Pendinnick.' He came towards Lise, stretching the cord between his hands. Lise shrank away, raising her arms to defend herself, and he jerked his head in Aaron's direction. 'Don't be just standin' there, Moxey. Hold 'er fer me.'

Aaron approached Lise from behind, so that any hope she might have had of him looking into her face and recognising her evaporated. He overpowered her easily, holding both her arms behind her back with his big hands while Flinders secured her wrists with the cord so tightly that it bit into her flesh painfully.

'When we get 'er t'the hoss, we'll bind 'er ankles too and fling her over like a sack o' grain,' he said with satisfaction, and Lise realised he was enjoying every moment of this.

'So 'ow about our wages?' he asked Cordelia.

'You'll be paid when the job is done,' she said coldly.

'Ooh, I think not. We do nuthin' till the money's in me 'and.' He fixed her with a truculent glare. 'Not that I don't trust ya, but better safe than sorry.'

Cordelia drew herself up to her full height. 'My sentiments exactly. How do I know you will do what I require once payment is in your pocket? I suggest a compromise. I will accompany you to see that the task is carried out satisfactorily, and *then* I will pay you. Do we have a deal?'

'S'pose so.' Flinders sounded less than pleased. 'You got yer own 'oss, I 'ope, 'cos while this one is light enough, you, if I may say . . .' He broke off, perhaps having second thoughts about the wisdom of insulting Miss Pendinnick.

'Of course,' Cordelia snapped. 'A horse is saddled and ready. I have always had every intention of coming with you to see the deed done.'

Lise's heart had sunk even further. Any chance she might have had of escape had disappeared. Aaron and this horrible little man would be sure to carry out Cordelia's instructions to the letter, or miss out on their payment, which must be substantial. Not many men would be willing to commit murder without proper recompense.

'Meet me on the drive,' Cordelia ordered.

''Ang about, miss,' Flinders said. 'You ain't gonna leave us in the dark, I 'ope.'

At the foot of the steps, Cordelia stopped, holding the lamp aloft. 'Make haste, then. And wait for me on the path.'

As the men bundled their captive past her, she hissed into Lise's ear: 'You'd have thought twice about crossing me if you had known what would happen, I imagine.'

Lise swung her head round to look her straight in the face. 'I'd do it again in a heartbeat!' She spoke the words defiantly, determined not to give her aunt the satisfaction of seeing her cowed, then allowed the men to push her out of the door and into the cool fresh evening air.

'How are you feeling now, my dear?' Sister Bridget entered the small bare cell where Cecile had been resting for most of the day and fixed her with the piercing look that Cecile was beginning to grow familiar with.

'Better, I think, thank you,' she said.

'Well enough to get up and join us for supper, perhaps?' the nun suggested.

'I can try.'

Gingerly Cecile raised herself from the thin pillow and swung her legs down from the cot and on to the bare board floor, but as she attempted to stand, the dizziness swept over her again and she was forced to sit down quickly.

'Hmm. Perhaps not.' Sister Bridget frowned. 'It is too soon, perhaps. Better you take some sustenance here and have a good night's rest. Tomorrow is another day.'

'I am sorry,' Cecile said weakly.

'Nonsense. This is no fault of yours. I will send Sister Margaret to sit with you for a while until Compline. She is much closer in age to you and will make for better company than I. In fact, she has to be disciplined on occasions for frivolity and talking too much when she should be observing silence.' But she said it with a smile. She was rather fond of Sister Margaret, Cecile thought.

A few minutes after the older nun had left, Sister Margaret appeared in the doorway with a tray, which she set down on the bare table. This morning, when she had answered the door, her nervousness had been the only thing Cecile had noticed about her. Now, however, she saw a button nose and rosy cheeks, eyes that were almost silver in colour, and a smiling mouth.

'I've brought you soup and a roll, and something to drink, and I am to sit with you while you eat,' she said, and added mischievously: 'Do try not to spill it on the blanket. I don't want to have more washing to do today. My hands are sore enough already.'

'I could sit at the table,' Cecile suggested.

Sister Margaret looked doubtful. 'Sister Bridget said you were dizzy when you tried to get up,' she said. 'If I were to allow you to faint, I would likely have to recite at least a dozen rosaries, and that wouldn't be good for my poor sore fingers either.'

'I won't faint, I promise,' Cecile said. 'I expect I just got up too quickly. And you can hold my arm and steady me just in case.'

With the young nun's help, she reached the chair safely and sat down gratefully.

The soup was delicious – a meaty broth with vegetables fresh from the nunnery garden, Sister Margaret told her. It was the first meal Cecile had really enjoyed for days, a sure sign she was getting better, she thought. As she ate, Margaret sat on the cot beside her chair, chatting about the events of the day, the highlights of which seemed to be the various services, some sung in Latin and some in English, and the quiet periods for contemplation and reading the Bible. Between these hours dedicated to religious pursuits, it seemed there was nothing but work: cleaning, cooking, digging in the garden or, as Margaret had been doing today, the laundry. Cecile had thought her own life restricted enough, and struggled to understand why any young woman would choose this spartan life far distant from civilisation.

'Why was this remote spot chosen for a nunnery?' she asked.

Sister Margaret smiled. 'It was not chosen exactly. The house was the family home of Mother Theresa. When she was left a widow some seventy years ago, she was called by God to serve him and she founded our little order. At first there was only Mother Theresa, her sister and two of her friends, but as word spread, others came. We number thirteen now: our Mother Superior and twelve of us ordinary nuns, just as the Lord Jesus had his twelve disciples.'

'How long have you lived here?' Cecile asked.

'Three years. Like the others, I was called. I had a young man, but he met his death fighting the French, and I found comfort in the House of God. I try very hard to serve Him, but I am afraid I am not always as good as I should be. I pray every night that I will learn to curb my selfish thoughts and thoughtless actions so as to be worthy of the life I have chosen.'

'You lost a young man!' Cecile was overcome by sympathy. 'I am so sorry to learn that.'

'It was God's will,' Sister Margaret said simply.

'Oh, I couldn't bear it if I lost . . .' Cecile broke off, biting her lip.

'The young man who brought you here?' Sister Margaret asked.

Cecile nodded, blushing. 'He was afraid we might be turned away if he told the truth. But yes, we are to be married. Only please, don't mention it to anyone. For all I know, my father may already be in pursuit of us. And if he finds us . . .'

Sister Margaret smiled her sweet smile. 'Don't worry. I can keep a secret. I may have to confess to Father O'Malley when he next comes, but by then you will be long gone.' She pursed her lips together almost playfully, and went on: 'And I think I may need to say five decades of Hail Marys to ask for forgiveness for myself and a happy outcome for you. But now I must get back to the kitchen with your dishes, and then it will be time for Night Prayer, and after that the Great Silence. But I will see you in the morning after Vigils, and hopefully you will be completely well by then, and able to go on your way.'

As she made for the door, a sudden cold shiver ran down Cecile's spine and a feeling of terrible dread made her blood turn to ice, though she had no idea why. Just a moment ago she had been feeling positive and happy; now she was trembling and on the verge of tears. Something terrible was going to happen. Or was happening already. Her first thought was for Sam, but she knew that wasn't it. Much as she loved him, close as they were, there was something about this that was more immediate, as if the bad thing, whatever it was, was happening to her.

Lise. Her twin. The other half of herself. Lise was in mortal danger.

'Please . . . Sister!' It was a cry of anguish, and the nun turned, startled.

'Whatever is wrong?'

'Please . . .' Cecile's terrified gaze lighted on the rosary that hung from Sister Margaret's belt, and she reached for it, her fingers closing over the silver crucifix above the rows of beads. She hadn't been brought up in a religious household. Had never been encouraged to kneel at the foot of her bed before retiring, or set foot inside a place of worship. But now, here, in this peaceful place where every minute of every day was dedicated to the service of God and the Lord Jesus, she was overcome with the need to plead for His intervention.

Clutching the rosary tightly, she looked up into the young nun's face.

'Will you pray with me?' she begged.

The three horses tracked in Indian file across the open moorland above Porthmeor. Dyfan Flinders led the way, Aaron followed with Lise slung face down in front of him, and Cordelia brought up the rear, riding side-saddle. Darkness was falling, hastened by storm clouds that had gathered since they had set out, when Dyfan came to a halt, straining his eyes in the gloom to see what he was looking for.

'Where is this damned mine shaft?' Cordelia called to him. 'This is taking too long. And there is a storm brewing.'

Even as she spoke, the first drops fell heavily, lightning forked the sky ahead of them and thunder rumbled overhead.

As another flash lit up the bleak landscape, Dyfan pointed and called out: 'Over yonder.' He turned his horse in the direction of a small cluster of rough stone ruins, and the others followed as the rain fell faster and harder, soaking them through in moments.

Lise groaned softly. She had been senseless for much of the journey as the discomfort of her position slung across Aaron's horse, the constant jolting back and forth and the stink of the sweaty skin she inhaled with each breath overcame her. Now the rain beating down on the back of her neck below the elaborate curls of her wig, and the clammy cold of her soaked gown across her back revived her a little, and her senses were flooded again with the hopelessness of her situation.

As they reached the ruins of what had once been a tin mine, Dyfan slowed, dismounted and continued on foot, leading his horse by the bridle. He had no wish to find the site of the shaft by stumbling into it.

'Wait there!' he called to the others.

The horses were drawn to a halt, and Lise struggled to shift position, desperate to somehow make Aaron aware of her true identity. Whether he would help her, or whether he would assist the other man in finishing their grisly work she did not know, but it was her last hope. She lifted her head, twisting her neck to face in his direction, and reached an arm back, managing to free her arm enough to grasp his leg, but he merely swatted her hand away as if she was no more than an irritating fly. All he was seeing, of course, was the elaborate powdered wig. She tugged at it, ignoring the sharp needles of pain as it caught on her own hair and wishing Bessie hadn't fixed it so securely when she'd put it on this morning.

Another awful thought occurred to her. Bessie. Why hadn't the maid missed her and come to look for her? She might have done, of course, and perhaps Cordelia had fed her some story to explain Lise's absence. But what if her evil aunt had realised that Bessie must be in on the plan? How might she have dealt with her? Had she administered a generous dose of whatever it was that was keeping Godfrey sedated? Or worse? Lise now knew to her cost that there was nothing Cordelia was not capable of.

Another flash of lightning illuminated the darkness, and Dyfan could be seen waving to them and shouting something. His words were lost in another rumble of thunder, but his meaning was clear enough. They were to dismount and join him. Cordelia wasted no time, slithering easily to the ground, and Aaron followed suit, then hauled Lise down and untied her ankles, grabbing her arm and dragging her towards where Dyfan waited. Her legs, stiff and numb, almost gave way beneath her and she stumbled awkwardly behind him, half sobbing yet still searching for a way to alert him. The wig was the key. As they covered the uneven ground, sharp gorse and heather scraping her bare ankles, she managed to raise her free arm to tug again at the elaborate curls. She felt it shift a little, and then a little more, but they were now only feet away from Dyfan and the old mine shaft. In desperation, she grasped the webbing and yanked at it as hard as she could and, glory be, she felt it come free.

'Aaron!' she cried, tossing the wig aside and shaking her own hair loose so that it tumbled around her shoulders. 'Aaron – look at me!'

He broke stride, turning his head. 'What . . . ?'

'Aaron! It's me – Lise!'

Yet another flash of lightning. In its light she saw the utter confusion on his good-looking face. Clearly he couldn't believe his eyes.

'Don't do this, Aaron!' she begged. And for long, breathless moments she had no idea how he would react.

Chapter Twenty-Five

As Aaron hesitated, staring at Lise in stunned disbelief, Dyfan started towards them. 'Get a move on! I'm wet t'the skin!'

Still Aaron made no move. It was as if he was frozen to the spot by shock. Dyfan reached them, grabbing Lise's arm roughly. 'Yeller, are ya? Y're no better than Stannard – 'e 'ad no stomach fer it either. Give 'er 'ere!' He dragged Lise from Aaron's grasp and propelled her across the rough wet scrub to where Cordelia stood waiting beside the mine shaft. 'D'you wanna do the deed, miss? I reckon you'd like to. One good shove an' she'll be gone.'

Lise's legs were shaking so that she stumbled and almost fell, and Flinders jerked her upright to face her evil aunt.

'See what happens to those who cross me?' Cordelia snarled. 'Your sister is out of my reach now, but I doubt she'll be back. And if she is . . . well, you will profit once again, Flinders.'

Lightning lit the scene once more, and Lise could see that the rain had left Cordelia's wig bedraggled and that the beauty spot had slid down her cheek, but her painted mouth was still twisted in a cruel and triumphant smile.

She stared with all the defiance she could muster into the loathsome face. 'You will rot in hell!' she spat at her aunt.

'But you will precede me.' Cordelia glanced at Dyfan. 'Bring her closer, Flinders. Right to the edge.'

As Dyfan did as he was bid, Lise drew a long, trembling breath. Aaron was still some feet away, rooted to the ground. He might not be able to bring himself to throw her into the mine shaft, but it seemed she could not look to him for salvation. He didn't want to jeopardise his lucrative sideline, she supposed. She raised her eyes heavenward, her lips moving in a silent prayer, and waited for the push that would send her tumbling down into the depths of the earth.

And then, just when she thought all was lost, it seemed that everything happened at once. A yell that might almost have been someone calling her name. Footsteps racing through the wet brush. The figure of a man materialising out of the darkness, barrelling into Dyfan, forcing the two of them backwards. She landed heavily on the sodden ground as a fist met Dyfan's jaw and he too went reeling.

Lise scrambled to her feet, too stunned to be able to make out what was happening. She only knew that she was free, and that her saviour and Dyfan, who had recovered himself, were engaged in a fierce fight. But as she gathered up her skirts, preparing to run, Cordelia grabbed her arm.

'Oh no you don't, miss!' she snarled. 'Moxey! Help me hold her!'

Aaron, who had seemingly recovered the use of his legs, was moving towards them.

'Aaron – please!' Lise gasped, afraid that he was about to do Cordelia's bidding. Instead, to her surprise and relief, he began trying to wrest her from her aunt's grasp in a desperate tug-of-war, back and forth, back and forth.

The ending came with unexpected suddenness. With one ferocious tug, Aaron somehow tore Lise free of Cordelia's grasping hands and they went down together in a heap on the scratchy wet ground, whilst Cordelia, equally unbalanced, staggered backwards.

Towards the mine shaft!

Instinctively Lise lunged forward in a mindless attempt to save the evil woman, but Aaron held her fast, and she watched helplessly as Cordelia toppled backwards. Her scream as she fell seemed to go on for an eternity, and Lise pressed her hands to her mouth, sobbing in shock and horror.

'She's gone. You're safe.' Aaron scrambled up and pulled her to her feet. Only then did she see that her mystery saviour had finally got the better of Dyfan, and was kneeling over his prone body, pressing him into the ground.

'Shall we throw him down after her?' Aaron suggested.

'No – I won't be party to murder, Aaron.' Shocked yet again, Lise recognised the man's voice. Billie Moxey!

'It's what he deserves,' Aaron argued.

'Maybe. But I say we just leave him here. He'll either find his way home or he won't.' Billie looked up at Lise. 'Are you hurt, lovely?'

'I'm alive, thanks to you. That's all that matters,' Lise said. 'But how did you come to be here?'

'Followed our Aaron. I lost you for a bit in the pitch black, and I only just found you in time because I knew Flinders was making for a disused mine shaft. It were a lucky guess and no mistake.' He hauled Dyfan to his feet, cracked his left fist into the man's jaw and followed it swiftly with a sickening punch to his stomach. As Flinders went down hard, he dusted off his hands and turned to his brother. 'Now let's get Lise to safety before that bastard recovers his senses.'

A weight seemed to have lifted from Cecile's shoulders. She raised her eyes from the rosary Sister Margaret had brought for her to where the young nun sat, counting the beads of her own rosary, her lips moving in silent prayer. She had begged leave to be excused Night Prayer, explaining to Sister Bridget that Cecile seemed to be in some distress, and asked if she might be allowed to remain with her until she was calmer, something the older nun had willingly agreed to. Sister Bridget was renowned for her kindness and compassion and, besides, she was curious about the young woman who had arrived so unceremoniously on their doorstep, though she had not yet discussed her suspicions with anyone. Perhaps, if Sister Margaret could establish a rapport with her, what Sister Bridget knew she must do before allowing Cecile to leave the convent would be easier.

Sister Margaret had given Cecile a small prayer card along with the rosary and asked if she could read. 'Just follow the words, then, and count the beads as you do. It doesn't matter if you get it wrong sometimes; the Lord God will forgive you. I'll say the first decade with you, and after that we will each be silent with our thoughts and prayers.'

How long they had sat this way in silence, Cecile had no idea, but quite suddenly she felt different, free of the terrible anxiety that had weighed her down.

'Sister,' she said softly. To interrupt the nun whilst she was praying seemed somehow sacrilegious.

Sister Margaret looked up questioningly, the beads still between her fingers. 'Yes?'

'I believe . . .' Cecile hesitated, almost afraid to say it. 'I believe our prayers have been answered. The awful feeling I had – it's gone.'

Sister Margaret took in the sweet face, now smooth where before it had been puckered with anxiety, the eyes clear with a sense of wonder, the tiny awed smile lifting her lips.

'Praise be!' There was joy in her voice.

'How can I ever thank you?' Cecile asked.

The nun shook her head, smiling. 'I need no thanks. It is you the Lord God heard, and He who must be thanked. Let us say one more rosary together, with gratitude in our hearts.'

She moved her fingers to the first bead and began aloud: 'Our Father, Who art in Heaven . . .'

Cecile followed suit, and although she stumbled a little over the Salve Regina, her heart was indeed full of gratitude. She still did not know what the dread she had experienced had meant, only that it concerned her twin, and she did not understand why the burden had lifted, nor even if it was simply a trick of her mind. What she did know was that it felt like a miracle. And she vowed that when she and Sam found a place to settle, she would seek out a church and a priest and learn more of the religion of which she was completely ignorant. If it could bring her the peace she felt in this place, and which she saw in the serene faces of the sisters who had cared for her, she would be truly blessed.

It was, of course, out of the question that Lise, Billie and Aaron could return to St Ives that night. All three were soaked to the skin, and the horses were tired. The brothers decided that it would be best to find lodging at the first hostelry they came across.

'You can ride with me,' Billie told Lise.

'In front o' 'im, not as you did with me – like a sack o' taters!'

'No!' Lise said sharply. She couldn't bear the thought of riding as she had with Zach. Not now, when her heart was breaking. It would be too painful to have Billie's arms about her waist rather than Zach's. To feel Billie's breath on her neck, to be thrown back against his body as she had been with the man she loved and feared she had lost for ever. In any case, she had recognised the horse Cordelia had ridden. 'I'll ride Lady.'

The two brothers exchanged puzzled glances. *Lady*?

'But . . . you can't ride!' Billie protested.

'Oh, but I can. Zach taught me. I am not very used to the side-saddle, but I know the horse. She belongs to Cecile. I have been feeding her carrots each morning. I'm sure I can manage.'

'Who is Cecile?' Aaron asked, mystified.

'The person you believed me to be until I removed the wig.' Lise could not help but smile as she realised that neither of the Moxey boys knew of her sister's existence, or any of the story of how she had come to be at Polruan House. Unless of course Gussie had told them. 'I'll explain later, when we're warm and dry.'

'And wi' a jar o' good ale inside us,' Billie said. 'She's right, Aaron, let's be goin', afore I 'ave t'bust me fists again on that varmint.'

'Thank the Lord you did,' Aaron said with feeling.

Thankfully the storm seemed to have passed. Before they started out, the men had removed their shirts and wrung them out, and Lise had done her best to do the same with her skirts, and by the time they reached a hostelry, their clothing, though still damp, was beginning to dry out.

Once they were seated on wooden settles in the tavern with their much-needed refreshment, Lise began to explain, telling them that she had an identical twin sister who had been believed drowned in the same shipwreck from which she and her mother had been rescued. But that unbeknownst to them, Cecile had been found on the shore, half dead, and returned to their father.

'Ye gods!' Billie exclaimed. 'Pendinnick's yer father?'

Lise nodded, and went on with her story. She had no intention of revealing the true reason for her being at Polruan House. Though she trusted Billie, Aaron had been working with the man tasked with disposing of her, and might still have connections with other members of the gang. She was horribly afraid Zach was dead, but if he had somehow survived and returned to Porthmeor, his life could be endangered yet again if Godfrey got wind of the existence of evidence of the wreckings. Cordelia might no longer be a threat, but Godfrey was almost as deeply involved in the crimes as she had been. She hoped he was merely weak, rather than wicked, but the evidence would be taken as proof that he too was responsible for the loss of innocent lives. That would be the last thing he would want, and he might well be willing to do whatever was necessary to stop the find being made public.

She couldn't risk that. So instead she simply spoke of Cecile's situation and her desperation to escape to be with her lover, Sam Penrose, coachman at Polruan.

'He and Zach are friends,' she said. 'Zach saw me in St Ives and realised that I was identical to Cecile in every way. A plan was conceived. Zach visited me and talked me into going along with it. It was Annie who told me that Cecile was indeed my twin sister, and also that my mother had disappeared after going to Polruan to try to bring her home. She tried to persuade me against what we had planned, but I would have none of it. Cecile and I swapped places, and she and Sam left. Unfortunately, Cordelia realised I was an imposter, and you know the rest.'

'If I'd known it was you I'd been hired to deal with, I'd never . . .' Aaron broke off, shamefaced.

'I'm glad it was you.' Lise sipped her drink. 'If it had been a stranger, I might now be the one at the bottom of the mine shaft instead of Cordelia.'

'And if it hadn't been Aaron, I would never have followed and been there to give that rogue a hiding,' Billie added. 'But where was Zach Carver? How could he have allowed this to happen?'

'Cordelia took him to France, and he's still there.' Lise swallowed hard. 'I don't even know if he's alive or dead. Cordelia said she was having him dealt with, and it may well be that the men she employed there will carry out their instructions to the letter. Zach might not have been as fortunate as I.'

They were silent for a moment, Lise too choked to continue and the men unsure of what to say.

'I am so sorry,' Aaron said eventually. 'I never knew murder was intended. I thought we was just to take you out on the moors and leave you there.'

Lise frowned, suddenly remembering Dyfan's words to Aaron when he had hung back, unwilling to deliver her to the gaping void of the mine shaft.

'Who's Stannard?' she asked.

'Stannard? He was the Pendinnick enforcer, many years ago. I never knew 'im, but Dyfan Flinders was 'is apprentice, if you like. Dyfan often speaks of him, an' scornfully. Whilst Stannard was 'appy to 'and out beatings to men who crossed the family, there was some tasks 'e drew the line at. Violence against women for one, murder another. Dyfan 'as no such scruples. 'E despises weakness. After one such failure to do 'is duty, Stannard were given his marching orders and Dyfan took 'is place.'

Lise was silent for a moment, digesting this – and trying not to attach too much hope to the crazy idea that had occurred to her.

'How long ago was this?' she asked.

Aaron blew breath over his lip. 'Oh, when I were not much more'n a twinkle in me father's eye, I reckon. Twenty-odd year, maybe?'

The breath caught in Lise's throat, and her heart began to

race. Was it possible – was it just possible – that the task this Stannard had failed to carry out was the one involving her mother? Might she still be alive somewhere? But that could not be. If she had escaped, surely she would have come home to St Ives? Perhaps Dyfan Flinders had been sent to finish what his companion had been unable to do. Her heart sank again as she realised there was almost no chance that her mother could still be alive. Emotion overcame her and, as tears filled her eyes, Billie patted her hand.

'I reckon 'tis time you went to bed,' he said.

Lise nodded without speaking, and rose and made her way to the room the innkeeper had prepared for her.

Godfrey Pendinnick was much more alert since Cordelia had not been around to ply him with overdoses of his medication, and was awake early next morning and calling for his breakfast.

'Aw right, aw right. Give me a chance.' Bessie waddled into the study with a tray of tea to find her employer sitting up on the chaise, but as choleric and bad tempered as ever.

'Where's Cecile?' he snapped.

'I really couldn't say,' Bessie snapped back. 'I ain't seen 'er since yesterday mornin', an' 'er bed ain't been slept in. Truth to tell, I'm worried out o' me mind.'

'Well, you'd best find her, and quickly,' Godfrey growled. 'And Cordelia – don't tell me you can't find her either.'

'Well, I can't. Seems as 'ow they've both 'ad enough o' you. You'll just 'ave t'put up wi' me.' Bessie had been with the Pendinnicks long enough to know she could speak as she liked to Godfrey and get away with it, though she had to watch her tongue with Cordelia.

'Hmm.' Godfrey snorted. 'As long as you don't desert me too.'

Bessie shrugged. 'Where would I go at my age?' She put the cup of tea down on the small table at Godfrey's elbow, then headed for the door, where she turned with a nod. 'Just drink yer tea, an' I'll bring ee summat to eat soon as 'tis ready.'

Sam was at the gates of the nunnery early, and to his surprise and delight, Sister Margaret invited him inside and took him to Cecile's cell, where she was eating breakfast.

'We believe our patient will be well enough to leave today,' the nun said. 'But where will you go?'

Sam frowned, unaware that Cecile had confided in her. 'To Launceston, of course.'

'Of course.' Sister Margaret exchanged a secret smile with Cecile. 'But before you go, there is someone Sister Bridget wants you to meet. She will bring her to you when you have finished your breakfast.'

'Who can it be?' Cecile asked, puzzled, as the young nun left the cell.

Sam shrugged. 'You'll find out soon enough.' He bent to kiss her cheek. 'You do look better. How do you feel?'

'Fine. They have looked after me very well here. It's a wonderful place, Sam. So peaceful and happy, and full of love. If it wasn't for you, I'd be tempted to remain here myself.'

'Don't you say such things!' Sam protested.

'I wouldn't, of course. I can't wait to be on our way. Do you think we might be able to find lodgings in Launceston? Is it far enough away from Porthmeor to be safe, do you think?'

'We'll see,' Sam said.

'I keep thinking about Lise.' Cecile finished her porridge and put down the spoon. 'Last night I had the most awful feeling that something was very wrong – something that concerned her. Sister Margaret prayed with me, and after a while the feeling went away. But I still keep wondering. Do you think she is safe?'

'Zach'll make sure she is,' Sam said confidently. 'He won't see any harm come to her.'

'He loves her very much, doesn't he?' Cecile said. 'I am so happy that she has found someone to love too.'

Sam went to the door of the cell and looked out, anxious to get the meeting Sister Margaret had spoken of over with so that they could be on their way. He saw two nuns heading in their direction.

'They're coming, I think,' he said, retreating hurriedly into the cell.

Cecile rose, smoothing down her skirts and tidying her hair as best she could with her fingers.

There was a tap at the door, and Sister Bridget entered, then stood aside for her companion, who was clad identically in the garb of the order. It was almost impossible to guess her age; like all the nuns, her face was smooth, serene and almost devoid of wrinkles. But it was her eyes that Cecile found herself staring into. Bright, and blue as periwinkles. Eyes that were the exact same colour as her own.

Chapter Twenty-Six

The breath caught in Marguerite's throat, those beautiful blue eyes widened, and she grasped the crucifix that hung around her neck with hands that trembled.

'You see?' Sister Bridget said. 'She looks exactly as you did when you sought sanctuary with us all those years ago.'

For a moment Marguerite's lips moved soundlessly, then she opened her arms wide and spoke in a soft, breathless tone that was full of wonder. Just one word.

'Cecile.'

'I think we should leave them alone for a little while, don't you?' Sister Bridget said to Sam, drawing him towards the door. Utterly dumbfounded, he offered no resistance.

'Mama?' Cecile whispered in disbelief. 'Mama? Is it really you?'

Marguerite nodded. 'And you are my beloved daughter.'

'But Papa told me . . .'

'That I was dead?'

'Yes. I've visited your grave often. What I believed to be your grave . . . Why would he do that?'

'He may well believe it,' Marguerite said. 'If that is what Cordelia told him.'

'But . . .' Cecile was still trying to process all this. 'But . . . if you were still alive, why didn't you come back for me? Why have you become a nun? Why—'

'Because I believed you were dead, too. Both of you. You may not remember, Cecile, but you once had a twin sister. Lise.' Marguerite's eyes misted with unshed tears. 'You were my two beautiful little girls. My reason for living.'

'I know,' Cecile said. 'I've met her. She's the reason I was able to escape with Sam. She—'

Marguerite gasped. 'Lise is alive too? Oh my dear, I can't believe this.'

'But why did you think we were both dead?' Cecile asked.

'If you will allow me the time, I will explain. But I warn you, it is a long story.'

'What does that matter?' Cecile cried. 'Please . . . I have to know everything!'

'Then come, sit beside me. We've been too long apart, Cecile. It all began when I was forced to wed your father against my will. I don't want to speak ill of him to you; suffice it to say he could never make me happy. Then there was his sister, Cordelia. She had been the only woman in his life before he wed me, and I believe she was jealous of me. Whatever, she did everything possible to make my life a misery. My only joy was in you and Lise, my beautiful babies. I thought that was the way it would be for ever. And then . . .' She hesitated, bowing her head. 'Before your father came into my life, I had a sweetheart, a soldier. He was away, fighting in India, when Godfrey brought me to England from my native France. The years had passed and I never thought to see him again. And then one day he came to find me. Oh, the joy of it! He planned to take me and the two of you home to France with him.' Her face lit up now as she remembered, then clouded again. 'But it all ended in tragedy.'

'The shipwreck,' Cecile said.

'You know about that?'

'Lise told me. She knew about it from the old woman she lives with.'

'She is still with Annie?' Marguerite asked in amazement.

'Yes.' Cecile did not think this was the moment to explain that Lise might well be at Polruan House.

'Dear Annie! It was her husband George who rescued us from the wreck and took us to his home in St Ives. Jean-Claude, my lover, had swum to shore with you and intended to come back for me and Lise, but he never made it. He was stoned by the men on the beach, and must have drowned. I believed you had drowned too. It was only much later that I learned that you had been found, recognised and returned to your father. And that was when I made another fateful decision: to come to Polruan and find you. My plan was to take you back to St Ives with me, but if that had been impossible, I would have fetched Lise and returned to your father. Little though I wanted that, I thought it would be best for you girls, and at least we would all three be together. I would have willingly endured the resumption of my marriage for that.'

'I think I remember you being there,' Cecile said. 'And I found a locket in a dresser drawer that must have belonged to you. It contains two likenesses. Lise and me.'

Marguerite nodded. 'It was my most precious possession. I thought it was lost. But if it was hidden in a drawer . . . It would not surprise me if Cordelia had stolen it out of spite. And that was the least of her crimes.'

'What do you mean?' Cecile asked.

'You wanted to know how I came to be here,' Marguerite said. 'And I shall tell you.'

* * *

How clearly she remembered the day she had gone to Polruan House to find her daughter. She had recently learned from Annie's husband George that Cecile had not drowned, as she had believed, but had been rescued and returned to Godfrey safe and sound. George had heard it from mariners he sometimes worked with, and also that the Pendinnicks were now living in Porthmeor.

She had talked things over with Annie, who had agreed to take care of Lise whilst she was gone. Annie had been sad to think she might lose the mother and daughter she had come to think of as her own family, but understood that Marguerite must do everything in her power to reunite the twins and hold Cecile in her arms again. Marguerite had set out by coach; then, when it could take her no further, she had walked the last ten miles to Polruan House.

A lump rose in her throat now as she remembered the joy that had coursed through her veins and lifted her heart at the sight that had met her eyes – a little girl, identical to the one she had left behind in St Ives, playing on the lawn, watched over by a plump, motherly figure in maid's uniform. Her first instinct was to run to her daughter, take her in her arms and never let her go. But Cecile might not remember her, and the last thing Marguerite wanted was to frighten her.

She approached the maid, who was staring at her suspiciously.

'I am Marguerite, her mother,' she said.

And then, like an evil wraith from the past, Godfrey was striding across the lawn towards them, clearly as amazed and delighted to see her as she had been to see Cecile.

'Marguerite!' he exclaimed. 'You are alive! You have come back to me!'

Perhaps if Godfrey had not been every bit as obsessed with her as he had ever been, things might have turned out differently.

But as it was, he refused to so much as let her out of his sight, so afraid was he that he would lose her again. She became a virtual prisoner in the house and garden, and was once again forced to endure sleeping in his bed. To make matters worse, Cordelia was ever present, all her old jealousy reignited, and ready to take out her fury at once more being usurped on the sister-in-law she loathed and resented. Yet, strangely, Godfrey seemed quite unaware that she was venting her spite on Marguerite at every opportunity.

Marguerite's only pleasure came in resurrecting her relationship with Cecile. But she knew now that she could never bring Lise to this dark and unhappy home. Could not live the rest of her life under the domination of her husband, and see both her daughters become his playthings, which was clearly how he viewed Cecile. He idolised her, and she wanted for nothing materially, yet she too was a prisoner of his possessiveness. The only way to resolve the situation was to get Cecile away to St Ives, where they would be safe until she could find a passage home to France for the three of them.

But how? This was exactly what she and Jean-Claude had tried to do, and that had ended in disaster.

Long months passed, and Marguerite was beginning to doubt that her chance would ever come. She fretted constantly about Lise, still in St Ives. She had no doubt that Annie would take good care of her, but Annie must be wondering why there had been no word from Marguerite, and Lise would be missing her. And then one day Godfrey told her regretfully that he must spend a few nights away from home making arrangements for the onward transmission of his contraband. 'Cordelia will take good care of you,' he said as he kissed her goodbye.

The moment he rode out of sight, she began plotting her escape. Cordelia would be only too happy to have her gone, and perhaps would be glad to be rid of Cecile too. Surely she would do nothing to stop her. Little did Marguerite know that Cordelia had other plans entirely for her, plans that would mean there was no danger of her returning to Polruan House ever again, and Cordelia would once more be the queen bee in the hive.

Marguerite visited the stables and ordered the coachman to make preparations, as she wished to take Cecile for an outing. Since she was the master's wife, and had been here long enough to be established as such, he raised no objection, and once more Marguerite went to Cecile's room to pack some of her things, just as she had done that other, fateful time. Cecile was with Bessie – Marguerite didn't want her to know that she would soon be leaving Polruan House for good, in case she inadvertently gave the game away. She took the bag out to the stables, ensured that the stable boy was occupied elsewhere, and secreted it beneath the seat of the coach.

It was as she returned to the house that she was confronted by Cordelia, who was waiting outside the side door, hands hidden in the folds of her skirt, an artful smile on her face. A smaller door in the wall beside her, which Marguerite had never noticed before, stood open.

'There's something I want to show you, my dear sister,' she said silkily. And thrust Marguerite down the steps into the cellar.

'The last thing I remember is her face the moment before she pushed me into the cellar,' Marguerite said. 'I'd always known she was evil, but . . .' She crossed herself, then clasped the crucifix that hung around her neck. 'I truly believe that if the devil has offspring in human form, it is Cordelia.'

Cecile was speechless, horrified by the story that was unfolding, and Marguerite went on. 'I must have cracked my head on the stone steps as I fell. Although I have vague memories of regaining consciousness for short periods – the dark, the pain in my head and neck and shoulder, and the cold and damp – otherwise there was nothing until I found myself propped up in front of a man on a horse. There was another man too, and they were arguing. The man who was holding me fast was saying, "I won't do it. It's beyond the pale." And the other one was berating him for cowardice. The next thing I knew, we had reached the place that I now know was this nunnery. "She'll be safe here," the first man said, and his companion swore and rode off as my saviour rang the bell. He lifted me down from his horse and waited until a nun appeared. "Take care of her," he said, and then he was gone. Once again, things became hazy. I was told later that it was days before I fully recovered my senses, and by then I had been cared for with the utmost love and kindness, such as I had never known.'

'And that is why you remained here?' Cecile asked.

'For a while, yes, though of course when I recovered, I intended to leave in search of you and Lise. Except that before I could, I was told you were both dead. Mother Jeanne broke the news to me. A man had come bearing a message. "Both your girls have met their maker. *Both of them*." I couldn't understand how the man would know I had two children, but I was sure the message had come from Cordelia, and that she must have somehow discovered that Lise had been with me in St Ives. I truly believed that she had done away with you both. I might have been outside her reach, but she was determined to ensure that I never went back to Polruan House. And I never did. If I had lost my babies, I had no reason to return to that cruel world. I was safe here. In the peace of this wonderful refuge I found God, and a faith that sustained me in my darkest hours. Only now do I know that I was wrong to remain here. Only now do I know that Cordelia's final cruelty was to make me believe that both my beloved children were dead.'

'Oh, Mama.' Cecile reached for her mother's hands, and the connection between them was as warm and comforting as a sunbeam after a long, hard winter.

They embraced, and Cecile buried her face in Marguerite's shoulder, tears rolling unchecked down her cheeks and soaking the nun's habit. For long moments she was overwhelmed by emotion, then, suddenly, a horrendous thought occurred to her as she remembered the dark despair that had enveloped her last night.

Lise! Was her twin still at Polruan? And if she was, might she be in terrible danger from Cordelia?

'Mama!' she said urgently. 'There's something I have to tell you. Sam isn't my brother as I told Sister Bridget. Well, of course you know he is not your son, but for all you know he could be my father's, my half-brother. But he is not. We are in love and Papa would never have allowed us to be together, so we are running away together.'

'Oh, Cecile!' Marguerite smiled. 'How strange that you should be forced to do the very same thing that Jean-Claude and I did! But it will end better for you, I know it will.'

'But that is not all, Mama. In order for me to make my escape, Lise has taken my place. Suppose Cordelia should discover the truth? If she is capable of such dreadful things, what danger might Lise be in?'

She hurried to the cell door, calling Sam's name, and when he appeared, she grasped his arm, her face white with panic.

'Sam, you must ride back to Polruan immediately. Such things I have learned about Aunt Cordelia and what she is capable of, and I fear for Lise. You must find her and take her to safety. Please – go without delay. I will remain here with Mama until you return.'

Though he didn't fully understand, Sam recognised the urgency of the situation and wasted no time in leaving.

Sam had ridden full pelt to Polruan, not knowing what sort of reception awaited him. But neither Lise nor Cordelia was there, and neither Bessie nor Godfrey knew where they were. Godfrey, who it seemed was laid up, was his usual bad-tempered self, complaining that the two people who should be here tending to him had seemingly abandoned him, and a concerned Bessie said that Cordelia had been missing since last evening, and Lise even longer.

'I can only 'ope she's gone 'ome to St Ives. Miss Cecile's horse is missin' too,' she added. 'But what's 'appened to Miss Cordelia, I don't know. 'Tis very strange.'

The fact that Lady was not in the stables gave Sam hope, but he didn't like the fact that Cordelia seemed to have disappeared.

'Did anyone suspect that Lise was pretending to be Cecile?' he asked, and although Bessie assured him she'd heard nothing to suggest that, he was still uneasy.

'What about Zach Carver?'

Bessie shook her head. 'I ain't seen hide nor hair o' 'im since Miss Cordelia took 'im to France wi' 'er,' she said.

'They've been to France?'

'Aye. Some merchant over there cheated Mr Godfrey. 'E weren't fit to go 'imself, so Miss Cordelia went, and took Zach Carver wi' 'er.'

So, either Zach had taken Lise home to St Ives, unbeknown to Bessie, or he was still on the other side of the Channel and of no help to Lise should she have needed it. He'd ride on to

St Ives, he decided, and after he had drunk a much-needed jar of tea and eaten some rabbit pie that had been baked that very morning, he set off, hoping desperately that he would find Lise safe and well.

Lise could scarcely believe her eyes when she answered a knock at the cottage door and found Sam standing there.

'Sam!' she gasped, her first thought for her twin. 'What is wrong?'

Sam wiped his sweaty brow with his sleeve. 'Cecile's fine – now. 'Twas you we were worried about. My, but you're a sight for sore eyes and no mistake. I've been to Polruan House, and when they said you and Miss Cordelia were both missing, I came straight here to make sure you were all right. She's an evil one, Lise.'

'And don't I know it,' Lise said ruefully. She opened the door wide. 'You'd better come in.'

'Who be it?' Annie's anxious voice called from the kitchen. Shaken as she was over what had befallen Lise, she feared that more trouble had come to their door.

'It's only Sam,' Lise reassured her, showing him in. Annie was still eyeing him with suspicion, and she added: 'Zach's friend. Cecile's intended.'

Annie snorted. 'Well, I hope you'll be tellin' 'im the trouble they landed you in.'

'I did it of my own free will, Annie. You know that – and the reason why. Though I don't believe Sam does.' She indicated one of the kitchen chairs. 'Sit down, Sam, you look done in. Annie will fetch you something to drink, and I'll tell you everything that has happened. But first I want to know how you and Cecile have fared.'

* * *

With a jar of ale in front of him, and glossing over just how ill Cecile had been, Sam explained that he had left her in a nunnery where she would be safe until his return. He decided not to tell Lise just yet the astonishing news that they had learned this morning – that Marguerite was alive, and a member of the religious order where they had sought shelter. That would be an enormous diversion, and he was anxious to hear Lise's story first.

'What did you mean when you said you knew all too well what an evil woman Cordelia is?' he asked. 'Did she try something wicked with you?'

'She did,' Lise said grimly.

''Tis lucky she didn't end up down a mine shaft,' Annie put in. ''Tis only thanks to the Moxey boys next door that she escaped wi' 'er life. That Cordelia 'ad paid 'andsomely ter 'ave 'er done away with. But she got 'er comeuppance an' no mistake. She won't be no danger to anyone ever agin.'

'She's dead?' Sam asked, incredulous.

Lise nodded. 'She's the one who ended up in the mine shaft. I was fortunate indeed to escape.' Her eyes clouded and she bent her head. 'I'm very afraid Zach has not been so lucky.'

'What?' Sam set his tankard down on the table so hard that some spilled over. 'Bessie told me he'd gone to France with Cordelia.'

'That's true. But she realised I was not Cecile, and that he must be a part of the deception. She told me she had arranged for him to be murdered there. I don't know whether her instructions were carried out, but he has not returned and I fear the worst.'

'Oh, dear God, no!' Sam was visibly upset at the news that his friend might be dead. 'What have we done, me and Cecile? This is all down to us.'

'No,' Lise said firmly. 'I might never have agreed to the plan if I hadn't had reasons of my own. For safety's sake, we told no one, Zach and I. But now, if he is dead, you are the only person I can confide in. Zach was working to bring the Pendinnicks to justice, and there are things hidden in that house that prove they were behind the wreckings, as well as the smuggling. He had been unable to find what he was looking for, and I agreed to make a search – something I was willing to risk for reasons of my own. I succeeded where he had failed, and it almost cost me my life. But I am determined this will come to light, and if Zach never returns, I don't know anyone but you who could help me achieve that. Perhaps Cordelia was the prime mover – I believe now that she was – but my father was complicit. They were behind the wrecking of the ship that tore me from my family. Separated me from my sister. Caused the death of Mama's lover.' She paused and raised her eyes to Sam's. 'And I believe them responsible for her death. She returned to Polruan House to fetch Cecile and never came back. She is supposed to be buried in Porthmeor churchyard, but according to Cordelia, she too is at the bottom of a mine shaft.'

It was time. Sam could keep silent no longer.

'Lise,' he said, his eyes holding hers. 'Your mother is not dead. The man charged with disposing of her couldn't do it. You know I said that I have left Cecile in a nunnery? She is not alone. Your mother is with her. She has been there these twenty-odd years, and is well and happy. She believed both of you to be dead, and so she took vows. But she is so delighted to have been proved wrong, and can no more wait to be reunited with you than I imagine you can to be with her.'

Chapter Twenty-Seven

Lise was in utter disbelief as she accompanied Sam on the long ride back to the nunnery. Cordelia's wickedness had indeed known no bounds, and she could feel no shred of pity for her terrible end, even though she had instinctively reached out to try to save her.

That Mama was alive, had been all these years, was unbelievable, but for all her joy at knowing she was on her way to be reunited with her, she could not dispel the pain of fearing Zach had gone from her life for ever. It was as if the price of having her mother back was losing the love of her life. If he was indeed dead, all that was left to her were her memories, the most precious of which was their parting in the churchyard, when they had declared their love for one another and shared a kiss that had electrified her body and touched her soul.

As they breasted a rise and the long, low building came into view in a fold of the moors, Lise took a deep breath and pushed all the dark thoughts to the back of her mind. Mama deserved nothing less. Sam dismounted and pulled the bell rope at the entrance gate, and Lise felt herself begin to quiver with anticipation and nervousness. How would the years have changed Marguerite? She would be older, of course, but what effect would a life of prayer and devotion, cut off from the outside

world, have had on her? Suddenly Lise was afraid that she
would no longer be the mother she knew and loved.

The door opened and a young nun stood there, clad all in
grey. Lise shrank inwardly. She had been through so much,
faced danger and even death with defiance and courage, yet
now she was overcome by a feeling of inadequacy and trepidation.

'Sister Margaret,' Sam said.

The nun smiled, the sweetest smile Lise had ever seen. 'Sam.
And you must be Lise. I bid you welcome. Come inside. Cecile
and Sister Theresa will be so happy to see you.'

For a moment Lise was unable to move a muscle, and Sam
took her arm, urging her over the threshold.

Two figures stood in the deep shadow of the entrance hall.
One was Cecile. The other . . . Though only her face was visible
peeping out between the folds of her veil, Lise recognised her
instantly.

'Mama,' she whispered, half afraid to approach her.

'Lise.'

Marguerite opened her arms, and Lise ran into them.

'Well!' Gussie Moxey folded her arms across her ample stomach
and glared at Aaron, who was seated at the breakfast table
making short work of a fillet of mackerel. 'All I do hope is
you've learned yer bliddy lesson.'

'Yeah.' Aaron munched on a mouthful of bread and dripping.
'Reckon I 'ave. A lot o' things I might be, but I ain't no
murderer.'

'I should 'ope not! Make no mistake, I be proud o' what you
did when push came to shove. But more fool you fer gettin'
mixed up wi' the likes of Dyfan Flinders in the fust place.'

'Aaron's goin' to come in wi' me,' Billie said. 'We'm gonna

git ourselves a bigger boat, catch more fish, make more money.'

Gussie snorted. 'I wouldn't too hasty doin' that if I was you. You don't want to put yerself in debt till our Aaron's proved he can pull his weight.'

'He will,' Bille said. 'I'll make sure of it.'

He grinned at his brother. There was a new closeness between them now, born of the horrendous experience they had shared. Aaron would likely always be something of a rogue – a leopard could never change its spots entirely – but Billie was confident there would be no more forays into the darkest depths of the Cornish underworld.

'An' 'tis time the both of yer found yerselves a nice girl, got out o' my hair and settled down. I could do with a bit o' peace in me old age,' Gussie told them sternly. 'Now, do ee want another jar o' tea? I reckon the pair o' you 'as earned it.'

As Bessie entered the room with his breakfast tray, Godfrey pulled himself up on his pillows, glowering.

'Not you again, you old crone. Where is Cecile? And Cordelia? Why have they deserted me?'

Bessie set down the tray. 'I told yer yesterday, I don't know where they've got to. I'm thinkin' mebbe Miss Cordelia's gone back to France.'

'France? Why the devil would she go to France?' Godfrey asked irritably. 'And Marguerite, where is she? I haven't set eyes on her for days.'

Bessie's eyes narrowed. 'Well o' course you ain't. She's bin dead an' gone fer years. And 'twas you as sent Miss Cordelia to France t'sort out the trouble with yer merchant there, though she never did get the business finished as I understand it.'

'What are you talking about, woman?'

Bessie shook her head. Mr Pendinnick's leg might be healing, but the blow to his head seemed to have affected his mind. Well, it wasn't for her to tell him so. The doctor could do that, and take the brunt of the master's bad temper when he did. But unless things changed for the better, she couldn't see he'd ever be able to run his business again, especially if his sister never came back, and that was no bad thing in her opinion.

'Just eat yer eggs an' don't worry yerself about it,' she said, and bustled out of the room.

'I'm worried about Papa,' Cecile said.

She and Lise had spent a few happy hours with Marguerite – or Sister Theresa as she now was. They had tried to persuade her that she should leave the convent and return to St Ives with Lise, but to no avail. Much as she loved them, delighted as she was to meet them as grown women, and however pleased she would be to see them whenever they could find the time to visit, this was now her home and she had promised her life to the service of God. When it was time for Vespers, the two of them had bidden her a tearful goodbye, and promised they would come to see her again very soon.

Now they stood outside the gates of the nunnery talking over all that had happened and trying to decide what to do next.

Sam gave Cecile a quizzical look, but Lise understood. She too had felt oddly responsible for their father, and in any case, it seemed the twins could communicate with one another without the need for words.

'I could call at Polruan House on my way back to St Ives,' she said, though her heart sank at the prospect. 'He may still be bed-bound, and with Cordelia dead . . .'

' . . . he'll be all alone,' Cecile finished for her. 'But you can't go there, Lise, after what happened to you.' She turned to Sam. 'I think we should go back.' Seeing the look on his face, she added quickly: 'He won't stop us being together now. We know too much. The threat of a word to the authorities should ensure his compliance, and if not . . . we'll simply leave again.'

'An' what if yer taken bad again?' Sam said firmly. 'I'll go if you think someone should, but you must stop 'ere wi' your mother and the nuns.'

Daunted by the thought of the arduous journey, and remembering how ill she had been, Cecile agreed far more swiftly than either Sam or Lise had anticipated.

'Just as long as you promise to make sure he is safe and well,' she said.

And so it was settled. Cecile was received back into the convent, and Lise and Sam left to ride south.

Though he tried to persuade her otherwise, Lise insisted on going with Sam to Polruan House, where they found Bessie in the garden gathering herbs. When she saw them walking towards her, she dropped her basket in surprise.

'Oh my life! Why be you two 'ere? What's 'appened now?'

'All's well, Bessie,' Lise assured her, and Sam explained that they had come because Cecile was anxious about her father now that Miss Cordelia was no longer here.

''Ow d'you know that?' Bessie demanded, her face a picture of astonishment.

'It's a long story,' Sam said. 'But I can tell you she won't be coming back.' He turned to Lise. 'Why don't you go and look in on your pa while I tell Bessie all that's happened.'

Lise nodded. 'I think as long as he has Bessie, he'll be well looked after. But I will go in and see him just to set my mind, and Cecile's, at rest.'

She left them sitting on a garden bench, where Bessie had subsided, and went into the house, shuddering as she passed the

311

door to the cellar. Inside, it was dim as always – no sun ever seemed to reach these rooms and passages. Only Godfrey's study, looking out as it did over the gardens, was less than suffocating. She entered with some trepidation, though she would no longer be obliged to act as Cecile would if he began trying to get close to her again. But almost at once, she realised there was little danger of that.

Though Godfrey was sitting up in bed, there was a vacant look in his eyes, and one hand picked ceaselessly at the covers whilst the other lay curled into a claw.

'Papa?' she said, but there was no recognition in those distant eyes.

'Who are you?' he demanded.

'I am your daughter. Don't you recognise me?'

'I do not have a daughter. Are you an intruder, come to rob us?' He was becoming agitated, fiddling ever more furiously with the bed covering.

'How is your leg?' Lise asked. 'Are you able to stand on it now?'

'How would I know?' he snapped. 'That old witch Bessie won't let me get up. She used to be such a pretty young thing, and now . . .' He huffed heavily, spittle flying from the corners of his mouth.

'She is looking after you then?' Lise said.

'I suppose so. She feeds me, attends to my toilet. I should be grateful, I suppose. What more can I expect? You'd best go now. Leave me alone. I want to sleep.'

'Very well. I'll leave you in peace.' Lise steeled herself to touch the hand that lay on top of the covers. It felt stiff and puffy, and there was not the slightest response to her contact.

Somewhat shocked, she returned to the garden, where Sam and Bessie were still talking.

'Well, thank the good Lord you escaped wi' yer life!' Bessie greeted her, and Lise knew that Sam had told her of the dreadful events that had occurred. 'I allus knew Miss Cordelia was a bad 'un, but I never guessed just 'ow bad.'

'Papa is acting very strangely,' Lise said, changing the subject. 'He seems much worse than he was. Is it the fall from his horse that is the cause, do you think?'

'Doctor says so. Reckons he might be bleeding inside his head from where he banged it. He don't seem t'think there's much can be done. 'Twill either heal itself or it won't.'

'He says you are taking good care of him,' Lise ventured.

Bessie snorted. 'Huh! I'll tell ee this much – he's a sight easier to deal with now than what 'e were before!' she said with what sounded like satisfaction.

'And you'll continue to do so?' Lise asked.

'What d'yer think? Course I will.'

'Then I'd best be going,' Lise said. 'I'm on my way home to St Ives. But I will call again soon. And so will Cecile when she is able to travel.'

'I'm thinking,' said Sam, 'that we might come back here. If Godfrey is in such a bad way, he's in no state to keep us apart, and Cecile'd like to be near, I reckon.'

That news lifted Lise's heart. To have her twin nearby was almost more than she had dared hope for. This part of the county was home for both of them, Sam would be more likely to find work and, as he had said, Cecile would be able to keep a watchful eye on her father, and spend time with him in what might be the last few years left to him.

Yet as she set out for St Ives, she was dreading the empty space in her life that Zach had left, and that would never be filled again.

* * *

313

Dyfan Flinders was furious. Not only had he taken a bad beating at the hands of Aaron Moxey's brother, not only had he been left to find his horse and make his way home sore, bleeding and soaked to the skin, but the purse of payment for his trouble was at the bottom of the mine shaft along with Cordelia Pendinnick. And Dyfan Flinders was not a man to let such a humiliation go unchallenged. Lucky he knew where to find the Moxey boys, he thought grimly, as he selected a couple of suitable weapons. Lucky he knew that Billie Moxey would be going out with his fishing boat alone. All he had to do was waylay him, and the bastard wouldn't be giving him or anybody else any more trouble. He'd deal with his yellow-livered brother later.

Dusk was falling as he hid himself in the shadow of an old boathouse and waited, chewing on a wad of baccy and watching. Before long, his patience was rewarded. Billie Moxey, making for his boat, and alone.

Dyfan extracted the knife from the leather sheath on his belt, then crept up behind him, seizing Billie with an arm encircling his chest and holding the knife to his throat. He could make this quick, or he could spin it out, and he fancied spinning it out. He wasn't going to let the bastard get off so lightly, not after what he'd done. This time, he had the upper hand. With a sharp blade pressing against his jugular vein, one false move would be the end of Billie Moxey.

"Ow d'yer like this, then?' Dyfan hissed in his ear. 'We'm goin' somewhere nice and quiet.' He began edging back into the shadow of the boathouse, pressing the knife so hard into Billie's throat that he broke the skin and drew blood.

'Hoi! What be afoot?' The yell was accompanied by the sound of boots on cobbles, and Aaron came into sight, running as fast as his legs would carry him.

'Stop right thar, or yer brother's a dead man!' Dyfan yelled back, and Aaron slithered to a halt, horrified at the sight that met his eyes.

'What y'doin'?'

'Gettin' me revenge. Glad yer 'ere to watch!' Again he slid the blade across Billie's throat, just hard enough that Billie could feel it, and at the same time pressed hard on Billie's Adam's apple with his thumb, eliciting a gurgle from his prisoner.

Aaron took a step forward, only to stop again as Dyfan's hold tightened around Billie's neck. What the hell could he do?

'Bastard!' he yelled, looking around him wildly for inspiration. Just for a moment, he saw someone move in the shadows at the far side of the shack, before they disappeared and he was left wondering if he had imagined it. Then, to his amazement, a man materialised behind Dyfan and Billie, holding some heavy object aloft before bringing it down hard on the man's skull. Aaron heard the sharp crack, saw the knife slip from Dyfan's hand as he went down like a felled tree. Aaron moved swiftly then, kicking the knife out of Dyfan's reach, though he looked to be out cold. Billie staggered a little, clutching his throat and gasping for breath. Only then did Aaron look at the man emerging from the shadows, the man who had saved his brother. And recognised him.

It was none other than Zach Carver.

Zach walked to the harbour wall and tossed away the iron bar he'd grabbed when he had seen what was occurring. It sank below the surface instantly. Then, leaving Dyfan Flinders where he lay, the three men walked back towards the Moxey cottage, both Aaron and Billie profuse in expressing their gratitude for what Zach had done.

'I'd be a goner if 'tweren't fer you,' Billie said. His voice was still hoarse and blood from the flesh wound was trickling down his neck and into the rough fabric of his shirt. 'I can never thank ee enough.'

'From what I hear, it's nothing but a favour repaid,' Zach said. When he had landed back in England, he had gone straight to Polruan House, where Bessie had told him something of what had happened.

'We couldn't see Lise harmed,' Billie said. 'We only did what were right. But 'ow come you was able to 'elp us?'

'I was on the quayside and heard shouts, so I investigated and saw what was going on,' Zach said. 'By sheer good fortune, I spotted that iron bar lying where somebody'd left it.'

'Did you kill'un, do ee think?' Aaron asked hopefully. If Flinders was still alive, he'd doubtless be back, with some of his cronies for support, to extract his revenge.

Zach shrugged. 'Who knows? If I did, it's no more than he deserves.'

'Well, you certainly 'it 'im 'ard enough! And thank God yer did!' Aaron could still hear the crack of the iron bar on Dyfan's skull echoing in his ears. 'Reckon I'd best go in first, our Billie, an' warn Ma. If she sees you like that, she'll 'ave a fit.'

Zach stopped at the house next door. 'I'll leave you here, lads. There's someone I came to see.'

Billie and Aaron exchanged knowing looks. But for once, neither of them felt any resentment. They owed too much to Zach Carver.

'Thanks again. An' I reckon Lise'll explain why that bastard 'ad it in fer me,' Billie said.

'A long tale it is too,' Aaron added.

Zach's eyes narrowed in curiosity, but he was too anxious to see the love of his life to delay any longer.

He raised his hand to knock at the door.

* * *

When she had seen who the caller was, Annie had tactfully left the two of them alone, and for long minutes Zach cradled Lise in his arms while she wept into his chest, too overcome with emotion to speak. Then he kissed her gently, pulled out a chair for her to sit at the kitchen table, and seated himself beside her, reaching for her hands.

'I feared for your safety, Lise. When Cordelia left me in France, I could only think that she suspected something, and intended to return home sooner than you expected and surprise you. I did all I could to get back to England swiftly myself, but it did not prove easy. And all the while I was tortured by thoughts of you in terrible danger, and me not here to protect you.'

'And I thought you were dead! Cordelia said she'd hired some thugs to do away with you. Oh, Zach . . .'

Zach smiled, a twisted, humourless smile. 'Oh, they tried. Fortunately I am well able to take care of myself. But you . . . When I landed, I went first to Polruan House, and learned from Bessie that Cordelia had tried to have you killed, but that the Moxey boys rescued you and it is Cordelia who is dead. How did that come about?'

Lise raised her eyes to his. 'She discovered me in the cellar and locked me in. I was taken up on to the moors, where I was to be thrown down a mine shaft. It's only thanks to Billie and Aaron that I escaped.'

'Ah, I think I understand,' Zach mused to himself. Billie Moxey's attacker was likely the ruffian Cordelia had hired, and, thwarted, he'd wanted revenge.

'What?' Lise asked, looking puzzled.

Zach shook his head. That would keep. There were far more important things to talk about. 'The cellar,' he said. 'I didn't know there was one.'

'I think it might once have provided a passage down to the

cove,' Lise said. 'But it's no longer in use. For very good reason.' A broad smile lifted her cheeks and sparkled in her eyes. 'The proof you sought is all hidden there. Not by my father, but by Cordelia.'

'Cordelia,' Zach repeated. 'I should have known. So it is still there?'

'It must be. There was no opportunity for her to remove it. What will you do?'

Zach was silent for a long moment, thinking. 'Perhaps we should leave it where it is,' he said at last. 'Cordelia is dead – she has paid the ultimate price for her wickedness – and Godfrey, it seems, is unlikely to ever be capable of resuming his illicit dealings. Should he recover, then I dare say the evidence could be used as a lever to ensure he desists. I rather think, Lise, that thanks to you and your courage, we have achieved our objective. Are you in agreement?'

'I am,' Lise said. The strangely protective feeling she had for her father had returned. He was an old man, a very sick old man. There was nothing to be gained by punishing him further. 'But I have so much else to tell you,' she added after a moment. 'Things you will scarcely believe. Good things.'

'I'll hear them later.' Zach pulled her towards him. 'You are safe. That's the only thing that matters to me. And I promise you, Lise, I shall take good care that you are never in danger again. I intend to spend the rest of my life making you happy.'

She was in his arms, his lips on hers, and in that moment, nothing else mattered to Lise either.

Chapter Twenty-Eight

Over the next weeks, things moved at a breakneck pace. With Godfrey no longer in any position to prevent them being together, Cecile had moved back into her old home – joyfully reunited with an excited Moll – and Sam had resumed his job in the stables. Now that there was no necessity for them to elope, they would wed here, they decided, and after the wedding they were going to set up home in a cottage in Porthmeor.

But they were not the only ones planning their nuptials. After all that had happened, Lise and Zach were determined never to be parted again.

'Why don't we make it a double wedding?' Zach suggested. 'If Cecile and Sam are agreeable, of course.'

Lise's face lit up. 'That would be wonderful! And Cecile won't object. She'll be as thrilled as I am, I know. The two of us together, sharing the happiest day of our lives, after all the lost years! And you and Sam are such close friends too. It's so fitting.'

Just one thing was worrying Lise. Where were she and Zach going to live when they were married? She assumed that Zach would return to his family's farm now that he'd achieved his objective and was no longer in the employ of Godfrey Pendinnick, but it was far – much too far – from St Ives.

'I can't leave Annie,' she told him. 'She's been a second mother to me, and now that she's old and sick, I want to stay here and look after her.'

'And so you shall,' Zach assured her. 'I don't intend to return to the farm. I am going to seek employment as a riding officer, as my brother did, so that I can continue to do all I can to thwart the evil trade that blights these coasts – and I can do that from St Ives as well as anywhere else.'

'Oh, Zach . . .' Delighted as she was that she would not have to choose between him and Annie, Lise couldn't help the prickle of fear that ran down her spine. She now knew all too well how ruthless the smugglers and wreckers could be, and the dangers faced by those who would attempt to bring them to justice. 'Are you sure?'

He nodded. 'My mind is made up, Lise. I've gone some way to avenging my brother's death, but it's not far enough. I hope I do not end up as he did, but if that is the price I have to pay, then so be it.'

The fear was knotting her throat now, but at the same time she felt a swell of pride for this brave and determined man who was to become her husband.

And so it was decided. A date was set, banns were called, and the sisters shopped together for wedding gowns – a bustle and demure puff sleeves for Cecile, a simply draped design for Lise, who would not contemplate wearing a corset. Invitations were issued, and preparations made for entertaining the guests after the ceremony, and all the while the two girls were overjoyed that they were together at last, sharing in every way.

On the eve of the wedding, Zach arranged for a gig to take Lise and Annie to Polruan, where they would stay overnight. He was there to meet them, and when Cecile had ushered Annie inside and the gig had departed, he took Lise in his arms.

'By this time tomorrow, you will be my wife,' he told her.

'I know. It's like a dream.' She smiled up at him. 'To think we would never have met if it hadn't been for—'

'Don't think about that now.' He lifted her chin, returning her smile, and then slowly lowered his lips to hers. A sweet, tender kiss that was a promise for the future that lay ahead of them.

'Until tomorrow,' he said softly.

'Tomorrow,' Lise echoed.

'Well, what a picture you two d'make. The most beautiful brides I ever did see.' Bessie stood back, tears in her eyes, as she surveyed Lise and Cecile, dressed in their wedding finery. 'I only wish I could be there to see you wed, but I can't leave yer father.'

'You've been so good to him since he fell ill,' Cecile said.

Bessie shrugged. 'Somebody 'as t'look after him, for the good Lord alone knows he can't look after 'imself – if ever he could,' she added darkly.

The sisters exchanged a look; they knew what the maid was alluding to. For almost all of his life, Cordelia had been at his side. Whilst it might have appeared to the outside world that he was the one with the power, it had been she who had planned, plotted and pulled the strings so that he had danced like a marionette. She had disposed of the one woman who had posed a threat to her dominance, and been ready to dispose of another.

But they weren't going to dwell on that today.

'We'll go down and see him now . . .'

' . . . that we're ready.' Lise looked at her sister and they both exploded into giggles. Already they were finishing one another's sentences.

Bessie tweaked Cecile's skirts and made a tiny adjustment to the neckline of Lise's gown, then stood aside. 'You'll do,' she said with a nod of approval, and followed them down the stairs.

Godfrey Pendinnick was dozing, dreaming as he so often did of his early life, when the rustle of taffeta beside his bed roused him. He opened his eyes blearily and thought for a moment he was still asleep and dreaming.

'Marguerite,' he whispered, his voice low, and as dry as his cracked lips.

'No, Papa, it's Cecile.'

'And Lise.'

'We're here so that you can see us in our wedding gowns.'

'We are both to be wed today.'

Godfrey gave a small impatient shake of his head. What was going on? Why were there two Marguerites here? Was he dying? He vaguely remembered once being told that the long-dead came calling when one was nearing the end of one's life. He'd never believed it, but this . . .

'We have to go now, but we'll be back after the ceremony,' Cecile said.

'And we'll come and see you again then,' Lise added.

Then they were gone, and there was nothing but the faint scent of what had been Marguerite's favourite perfume left to tell him they had ever been there.

'Well, I hope you be as proud of them as I be.' It was Bessie, bustling in. 'It'll be just you and me now.'

'Oh, let me be, you old crone,' Godfrey muttered irritably.

'Don't you fret, I'm not about to do that.'

Though he was becoming drowsy again and scarcely registered what Bessie had said, the words must have stirred something deep in his memory. Strange how people and events from the past came to him as clearly as yesterday when he had difficulty remembering what had happened just hours ago.

He let his eyes drift closed and thought about the first time he and Cordelia had come to Polruan House. Amos Fletcher, the old smuggler who had given him the wherewithal to set up his business, taught him his trade and bequeathed him this house. And the elderly housekeeper – Hetty, was it? – who had tried to keep them from seeing him. Now history was repeating itself. He'd turned into Fletcher, and Bessie into Hetty.

Godfrey harrumphed to himself, and drifted back into sleep.

The tiny church was almost full. The story of Cecile Pendinnick's twin come back from the dead had spread through the village and beyond, and there were many who had been eager to set eyes on the girls who were, it was said, as alike as peas in a pod. None of the wreckers had shown their faces, though, nor Godfrey's smugglers. News of Cordelia's unexplained disappearance had rattled them, and as one they had decided to lie low.

It was women, in any case, who loved a wedding. And those who had come were making the most of it, gossiping and chattering, speculating about the guests who occupied the front pews. There was an old woman wrinkled as only a working woman could be, though the garb she wore looked respectable enough, who had been supported up the aisle to her place by a nun – whatever next? – with another old woman, plump as a cockerel fattened up for Christmas, and giving off the distinctive odour of fish, following close behind.

Then there were the folk on the other side of the aisle, where the groom's family always sat, though in this case there were two grooms, and none of the guests looked like gentry. It certainly was enough to keep tongues wagging for weeks to come.

When Zach and Sam entered the church and walked to their places, the murmurs were of approval. Sam was well known in Porthmeor and well liked, and both he and Zach were so good looking, and so smart in their formal attire, that the hearts of young girls beat faster as they made their way up the aisle.

'But who's goin' to give the girls away?' one woman whispered loudly, and was answered only by shrugs and expressions that said 'Who knows?' What had become of Godfrey was common knowledge; there was no way he would be walking them up the aisle.

The organist had begun to play, and a hush fell over the congregation, whilst in the porch the bridal party waited. Lise and Billie Moxey, Cecile and Aaron. There had never been any question in their minds as to who should give them away. Billie and Aaron had saved Lise's life.

At a nod from the churchwarden, the Moxey boys offered their arms, and Lise and Cecile took them. The moment had arrived. They were going to wed the only men either of them had ever loved, and they were doing it together.

As Lise and Cecile entered the church, Marguerite turned to look at them, and suddenly tears were running down her cheeks. Her daughters. Her beautiful daughters, whom she had thought she had lost for ever. Visions of radiance that seemed to light up the little church. She clutched at the crucifix that hung around her neck, holding it fast and breathing a silent prayer of thanks and wonder.

She glanced at Annie, standing beside her, then reached out and took her frail hand. Dear Annie, who had raised Lise to be the fine woman she was today. What would have become of her had it not been for Annie? Tears were running down the old woman's wrinkled cheeks too and Marguerite squeezed her hand, though neither of them could take their eyes off the vision of loveliness that was Lise.

I have been so blessed, Marguerite thought. If only I could share this moment with Jean-Claude! Just then, a ray of sunlight slanted through the stained-glass windows and lit a path across the aisle to the pew where Marguerite stood, and a shard of joy pierced her heart. She'd often felt his presence across the years, and now he was here with her, sharing her pride and her joy, watching the little girl for whom he had given his life walk up the aisle towards her future husband, the sister he had had to leave behind beside her.

For a brief moment both girls looked up, directly into that ray of sunlight, and an expression of something like wonder crossed both their faces. It was as if it was meant especially for them. They turned towards their mother, smiling at her, and it seemed that she was caught in the bright path of sunlight too.

And there ahead of them, Zach and Sam waited at the chancel steps. Billie and Aaron stood aside, and Lise and Cecile moved hand in hand towards the men they loved, and into a shared future.